Praise for #1 *New York Times* bestselling author

NORA ROBERTS

"Roberts is deservedly one of the best known
and most widely read of all romance writers..."
—*Library Journal*

"The publishing world might be hard-pressed
to find an author with a more diverse style
or fertile imagination than Roberts."
—*Publishers Weekly*

"Roberts has a warm feel for her characters
and an eye for the evocative detail."
—*Chicago Tribune*

"Characters that touch the heart, stories that intrigue,
romance that sizzles—Nora Roberts has mastered it all."
—*Rendezvous*

"Roberts' style has a fresh, contemporary snap."
—*Kirkus Reviews*

"Some estimates have [Nora Roberts]
selling 12 books an hour, 24 hours a day,
7 days a week, 52 weeks a year."
—*New York Times*

Dear Reader,

You may find that the characters in this collection seem familiar, and you would be right! Many of you have already met Nikolai Davidov and Ruth Bannion in *New York Times* bestselling author Nora Roberts's beloved book *Considering Kate*. This collection will take you from the first time they meet to their declaration of love.

In *Reflections,* Nikolai has gone to Connecticut to convince his friend and former dance partner Lindsay Dunne to return to New York City and perform with him again. Yet Lindsay has changed, and doesn't seem to be in any hurry to revive her career. While teaching ballet to architect Seth Bannion's daughter, Ruth—and clashing over his plans for the girl's future—Lindsay may have found something worth even more to her than dance. But choosing one dream over another is never easy…and this ballerina has a very tough decision to make.

In *Dance of Dreams,* some time has passed and we find Ruth Bannion pursuing a dance career in the Big Apple. Nikolai, of course, remembers Ruth, and is intrigued by her just as much now as he was when he first met her in Lindsay's studio—and he can't wait to partner with her! Ruth has grown into a woman—a beautiful, determined woman. But it is Nikolai's job to mentor her and teach her the ways of the stage—not the ways of love. Yet the more time they spend together, the harder it is for Nikolai to stick to his lesson plan….

These stories of passion—both on and off the stage— are sure to inspire each of us to go after our own special dreams with as much determination as these heroes and heroines do!

The Editors
Silhouette Books

NORA ROBERTS

Reflections & Dreams

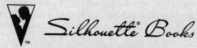

Silhouette Books

Published by Silhouette Books

America's Publisher of Contemporary Romance

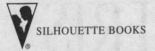

SILHOUETTE BOOKS

Recycling programs for this product may not exist in your area.

REFLECTIONS & DREAMS

ISBN-13: 978-0-373-28170-1

Copyright © 2001 by Harlequin Books S.A.

The publisher acknowledges the copyright holder of the individual works as follows:

REFLECTIONS
Copyright © 1983 by Nora Roberts

DANCE OF DREAMS
Copyright © 1983 by Nora Roberts

This edition published by arrangement with Harlequin Books S.A.

For questions and comments about the quality of this book, please contact us at CustomerService@Harlequin.com.

® and TM are trademarks of Harlequin Books S.A., used under license. Trademarks indicated with ® are registered in the United States Patent and Trademark Office, the Canadian Trade Marks Office and in other countries.

Visit Silhouette Books at www.Harlequin.com

Printed in U.S.A.

CONTENTS

REFLECTIONS

Chapter 1

The wind had cooled the air. It blew dark clouds across the sky and whistled through the leaves, now hinting at fall. Along the roadside the trees appeared more yellow than green, and touches of flame and scarlet were beginning to show. The day was poised in September, just as summer was turning autumn. The late afternoon sunshine squeezed between the clouds, slanting onto the roadway.

The air smelled of rain. Lindsay walked swiftly, knowing the clouds could win out at any moment. The breeze lifted and tossed the strands of her silvery blond hair, and she pushed at them with annoyance. She would have been wiser to have left it neatly pinned at the nape of her neck, she thought.

Had she not been so pressed for time, Lindsay would have enjoyed the walk. She would have reveled at the hint of fall and the threatening storm. Now, however, she hurried along the roadway wondering what else could go wrong.

In the three years since she had returned to Connecticut to teach, she had experienced some rough moments. But this, she decided, was among the top ten for frustration value. Backed up plumbing in the studio, a forty-five minute lecture from an overeager parent on her child's prowess, two torn costumes and a student with an upset stomach—these minor annoyances had culminated with her temperamental car. It had coughed and moaned as usual when she had turned the ignition, but then it had failed to pull itself together. It simply had sat there shuddering until Lindsay had admitted defeat. This car, she thought with a rueful smile, is about as old as I am, and we're both tired.

After taking a hopeless look under the hood, Lindsay had gritted her teeth and begun the two-and-a-half-mile hike home from the studio.

Of course, she admitted as she trudged along under the shifting sunlight, she could have called someone. She sighed, knowing her temper had set her off. Ten minutes of brisk walking had cooled it. Nerves, she told herself. I'm just nervous about the recital tonight. Not the recital, technically, she corrected, stuffing her hands into her pockets. The girls are ready; rehearsals had been perfect. The little ones are cute enough that mistakes won't matter. It was the times before and after the recitals that distressed Lindsay. And the parents.

She knew that some would be dissatisfied with their children's parts. And more still who would try to pressure her into accelerating the training. Why wasn't their

Pavlova on *pointe* yet? Why did Mrs. Jones's ballerina have a bigger part than Mrs. Smith's? Shouldn't Sue move on to the intermediate class?

So often Lindsay's explanations on anatomy, growing bones, endurance and timing met with only more suggestions. Normally, she used a mixture of flattery, stubbornness and intimidation to hold them off. She prided herself on being able to handle overzealous parents. After all, she mused, hadn't her mother been exactly the same?

Above all else, Mae Dunne had wanted to see her daughter on stage. She herself was short-legged, with a small, compact body. But she had possessed the soul of a dancer. Through sheer determination and training, she had secured a place in the *corps de ballet* with a small touring company.

Mae had been nearly thirty when she married. Resigned that she would never be a principal dancer, she had turned to teaching for a short time, but her own frustrations made her a poor instructor. Lindsay's birth had altered everything. She could never be a prima ballerina, but her daughter would.

Lessons for Lindsay had begun at age five with Mae in constant attendance. From that time on, her life had been a flurry of lessons, recitals, ballet shoes and classical music. Her diet had been scrupulously monitored, her height agonized over until it was certain that five-feet-two was all she would achieve. Mae had been pleased. Toe shoes add six inches to a dancer's height, and a tall ballerina has a more difficult time finding partners.

Lindsay had inherited her mother's height, but to

Mae's pride, her body was slender and delicate. After a brief, awkward stage, Lindsay had emerged as a teenager with fawnlike beauty: fragile blond hair, ivory skin, and Viking blue eyes with brows thin and naturally arched. Her bone structure was elegant, masking a sturdy strength gained from years of training. Her arms and legs were slim with the long muscles of a classical dancer. All of Mae's prayers had been answered.

Lindsay looked the part of a ballerina, and she had the talent. Mae didn't need a teacher to confirm what she could see for herself. There were the coordination, the technique, the endurance and the ability. But more, there was the heart.

At eighteen Lindsay had been accepted into a New York company. Unlike her mother, she did not remain in the *corps*. She advanced to soloist, then, the year she turned twenty, she became a principal dancer. For nearly two years it seemed that Mae's dreams were reality. Then, without warning, Lindsay had been forced to give up her position and return to Connecticut.

For three years teaching dance had been her profession. Though Mae was bitter, Lindsay was more philosophical. She was a dancer still. That would never change.

The clouds shifted again to block out the sun. Lindsay shivered and wished she had remembered her jacket. It sat in the front seat of her car, where, in the heat of her temper, she had tossed it. Her arms were now bare, covered only at the shoulders by a pale blue leotard. She had pulled on jeans, and her leg-warmers helped, but she thought longingly of the jacket. Because thinking of it failed to warm her, Lindsay quickened her pace to a jog. Her muscles responded instantly. There was a fluidity to the motion, a grace instinctive rather than planned. She began to enjoy the run. It was her nature to hunt for pleasure and to find it.

Abruptly, as if a hand had pulled the plug, the rain began. Lindsay stopped to stare up at the churning, black sky. "What else?" she demanded. A deep roar of thunder answered her. With a half-laugh, she shook her head. The Moorefield house was just across the street. She decided to do what she should have done initially: ask Andy to drive her home. Hugging her arms, she stepped out into the road.

The rude blast of a horn had her heart bounding to her throat. Her head snapped around, and she made out the dim shape of a car approaching through the curtain of rain. Instantly she leaped out of the way, slipping on the wet pavement and landing with a splash in a shallow puddle.

Lindsay shut her eyes as her pulse quickened. She heard the high squeal of brakes and the skid of tires. Years from now, she thought as the cold wetness soaked through her jeans, I'll laugh at this. But not now. She kicked and sent a small spray of water flying.

"Are you out of your mind?"

Lindsay heard the roar through the rain and opened her eyes. Standing over her was a raging, wet giant. Or a devil, she thought, eyeing him warily as he towered over her. He was dressed in black. His hair was black as well; sleek and wet, it enhanced a tanned, raw-boned face. There was something faintly wicked about that face. Perhaps it was the dark brows that rose ever so slightly at the ends. Perhaps it was the strange contrast of his eyes, a pale green that brought the sea to mind. And at the moment, they were furious. His nose was long and rather sharp, adding to the angular impression of his face. His clothes were plastered against his body by the rain and revealed a firm, well-proportioned frame. Had she not been so absorbed with his face, Lindsay would have admired it professionally. Speechless, she only stared up at him, her eyes huge.

"Are you hurt?" he demanded when she failed to answer his first question. There was no concern in his voice, only restrained anger. Lindsay shook her head and continued to stare. With an impatient oath, he took her arms and pulled her up, lifting her well off the ground before he set her on her feet. "Don't you look where you're going?" he tossed out, giving her a quick shake before releasing her.

He was not the giant Lindsay had first imagined. He was tall, certainly—perhaps a foot taller than herself— but hardly a bone-crushing giant or satanic apparition. She began to feel more foolish than frightened.

"I'm terribly sorry," she began. She was fully aware that she had been at fault and equally willing to admit it. "I did look, but I didn't..."

"Looked?" he interrupted. The impatience in his tone barely covered a deeper, tightly controlled fury. "Then perhaps you'd better start wearing your glasses. I'm sure your father paid good money for them."

Lightning flashed once, slicing white across the sky. More than the words, Lindsay resented the tone. "I don't wear glasses," she retorted.

"Then perhaps you should."

"My eyes are fine." She pushed clinging hair from her brow.

"Then you certainly should know better than to walk out into the middle of the street."

Rain streamed down her face as she glared at him. She wondered that it didn't turn to steam. "I apologized," she snapped, placing her hands on her hips. "Or had begun to before you jumped on me. If you expect groveling, you can forget it. If you hadn't been so heavy on the horn, I wouldn't have slipped and landed in that stupid puddle." She wiped ineffectually at the seat of her pants. "I don't suppose it occurs to you to apologize?"

"No," he answered evenly, "it doesn't. I'm hardly responsible for your clumsiness."

"Clumsiness?" Lindsay repeated. Her eyes grew round and wide. *"Clumsiness?"* On the repetition, her voice broke. To her, there was no insult more vile. *"How dare you!"*

She would take the dunk in the puddle, she would take his rudeness, but she would not take that. "You're the most deplorable excuse for a man I've ever met!" Her face was aglow with passion now, and she pushed impatiently at the hair the rain continued to nudge into her eyes. They shone an impossibly vivid blue against her flushed skin. "You nearly run me down, frighten me to death, push me into a puddle, lecture me as if I were a near-sighted child and now, *now* you have the nerve to call me *clumsy!*"

A winglike brow raised up at the passion of her speech. "If the shoe fits," he murmured, then stunned her by grabbing her arm and pulling her with him.

"Just what are you doing?" Lindsay demanded, trying for imperviousness and ending on a squeak.

"Getting out of this damn downpour." He opened the car door on the driver's side and shoved her, without ceremony, inside. Automatically, Lindsay scooted across the seat to accommodate him. "I can hardly leave you out in the rain." His tone was brusque as he moved in beside her at the wheel and slammed the door behind him. The storm battered against the windows.

He dragged his fingers through the thick hank of hair that was now plastered against his forehead, and Lindsay was immediately taken with his hand. It had the wide palm and long-fingered extension of a pianist. She almost felt sympathy for his predicament. But then he turned his head. The look was enough to erase any empathy.

"Where were you going?" he asked. The question was curt, as though it had been put to a child. Lindsay straightened her wet, chilled shoulders.

"Home, about a mile straight down this road."

The brows lifted again as he took a good, long look at her. Her hair hung limp and straight around her face. Her lashes were darkened and curled without the aid of mascara, framing eyes almost shockingly blue. Her mouth pouted, but it obviously did not belong to the child he had first taken her for. Though unpainted, it was clearly a woman's mouth. The naked face had something beyond simple beauty, but before he could define it, Lindsay shivered, distracting him.

"If you're going to go out in the rain," he said mildly as he reached toward the back seat, "you should take care to dress for it." He tossed a tan jacket into her lap.

"I don't need..." Lindsay began, only to break off by sneezing twice. Teeth clenched, she slipped her arms into the jacket as he started the engine. They drove in silence with the rain drumming on the roof.

It occurred to Lindsay all at once that the man was a total stranger. She knew virtually everyone in the small seacoast town by name or by sight, but never had she seen this man. She would hardly have forgotten that face. It was easy, in the slow-moving, friendly atmosphere of Cliffside, to be casual, but Lindsay had also spent several years in New York. She knew the very real dangers of accepting rides from strangers. Surreptitiously, she inched closer to the passenger door.

"A bit late to think of that now," he said quietly.

Lindsay's head snapped around. She thought, but couldn't be certain, that his mouth lifted slightly at the corner. She angled her chin. "Just there," she said coolly, pointing to the left. "The cedar house with the dormers."

The car purred to a halt in front of a white picket fence. Pulling together all her dignity, Lindsay turned to him again. She fully intended to make her thanks frosty.

"You'd better get out of those wet clothes," he advised before she could speak. "And next time, look both ways before you cross the street."

She could only make a strangled sound of fury as she fumbled for the door handle. Stepping back into the torrent of rain, she glared across the seat. "Thanks heaps," she snapped and slammed the door peevishly. She dashed around the back of the car and through the gate, forgetting she still wore a stranger's jacket.

Lindsay stormed into the house. With her temper still simmering, she stood quite still, eyes shut, calling herself to order. The incident had been infuriating, outrageously so, but the last thing she wanted was to have to relate the entire story to her mother. Lindsay was aware that her face was too expressive, her eyes too revealing. Her tendency to so visibly express her feelings had been only another asset in her career. When she danced *Giselle,* she felt as Giselle. The audience could read the tragedy on Lindsay's face. When she danced, she became utterly rapt in the story and in the music. But when her ballet shoes came off and she was Lindsay Dunne again, she knew it was not wise to let her thoughts shout from her eyes.

If she saw that Lindsay was upset, Mae would question her and demand a detailed account, only to criticize in the end. At the moment, the last thing that Lindsay wanted was a lecture. Wet and tired, she wearily began to climb the stairs to the second floor. It was then that she heard the slow, uneven footsteps, a constant reminder of the accident that had killed Lindsay's father.

"Hi! I was just dashing upstairs to change." Lindsay pulled back the wet hair from her face to smile at her mother, who stood at the foot of the stairs. Mae rested her hand on the newel post. Though her carefully coiffed hair had been dyed an ageless blond and her makeup had been skillfully applied, the effect was spoiled by Mae's perpetual expression of dissatisfaction.

"The car was acting up," Lindsay continued before the questioning could begin. "I got caught in the rain before I got a lift. Andy will have to give me a ride back tonight," she added in afterthought.

"You forgot to give him back his jacket," Mae observed. She leaned heavily on the newel post as she looked at her daughter. The damp weather plagued her hip.

"Jacket?" Blankly, Lindsay looked down and saw the wet, too-long sleeves that hung over her arms. "Oh no!"

"Well, don't look so panic-stricken," Mae said testily as she shifted her weight. "Andy can manage without it until tonight."

"Andy?" Lindsay repeated, then made the connection her mother had guessed at. Explanations, she decided, were too complicated. "I suppose so," she agreed casually. Then, descending a step, she laid her hand over her mother's. "You look tired, Mother. Did you rest today?"

"Don't treat me like a child," Mae snapped, and Lindsay immediately stiffened. She drew her hand away.

"I'm sorry." Her tone was restrained, but hurt flickered into her eyes. "I'll just go up and change before dinner." She would have turned, but Mae caught at her arm.

"Lindsay." She sighed, easily reading the emotions in the wide, blue eyes. "I'm sorry; I'm bad-tempered today. The rain depresses me."

"I know." Lindsay's voice softened. It had been a combination of rain and poor tires that had caused her parents' accident.

"And I hate your staying here taking care of me when you should be in New York."

"Mother…"

"It's no use." Mae's voice was sharp again. "Things won't be right until you're where you belong, where you're meant to be." Mae turned, moving down the hall in her awkward, uneven gate.

Lindsay watched her disappear before she turned

to mount the stairs. Where I belong, she mused as she turned into her room. Where is that really? Closing the door, she leaned back against it.

The room was big and airy with two wide windows side by side. On the dresser that had been her grandmother's was a collection of shells gathered from a beach barely a mile from the house. Set in a corner was a shelf stacked with books from her childhood. The faded Oriental rug was a prize she had brought back with her when she had closed up her New York apartment. The rocking chair was from the flea market two blocks away, and the framed Renoir print was from a Manhattan art gallery. Her room, she thought, reflected the two worlds in which she had lived.

Over the bed hung the pale pink toe shoes she had worn in her first professional solo. Lindsay walked over to them and lightly fingered the satin ribbons. She remembered sewing them on, remembered the stomach-churning excitement. She remembered her mother's ecstatic face after the performance and her father's gently awed one.

A lifetime ago, she thought as she let the satin fall from her fingers. Back then she had believed that anything was possible. Perhaps, for a time, it had been.

Smiling, Lindsay let herself remember the music, the movement, the magic and the times she had felt her body was without bounds, fluid and free. Reality had come afterward, with unspeakable cramping, bleeding feet, strained muscles. How had it been possible, again and again, to contort her body into the unnatural lines that made up the dance? But she had done it, and she had pushed herself to the limits of ability and endurance. She had given herself over, sacrificing her body and the years. There had been only the dance. It had absorbed her utterly.

Shaking her head, Lindsay brought herself back. That, she reminded herself, was a long time ago. Now, she had other things to think about. She stripped out of the damp jacket, then frowned at it. What do I do with this? she wondered.

The owner's blatant rudeness came back to her. Her frown deepened. Well, if he wants it, he can just come back for it. A quick scan of the material and the label told her it was not a piece of clothing to be carelessly forgotten. But the mistake was hardly her fault, she told herself as she walked to the closet for a hanger. If he hadn't made her so mad, she wouldn't have forgotten to give it back to him.

She hung the jacket in her closet and began to peel off her own wet clothes. She slipped a thick, chenille robe over her shivering skin and closed the closet doors. She told herself to forget the jacket and the man it belonged to. Neither of them, she decided, had anything to do with her.

Chapter 2

It was a different Lindsay Dunne who stood greeting parents two hours later. She wore a high-necked, ruffled lawn blouse with a full, knife-pleated skirt, both in a rain-washed shade of blue. Her hair was neatly braided and coiled at each ear. Her features were calm and composed. Any resemblance to the wet, furious woman of the early evening had vanished. In her preoccupation with the recital, Lindsay had completely forgotten the incident in the rain.

Chairs had been set up in rows from which parents could watch their children's performance. Behind the audience was a table on which coffee and assorted cookies had been arranged. Throughout the room Lindsay could hear the buzz of conversation, and it made her recall the innumerable recitals of her own past. She tried not to hurry through the handshakings and questions, but her mind flitted to the adjoining room, where two dozen girls were busy with tutus and toe shoes.

She was nervous. Underneath the calm, smiling exterior, Lindsay was every bit as nervous as she had been before every one of her own recitals. But she managed to field questions smoothly, knowing almost invariably in advance what they would be. She'd been here before, as a preschooler, a junior, an intermediate and as a senior dancer. Now she was the instructor. Lindsay felt there was no aspect of a recital that she had missed in her lifetime. Yet she was still nervous.

The quiet Beethoven sonata she had placed on the CD player had been an attempt to quiet her own nerves as much as to create atmosphere. It was foolish, she told herself, for a seasoned professional—an established instructor—to be nervous and tense over a simple recital. But there was no help for it. Lindsay's heart was very close to the surface when it came to her school and her students. She wanted badly for the evening to be a success.

She smiled, shaking hands with a father whom she was certain would rather be at home watching a ball game. The finger he eased surreptitiously under his collar made it plain that he was uncomfortable in the restricting tie. If Lindsay had known him better, she would have laughed, then whispered to him to remove it.

Since she had started giving recitals more than two years before, one of Lindsay's main objectives had been to keep the parents at ease. Her rule of thumb was that comfortable parents made a more enthusiastic audience, and a more enthusiastic audience could generate more students for the school. She had founded the school by word of mouth, and it was still a neighbor's recommendation to a neighbor, a satisfied parent's suggestion to an acquaintance, that kept it working. It was her business now, her living as well as her love. She considered herself fortunate to have been able to combine the two for a second time in her life.

Aware that many of the dancers' families had come out of a sense of duty, Lindsay was determined to give them a good time. In each recital, she tried not only to vary the program but to see to it that every dancer had a part especially choreographed for her talent and ability. She knew that not all mothers were as ambitious for their children as Mae, nor were all fathers as supportive as hers had been.

But they came anyway, she thought, looking around her at the group huddled in her studio. They drove out in the rain, giving up a favorite television show or an after-dinner snooze on the sofa. Lindsay smiled, touched again by the perpetually unnoticed selflessness of parents dealing with their children.

It struck her then—strongly, as it did from time to time—how very glad she was to have come home, how very content she was to remain here. Oh, she had loved New York, the continual throb of life, the demands, the undeniable excitement, but the simple pleasure of the close-knit town and the quiet streets more than satisfied her now.

Everyone in the room knew each other, either by sight or by name. The mother of one of the senior dancers had been Lindsay's sitter almost twenty years before. She'd worn a ponytail then, Lindsay remembered as she looked at the woman's short, sculptured hairstyle. It had been a long ponytail tied up with colored yarn. It had swung when she walked, and Lindsay had found it beautiful. Now the memory warmed her and eased her nerves.

Perhaps everyone should leave at some point, then come back to their hometown as an adult, she reflected, whether they settled down there again or not. What a revelation it is to see the things and people we knew as children through an adult's perspective.

"Lindsay."

Lindsay turned to greet a former schoolmate, now the mother of one of her smallest dancers. "Hello, Jackie. You look wonderful."

Jackie was a trim and competent brunette. Lindsay recalled that she had been on an amazing number of committees during their high school years. "We're awfully nervous," Jackie confessed, referring to herself, her daughter and her husband as one.

Lindsay followed Jackie's eyes across the room and spotted the former track star turned insurance executive whom Jackie had married within a year of graduation. He was talking with two elderly couples. All the grandparents are here as well, Lindsay thought with a smile.

"You're supposed to be nervous," Lindsay told her. "It's traditional."

"I hope she'll do well," Jackie said, "for her sake. And she wants so badly to impress her daddy."

"She'll be just fine," Lindsay assured her, giving the nervous hand a squeeze. "And they'll all look wonderful, thanks to the help you gave me with the costumes. I haven't had a chance to thank you yet."

"Oh, that was a pleasure," Jackie assured her. She

glanced toward her family again. "Grandparents," she said in an undertone, "can be terrifying."

Lindsay laughed softly, knowing how these particular grandparents doted on the tiny dancer.

"Go ahead, laugh," Jackie invited scornfully, but a self-deprecating smile touched her lips. "You don't have to worry about grandparents yet. Or in-laws," she added, giving the word a purposefully ominous tone. "By the way," Jackie's change of tone put Lindsay on immediate alert. "My cousin Tod...you remember?"

"Yes," Lindsay answered cautiously as Jackie paused.

"He's coming through town in a couple of weeks. Just for a day or so." She gave Lindsay a guileless smile. "He asked about you the last time he phoned."

"Jackie..." Lindsay began, determined to be firm.

"Why don't you let him take you out to dinner?" Jackie continued, cutting off Lindsay's chance to make a clean escape. "He was so taken with you last year. He'll only be in town for a short time. He has a marvellous business in New Hampshire. You know, hardware; I told you."

"I remember," Lindsay said rather shortly. One of the disadvantages of being single in a small town was continually having to dodge matchmaking schemes by well-meaning friends, she thought. The hints and suggestions for partners had been dropped more frequently now that Mae was improving steadily. Lindsay knew that in order to avoid a deluge, she must set a precedent. She must be firm.

"Jackie, you know how busy I am...."

"You're doing a wonderful job here, Lindsay," Jackie said quickly. "The girls all love you, but a woman needs a diversion now and then, doesn't she? There's nothing serious between you and Andy?"

"No, of course not, but…"

"Then there certainly isn't any need to bury yourself."

"My mother…"

"She looked so well when I dropped off the costumes at your house the other day," Jackie went on relentlessly. "It was wonderful to see her up and around. She's finally putting on a bit of weight, I noticed."

"Yes, she is, but…"

"Tod should be in town a week from Thursday. I'll tell him to give you a ring," Jackie said lightly before turning to weave her way through the crowd to her family.

Lindsay watched her retreat with a mixture of irritation and amusement. Never expect to win over someone who won't let you finish a sentence, she concluded. Oh well, she thought, one cousin with a nervous voice and slightly damp palms won't be too bad for an evening. Her social calendar wasn't exactly bulging with appointments, and fascinating men weren't exactly lining up at her front door.

Lindsay pushed the prospective dinner date to the back of her mind. Now wasn't the time to worry about it. Now was the time to think of her students. She walked across the studio to the dressing room. Here, at least, her authority was absolute.

Once inside, she leaned back against the closed door and took a long, deep breath. Before her, pandemonium ruled, but this was the sort of chaos she was immune to. Girls chattered excitedly, helping each other into costumes or trying out steps one final time. One senior dancer calmly executed *pliés* while a pair of five-year-olds played tug of war with a ballet shoe. All around there was the universal backstage confusion.

Lindsay straightened, her voice rising with the gesture. "I'd like your attention, please." The soft tone carried over the chattering and brought all eyes to her.

"We'll begin in ten minutes. Beth, Josey," she addressed two senior dancers with a nod, "if you'd help the little ones." Lindsay glanced at her watch, wondering why the piano accompanist was so late. If worse comes to worst, she would use the CD player.

She crouched to adjust the tights on a young student and dealt with questions and nerves from others.

"Ms. Dunne, you didn't let my brother sit in the front row, did you? He makes faces. Awful ones."

"Second row from the back," Lindsay countered with a mouthful of hairpins as she completed repairs on a tousled coiffure.

"Ms. Dunne, I'm worried about the second set of *jetés.*"

"Just like rehearsal. You'll be wonderful."

"Ms. Dunne, Kate's wearing red nail polish."

"Hmm." Lindsay glanced at her watch again.

"Ms. Dunne, about the *fouettés...*"

"Five, no more."

"We really ought to be wearing stage makeup so we don't look washed out," a diminutive dancer complained.

"No," Lindsay said flatly, suppressing a smile. "Monica, thank goodness!" Lindsay suddenly called out with relief as an attractive young woman entered through the back door. "I was about to drag out the CD player."

"Sorry I'm late." Monica grinned cheerfully as she shut the door at her back.

Monica Anderson at twenty was pretty in a healthy, wholesome way. Her bouncy blond hair adorned a face that featured a dash of freckles and large, hopeful, brown eyes. She had a tall, athletic body and the purest heart of anyone Lindsay had ever known. She collected stray cats, listened to both sides of every argument and never thought the worst of anyone, even after being confronted with it. Lindsay liked her for her simple goodness.

Monica also possessed a true gift for piano accompaniment. She kept tempo, playing the classics truthfully, without the embellishments that would detract from the dancers. But she was not, Lindsay thought with a sigh, overly obsessed with punctuality.

"We've got about five minutes," Lindsay reminded her as Monica maneuvered her generously curved body toward the door.

"No problem. I'll go out in just a second. This is Ruth," she continued, gesturing to a girl who stood just to the side of the door. "She's a dancer."

Lindsay's attention shifted from the tall, busty blonde to the finely boned girl. She noted the exotic, almond-shaped eyes and the full, passionate mouth. Ruth's straight, black hair was parted in the center to frame her small, triangular face and hung down just past her shoulder blades. Her features were uneven, and while individually they might have been unremarkable, in combination they were arresting. She was a girl on the brink of womanhood. Though her stance was easy and full of confidence, there was something in the dark eyes that bespoke uncertainty and nervousness. The eyes caused Lindsay's smile to warm as she held out her hand.

"Hello, Ruth."

"I'll go give them a quick overture and quiet things down," Monica interjected, but as she turned to go, Ruth plucked at her sleeve.

"But, Monica…" Ruth protested.

"Oh, Ruth wants to talk to you, Lindsay." She gave her cheerful, toothy smile and turned once more toward the door. "Don't worry," she said to the younger girl, "Lindsay's very nice. I told you. Ruth's a little nervous," she announced as she backed out the door leading to the studio.

Amused, Lindsay shook her head, but as she turned back, she saw Ruth's heightened color. At ease with strangers herself, she still recognized one who was not. She touched the girl's arm lightly. "There's only one Monica," she stated with a new smile. "Now, if you'll give me a hand lining up the first dancers, we should be able to talk."

"I don't want to be in the way, Ms. Dunne."

In answer, Lindsay gestured behind her to the backstage confusion. "I could use the help."

Lindsay was easily capable of organizing the dancers herself, but she knew, watching Ruth relax, that she had made the right gesture. Intrigued, she watched the way the girl moved, recognizing natural grace and trained style. Lindsay then turned to give her full attention to her students. In a few moments, a restrained hush fell over the room. After opening the door, she gave a quick signal to Monica. The introductory music began, then the youngest of Lindsay's students glided into the studio.

"They're so cute at this stage," she murmured. "There's very little they can do wrong." Already some of the pirouettes had touched off smatterings of applause. "Posture," she whispered to the small dancers. Then to Ruth: "How long have you been studying?"

"Since I was five."

Lindsay nodded while keeping her eyes trained on the tiny performers. "How old are you?"

"Seventeen."

It was stated with such determination that Lindsay lifted a brow.

"Just last month," Ruth added with a tinge of defense. Lindsay smiled but continued to watch the dancers.

"I was five, too. My mother still has my first pair of ballet shoes."

"I saw you dance in *Don Quixote*." The words tumbled out swiftly. Lindsay turned to see Ruth staring at her, her bottom lip trapped between her teeth.

"Did you? When?"

"Five years ago in New York. You were wonderful." The eyes were so filled with awe and admiration that Lindsay lifted a hand to the girl's cheek. Ruth stiffened, but Lindsay, puzzled, smiled nonetheless.

"Thank you. It was always my favorite ballet. So full of flash and fire."

"I'm going to dance Dulcinea one day." Some of the nerves had faded from the voice. Now Ruth's eyes were direct on Lindsay's.

Studying her, Lindsay thought she had never seen

more perfect looks for the part. "Do you want to continue your training?"

"Yes." Ruth moistened her lips.

She tilted her head, still studying. "With me?"

Ruth nodded before the word would come. "Yes."

"Tomorrow's Saturday." Lindsay lifted her hand to signal the next group of dancers. "My first class is at ten. Can you come at nine?" The triumphant preschoolers forged back into the dressing room. "I'll want to check the progress of your training to see where to place you. Bring ballet and toe shoes."

Ruth's eyes shimmered with excitement. "Yes, Ms. Dunne. Nine o'clock."

"I'd also like to speak with your parents, Ruth, if one or both of them could come with you."

Monica changed tempo to introduce the next group.

"My parents were killed in an accident a few months ago."

Lindsay heard the quiet pronouncement as she nudged the next group out on stage. Over their heads, her eyes met Ruth's. She saw that the light in them had dimmed. "Oh, Ruth, I'm terribly sorry." Sympathy and distress deepened Lindsay's tone. She knew the feel of tragedy. But Ruth shook her head briskly and avoided the touch of her hand. Suppressing the instinctive need to comfort, Lindsay stood silently while Ruth composed herself. She recognized a very private person, one who was not yet ready to share her emotions.

"I live with my uncle," Ruth continued. There was nothing of her feelings in her voice. It was low and smooth. "We've just moved into the house on the edge of town."

"The Cliff House." Fresh interest sparkled in Lindsay's eyes. "I'd heard it'd been sold. It's a fabulous place." Ruth merely looked off into space. She hates it, Lindsay decided, again feeling a profound tug of sympathy. She hates everything about it. It was difficult to keep her tone practical. "Well, then, perhaps your uncle could come in with you. If it's not convenient, have him phone me. I'm in the book. It's important that I speak with him before we outline your routine."

A sudden smile illuminated Ruth's face. "Thank you, Ms. Dunne."

Lindsay turned away to quiet a pair of youngsters. When she looked again, Ruth had gone.

An odd girl, she mused, obliging one of the little ones by picking her up. *Lonely.* The word seemed too suitable, and Lindsay nuzzled against the neck of the small child she held. She had had little time for loneliness, but she recognized it. It saddened her to see it reflected in the eyes of one so young.

She wondered what the uncle was like as she watched her intermediate students carry out a short routine from *Sleeping Beauty.* Is he kind? Is he understanding? She thought again of the large, dark eyes and sighed. Monica had found another stray, and Lindsay knew she had already involved herself. Smiling, she kissed the little ballerina's cheek, then set her down.

Tomorrow, Lindsay decided, we'll see if she can dance.

Lindsay began to wonder if the rain would last forever. It was warm—even cozy—in her bed, but the night wore on, and she was still wide awake. It was odd, she thought, because usually the patter of lingering rain and the soft quilt around her would have induced sleep. She thought perhaps it was leftover tension from the recital which kept her mind alert.

It had gone well, she recalled, pleased. The little ones, shaky posture and all, had been as appealing as she had hoped, and the older girls had demonstrated all the poise and grace she could have asked of them. If only she could lure some boys into class! She sighed. But she had to put that out of her mind. The recital had gone well, her students were happy. Some of them showed potential. But soon her thoughts drifted to the dark-haired girl, Ruth.

Lindsay had recognized ambition there but wondered if she would find talent. Remembering Ruth's eyes and the need and vulnerability she had seen there, she hoped she would. She wants to dance Dulcinea, she remembered with a wistful smile. Lindsay felt a small ache, knowing how many hopes could be dashed to the ground in the world of dance. She could only hope Ruth's weren't, for something in the young, poignant face had touched a chord in her. There had been a day not so long ago when dancing Dulcinea had been only a wish for Lindsay as well. She thought perhaps she had come full circle.

Lindsay closed her eyes, but her mind continued to race.

She briefly considered going down to the kitchen for some tea or hot chocolate. She sighed into the darkness. The noise would disturb her mother. Mae slept lightly, especially in the rain. Lindsay knew how difficult it was for her mother to deal with all the disappointments she had been handed. And the tragedy.

Mae's aching hip would be a continual reminder of the death of her husband. Lindsay knew that Mae had not always been happy, but her father had been so quietly supportive. His loss had been hard on Mae, who had awakened from a coma confused and in pain, unable to understand how he could have been taken from her. Lindsay knew her mother could never forget her husband's death, her own injuries and painful therapy and the abrupt end of her daughter's career.

And now that Mae was finally accepting Dad's death, Lindsay reflected, and could get around a bit more, she thought of nothing but Lindsay's return to professional dancing.

Lindsay rolled to her side, curling her arm under her pillow. The rain splashed on the window glass, excited by the wind. What would it take to resign her mother to the inevitable, she wondered. What would it take to make her happy? Would she ever be able to do both? The look on her mother's face as she had stood at the base of the stairs that afternoon came back to her. With the image came the familiar helplessness and guilt.

Rolling onto her back, Lindsay stared at the ceiling. She had to stop thinking about it. It was the rain, she decided, just the rain. To ease her insomnia, she began to go over the details of the day.

What an afternoon it had been. The varied complications now brought on a smile. Still, for a Friday class in which older girls were always thinking about their Saturday night dates and the younger ones were just thinking about Saturday, it had gone fairly well. And everything had worked out, except for that blasted car!

The thought of her broken-down car pushed the memory of the man in the rain back into Lindsay's mind. Frowning, she turned her head so that she faced the closet. In the near-perfect darkness, it was impossible to see the door itself, much less what was inside it. But Lindsay continued to frown. I wonder, she thought, if he'll come back for his jacket.

He had been so rude! Indignation welled up again, replacing her earlier depression. She much preferred it. He was so superior? *If you're going to go out in the rain...* In her mind she mimicked his low, controlled voice.

A wonderfully appealing voice, she reflected. Too bad it has to come out of such an unappealing man. Clumsy, she thought, fuming all over again. And he had the nerve to call me clumsy! She rolled onto her stomach and pounded the pillow before placing her head on it. I hope he does come back for his jacket, she decided. This time I'll be ready for him. It gave her a great deal of pleasure to imagine a variety of situations in which she returned the borrowed jacket. Haughtily, disdainfully, benevolently...she would hold the upper hand and humiliate the objectionable man whose eyes and cheekbones now haunted her. When next they met, it would not be raining. She would not be at a disadvantage—soaking wet and sneezing. She would be witty, poised...devastating. She smiled to herself as she drifted off to sleep.

Chapter 3

Rain had accumulated in puddles. The morning sun glistened on their surfaces in a splash of colors, while beads of moisture still clung to the grass. There was just a trace of fog misting over the ground. Andy turned up the car heater to combat the chill as he watched Lindsay walk through the front door of her house. She was, to him, the most gorgeous creature in the world. In point of fact, Andy felt Lindsay was beyond the real world. She was too delicate, too ethereal to be of the earth.

And her beauty was so pure, so fragile. It tied his stomach into knots when he saw her. It had been so for fifteen years.

Lindsay smiled and lifted a hand in greeting as she moved down the concrete walk toward the car. In her smile he saw the affection, the friendship she had always offered to him. Andy returned both the smile and the wave. He had no illusions about his relationship with Lindsay. Friendship and no more. It would never be anything else. Not once in all the time he had known her had she encouraged him beyond the borders of friendship.

She's not for me, Andy mused as Lindsay swung through the gate. But he felt the familiar surge when she opened the car door and slid in beside him. Her scent was always the same, light and fresh with a touch of the mysterious. He always felt too big when she was beside him. Too broad, too clumsy.

Lindsay smiled into his wide, square-jawed face and kissed him with quick friendliness. "Andy, you're a lifesaver." She studied his face, liking it as always; the dependable dark eyes, the strong bones, the slightly disheveled brown hair reminiscent of a family dog. And like a family pet, he made her feel comfortable and just a little maternal. "I really appreciate your driving me to the studio this way."

He shrugged broad shoulders. Already the surge had mellowed into the familiar warmth he felt whenever she was near. "You know I don't mind."

"I know you don't," she acknowledged as he pulled away from the curb. "So I appreciate it even more." As was her habit, she slid sideways in the seat as she spoke. Personal contact was vital to her. "Your mom's coming by to spend some time with mine today."

"Yeah, I know." Andy drove down the street with the relaxed attention of one who had followed the same route uncountable times. "She's going to talk her into taking that trip to California this winter."

"I really hope she does." For a moment Lindsay allowed her mind to linger on her mother's restless, unhappy face. "She could use a change."

"How's she doing?"

Lindsay let out a long sigh. There was nothing she felt she could not discuss with Andy. She'd had no closer friend since childhood. "Physically, so much better. There's a great improvement even in the last three months, but otherwise..." She linked her fingers together, then turned her hands palms up, a gesture she used as others used a shrug. "Frustrated, angry, restless. She wants me to go back to New York to dance. She can't see it any other way. It's tunnel vision; she's refused to accept the fact that picking up where I left off is virtually impossible. Three years away, three years older." She shook her head and lapsed into thoughtful silence. Andy gave her a full minute.

"Do you want to go back?"

She looked back at him now, and though the frown brought a line between her brows, it was one of concentration and not annoyance. "I don't know. I don't think so. I did it all once, and I'm very content here, but..." She sighed.

"But?" Andy turned left and absently waved to a pair of youngsters on bicycles.

"I loved it when I was doing it, even though so much of the life is brutal. I loved it." She smiled, relaxing against the seat again. "Past tense, you see. But Mother continually pushes it into the present. Even if I wanted it—wanted it desperately—the chance that the company would have me back is so—so slim." Her eyes wandered to the familiar houses. "So much of me belongs here now. It feels right, being home. Do you remember that night we snuck into the Cliff House?" Her eyes were alight again, laughing. Andy responded with a grin.

"I was scared to pieces. I still swear I saw the ghost."

Lindsay's laugh was a light, bubbling sound. "Ghost or no ghost, it's the most fantastic place I've ever seen. You know, it was finally sold."

"I'd heard." Andy shot her a look. "I remember you swearing you'd live there one day."

"We were young," she murmured, but the sadness she felt at the memory was warm and not unpleasant. "I wanted to live high up above the town and feel important. All those marvelous rooms stacked on top of each other, and those endless corridors," she recalled out loud.

"The place is a labyrinth," he remarked unromantically. "There's been a lot of work going on up there."

"I hope they haven't ruined the atmosphere."

"What, spider webs and field mice?"

Lindsay wrinkled her nose. "No, idiot, the stateliness, the magnificence, the arrogance. I've always imagined it with the gardens blooming and the windows wide open for parties."

"The place hasn't had a window open in more than a decade, and the garden has the toughest weeds in New England."

"You," she said gravely, "have no vision. Anyway," she continued, "the girl I'm seeing this morning is the niece of the man who bought the place. Know anything about him?"

"Nope. Mom might; she's always up on the town's latest gossip."

"I like the girl," Lindsay mused, conjuring up a picture of Ruth's poignant beauty. "She has rather a lost look. I'd like to help her."

"You think she needs help?"

"She seemed like a bird who wasn't quite certain whether the hand held out to her would squeeze or stroke. I wonder what the uncle's like."

Andy pulled into the studio parking lot. "How much could you find wrong with the man who bought the Cliff House?"

"Very little, I'm sure," she agreed, slamming her door behind her as Andy slammed his.

"I'll take a look at your car," he volunteered, and moving to it, lifted the hood. Lindsay walked to stand beside him. She scowled at the engine.

"It looks dreadful in there."

"It might help if you'd have it serviced once in a while." He grimaced at the grime-coated engine, then gave a disgusted look at the spark plugs. "You know, there are things that need to be replaced other than gas."

"I'm a mechanical failure," Lindsay said carelessly.

"You don't have to be a mechanic to take minimal care of a car," Andy began, and Lindsay groaned.

"A lecture. It's better to plead guilty." She threw her arms around his neck and kissed both his cheeks. "I'm incompetent. Forgive me."

Lindsay watched the grin flash just as she heard another car pull into the lot. With her arms still around Andy's neck, she turned her head. "That must be Ruth," she thought aloud before releasing him. "I really appreciate your checking out the car, Andy. If it's anything terminal, try to break it to me gently."

Turning around to greet Ruth, Lindsay was struck

dumb. The man who approached with the girl was tall and dark. Lindsay knew how his voice would sound before he spoke. Just as she knew his taste in jackets.

"Marvelous," she said just under her breath. Their eyes locked. She decided he was not a man who surprised easily.

"Ms. Dunne?" There was a hesitant question in Ruth's voice. Shock, distress and annoyance were all easily read on Lindsay's face. "You did say I should be here at nine?"

"What?" Lindsay stared a moment. "Oh, yes," she said quickly. "I'm sorry. I've had some car trouble; I was a bit preoccupied. Ruth, this is my friend Andy Moorefield. Andy, Ruth…"

"Bannion," Ruth supplied, visibly relaxing. "And my uncle, Seth Bannion."

Andy discouraged handshakes by holding out his grimy palms and grinning.

"Ms. Dunne." Seth's tone was so bland, Lindsay thought perhaps he hadn't recognized her after all. A glimpse of his face, however, scotched the theory. Recognition was mixed with mockery. Still, the handshake was unquestionably polite, his fingers making firm but brief contact with hers. Two can play at this game, she decided.

"Mr. Bannion." Her tone was politely distant. "I appreciate your coming with Ruth this morning."

"My pleasure," he returned. Lindsay eyed him suspiciously.

"Let's go inside," she said directly to Ruth. Moving toward the building, she waved a quick farewell in

Andy's direction, then dipped into her jacket pocket for the keys.

"It's nice of you to see me early this way, Ms. Dunne," Ruth began. Her voice was much as it had been the night before: low with a faint tremor that betrayed nerves barely under control. Lindsay noted that she clung to her uncle's arm. She smiled, touching the girl's shoulder.

"It helps me to see students individually the first time." She felt the slight resistance and casually removed her hand. "Tell me," she went on as she unlocked the studio door, "whom did you study under?"

"I've had several teachers." As she answered, Ruth stepped inside. "My father was a journalist. We were always traveling."

"I see." Lindsay glanced up at Seth, but his expression remained neutral. "If you'll just make yourself comfortable, Mr. Bannion," she said, matching his seamless politeness, "Ruth and I will work at the barre for a few moments."

Seth merely gave Lindsay a nod, but she noticed that he lightly touched Ruth's hand before he moved to a seat.

"The classes are on the small side," she began as she slipped out of her jacket. "In a town this size, I suppose we have a fairly good number of students, but we're not turning them away in droves." She smiled at Ruth, then drew white leg-warmers over her dark green tights. She wore a chiffon overskirt in a shade of sea green. Lindsay realized abruptly that the color was identical to Seth's eyes. She scowled as she reached for her ballet shoes.

"But you like to teach, don't you?" Ruth stood a few

feet from her. Lindsay looked up to see her, slim and uncertain in a rose pink leotard that enhanced her dark coloring. Lindsay cleared her expression before she rose.

"Yes, I do. Barre exercises first," she added, gesturing to Ruth as she herself moved to the mirrored wall. Placing her hand on the barre, she indicated for Ruth to stand in front of her. "First position."

Both figures in the mirror moved simultaneously. Both women were poised together, of nearly identical height and build. One was all light, the other stood as a dark shadow, waiting.

"Grand plié."

With seemingly no effort, they dipped into deep knee bends. Lindsay watched Ruth's back, her legs, her feet for posture, positioning, style.

Slowly she began to take Ruth through the five positions, working her thoroughly. The *pliés* and *battements* were well-executed, she observed. Lindsay could see by the gesture of an arm, the movement of a leg, the love Ruth had for the dance. She remembered herself a decade before, achingly young, full of dreams and aspirations.

She smiled, recognizing a great deal of herself in Ruth. It was easy to empathize with the girl and in their joint motions to forget everything else. As her body stretched, her mind moved in close harmony.

"Toe shoes," she said abruptly, then walked away to change the CD. As she did, her eyes passed over Seth. He was watching her, and she thought there might have been something soothing in his look had it not been so uncompromisingly direct. Still, she met his eyes levelly as she slipped Tchaikovsky into the player. "We'll be about a half-hour yet, Mr. Bannion. Shall I make you some coffee?"

He didn't answer with the immediacy she expected from a casual question. The ten seconds of silence left Lindsay oddly breathless. "No," he paused, and she felt her skin grow warm. "Thank you."

When she turned away, the muscles that had been loosened at the barre were taut again. She swore under her breath but wasn't certain if she cursed Seth or herself. After gesturing for Ruth to stand in the center of the room, Lindsay walked back to the barre. She would start *adagio,* slow, sustained steps, looking for balance and style and presence. Too often in her students she found a desire only for the flash: dizzying *pirouettes, fouettés, jetés.* The beauty of a long, slow move was forgotten.

"Ready?"

"Yes, Ms. Dunne."

There was nothing shy about the girl now, Lindsay thought. She caught the light in Ruth's eyes.

"Fourth position, *pirouette,* fifth." The execution was clean, the line excellent. "Fourth position, *pirouette, attitude."* Pleased, Lindsay began to take a slow circle around Ruth. "*Arabesque.* Again. *Attitude,* hold. *Plié.*"

Lindsay could see that Ruth had talent, and more important, she had endurance and drive. She was further gifted with the build and face of a classical dancer. Her every move was an expression of her love for the art, and Lindsay responded to her involvement. In part, Lindsay felt pain for the sacrifices and self-denial that lay ahead for Ruth, but her joy overpowered it. Here was a dancer who would make it. Excitement began to course through Lindsay's body. *And I'm going to help her,* she thought. There's still quite a bit she needs to learn. She doesn't yet know how to use her arms and hands. She has to learn to express more emotion through her face and body. But she's good—very, very good....

Nearly forty-five minutes had passed. "Relax," Lindsay said simply, then walked over to switch off the CD player. "Your several teachers appear to have done a good job." Turning back, she saw the anxiety had returned to Ruth's eyes. Instinctively, she moved to her, placing her hands on her shoulders. The withdrawal was unspoken, but feeling it, Lindsay removed her hands. "I don't have to tell you that you've a great deal of talent. You're not a fool."

She watched her words sink in. The tension seemed to dissolve from Ruth's body. "It means everything to have you say it."

Surprise lifted Lindsay's brows. "Why?"

"Because you're the most wonderful dancer I've ever seen. And I know if you hadn't given it up, you'd be the most famous ballerina in the country. I've read things, too, that said you were the most promising American dancer in a decade. Davidov chose you for his partner, and he said you were the finest Juliet he ever danced with, and..." She stopped abruptly, ending the uncharacteristically long speech. Color deepened her cheeks.

Though sincerely touched, Lindsay spoke lightly to ease the embarrassment. "I'm very flattered. I don't hear nearly enough of that sort of thing around here." She paused, resisting the instinctive move to touch the girl's shoulder again. "The other girls will tell you I can be a very difficult teacher, very demanding and strict with my advanced students. You'll work hard."

"I won't mind." The gleam of anticipation had returned.

"Tell me, Ruth, what do you want?"

"To dance. To be famous," she answered immediately. "Like you."

Lindsay gave a quick laugh and shook her head. "I only wanted to dance," she told her. For a moment, the amusement flickered out. "My mother wanted me to be famous. Go, change your shoes," she said briskly. "I want to talk to your uncle now. Advanced class on Saturday is at one, *pointe* class at two-thirty. I'm a demon on punctuality." Turning, she focused on Seth. "Mr. Bannion...shall we use my office?"

Without waiting for an answer, Lindsay walked to the adjoining room.

Chapter 4

Because she wanted to establish her authority from the outset, Lindsay moved behind her desk. She felt neat and competent, light-years away from the first time she had met Seth. With a gesture for him to do likewise, she sat. Ignoring the instruction, Seth stood, scanning the photographs on her wall. She saw that he had focused on one of herself and Nick Davidov in the final act of *Romeo and Juliet*.

"I managed to get my hands on a poster from this ballet and sent it to Ruth some years back. She has it in her room still." He turned back but didn't move to her. "She admires you tremendously." Though his tone was even, Lindsay understood he felt the admiration implied responsibility. She frowned, not because she was loath to take it, but because he gave it to her.

"As Ruth's guardian," she began, circling around his

statement, "I feel you should know precisely what it is she'll be doing here, what's expected of her, when the classes are set and so forth."

"I believe you're the expert in this field, Ms. Dunne." Seth's voice was quiet, but Lindsay wasn't certain his mind was on his words. Again his eyes roamed her face inch by inch. It was odd, she thought, that his manner and tone could be so formal while his gaze was so personal. She shifted, suddenly uncomfortable.

"As her guardian…"

"As her guardian," Seth interrupted, "I'm aware that studying ballet is as necessary to Ruth as breathing." He came closer now, so that she had to tilt her head back to keep her eyes on his. "I'm also aware that I have to trust you…to an extent."

Lindsay lifted a brow curiously. "To what extent is that?"

"I'll know better in a couple of weeks. I like my information to be more complete before I make a decision." The eyes that were fixed on her face narrowed ever so slightly. "I don't know you yet."

She nodded, miffed without knowing precisely why. "Nor I you."

"True." He took the statement without a change of expression. "I suppose that's a problem that will solve itself in time. It's difficult for me to believe that the Lindsay Dunne I saw dance Giselle is clumsy enough to fall into puddles."

She sucked in her breath, staring at him in outraged amazement. "You nearly ran me down!" All the restraint she had practiced that morning vanished. "Anyone who comes barreling down a residential street in the rain that way should be arrested."

"Fifteen miles an hour isn't considered barreling," he countered mildly. "If I'd been doing the speed limit, I *would* have run you down. You weren't looking where you were going."

"Most people take a little care to learn the streets when they move into a new neighborhood," Lindsay retorted.

"Most people don't go for walks in rain storms," he returned. "I've an appointment shortly," he continued before she could answer. "Shall I write you a check for Ruth's tuition?"

"I'll send you a bill," she told him icily, walking past him to open the door.

Seth followed her, then pausing, crowded her into the jamb as he turned to face her again. Their bodies brushed in brief, potent contact. Every coherent thought veered out of Lindsay's brain. Tilting her head, she stared up at him, surprised and questioning, while her body reacted with instinctual knowledge.

For a moment he stayed, his eyes again making their slow, intruding study before he turned and walked to Ruth.

Off and on during the day, Lindsay's thoughts returned to Seth Bannion. What sort of man was he? On the surface he appeared to be conventional enough. But there was something more beneath. It wasn't just the glimpse of his temper she had witnessed in their first meeting. She had seen something in his eyes, felt something in the touch of his body. It was an energy that went further than the physical. She knew that volcanoes were usually calm and well-mannered on the surface but that there was always something hot and dangerous underneath.

It's nothing to me, she reminded herself, but her thoughts drifted back to him more often than she liked. He interested her. And so did his niece.

Lindsay watched Ruth during her first two classes, looking for more than technique and movement. She wanted to discover attitude and personality. Outgoing herself, Lindsay found it difficult to understand the guards the girl had built. She made no move to reach out to any of her fellow students nor to accept any overtures made to her. She was not unfriendly nor impolite, simply distant. It would be her fate, Lindsay knew, to be labeled a snob. But it isn't snobbery, Lindsay mused as she took her class through *glissades.* It's overwhelming insecurity. Lindsay recalled the instant withdrawal when she had laid her hands on Ruth's shoulders. She remembered how Ruth had been clinging to Seth before the morning session. He's her anchor at the moment; I wonder if he knows it, she mused. How much does he know about her doubts and her fears and the reason for them? How much does he care?

Lindsay demonstrated a move, her body lifting effortlessly to *pointe,* her arms rising slowly. His doubts about her training seemed to Lindsay inconsistent with his patience in sitting through the morning session.

It annoyed her that once again he had insinuated himself into her thoughts. Thrusting him out, Lindsay concentrated fully on the last of her classes. But even as her final student dashed through the front door, leaving her alone, her defenses slipped. She remembered the exploring way he had looked at her and the quiet, even texture of his voice.

Trouble, she thought as she stacked CDs. *Complications.* I'm beginning to enjoy life without complications. She glanced around with a satisfied smile.

My studio, she thought chauvinistically. I'm making something out of it. It might be small and filled with girls who won't dance to anything but top-forty rock after they hit sixteen, but it's mine. I'm making a living doing something I enjoy. What else could anyone want? Irresistibly, her eyes were drawn down to the CD she still held in her hand. Without hesitation, she inserted it into the player.

She loved her students, and she loved teaching them, but she also loved the empty studio. She had found satisfaction in the past three years of instructing, but there was something private—something nourishing—in dancing for the sheer sake of it. It was something her mother had never understood. To Mae, dancing was a commitment, and obsession. To Lindsay, it was a joy, a lover.

Ruth had brought back memories of Dulcinea. It had always been a favored role of Lindsay's because of its enthusiasm and power. Now, as the music poured into the room, she remembered vividly the flow of movement and the strength.

The music was fast and richly Spanish, and she responded to it with verve. Her body came to life with the need to dance. The challenge of the story came back to her to be expressed with sharp arm movements and *soubresauts.* There was energy and youth in the short, quick steps.

As she danced, the mirror reflected the gently flowing chiffon, but in Lindsay's mind, she wore the stiff tutu in black lace and red satin. There was a full-blossomed rose behind her ear and a Spanish comb in her hair. She was Dulcinea, all spirit, all challenge, with the energy to dance endlessly. As the music built toward the finish, Lindsay began her *fouettés*. Around and around with speed and style she twirled herself. It seemed she could go on forever, like the ballerina on a music box, effortlessly spinning to the tune. And as the toy stopped with the music, so did she. She threw a hand over her head and the other to her waist, styling for the sassy ending.

"Bravo."

With both hands clasped to her speeding heart, she whirled. There, straddling one of her small, wooden chairs, was Seth Bannion. She was breathing heavily, both from the exertion of the dance and from the shock of discovering she had not been alone. Her eyes were huge, still dark with excitement, her skin wildly flushed.

The dance had been for herself alone, but she felt no infringement on her privacy. There was no resentment that he had shared it with her. Even her initial surprise was fading to be replaced by an inner knowledge that he would understand what she had been doing and why. She didn't question the feeling, but stood, waiting as he rose and moved to her.

He kept his eyes on hers, and something more than breathlessness began to flutter inside her breast. The look was long and personal. Her blood, already warmed from the dance, heated further. She could feel it tingle under the surface of her skin. There was a feathery dryness in her throat. She lifted one of the hands she still held against her breast and pressed it to her lips.

"Magnificent," he murmured with his eyes still locked on hers. He took the hand she had pressed to her lips and brought it to his own. Her pulse was still racing at her wrist, and his thumb grazed it lightly. "You make it seem so effortless," he commented. "I hardly expect you to be out of breath."

The smile he gave her was as potent as it was unexpected. "I feel I should thank you, even though the dance wasn't for me."

"I didn't…I wasn't expecting anyone." Her voice was as jumpy as her nerves, and Lindsay sought to discipline them both. She began to remove her hand from his and was surprised when Seth resisted, holding her fingers an extra moment before releasing them.

"No, I could see you weren't." He took yet another careful scan of her face. "I'd apologize for intruding, but I'm not in the least bit sorry to have been your audience." He possessed considerably more charm than Lindsay had given him credit for. It made it difficult to separate her response to the dance from her response to him. She thought the slight wings at the tips of his brows were fascinating. Only when the left one tilted up did she realize she'd been staring and that he was amused by it. Annoyed with her own lack of sophistication, she turned to the CD player.

"I don't mind," she told him carelessly. "I always worked better with an audience. Was there something you wanted to talk to me about?"

"My knowledge of ballet is limited. What was the dance from?"

"Don Quixote." Lindsay slipped the CD back into its case. "Ruth reminded me of it last night." She faced Seth again with the CD held between them. "She intends to dance Dulcinea one day."

"And will she?" Seth took the CD from her hands, setting it aside as if impatient with the barrier.

"I think so. She has exceptional talent." Lindsay gave him a direct look. "Why did you come back here?"

He smiled again, a slow, somehow dashing smile she knew women found difficult to resist. "To see you," he said and continued to smile as surprise reflected clearly on her face. "And to talk about Ruth. It simply wasn't possible this morning."

"I see." Lindsay nodded, prepared to become the instructor again. "There is quite a bit we need to discuss. I'm afraid I thought you weren't terribly interested this morning."

"I'm very interested." His eyes were on hers again. "Have dinner with me."

It took Lindsay a moment to react, as her mind had jumped forward to plans for Ruth. "Dinner?" She gave him an ingenuous stare as she tried to decide how she felt about the idea of being with him. "I don't know if I want to do that."

His brows lifted at her bluntness, but he nodded. "Then you apparently haven't any great objection. I'll pick you up at seven." Before she could comment, Seth walked back to the door. "I already know the address."

When she had bought it, Lindsay had thought the pelican gray dress would be clean and sophisticated. It was made of thin, soft wool and was closely tailored with a mandarin collar. Critically studying herself in it, she was pleased. This was a far different image than the dripping, babbling mess who had sat in a roadside puddle, and more different, still, from the dreamy, absorbed dancer. The woman who stared back at Lindsay from the glass was a confident, mature woman. She felt as comfortable with this image as she felt with all her other roles. She decided that this aspect of Lindsay Dunne would deal most successfully with Seth Bannion. Lindsay brushed her long mane of hair over one shoulder and braided it loosely as she thought of him.

He intrigued her, perhaps because she hadn't been able to pigeonhole him, as she often did with the people she met. She sensed he was complex, and complexities always had interested her. Or perhaps, she thought, fastening thick, silver hoops to her ears, it was just because he had bought the Cliff House.

Moving to the closet, Lindsay took out his jacket and folded it. It occurred to her suddenly that it had been some time since her last real date. There had been movies and quick dinners with Andy, but thinking back on them, she decided those times hardly counted as dates. Andy's like my brother, she mused, unconsciously toying with the collar of Seth's jacket. His scent still clung to it, faint but unmistakably male.

How long has it been since I went out with a man? she wondered. Three months? Four? Six, she decided with a sigh. And in the past three years, no more than a handful of times. Before that? Lindsay laughed and shook her head. Before that, a date had been the next performance scheduled.

Did she regret it? For a moment she studied herself

seriously in the glass. There was a young woman there whose fragile looks were deceptive, whose mouth was generous. No, she'd never regretted it. How could she? She had what she wanted, and whatever she had lost was balanced on the other end of the scale. Glancing up, she saw the reflection of her toe shoes in the mirror as they hung over her bed. Thoughtfully, she stroked the collar of Seth's jacket again before gathering it up with her purse.

Her heels clicked lightly on the stair treads as she came down to the main floor. A quick glance at her watch assured her that she had a few minutes to spare. Setting down the jacket and her purse, Lindsay walked back toward her mother's rooms.

Since Mae's return from the hospital, she had been confined to the first floor of the house. Initially, the stairs had been too much for her to manage, and afterward, the habit of avoiding them had set in. The arrangement afforded both women privacy. Two rooms off the kitchen had been converted to serve as Mae's bedroom and sitting room. For the first year, Lindsay had slept on the sofa in the living room to be within calling distance. Even now she slept lightly, ever alert for any disturbance in the night.

She paused at her mother's rooms, hearing the low drone of the television. After knocking softly, she opened the door.

"Mother, I…"

She stopped when she saw Mae sitting in the recliner. Her legs were propped up as she faced the television, but her attention was focused on the book in her lap. Lindsay knew the book well. It was long and

wide and leather-bound to endure wear. Nearly half of
its oversized pages were crammed with clippings and
photos. There were professional critiques, gossip column tidbits and interviews, all expounding on Lindsay
Dunne's dancing career. There was the earliest story
from the *Cliffside Daily* to her final review in the *New
York Times.* Her professional life—and a good portion
of her personal one as well—were bound in that book.

As always, when she saw her mother poring over the
scrapbook, Lindsay was struck by waves of guilt and
helplessness. She felt her frustration rise as she stepped
into the room.

"Mother."

This time Mae glanced up. Her eyes were lit with excitement, her cheeks flushed with it. "'A lyrical dancer,'"
she quoted without looking back at the clipping, "'with
the beauty and grace of a fairy tale. Breathtaking.' Clif-
ford James," Mae continued, watching Lindsay as she
crossed the room. "One of the toughest dance critics in
the business. You were only nineteen."

"I was overwhelmed by that review," Lindsay remembered, smiling as she laid her hand on her mother's shoulder. "I don't think my feet touched ground
for a week."

"He'd say the same thing if you went back today."

Lindsay shifted her attention from the clipping and
met her mother's eyes. A thin thread of tension made
its way up her neck. "Today I'm twenty-five," she reminded her gently.

"He would," Mae insisted. "We both know it. You…"

"Mother." Sharply, Lindsay cut her off, then, appalled by her own tone, crouched down beside the chair.

"I'm sorry, I don't want to talk about this now. Please."
She lifted their joined hands to her cheek, and sighing, wished there could be more between them than the
dance. "I've only another minute or two."

Mae studied her daughter's dark, expressive eyes and
saw the plea. She shifted restlessly in her chair. "Carol
didn't say anything about your going out tonight."

Reminded that Andy's mother had spent part of the
day with her mother, Lindsay rose and began a cautious explanation. "I'm not going out with Andy." She
straightened the line of her dress.

"No?" Mae frowned. "Who, then?"

"The uncle of a new student of mine." Lindsay
brought her head up to meet Mae's eyes. "She has potential, a truly natural talent. I'd like you to see her."

"What about him?" Mae brushed off the thought of
Lindsay's student and stared down at the open scrapbook.

"I don't know him very well, of course. He's bought
the Cliff House."

"Oh?" Mae's attention returned. She was aware of
Lindsay's fascination with the house.

"Yes, they've just recently moved in. It seems Ruth
was orphaned a few months ago." She paused, remembering the sadness lurking in the girl's eyes. "She interests me very much. I want to speak to her uncle
about her."

"So you're having dinner."

"That's right." Annoyed at having to justify a simple date, Lindsay moved to the door. "I don't suppose
I'll be very late. Would you like anything before I go?"

"I'm not a cripple."

Lindsay's eyes flew to her mother's. Mae's mouth

was set, her fingers gripped tight on the edges of the book. "I know."

Then there was a silence between them that Lindsay felt unable to break. Why is it, she wondered, that the longer I live with her, the wider the gap? The doorbell sounded, overloud in the quiet. Studying her daughter, Mae recognized the indecision. She broke the contact by looking back at the pages in her lap.

"Good night, Lindsay."

She tasted failure as she turned to the door. "Good night."

Briskly, Lindsay walked down the hall, struggling out of the mood. There was nothing I could have done differently, she told herself. Nothing I could have altered. Suddenly she wanted escape, she wanted to open the front door, to step outside and to keep going until she was somewhere else. Anywhere else. Someplace where she could take her time discovering what it was she really wanted of herself. Lindsay pulled open the door with a hint of desperation.

"Hi." She greeted Seth with a smile as she stepped back to let him in. The dark suit was perfect for his lean, elegant build. Still, there was something slightly sinful about his face. It was dark and narrow and knowing. Lindsay found she liked the contrast. "I suppose I need a coat; it's turned cold." She walked to the hall closet to take out a coat of dark leather. Seth took it from her.

Wordlessly, she allowed him to slip the coat over her while she wondered about basic chemistry. It was odd, she thought, that one person should have such a strong physical reaction to another. Wasn't it strange that nearness or a touch or just a look could increase the heartbeat or raise the blood pressure? Nothing else was required—no personal knowledge, no amiability—just that chance mixture of chemicals. Lindsay didn't resist when Seth turned her to face him. They stood very close, eyes holding, as he brought his hand from her shoulder to adjust the collar of her coat.

"Do you think it's strange," she asked thoughtfully, "that I should be so strongly attracted to you when I thought you were quite horrible the first time I met you, and I'm still not completely sure you're not?"

His grin was different from his smile, she noted. The smile was slow, while the grin was a quick flash. All of his features responded at once. "Are your sentences always so frank and so convoluted?"

"Probably." Lindsay turned away, pleased to have seen the grin. "I'm not very good at dissimulating, and I suppose I talk as I think. Here's your jacket." She handed it to him, dry and neatly folded. Her smile came easily. "I certainly didn't expect to return it to you under these circumstances."

Seth took it, glancing at it briefly before bringing his eyes back to hers. "Did you have other circumstances in mind?"

"Several," Lindsay answered immediately as she picked up her purse. "And you were extremely uncomfortable in all of them. In one, you were serving a ten-year stretch for insulting dancers on rainy afternoons. Are we ready?" she asked, holding out her hand to him in a habitual gesture. His hesitation was almost too brief to measure before he accepted it. Their fingers interlocked.

"You're not what I expected," Seth told her as they stepped out into the chill of the night.

"No?" Lindsay took a deep breath, lifting her face

to try to take in all the stars at once. "What did you expect?"

They walked to the car in silence, and Lindsay could smell the spicy aroma of mums and rotting leaves. When they were in the car, Seth turned to her to give her another of the long, probing looks she had come to expect of him.

"The image you were portraying this morning was more in line with what I expected," he said at length. "Very professional, very cool and detached."

"I had fully intended to continue along those lines this evening," Lindsay informed him. "Then I forgot."

"Will you tell me why you looked ready to run for your life when you answered the door?"

She lifted a brow. "You're very perceptive."

With a sigh, Lindsay sat back against the seat. "It has to do with my mother and a constant feeling of inadequacy." She twisted her head until her eyes met his. "Perhaps one day I'll tell you about it," she murmured, not pausing to ponder why she felt she could. "But not tonight. I don't want to think about it anymore tonight."

"All right." Seth started the car. "Then perhaps you'll let a new resident in on who's who in Cliffside."

Lindsay relaxed, grateful. "How far away is the restaurant?"

"About twenty minutes," he told her.

"That should about do it," she decided, and she began to fill him in.

Chapter 5

Lindsay felt comfortable with Seth. She told him amusing stories because she liked the sound of his laughter. Her own mood of panic and desperation was gone. As they drove, she decided she wanted to know him better. She was intrigued and attracted, and if something volcanic erupted, she'd risk it. Natural disasters were rarely dull.

Lindsay knew the restaurant. She had been there once or twice before when a date had wanted to impress her. She knew that Seth Bannion wouldn't feel the need to impress anyone. This was simply the sort of restaurant he could choose: quiet, elegant, with superior food and service.

"My father brought me here once," Lindsay remembered as she stepped from the car. "On my sixteenth birthday." She waited for Seth to join her, then offered her hand. "I hadn't been allowed to date until then, so he took me out on my birthday. He said he wanted to be my first date." She smiled, warmed by the memory. "He was always doing things like that...small, incredible things." Turning, she found Seth watching her. Moonlight showered over both of them. "I'm glad I came. I'm glad it was with you."

He gave her a curious look, then trailed a finger down her braid. "So am I."

Together they walked up the steps that led to the front door.

Inside, Lindsay was attracted to the long, wide window that revealed an expanse of the Long Island Sound. Sitting in the warm, candlelit restaurant, she could all but hear the waves beat against the rocks below. She could almost feel the cold and the spray.

"This is a wonderful place," she enthused as they settled at their table. "So elegant, so subdued, yet open to all that power." There was a smile on her lips as she turned back to Seth. "I like contrasts, don't you?" The candlelight caught the dull gleam of silver at her ears. "How dull life would be if everything fit into a slot."

"I've been wondering," Seth countered as his eyes flickered from the thick hoops to the delicate planes of her face, "exactly where you fit in."

After a quick shake of her head, Lindsay looked back out the window. "I often wonder that myself. You know yourself well, I think. It shows."

"Would you like something to drink?"

Lindsay turned her head at Seth's question and saw a waiter hovering at his elbow. "Yes." She smiled at him before she gave her attention back to Seth. "Some white wine would be nice, I think. Something cold and dry."

His eyes remained on hers while he ordered. There's something quietly tenacious in the way he looks at me, Lindsay decided, like a man who's finished one page of a book and intends to go on reading until the end. When they were alone, the silence held. Something fluttered up her spine, and she drew in a long breath. It was time to establish priorities.

"We need to talk about Ruth."

"Yes."

"Seth." Nonplussed that his look didn't waver, Lindsay added authority to her voice. "You have to stop looking at me that way."

"I don't think so," he disagreed mildly.

Her brow arched at his reply, but a hint of amusement touched her mouth. "And I thought you were so scrupulously polite."

"I'm adaptable," he told her. He was relaxed in his chair, one arm resting over the back as he studied her. "You're beautiful. I enjoy looking at beauty."

"Thank you." Lindsay decided she would grow used to his direct gaze before the evening was over. "Seth," she leaned forward, pushed by her own thoughts, "this morning, when I watched Ruth, I knew she had talent. This afternoon in class I was even more impressed."

"It was very important to her to study with you."

"But it shouldn't be." Lindsay continued quickly as she again observed the slight narrowing of his eyes. "I'm not capable of giving her everything she needs. My school's so limited in what it can offer, especially to a girl like Ruth. She should be in New York, in a school where her training could be more centered, more intense."

Seth waited while the waiter opened and poured their wine. He lifted his glass, studying the contents carefully before speaking. "Aren't you capable of instructing Ruth?"

Lindsay's brows shot up at the tone of the question. When she answered, her voice was no longer warm. "I'm a capable instructor. Ruth simply needs discipline and advantages available elsewhere."

"You're easily annoyed," Seth commented, then sipped his wine.

"Am I?" Lindsay sipped hers as well, trying to remain as pragmatic as he. "Perhaps I'm temperamental," she offered and felt satisfied with the cool tone. "You've probably heard dancers are high-strung."

Seth shifted his shoulders. "Ruth plans to take more than fifteen hours of training a week with you. Isn't that adequate?"

"No." Lindsay set down her glass and again leaned close. If he asked questions, she concluded, he couldn't be totally unreasonable. "She should be taking classes every day, more specialized classes than I could possibly offer because I simply don't have any other students with her abilities. Even if I could instruct her one on one, it wouldn't be enough. She needs partnering classes. I have four male students, all of whom come in once a week to polish their football moves. They won't even participate in the recitals."

A sound of frustration escaped. Her voice had become low and intense in her need to make him understand. "Cliffside isn't the cultural center of the east coast. It's a small Yankee town." There was an inherent, unrehearsed beauty in the way her hands gestured to accent her words. Music was in the movement, silent and sweet. "People here are basic, they're not dreamers. Dancing has no practical purpose. It can be a hobby, it can be an enjoyment, but here it isn't thought of as a career. It's not thought of as a life."

"Yet you grew up here," Seth pointed out, then added more wine to the glasses. It shimmered gold in the candlelight. "You made it a career."

"That's true." Lindsay ran a fingertip around the rim of her glass. She hesitated, wanting to choose her words carefully. "My mother was a professional dancer, and she was very…strict about my training. I went to a school about seventy miles from here. We spent a great deal of time in the car coming and going." Again she looked up at Seth, but the smile was beginning to play around her mouth. "My teacher was a marvel, a wonderful woman, half French, half Russian. She's almost seventy now and not taking students or I'd plead with you to send Ruth to her."

Seth's tone was as calm and undisturbed as it had been at the start of the conversation. "Ruth wants to study with you."

Lindsay wanted to scream with frustration. She took a sip of wine until the feeling passed. "I was seventeen, Ruth's age, when I went to New York. And I'd already had eight years of intense study in a larger school. At eighteen I started with the company. The competition for a place is brutal, and training is…" Lindsay paused, then laughed and shook her head. "It's indescribable.

Ruth needs it, she deserves it. As soon as possible if she wants to be a serious dancer. Her talent demands it."

Seth took his time in answering. "Ruth is little more than a child who's just been through a series of unhappy events." He signaled the waiter for menus. "New York will still be there in three or four years."

"Three or four years!" Lindsay set the menu down without glancing at it. She stared at Seth, incredulous. "She'll be twenty."

"An advanced age," he returned dryly.

"It is for a dancer," Lindsay retorted. "It's rare for one of us to dance much past thirty. Oh, the men steal a few extra years with character parts, or now and again there's someone spectacular like Fonteyn. Those are the exceptions, not the rules."

"Is that why you don't go back?" Lindsay's thoughts stumbled to a halt at the question. "Do you feel your career is over at twenty-five?"

She lifted her glass, then set it down again. "We're discussing Ruth," she reminded him, "not me."

"Mysteries are intriguing, Lindsay." Seth picked up her hand, turning it over to study her palm before he brought his eyes back to hers. "And a beautiful woman with secrets is irresistible. Have you ever considered that some hands were made for kissing? This is one of them." He took her palm to his lips.

Lindsay's muscles seemed to go fluid at the contact. She studied him, frankly fascinated with the sensations. She wondered what it would feel like to have his lips pressed to hers, firmly, warmly. She liked the shape of his mouth and the slow, considering way it smiled.

Abruptly, she brought herself out of the dream. *Priorities,* she remembered.

"About Ruth," she began. Though she tried to pull her hand away, Seth kept it in his.

"Ruth's parents were killed in a train accident barely six months ago. It was in Italy." There was no increased pressure on her fingers, but his voice had tightened. His eyes had hardened. Lindsay was reminded of how he had looked when he had loomed over her in the rain. "Ruth was unusually close to them, perhaps because they traveled so much. It was difficult for her to form other attachments. You might be able to imagine what it was like for a sixteen-year-old girl to find herself suddenly orphaned in a foreign country, in a town they'd been in for only two weeks."

Lindsay's eyes filled with painful sympathy, but he continued before she could speak. "She knew virtually no one, and as I was on a site in South Africa, it took days to contact me. She was on her own for nearly a week before I could get to her. My brother and his wife were already buried when I got there."

"Seth, I'm sorry. I'm so terribly sorry." The need to comfort was instinctive. Lindsay's fingers tightened on his as her other hand reached up to cover their joined ones. Something flickered in his eyes, but she was too overwhelmed to see it. "It must have been horrible for her, for you."

He didn't speak for a moment, but his study of her face deepened. "Yes," he said at length, "it was. I brought Ruth back to the States, but New York is very demanding, and she was very fragile."

"So you found the Cliff House," Lindsay murmured.

Seth lifted a brow at the title but didn't comment. "I wanted to give her something stable for a while, though I know she's not thrilled with the notion of settling into a house in a small town. She's too much like her father. But for now, I feel it's what she needs."

"I think I can understand what you're trying to do," Lindsay said slowly. "And I respect it, but Ruth has other needs as well."

"We'll talk about them in six months."

The tone was so final and quietly authoritative that Lindsay had closed her mouth before she realized it. Annoyance flitted over her face. "You're very dictatorial, aren't you?"

"So I've been told." His mood seemed to switch as she looked on. "Hungry?" he asked and smiled with slow deliberation.

"A bit," she admitted, but she frowned as she opened the menu. "The stuffed lobster is especially good here."

As Seth ordered, Lindsay let her eyes drift back out to the Sound. Clearly, she could see Ruth alone, frightened, stunned with grief, having to deal with the loss of her parents and the dreadful details that must have followed. Too well could she recall the panic she had felt upon being notified of her own parents' accident. There was no forgetting the horror of the trip from New York back to Connecticut to find her father dead and her mother in a coma.

And I was an adult, she reminded herself, already having been on my own for over three years. I was in my hometown, surrounded by friends. More than ever, she felt the need to help Ruth.

Six months, she mused. If I can work with her individually, the time wouldn't be completely wasted. And maybe, just maybe, I can convince Seth sooner. He's got to understand how important this is for her. Losing my temper isn't going to get me anywhere with a man like this, she acknowledged, so I'll have to find some other way.

On a site in South Africa, Lindsay reflected, going back over their conversation. Now what would he have been doing in South Africa? Even before she could mull over the possibilities, a jingle of memory sounded in her brain.

"Bannion," she said aloud and sent his eyebrow up in question. "S. N. Bannion, the architect. It just came to me."

"Did it?" He seemed mildly surprised, then broke a breadstick in half. He offered her a share. "I'm surprised you've had time to delve into architecture."

"I'd have to have been living in a cave for the past ten years not to know the name. What was it in… *Newsview?* Yes, *Newsview,* about a year ago. There was a profile of you with pictures of some of your more prestigious buildings. The Trade Center in Zurich, the Mac-Afee Building in San Diego."

"Your memory's excellent," Seth commented. The candlelight marbled over her skin. She looked as fragile as porcelain with eyes dark and vivid. They seemed to smile at him.

"Flawless," Lindsay agreed. "I also recall reading several tidbits about you and a large portion of the female population. I distinctly remember a department store heiress, an Australian tennis pro and a Spanish opera star. Weren't you engaged to Billie Marshall, the newscaster, a few months ago?"

Seth twirled the stem of his glass between his fingers. "I've never been engaged," he answered simply. "It tends to lead to marriage."

"I see." Absently, she chewed on the breadstick. "And that isn't one of your goals?"

"Is it one of yours?" he countered.

Lindsay paused, frowning. She took his parry quite seriously. "I don't know," she murmured. "I suppose I've never thought of it in precisely that way. Actually, I haven't had a great deal of time to think of it at all. Should it be a goal?" she thought aloud. "Or more of a surprise, an adventure?"

"So speaks the romantic," Seth observed.

"Yes, I am," Lindsay agreed without embarrassment. "But then, so are you or you'd never have bought the Cliff House."

"My choice of real estate makes me a romantic?"

Lindsay leaned back, still nibbling on the breadstick. "It's much more than a piece of real estate, and I've no doubt you felt that, too. You could have bought a dozen houses, all more conveniently located and in less need of repair."

"Why didn't I?" Seth asked, intrigued with her theory.

Lindsay allowed him to top off her glass again but left it untouched. The effect of the wine was already swirling pleasantly in her head. "Because you recognized the charm, the uniqueness. If you were a cynic, you'd have bought one of the condos twenty miles further up the coast which claim to put you in touch with genuine New England scenery while being fifteen convenient minutes from the Yankee Trader Mall."

Seth laughed, keeping his eyes on her while their meal was served. "I take it you don't care for condos."

"I detest them," Lindsay agreed immediately. "Arbitrarily, I'm afraid, but that's strictly personal. They're perfect for a great number of people. I don't like…" She trailed off, hands gesturing as if to pluck the word from the air. "Uniformity," she decided. "That's strange, I suppose, because there's so much regimentation in my career. I see that differently. Individual expression is so vital. I'd so much rather someone say I was different than I was beautiful." She glanced down at the enormous serving of lobster. "*Innovative* is such a marvelous word," she stated. "I've heard it applied to you."

"Is that why you became a dancer?" Seth speared a delicate morsel of lobster into melted butter. "To express yourself?"

"I think it might be that because I was a dancer, I craved self-expression." Lindsay chose lemon over butter. "Actually, I don't analyze myself often, just other people. Did you know the house was haunted?"

"No." He grinned. "That wasn't brought up during settlement."

"That's because they were afraid you'd back out." Lindsay speared a piece of lobster. "It's too late now, and in any case, I think you'd enjoy having a ghost."

"Would you?"

"Oh, yes, I would. Tremendously." She popped the lobster into her mouth, leaning forward. "It's a romantic, forlorn creature who was done in by a narrow-minded husband about a century ago. She was sneaking off to see her lover and was careless, I suppose. In any case, he dropped her from the second-floor balcony onto the rocks."

"That should have discouraged her adulterous tendencies," Seth commented.

"Mmm," she agreed with a nod, hampered by a full mouth. "But she comes back now and again to walk in the garden. That's where her lover was waiting."

"You seem rather pleased about the murder and deceit."

"A hundred years can make almost anything romantic. Do you realize how many of the great ballets deal with death yet remain romantic? *Giselle* and *Romeo and Juliet* are only two."

"And you've played both leads," Seth said. "Perhaps that's why you emphathize with a star-crossed ghost."

"Oh, I was involved with your ghost before I danced either Giselle or Juliet," Lindsay sighed, watching the stars glitter over the water's surface. "That house has fascinated me for as long as I can remember. When I was a child, I swore I'd live there one day. I'd have the gardens replanted, and all the windows would glisten in the sun." She turned back to Seth. "That's why I'm glad you bought it."

"Are you?" His eyes ran the length of her slender throat to the collar of her dress. "Why?"

"Because you'll appreciate it. You'll know what to do to make it live again." His gaze paused briefly on her mouth before returning to her eyes. Lindsay felt a tingle along her skin. She straightened in her chair. "I know you've done some work already," she continued, feeling the Cliff House was a safe dinner topic. "You must have specific plans for changes."

"Would you like to see what's been done?"

"Yes," she answered immediately, unable to pretend otherwise.

"I'll pick you up tomorrow afternoon." He looked at her curiously. "Did you know you've an outrageous appetite for someone so small?"

Lindsay laughed, at ease again, and buttered a roll.

The sky was a deep, dark blue. The stars were low and bright, glimmering through a cloudy sky. Lindsay could feel the autumn wind shiver against the car as Seth drove along the coast. It added excitement to the romance of moonlight and wine.

The evening, she decided, had been much more pleasant than she had anticipated. From the first moment, she had enjoyed being with him. It surprised her that he could make her laugh. Lindsay knew there were times between dealing with her work and her mother that she became too serious, too intense. It was good to have someone to laugh with.

By unspoken agreement, they had steered away from controversial topics, keeping the conversation as light and palatable as the meal. She knew they would lock horns again over Ruth; there was no escaping it. Their desires for her were so totally diverse that no solution could be reached without a battle. Or two. But for the moment, Lindsay felt calm. Even as she wondered about the eye of the storm, she accepted it.

"I love nights like this," she said on a sigh. "Nights when the stars hang low and the wind talks in the trees.

You'd hear the water from the east side of your house." She turned to him as she spoke. "Did you take the bedroom with the balcony that hangs over the Sound? The one that has an adjoining dressing room?"

Seth turned to her briefly. "You seem to know the house well."

Lindsay laughed. "You could hardly expect me to resist exploring the place when it was just sitting there waiting."

Ahead, a few twinkling lights outlined Cliffside against the darkness. "Is that the room you've taken?"

"The huge stone fireplace and lofty old ceiling would have been enough by themselves, but the balcony... Have you stood on it during a storm?" she demanded. "It must be incredible with the waves crashing and the wind and lightning so close." Her eyes were trained on him so that she saw the tilt of his smile when it began.

"You like to live dangerously."

She wondered how his hair would feel between her fingers. Her eyes widened at the route her thoughts had taken. Carefully, she laced her fingers in her lap. "I suppose," she began, going back to his comment. "Perhaps I never have, except vicariously. Cliffside isn't exactly fraught with danger."

"Tell that to your ghost."

Lindsay chuckled. "*Your* ghost," she corrected as he pulled up in front of her house. "You've absolute claim on her now." While she spoke, Lindsay stepped from the car. The wind fluttered over her face. "It's truly fall now," she mused, looking about her at the quiet house. "We'll have a bonfire in the square. Marshall Woods will bring his fiddle, and there'll be music until midnight." She smiled. "It's a big event in town. I suppose it must seem very tame to someone who's traveled as much as you have."

"I grew up in a dot on the map in Iowa," he told her as they passed through the gate.

"Did you really?" Lindsay mulled over the information. "Somehow I pictured you growing up in a city, very urbane, very sophisticated. Why didn't you go back?" She stood on the first step of the porch and turned to him again.

"Too many memories."

With the height of the step and her evening shoes, Lindsay stood nearly level with him. There was a jolt of surprise in finding her eyes and mouth lined up with his. In his irises were tiny amber flecks. Without thinking, she counted them.

"There are thirteen," she murmured. "Six in one and seven in the other. I wonder if it's bad luck."

"If what's bad luck?" Her eyes were direct on his, but he could see her mind drift off, then snap back at his question.

"Oh, nothing." Lindsay brushed off the question, embarrassed by her lapse. "I have a tendency to daydream." Amusement moved over Seth's face. "Why are you smiling?"

"I was thinking back on the last time I walked my girl to her door with the front porch light shining behind her and her mother inside. I think I was eighteen."

Lindsay's eyes brightened with mischief. "It's a comfort to know you were eighteen once. Did you kiss her good-night?"

"Naturally. While her mother peeked through the living room drapes."

Slowly, Lindsay twisted her head and studied the dark, empty windows. With an arching brow, she turned back. "Mine's probably gone to bed by now," she decided. Laying her hands on his shoulders, Lindsay leaned forward to touch her lips lightly, quickly, to his.

In an instant of contact, everything changed. The bare brushing of lips was cataclysmic. Its effect rocketed through her with such velocity that she gasped. Carefully she drew away, still keeping her hands on his shoulders as they studied each other.

Her heart was knocking against her ribs as it had when she had stood in the wings before a difficult *pas de deux*. Anticipation soared through her. But this duet was unrehearsed and older than time. She dropped her eyes to his mouth and felt a hunger that was essentially physical.

They came together slowly, as if time would stop for them. There was a certainty as they slipped into each other's arms, as of old lovers reacquainting rather than meeting for the first time. Their lips touched and parted, touched and parted, as they experimented with angles. His hands slid inside her coat, hers inside his jacket. Warmth grew as the wind swirled a few autumn leaves around them.

Seth caught her bottom lip between his teeth to halt her roaming mouth. The tiny nick of pain shot trembles of desire through her. Passion flared. The slow, experimental kisses became one desperate demand. Her tongue moved with his. The hunger intensified, promising only to increase with each taste. Lindsay curved her arms up his back until she gripped his shoulders. She pressed hard against him as he took his mouth from hers to move it to the slender arch of her throat. His hair feathered against her cheek. It was soft and cool, unlike the heat of his mouth, and it seemed to draw her fingers into it.

She felt him tug the zipper of her dress down until his hands touched the naked skin of her back. They roamed, trailing down to her waist and up to the nape of her neck, flashing flames along the journey. The longing for him swelled so urgently that Lindsay trembled with it before his mouth at last returned to hers.

Her emotions began to swirl, rising to compete with the physical need. The onslaught made her dizzy, the intensity frightening her. She was discovering frailties she had not known she possessed. Struggling back to the surface, Lindsay brought her hands to his chest to push herself away. Seth freed her lips, though he kept her close in his arms.

"No, I..." Lindsay closed her eyes briefly, drawing back the strength she had always taken for granted. "It was a lovely evening, Seth. I appreciate it."

He watched her in silence a moment. "Don't you think that little speech is a bit out of place now?" Barely moving, he rubbed her lips with his.

"Yes, yes, you're right, but..." Lindsay turned her head and breathed deep of the cool, evening air. "I have to go in. I'm out of practice."

Seth took her chin in his hand, turning her face back to his. "Practice?"

Lindsay swallowed, knowing she had allowed the situation to get out of hand and having little idea how to regain control. "Please, I've never been any good at handling this sort of thing, and..."

"What sort of thing is that?" he asked her. There was no lessening of his grip on her, no weakening in the strength of his eyes.

"Seth." Her pulse was beginning to beat wildly again. "Please, let me go in before I make a total fool of myself."

All the uncertainty of her emotions beamed from her eyes. She saw anger flash in his before he crushed her mouth in a swift, powerful kiss.

"Tomorrow," he said and released her.

Breathless, Lindsay ran her hand through her hair. "I think I'd better not...."

"Tomorrow," he said again before he turned and walked back to his car.

Lindsay watched its taillights disappear. *Tomorrow,* she thought and trembled once in the chill of the night air.

Chapter 6

Because she arose late, it was past noon before Lindsay finished her barre and changed. She was determined to keep her afternoon at the Cliff House casual and dressed accordingly in a rust-colored jogging suit. Tossing the matching jacket over her arm, Lindsay bounded down the stairs just as Carol Moorefield let herself in.

Mrs. Moorefield was as unlike her son as night and day. She was petite and slender, with sleek brunette hair and sophisticated looks that never seemed to age. Andy's looks came straight from his father, a man Lindsay had seen only in photographs, as Carol had been a widow for twenty years.

When her husband had died, she had taken over his florist business and had run it with style and a keen business sense. She was a woman whose opinion Lindsay valued and whose kindness she had grown to depend on.

"Looks like you're geared up to do some running," Carol commented as she closed the front door behind her. "I'd think you'd want to rest up after your date last night."

Lindsay kissed the lightly powdered cheek. "How'd you know I'd had a date? Did Mother call you?"

Carol laughed, running a hand down the length of Lindsay's hair. "Naturally, but I could have told her. Hattie MacDonald," she supplied with a jerk of her head to indicate the house across the street. "She saw him pick you up and gave me the early bulletin."

"How nice that I made the Saturday evening information exchange," Lindsay said dryly.

Carol turned into the living room to drop her purse and jacket on the sofa. "Did you have a nice time?"

"Yes, I...yes." Lindsay suddenly found it necessary to retie her tennis shoes. Carol studied the top of her head but said nothing. "We had dinner up the coast."

"What sort of man is he?"

Lindsay looked up, then slowly began to tie her other shoe. "I'm not completely sure," she murmured. "Interesting, certainly. Rather forceful and sure of himself, and just a little formal now and again, and yet..." She recalled his attitude toward Ruth. "And yet, I think he can be very patient, very sensitive."

Hearing the tone, Carol sighed. Though she, too, knew Lindsay was not for Andy, a tiny part of her heart still hoped. "You seem to like him."

"Yes..." The word came out in a long, thoughtful stretch. Laughing, Lindsay straightened. "At least,

I think I do. Did you know he's S. N. Bannion, the architect?"

At the rate Carol's brows rose, Lindsay knew this was news. "Is he really? I thought he was going to marry some Frenchwoman, a race car driver."

"Apparently not."

"Well, this is interesting," Carol decided. She placed her hands on her hips as she did when she was truly impressed. "Does your mother know?"

"No, she…" Lindsay glanced back over her shoulder toward her mother's rooms. "No," she repeated, turning back. "I'm afraid I upset her last night. We haven't really spoken yet this morning."

"Lindsay." Carol touched her cheek, seeing the distress. "You mustn't let this sort of thing worry you."

Lindsay's eyes were suddenly wide and vulnerable. "I never seem to be able to do the right thing," she blurted out. "I owe her…"

"Stop it." Carol took her by the shoulders and gave them a brisk, no-nonsense shake. "It's ridiculous for children to go through life trying to pay back their parents. The only thing you owe Mae is love and respect. If you live your life trying to please someone else, you'll make two people unhappy. Now—" she stroked Lindsay's hair again and smiled "—that's all the advice I have for today. I'm going to go talk Mae into a drive."

Lindsay threw her arms around Carol's neck and gave one desperate squeeze. "You're so good for us."

Pleased, Carol squeezed back. "Want to come?" she invited. "We can drive for a while and have a fussy little lunch somewhere."

"No, I can't." She drew away. "Seth is picking me up soon to take me through his house."

"Ah, your Cliff House." Carol gave a knowledgeable nod. "This time you'll be able to wander about in broad daylight."

Lindsay grinned. "Do you think it'll lose some of its charm?"

"I doubt it." Carol turned to start down the hall. "Have fun, and don't worry about getting home to fix supper. Your mother and I will eat out." Before Lindsay could speak, the doorbell rang. "There's your young man," Carol announced and disappeared around the corner.

Lindsay turned to the door in a flurry of nerves. She had told herself that her response to Seth the night before had been abetted by the mood of the evening. It had been aided by her own lack of male companionship and his well-reported experience. It had been a moment only, nothing more. She told herself that now it was important to remember who he was and how easily he drew women. And how easily he left them.

It was important to channel their association into a careful friendship right from the outset. There was Ruth to think of. Lindsay knew that if she wanted what was right for Ruth, she had to keep her involvement with Ruth's uncle amicable. Like a business relationship, she decided, placing a hand on her stomach to quiet jarred nerves. Lightly friendly, no strings, nothing personal. Feeling herself settle, Lindsay opened the door.

He wore dark brown chinos and a bone-colored, crew-neck sweater. His raw physicality hit Lindsay instantly. She had known one or two other men who possessed this elemental sexual pull. Nick Davidov was one, and a choreographer she had worked with in the company was another. She recalled, too, that for them there had been women—never *a* woman—in their lives. Be careful, her brain flashed. *Be very careful.*

"Hi." Her smile was friendly, but the wariness was in her eyes. She slipped a small, canvas purse over her shoulder as she pulled the door shut behind her. Habitually, she offered her hand. "How are you?"

"Fine." With a slight pressure on her fingers, he stopped her from continuing down the porch steps. They stood almost precisely where they had stood the night before. Lindsay could all but feel the lingering energy in the air. Looking at him, she met one of his long, searching gazes. "How are you?"

"Fine," she managed, feeling foolish.

"Are you?" He was watching her carefully, deeply.

Lindsay felt her skin warm. "Yes, yes, of course I am." Annoyance replaced the guardedness in her eyes. "Why shouldn't I be?"

As if satisfied by her answer, Seth turned. Together they walked to his car. A strange man, Lindsay decided, unwittingly more intrigued than ever. Smiling, she shook her head. A very strange man.

As she started to slip into the car, she spotted three small birds chasing a crow across the sky. Amused, she followed their progress, listening to the taunting chatter. The crow arched toward the east and so did the trio of birds. Laughing, she turned, only to find herself in Seth's arms.

For a moment Lindsay lost everything but his face. Her being seemed to center on it. Her mouth warmed as his eyes lingered on hers. In invitation, her lips parted, her lids grew heavy. Abruptly she remembered what she had promised herself. Clearing her throat, she drew away. She settled herself in the car, then waited until she heard Seth shut the door before she let out a long, shaky breath.

She watched him move around the car to the driver's side. I'll have to start out in control of the situation and stay that way, she decided. She turned to him as he slid in beside her, and opted for bright conversation.

"Have you any idea how many eyes are trained on us at this moment?" she asked him.

Seth started the car but left it idling. "No, are there many?"

"Dozens." Though the car doors were closed, she lowered her voice conspiratorially. "Behind every curtain on the block. As you can see, I'm totally unaffected by the attention, but then, I'm a trained performer and used to center stage." Mischief was in her eyes. "I hope it doesn't make you nervous."

"Not a bit," Seth returned. In a quick move, he pinned her back against the seat, taking her mouth in a rapid, thrilling kiss. Though quick, it was thorough, leaving no portion of her mouth unexplored, no part of her system unaffected. When he drew away, Lindsay was breathing jerkily and staring. No one, she was certain, had ever felt what she was feeling at that moment.

"I hate to put on a dull show, don't you?" The words were low and intimate, stirring Lindsay's blood.

"Mmm," she answered noncommittally and slid cautiously away from him. This was not the way to stay in control.

The Cliff House was less than three miles from Lindsay's, but it stood high above the town, high above the rocks and water of the Sound. It was built of granite. To Lindsay's fascinated imagination, it seemed hewn from the cliff itself, carved out by a giant's hand. It was unrefined and fierce, a wicked castle perched at the very edge of the land. There were many chimneys, doors and windows, as the size of the place demanded them. But now, for the first time in more than a dozen years, Lindsay saw the house live. The windows sparkled, catching the sun, then holding it or tossing it back. There were no flowers yet to brighten the serious face of the house, but the lawn was neatly tended. And to her pleasure, there was smoke curling and drifting from the several chimneys. The driveway was steep and long, starting out from the main road, curving along the way and ending at the front of the house.

"It's wonderful, isn't it?" Lindsay murmured. "I love the way it has its back turned to the sea, as if it isn't concerned with any power but its own."

Seth stopped the car at the end of the drive, then turned to her. "That's a rather fanciful thought."

"I'm a rather fanciful person."

"Yes, I know," Seth observed, and leaning across her, unlatched her door. He stayed close a moment so that the slightest move would have brought their mouths together. "Strangely, on you it's attractive. I've always preferred practical women."

"Have you?" Something seemed to happen to Lindsay when he was close. It was as if many threads, thin but impossibly strong, wound their way around her until she was helpless. "I've never been very good at practicalities. I'm better at dreaming."

He twisted the end of a strand of her hair around his fingers. "What sort of dreams?"

"Foolish ones mostly, I suppose. They're the best kind." Quickly she pushed the door open and stepped outside. Closing her eyes, she waited for her system to drift back to normal. When she heard his door shut, she opened them again to study the house. Casual, friendly, she reminded herself and took a deep breath.

"Do you know," she began, "the last time I walked here, it was about midnight and I was sixteen." She smiled, remembering, as they moved up the narrow walk toward a skirting porch. "I dragged poor Andy along and crawled through a side window."

"Andy." Seth paused at the front door. "That's the weight-lifter you were kissing in front of your studio."

Lindsay lifted a brow, acknowledging the description of Andy. She said nothing.

"Boyfriend?" Seth asked lightly, jiggling the keys in his palm as he studied her.

Lindsay kept her look bland. "I outgrew boyfriends a few years back, but he's a friend, yes."

"You're a very affectionate friend."

"Yes, I am," she agreed. "I've always considered the two words synonymous."

"An interesting outlook," Seth murmured and unlocked the door. "No need to crawl in a side window this time." He gestured her inside.

It was as awesome as Lindsay remembered. The ceilings in the entrance hall were twenty feet high with the rough beams exposed. A wide staircase curved to the left, then split in two and ran up opposing sides of an overhanging balcony. The banister was polished mirrorlike, and the treads were uncarpeted.

The dusty, peeling wallpaper Lindsay remembered had been stripped away to be replaced by a new fabric of rich cream. A long, narrow Persian carpet was spread on the oak-planked floor. The sun was muted, reflected on the prisms of a tiered chandelier.

Without speaking, she walked down the hall to the first doorway. The parlor had been completely restored. There was a bold floral print on one wall, offset by the lacquered pearl-colored tones of the others. Lindsay took a slow tour of the room. She stopped by a small, eighteenth-century table, touching it lightly with a fingertip.

"It's wonderful." She glanced at the thinly striped brocade of the sofa. "You knew precisely what was needed. I could almost have pictured this room with a Dresden shepherdess on the mantel—and there it is!" She walked over to study it, moved by its delicacy. "And French carpets on the floor...." Lindsay turned back with a smile that reflected all her pleasure with the room. Hers was a fragile, timeless beauty suited to the antiques and silks and brocades that now surrounded her. Seth took a step closer. Her perfume drifted to him. "Is Ruth here?" she asked.

"No, not at the moment." He surprised them both by reaching out to run a fingertip down her cheek. "She's at Monica's. This is the first time I've seen you with your hair down," he murmured, moving his fingers from her skin to her hair, where he tangled them in its length. "It suits you."

Lindsay felt the threads of desire reaching out for her and stepped back. "I had it down the first time we met." She smiled, ordering herself not to be foolish. "It was raining, as I remember."

Seth smiled back, first with his eyes, then with his lips. "So it was." He closed the distance between them again, then trailed a finger down her throat. Lindsay shivered involuntarily. "You're amazingly responsive," he said quietly. "Is that always true?"

Heat was rushing through her, pulsing where his flesh touched hers. Shaking her head, she turned away. "That's not a fair question."

"I'm not a fair man."

"No," Lindsay agreed and faced him again. "I don't think you are, at least not in your dealings with women. I came to see the house, Seth," she reminded him briskly. "Will you show it to me?"

He moved to her again but was suddenly interrupted. A small, trim man with a dark, silver-speckled beard appeared in the doorway. The beard was full, beautifully shaped, growing down from his ears to circle his mouth and cover his chin. It was all the more striking as it was the only hair on his head. He wore a black, three-piece suit with a crisp, white shirt and a dark tie. His posture was perfect, militarily correct, his hands at ease by his sides. Lindsay had an immediate impression of efficiency.

"Sir."

Seth turned to him, and the tension seemed to slip from the room. Lindsay's muscles relaxed. "Worth." He nodded in acknowledgement as he took Lindsay's arm. "Lindsay, Worth. Worth, Ms. Dunne."

"How do you do, miss?" The slight bow was European, the accent British. Lindsay was captivated.

"Hello, Mr. Worth." Her smile was spontaneously open and friendly as was the offering of her hand. Worth hesitated with a brief glance at Seth before accepting it. His touch was light, a bare brushing of her fingertips.

"You had a call, sir," he said, returning his attention to his employer. "From Mr. Johnston in New York. He said it was quite important."

"All right, get him back for me. I'll be right in." He turned to Lindsay as Worth backed from the room. "Sorry, this shouldn't take long. Would you like a drink while you wait?"

"No." She glanced back to where Worth had stood. It was easier, she decided, to deal with Seth when he slipped into a formal attitude. Smiling, she wandered back to the window. "Go ahead, I'll just wait here."

With a murmur of assent, Seth left her.

It took less than ten minutes for Lindsay's curiosity to overpower her sense of propriety. This was a house she had explored in the dead of night when cobwebs and dust had been everywhere. It was impossible for her to resist exploring it when the sun was shining on a polished floor. She began to wander, intending to limit her tour to the main hall.

There were paintings to admire and a tapestry that took her breath away. On a table sat a Japanese tea set so thin, she thought it might shatter under her gaze. Too intrigued by the treasures she was discovering to remember her resolution to keep to the hall, she pushed open the door at the end of it and found herself in the kitchen.

It was a strange, appealing mixture of scrupulous efficiency and old-fashioned charm. The appliances were built-in, with stainless steel and chrome glistening everywhere. The counters were highly lacquered wood. The dishwasher hummed mechanically while a quiet little fire crackled in a waist-high hearth. Sunlight poured through the window illuminating the vinyl-covered walls and planked floors. Lindsay made a sound of pure appreciation.

Worth turned from his activity at a large butcher block table. He had removed his jacket, replacing it with a long, white, bibbed apron. An expression of astonishment ran across his face before he folded it into its habitual placid lines.

"May I help you, miss?"

"What a wonderful kitchen!" Lindsay exclaimed and let the door swing shut behind her. She turned a circle, smiling at the shining copper-bottomed kettles and pans that hung over Worth's head. "How clever Seth must be to have blended two worlds into one so perfectly."

"To be sure, miss," Worth agreed crisply. "Have you lost your way?" he asked and carefully wiped his hands on a cloth.

"No, I was just wandering a bit." Lindsay continued to do so around the kitchen while Worth stood correctly and watched her. "Kitchens are fascinating places, I think. The hub of the house, really. I've always regretted not learning to cook well."

She remembered the yogurts and salads of her professional dancing days, the occasional binges at an Italian or French restaurant, the rarely used refrigerator in her apartment. Eating had been something often overlooked in the crammed course of a day. Cooking had been out of the question.

"I'm baffled by anything more complex than a tuna casserole." She turned to Worth, still smiling. "I'm sure you're a marvelous cook." Lindsay stood just to the side of the window. The afternoon sun shone strong on her face, accentuating the fine bones and delicate complexion.

"I do my best, miss. Shall I serve you coffee in the parlor?"

Lindsay held back a sigh. "No, thank you, Mr. Worth. I suppose I'll just wander back and see if Seth is finished."

As she spoke, the door swung open and Seth walked through. "I'm sorry that took so long." The door closed soundlessly behind him.

"I barged into your kitchen without thinking." After casting a quick, apologetic glance at Worth, she moved to Seth. "Things have changed a bit since the last time I was here."

Some silent male message passed over her head between Seth and Worth before he took her arm to lead her through the door. "And you approve?"

She pushed her hair off her shoulder as she turned her face up to his. "I should reserve judgment until I see the rest, but I'm already captivated. And I *am* sorry," she continued, "about just walking into the kitchen that way. I got involved."

"Worth has a policy about women in the kitchen," Seth explained.

"Yes," Lindsay agreed wryly. "I think I know what the policy is. *Keep out.*"

"Very perceptive."

They moved through the downstairs rooms; the library, where the original paneling had been restored and polished to a glossy finish; a sitting room stripped of wallpaper and as yet unfinished; to Worth's quarters, spartan in cleanliness.

"The rest of the main level should be finished off this winter," Seth commented as they started up the staircase. Lindsay let her fingers trail over the banister. *How could wood feel this smooth?* she mused. "The house was solidly built, and there's generally only small bits of repair and redesigning to do," Seth continued.

The banister, she reflected, would have known the touch of countless palms and an occasional bottom. She grinned, thinking what a thrill it would be to slide all the way down from the third floor.

"You love this place," Seth stated, pausing at the landing, catching Lindsay between the banister and himself. They were close, and she tilted her head until she could meet his eyes. "Why?"

It was obvious he wanted an answer that was specific rather than general. Lindsay thought it through before speaking. "I think because it's always seemed so strong, so eternal. There's a fairy tale quality about it. Generation after generation, era after era, it endures."

Turning, Lindsay walked along the railing that overhung the first floor. Below, the line and space of the main hall ran parallel. "Do you think Ruth will adjust to living here? That she'll come to accept being settled in one place?"

"Why do you ask?"

Shrugging, Lindsay turned and began to walk with Seth down the hall. "Ruth interests me."

"Professionally."

"And personally," Lindsay countered, glancing up at his tone. "Are you against her dancing?"

He stopped at a doorway to fix her with one of his lengthy looks. "I'm not at all certain your definition of dancing and mine are the same."

"Maybe not," she acknowledged. "But perhaps Ruth's definition would be more to the point."

"She's very young. And," he added before Lindsay could retort, "my responsibility." Opening the door, he guided her inside.

The room was unmistakably feminine. Pale blue Priscilla curtains fluttered at the windows, and the shade was repeated in the counterpane. There was a white brick fireplace with a brass fan-shaped screen in front of the hearth. English ivy trailed from a brass pot on a piecrust table. Lining the walls were framed pictures of ballet stars. Lindsay saw the poster Seth had spoken of. Her Juliet to Davidov's Romeo. Memories flooded back.

"There's no doubt about whose room this is," she murmured, glancing at the pink satin ribbons on the bureau. She looked up to study Seth's chiseled features. He is a man, accustomed to seeing things exclusively from a man's perspective, she realized. He could easily have settled Ruth in a boarding school and sent her generous checks. Had it been difficult to make room for a girl and a girl's unique needs in his life?

"Are you a generous man on the whole, Seth," she asked curiously, "or is it selective?"

She saw his brow lift. "You have a habit of asking unusual questions." Taking her arm, he began to lead her back down the hall.

"And you've a talent for evading them."

"This is the room that should interest your ghost," Seth smoothly changed the subject.

Lindsay waited for Seth to open the door, then stepped inside. "Oh, yes!" She walked to the center and turned a quick circle. Her hair followed in a slow arch. "It's perfect."

Deep, curved window seats were cushioned in burgundy velvet, the shade picked up in the pattern of a huge Oriental rug. The furniture was old, heavy Victorian, gleaming from Worth's attentiveness. Nothing could have suited the high, wide room more. There was a blanket chest at the foot of the four-poster bed and pewter candlesticks on either side table.

"It's because you're an architect, I suppose," Lindsay said, admiringly. "You seem to know exactly what's needed."

The fireplace was stone and massive, sending images of thundering flames through Lindsay's mind. On a long, dark night the fire would roar, then crackle, then sizzle as the hours passed. She had a vivid flash of herself curled in the huge bed with Seth's body warming hers. A bit stunned by the clarity of the vision, she turned to wander about the room.

Too soon, she told herself. *Too fast.* Remember who he is. Silently she juggled the unexpected and unwanted emotions. At the French doors she paused, pushing them both open to step out. A rush of wind met her.

There was the raw sound of water against rock, the

scent of salt in the chilling air. Lindsay watched the clouds scrambling across the sky chased by the wild wind. She walked to the rail and looked down. The drop was sheer and deadly. The fierce waves battered the jagged rocks, receding only to gather force to strike again. Lost in the wild excitement of the scene, Lindsay was not fully aware of Seth close behind her. When he turned her toward him, her response was as unrestrained and inevitable as the moving clouds above, the pounding surf below.

Her arms reached up to circle his neck as he drew her close. They came together. Her mouth molded to his, the hunger instant. She didn't hesitate but answered the intimacies of the kiss, exploring with her tongue until his taste mixed with hers. When he touched her, she trembled, not from fear or resistance, but from pure pleasure.

His hand slid under her shirt, trailing briefly along her ribcage. He cupped her breast; she was small and his hand was large. Slowly, while he took the kiss deeper, he traced his finger over the swell. As she had longed to do, she tangled her fingers in his hair. There was an impossible surge of need. It ran through her quickly— a river changing course. The current was irresistible, dragging her along into more turbulent waters. His fingers warmed against her skin as they roamed, spreading waves of delight.

When he took his mouth from hers to ravage the cord of her neck, Lindsay felt her body suffused by a sudden heat. The chill of the wind was a shock to her face and only increased the excitement. His teeth brought tiny ripples of pain to blend with the pleasure. The sound of the surf echoed in her brain, but through it she heard him murmur her name. When his mouth returned to claim hers, she welcomed it eagerly. Never had desire been so quick, so all-consuming.

Seth tore his mouth from hers, bringing his hands to her shoulders to keep her close. His eyes locked on hers. In them, Lindsay recognized anger and passion. A fresh tremor of excitement sped up her spine. She would have melted back into his arms had he not held her away.

"I want you." The wind tossed his hair around his face. His brows were lowered, accentuating the slight upsweep at the tips.

Lindsay could hear her heartbeat increase to roar in her brain like the waves below. She was courting danger and knew it, but the extent of it began to seep through. "No." She shook her head even as she felt the flush of desire on her cheeks. "No." The ground was unsteady under her feet. She moved away to grip the rail and breathe deep of the cold, sea air. It left her throat raw and tingling. Abruptly, Seth took her arm and spun her around.

"What the hell do you mean, no?" His voice was deadly low.

Lindsay shook her head again. The wind threw her hair into her eyes, and she tossed it back, wanting to see him clearly. Something in his stance was as untamed and fierce as the surf below them. This was the volcano. It drew her, tempted her. "Just that," she said. "What happened just now was unavoidable, but it won't go beyond that."

Seth came closer. A strong hand took hold of the back of her neck. Lindsay could feel the weight and texture of each separate finger. "You don't believe that."

His mouth lowered swiftly to hers, but instead of demand, he used persuasion. He traced his tongue between her lips until they parted on a sigh. He plundered, but gently, devastatingly. Lindsay gripped his arms to keep her balance. Her breath was as trapped as it would have been had she tumbled over the edge of the balcony to cartwheel through the air to the rocks below.

"I want to make love with you." The movement of his lips against hers shot an ache of desire through her. Lindsay struggled away.

For a moment she didn't speak but stood, catching her breath and watching him. "You have to understand," she began, then paused for her voice to steady. "You have to understand the kind of person I am. I'm not capable of casual affairs or one-night stands." Again she tossed her hair from her eyes. "I need more than that. I haven't your sophistication, Seth, I can't—I won't—compete with the women you've had in your life."

She turned to move away, but he took her arm again, keeping her facing toward him. "Do you really think we can walk away from what's already between us?"

"Yes." The word came out sharply as doubts crowded her. "It's necessary."

"I want to see you tonight."

"No, absolutely not." He was close, and Lindsay backed away.

"Lindsay, I'm not going to let this pass."

She shook her head. "The only thing between us is Ruth. Things would be simpler if we'd both remember that."

"Simple?" He caught a strand of her hair. A half-smile played around his mouth. "I don't think you're the sort of woman who'd be satisfied with simplicity."

"You don't know me," she retorted.

He smiled fully now, and releasing her hair, took her arm to lead her firmly into the house. "Perhaps not, Lindsay," he agreed pleasantly, "but I will." The iron determination of his tone was not lost on Lindsay.

Chapter 7

It had been almost a month since Ruth had joined Lindsay's school. The weather had turned cold quickly, and already there was a hint of snow in the air. Lindsay did her best to keep the school's ancient furnace operating to its fullest capacity. With a shirt tied loosely at the waist over her leotard, she taught the final class of the day.

"*Glissade, glissade. Arabesque* on *pointe.*" As she spoke, Lindsay moved up and down the line of students, watching each critically for form and posture. She was pleased with her advanced *pointe* class. The students were good, possessing a firm understanding of music and movement. But the longer Ruth remained in the class, the more she stood apart from the others.

Her talent is so far above the ordinary, Lindsay thought, studying her for posture and flow. *She's being wasted here.* The now-familiar frustration overcame her, bordering on anger. And the look in her eyes, she thought as she signaled to one of the girls to keep her chin lifted, says, *"I want."* How do I convince Seth to let her go for it—and to let her go for it now before it slips away?

At the thought of Seth, Lindsay's attention wavered from her students. It locked on the last time she had seen him. If she were honest with herself, she'd admit that she'd thought of him over and over again these past weeks. She wanted to tell herself that the physical attraction she felt for him would fade. But remembering the strength, remembering the speed, she knew it was a lie.

"Tendu," Lindsay instructed and folded her arms over her chest. Still the memories of his touch, of his taste, lingered. Often she had caught herself wondering what he was doing—when she was drinking coffee in the morning, when she was alone in the studio in the evening, when she woke without cause in the middle of the night. And she had forced herself to resist the urge to question Ruth.

I will not make a fool of myself over this man, she thought.

"Brenda, hands." Lindsay demonstrated, fingers flowing with a movement of her wrist. The ringing of the phone caught her by surprise. She gave her watch a frown. No one ever called the studio during class. Instantly the thought rushed through her mind: *Mother.*

"Take over, Brenda." Without waiting for a reply, she raced back to her office and grabbed the phone.

"Yes, Cliffside School of Dance." Her heart fluttered in her throat.

"Lindsay? Lindsay, is that you?"

"Yes, I…" Her hand paused on its way to her lips. "Nicky." There was no mistaking the musical Russian accent. "Oh, Nick, how wonderful to hear your voice!" Monica's piano playing continued smoothly. Lindsay cupped her hand over her ear as she sat. "Where are you?"

"In New York, of course." There was a laughing lilt to his voice which she had always loved. "How is your school progressing?"

"Very well. I've worked with some very good dancers. In fact, there's one in particular I want badly to send up to you. She's special, Nick, beautifully built, and…"

"Later, later." As he cut off Lindsay's enthusiastic report of Ruth, she could almost see the quick brushing-away gesture that would have accompanied the words. "I've called to talk about you. Your mother does well?"

Lindsay's hesitation was barely a sigh. "Much better. She's been getting around on her own for some time now."

"Good. Very good. Then when are you coming back?"

"Nick." Lindsay moved her shoulders, then glanced at the wall at the photograph of herself dancing with the man on the other end of the phone. Three years, she mused. It might as well be thirty. "It's been too long, Nick."

"Nonsense. You're needed."

She shook her head. He had always been dictatorial. Perhaps, she thought, it's my fate to tangle with domineering men. "I'm not in shape, Nick, not for the merry-go-round. There's young talent coming up." Her mind drifted back to Ruth. "*They're* needed."

"Since when are you afraid of hard work and competition?"

The challenge in his voice was an old ruse that made Lindsay smile. "We're both aware that teaching dance for three years is entirely different from performing for three years. Time doesn't stand still, Nick, not even for you."

"Afraid?"

"Yes. A little, yes."

He laughed at the confession. "Good, the fear will push you to dance better." He broke in on her exasperated laugh. "I need you, *ptichka,* my little bird. I've almost finished writing my first ballet."

"Nick, that's wonderful! I had no idea you were working on anything."

"I have another year, perhaps two, to dance. I have no interest in character parts." During the slight pause, Lindsay heard the murmur of girls as they changed into their outdoor shoes. "I've been offered the directorship of the company."

"I can't say I'm surprised," Lindsay returned warmly. "But I am pleased, for you and for them."

"I want you back, Lindsay, back in the company. It can be arranged, you know, with some strings pulled."

"I don't want that. No, I…"

"There is no one to dance my ballet but you. She is Ariel, and Ariel is you."

"Oh, Nick, please." Lifting a hand, she pinched the

bridge of her nose between her thumb and forefinger. She had put the world he was offering behind her.

"No, no argument, not over the phone." She shook her head silently and shut her eyes. "When I've finished the ballet, I'm coming to Cliffdrop."

"Cliffside," Lindsay corrected. She opened her eyes as a smile came to her lips.

"Side, drop, I'm Russian. It's expected. I'll be there in January," he continued, "to show you the ballet. Then you'll come back with me."

"Nick, you make it sound so simple."

"Because it is, *ptichka.* In January."

Lindsay took the dead receiver from her ear and stared at it. How like Nick, she mused. He was famous for his grand, impulsive gestures, his total dedication to the dance. And he's so brilliant, she thought, replacing the receiver. So confident. He'd never understand that some things can be tucked away in a memory box and still remain precious and alive. For Nick it was all so simple.

She rose and walked over to study the photograph. It's the company first, last and always. But for me there are so many other factors, so many other needs. I don't even know what they are, only that I have them. She folded her arms across her chest, hugging her elbows. Maybe this was the time of decision. A flutter of impatience ran through her. I've been coasting for too long, she accused. Shaking herself back to the moment, Lindsay walked into the studio. Students were still milling about, reluctant to leave the warmth of the school for the cold outside. Ruth had returned to the barre alone to practice. In the mirror, her eyes followed Lindsay across the room. Monica looked up with her cheerful smile.

"Ruth and I are going to do a pizza and a movie. Want to come?"

"Sounds great, but I want to do a little more work on the staging for *The Nutcracker*. Christmas will be here before we know it."

Monica reached out to touch her hand. "You work too hard, Lindsay."

Lindsay squeezed Monica's hand, meeting the grave, concerned eyes. "I've just been giving that some thought." Both women glanced up as the door opened. A blast of cold air whooshed in with Andy. His normally pale complexion was reddened with cold, his huge shoulders hunched against it.

"Hi!" Lindsay held out her hands to take both of his. She chafed at the chill. "I didn't expect to see you tonight."

"Looks as though I timed it pretty well." He gave a quick look around as students pulled slacks and sweaters over their leotards. He greeted Monica casually; she, in turn, seemed to nod almost hopefully in Andy's direction.

"Hello, Andy," she seemed to stammer at last.

Ruth watched the simple exchange from across the room. It was so obvious, she thought, to everyone but the three of them. He was crazy in love with Lindsay, and Monica was crazy in love with him. She had seen Monica flush with anticipation the moment Andy had entered the studio. He, on the other hand, had seen only

Lindsay. How strange people are, she reflected as she executed a *grand plié*.

And Lindsay. Lindsay was everything Ruth ever hoped to be: a true ballerina, confident, poised, beautiful, with something elusive in her movements. Ruth thought she moved not like a butterfly or bird, but like a cloud. There was something light, something free, in each step, in each gesture. It wasn't with envy that Ruth watched her, but with longing. And she did watch her, closely, continually. And because she did so, Ruth felt she was growing to know Lindsay well.

Ruth admired Lindsay's openness, her free flow of emotions. She had warmth, which drew people to her. But there was more playing beneath the surface, much more, Ruth felt, than Lindsay was in the habit of revealing. Ruth doubted whether those hidden passions were often fully released. It would take something strong, like the dance itself, to release them.

As Ruth pondered these thoughts, the door opened again, and her uncle strode into the studio.

A smile sprang to Ruth's lips along with a greeting. She halted the latter to play the observer once more.

The jolt of the eye contact between Seth and Lindsay was quick and volcanic. Its flare was so short that had she not been watching so intensely, she would have missed it. But it was real and potent. She paused a moment, frowning thoughtfully at her mentor and her uncle. This was unexpected, and she didn't know how she felt about it. The attraction between them was as patently obvious to her as Monica's for Andy and Andy's for Lindsay.

Amazing, she decided, that none of them seemed

aware of the emotions at play among the four of them. She remembered the awareness in her parents' eyes when they had looked at each other. The vision brought both warmth and sadness. Ruth badly wanted to feel a part of that kind of love again. Without speaking, she moved to the corner of the room to remove her toe shoes.

The moment Lindsay had looked over and seen Seth, she had felt the power. It flooded her, then ebbed so swiftly she was certain that her legs had dissolved below the knees. No, the attraction hadn't faded. It had doubled. Everything about him was instantly implanted in her brain: his wind-tousled hair, the way he left his sheepskin jacket unbuttoned to the cold, the way his eyes seemed to swallow her the moment he stepped inside.

It seemed impossible that without even an effort she could completely obliterate everyone else from her consciousness. They might have stood alone, on an island, on a mountaintop, so complete was her absorption with him.

I've missed him, she realized abruptly. It's been twenty-six days since I've seen him, spoken to him. A month ago I didn't know he existed, and now I think about him at all sorts of odd, unexpected times. Her smile began of its own volition. Though Seth didn't return it, Lindsay stepped forward, extending her hands.

"Hello. I've missed seeing you."

The statement came spontaneously and without guile. She took Seth's hands as he studied her face.

"Have you?" He asked the question quietly, but the demand in his tone reminded Lindsay to use caution.

"Yes," she admitted. She took her hands from his and turned. "You know Monica and Andy, don't you?" Monica stood near the piano stacking sheet music, but Lindsay approached her now and claimed the task. "You don't have to bother with that," she said. "You and Ruth must be starving, and you'll miss that movie if you stay around too long." She rambled, annoyed with herself. Why, she asked herself, don't I ever think before I speak? She lifted her hand in farewell as loitering students trickled out. "Have you eaten, Andy?"

"Well, no, actually, that's why I stopped by." He glanced at Seth. "I thought maybe you'd like to grab a hamburger and take in a movie."

"Oh, Andy, that's sweet." She stopped shuffling music to smile at him. "But I've got some work to finish up. I've just turned down a similar offer from Monica and Ruth. Why don't you switch to pizza and go with them?"

"Sure, Andy." Monica spoke up rapidly, then struggled with a flush. "That'd be fun, wouldn't it, Ruth?"

At the entreaty in Monica's liquid brown eyes, Ruth smiled and nodded. "You weren't coming by for me, were you, Uncle Seth?" Ruth rose, pulling on jeans.

"No." He watched his niece's head disappear inside a bulky sweater, then pop through the neck opening. "I came to have a few words with Lindsay."

"Well, we should get out of your way." Monica moved with a grace unexpected in a large-boned girl. There was an athletic swing to her gait softened by her own early years at the barre. Grabbing her coat, she looked back at Andy. Her smile wasn't reserved, but hesitant. "Coming, Andy?" She saw the quick glance he aimed at Lindsay. Her heart sank.

"Sure." He touched Lindsay's shoulder. "See you tomorrow."

"Night, Andy." Rising on her toes, she gave him a light kiss. "Have a good time." The statement was made to all three. Andy and Monica walked to the door, both battling depression. Ruth trailed after them, a smile lurking at her mouth.

"Good night, Uncle Seth, Ms. Dunne." She pulled the studio door firmly shut behind her.

Lindsay stared at the closed panel a moment, wondering what had caused the gleam in Ruth's eyes. It had been mischief, pure and simple, and though it pleased her to see it, Lindsay wondered at its cause. Shaking her head, she turned back to Seth.

"Well," she began brightly, "I suppose you want to discuss Ruth. I think…"

"No."

Lindsay's thoughts paused in midstream, then backed up. "No?" she repeated. Her expression was one of genuine bafflement until Seth took a step closer. Then she understood. "We really should talk about her." Turning away, she wandered to the room's center. In the wall of mirrors, she could see their reflections. "She's far more advanced than any of my other students, far more dedicated, far more talented. Some were born to dance, Seth. Ruth is one of them."

"Perhaps." Casually, he shrugged out of his jacket and laid it on top of the piano. She knew instinctively that tonight he wouldn't be easy to deal with. Her fingers plucked at the knot in her shirt. "But it's been one month, not six. We'll talk about Ruth next summer."

"That's absurd." Annoyed, Lindsay turned to face him. It was a mistake, she discovered, as the reality of him was far more potent than the mirror image. She turned away again and began to pace quickly. "You make it sound as though this is a whim she'll outgrow. That's simply unrealistic. She's a dancer, Seth. Five months from now she'll still be a dancer."

"Then waiting shouldn't be a problem."

His logic caused Lindsay to close her eyes in a spurt of fury. She wanted badly to reason with him calmly. "Wasted time," she said with quiet control. "And in this situation, wasted time is a sin. She needs more— so much more—than I can give her here."

"She needs stability first." There was annoyance just under the surface of his voice. It mirrored Lindsay's own sentiments as the glass did their bodies.

"She has something," she tossed back, gesturing with both arms in frustration. "Why do you refuse to see it? It's rare and beautiful, but it needs to be nurtured, it needs to be disciplined. It only becomes more difficult to do that as time goes on."

"I told you before, Ruth's my responsibility." His voice had sharpened to a fine edge. "And I told you I didn't come to discuss Ruth. Not tonight."

Lindsay's intuition repressed her retort. She'd get no-where with him now, not this way, and it was possible to ruin the chance of any further opportunity. To win for Ruth, she needed patience.

"All right." She took a deep breath and felt her temper recede. "Why did you come?"

He walked to her, taking her firmly by the shoulders before she could move away. "You missed seeing me?" he asked as his eyes bored into hers in the glass.

"In a small town like this it's rare to go nearly a month without seeing someone." She tried to step away, but his fingers tightened.

"I've been working on a project, a medical center to be built in New Zealand. The drawings are nearly finished now."

Because the idea intrigued her, Lindsay relaxed. "How exciting that must be—to create something out of your head that people will walk in, live in, work in. Something that's solid and lasting. Why did you become an architect?"

"Buildings fascinated me." He began a slow massage of her shoulders, but her interest was focused on his words. "I wondered why they were built in certain ways, why people chose different styles. I wanted to make them functional and appealing to the eye." His thumb trailed up the nape of her neck and awakened a myriad of nerve endings. "I've a weakness for beauty." Slowly, while Lindsay's eyes were glued to the mirror, he lowered his mouth to tease the freshly aroused skin. A breath trembled through her lips to be sucked back in at the contact.

"Seth…"

"Why did you become a dancer?" His question interrupted her protest. He kneaded her muscles with his fingers and watched her in the mirror. He caught the desire flickering in her eyes.

"It was all there ever was for me." Lindsay's words were husky, clouded with restrained passion. She found it hard to concentrate on her own words. "My mother spoke of nothing else as far back as I can remember."

"So you became a dancer for her." He lifted a hand to her hair and drew out a pin.

"No, some things are meant to be. This was meant for me." His hand trailed up the side of her neck to bury itself in her hair. He drew out another pin. "It would have been dancing for me regardless of my mother. She only made it more important sooner. What are you doing?" She placed a hand over his as he began to withdraw another pin.

"I like your hair down, where I can feel it."

"Seth, don't..."

"You always wear it up when you're teaching, don't you?"

"Yes, I..." The weight of her hair pushed against the remaining pins until they fell to the floor. Her hair tumbled free in pale blond clouds.

"School's out," he murmured, then buried his face in its thickness.

Their reflection showed her the sharp contrast of his hair against hers, of his tanned fingers against the ivory skin of her throat. There was a magic about watching him brush the hair from her neck and lower his mouth while feeling his lips and fingers on her skin. Fascinated, she watched the couple in the wall of the mirrors. When he turned her so that flesh and blood faced flesh and blood, she felt no lessening of the trance. Totally involved, she stared up at him.

He lowered his mouth, and though her lips hungered, he feathered kisses along her jawline. His hands moved greedily through her hair while he teased her face with promising kisses. Lindsay began to burn for the intimacy that comes with the joining of mouth to mouth. But even as she turned her head to find his lips, he drew her away.

Waves of heat rose from her toes, concentrating in her lungs until she was certain they would explode from the pleasure. With his eyes locked on hers, Seth slowly untied the knot in her shirt. Barely touching her, he ran his fingers up her shoulders, lingering only a heartbeat away from the swell of her breasts. Gently, he pushed the shirt from her until it drifted soundlessly to the floor.

There was something stunningly sexual in the gesture. Lindsay felt naked before him. He had destroyed all her barricades. There was no longer room for illusions. Stepping forward, she rose on her toes to take his mouth with hers.

The kiss started slowly, luxuriously, with the patience of two people who know the pleasure they can bring to each other. The mouth is for tasting, and they assuaged a hunger that had grown sharp and deep with fasting. They supped without hurry, as if wanting to prolong the moment of full contentment.

Lindsay took her lips from his to explore. There was a hint of roughness at his jawline from the day's growth of beard. His cheekbones were long and close to his skin. Below his ear his taste was mysteriously male. She lingered there, savoring it.

His hands were on her hips, and his fingers trailed along the tops of her thighs. She shifted so that he might touch her more freely. On a long, gradual journey, he brought his hand to her breast. Her leotard was snug, hardly an intrusion between his palm and her flesh.

Their lips joined in a hot, desperate demand as their bodies strained, one against the other. His arms swept her closer, nearly bringing her off the floor. There was no longer comfort, no longer leisure, but the pain was exquisite.

As from down a long tunnel, Lindsay heard the ringing of the bell. She burrowed deeper into Seth. The ringing came again, and yet again, until its meaning sunk into her consciousness. She moved against him, but he caught her closer.

"Let it ring, damn it." His mouth took hers, swallowing the words.

"Seth, I can't." Lindsay struggled through the mists in her brain. "I can't…my mother."

He swore richly but loosened his hold. Pushing away, Lindsay rushed to answer the phone.

"Yes?" Passing a hand through her hair, she tried to gather enough of her wits to remember where she was.

"Miss Dunne?"

"Yes. Yes, this is Lindsay Dunne." She sat on the corner of her desk as her knees trembled.

"I'm sorry to disturb you, Miss Dunne. This is Worth. Might I find Mr. Bannion there?"

"Worth?" Lindsay slowly let air in and out of her lungs. "Oh, yes. Yes, he's here. Just a moment."

Her movements were slow and deliberate as she set the receiver beside the phone and rose. For a moment she stood in the doorway of her office. He was turned toward her, and his eyes met hers instantly as if he'd been waiting for her return. Lindsay stepped into the studio, resisting the need to clasp her hands together.

"It's for you," she told him. "Mr. Worth."

Seth nodded, but there was nothing casual in the way he took her shoulders as he passed. Briefly, they stood side by side. "I'll only be a moment."

Lindsay remained still until she heard the murmur of his voice on the phone. Whenever she finished a difficult dance, she always took a few moments to breathe. It was concentrated breathing, in-out, deep and slow, not the unconscious movement of air in the lungs. She took time to do so now. Gradually, she felt the flow of blood decrease, the hammer of her pulse quiet. The tingle just under her skin faded. Satisfied that her body was responding, Lindsay waited for her mind to follow suit.

Even for a woman who enjoyed taking risks, Lindsay knew the idiocy of her behavior. With Seth Bannion, the odds were too highly stacked against her. She was beginning to realize that she contributed to those odds. She was too attracted to him, too vulnerable to him. It didn't seem to matter that she had known him for only a matter of weeks.

Slowly, she walked to the shirt that lay on the floor. She stooped just as a movement in the mirror caught her eye. Again, her eyes locked with Seth's in the glass. Chilled pinpricks spread over her skin. Lindsay rose and turned. Now, she knew, was not the time for fantasies and illusions.

"A problem on a site," he said briefly. "I need to check some figures at home." He crossed to her. "Come with me."

There was no mistaking what he meant. To Lindsay, the simplicity and directness were overpoweringly seductive. With careful movements, she slipped back into her shirt.

"No, I can't. I've work to do, and then…"

"Lindsay." He halted her with a word and a hand to her cheek. "I want to sleep with you. I want to wake up with you."

She let out a long breath. "I'm not accustomed to dealing with this sort of thing," she murmured. She ran a hand through her loosened hair, then her eyes lifted to his again and held. "I'm very attracted to you. It's a bit beyond what I've felt before and I don't know quite what to do about it."

Seth's hand moved from her cheek to circle her throat. "Do you think you can tell me that and expect me to go home alone?"

Lindsay shook her head and put a decisive hand to his chest. "I tell you that, I suppose, because I'm not sophisticated enough to keep it to myself. I don't believe in lies and pretense." A faint line appeared between her brows as she continued. "And I don't believe in doing something I'm not totally sure is what I want. I'm not going to sleep with you."

"But you are." He put his hand over hers, capturing the other at the same time. "If not tonight, tomorrow; if not tomorrow, the day after."

"I wouldn't be so smug if I were you." Lindsay shook off his hands. "I'm never very obliging when told what I'm going to do. I make my own decisions."

"And you made this one," Seth said easily, but temper flared in his eyes. "The first time I kissed you. Hypocrisy doesn't suit you."

"Hypocrisy?" Lindsay held the words back a moment, knowing she would stutter. "The precious male ego! Refuse a proposition and you're a hypocrite."

"I don't believe *proposition* is a fully accurate term."

"Go sit on your semantics," she invited. "And do it elsewhere. I've got work to do."

He was quick. He grabbed her arm, jerking her against him before the command to step away could shoot from her brain to her feet. "Don't push me, Lindsay."

She pulled at her arm. It remained in his grip. "Aren't you the one who's pushing?"

"It appears we have a problem."

"*Your* problem," she tossed back. "I'm not going to be another set of blueprints in your file. If I decide I want to go to bed with you, I'll let you know. In the meantime, our main topic of conversation is Ruth."

Seth made an intense study of her face. Her cheeks had flushed with temper, her breath came quickly. A hint of a smile played on his mouth. "Right now you look a bit as you did when I watched you dance Dulcinea, full of passion and spirit. We'll talk again." Before Lindsay could comment, he gave her a long, lingering kiss. "Soon."

She managed to gather her wits as he crossed to the piano to retrieve his jacket. "About Ruth…"

He shrugged into his coat, all the time watching her. "Soon," he repeated and strode to the door.

Chapter 8

On Sundays Lindsay had no set schedule. Six days a week her time was regimented, given over to classes and paperwork and her mother. On Sunday she broke free.

It was late morning when she wandered downstairs. The aroma of coffee was strong, drawing her into the kitchen. She could hear her mother's slow, uneven movements before she pushed open the door.

"Morning." Lindsay crossed the linoleum floor to kiss Mae's cheek, then studied her neat, three-piece suit. "You're all dressed up." Pleasure warmed her voice. "You look wonderful."

Mae smiled as she touched her hair with a fussy hand. "Carol wanted to have lunch at the country club. Do you think my hair's all right?"

"It's lovely." Lindsay's heart lightened as she watched

her mother preen again. "But you know it's your legs everybody looks at. You've got great legs."

Mae laughed, a sound Lindsay had waited a long time to hear. "Your father always thought so." The tone was sad again. Lindsay slipped her arms around Mae's neck.

"No, don't, please." She held her close a moment, willing away the gloom. "It's so good to see you smile. Dad would want you to smile." When she felt Mae sigh, she held her closer. If it were possible, she would have transfused some of her own strength into her. Mae patted Lindsay's back, then drew away.

"Let's have coffee." She moved to sit at the table. "My legs might look good, but they're still attached to this hip, and they get tired easily."

Lindsay watched as her mother carefully settled herself, then turned to the cupboard. It was important to keep Mae's mood on the upswing. "I worked late yesterday with the girl I've been telling you about, Ruth Bannion." Lindsay poured two cups of coffee before walking to the refrigerator for milk. She added a generous dose to her mother's and left her own black. "She's exceptional, truly exceptional," she continued as she walked over to join Mae. "I've cast her as Carla in *The Nutcracker.* She's a shy, introverted girl who seems really confident only when she's dancing." Thoughtfully, Lindsay watched the steam curl up from the surface of her coffee. "I want to send her to New York, to Nick. Her uncle won't even discuss it." Not for four and a half more months, she thought grimly. Stubborn, immovable... "Are all men mules?" Lindsay demanded, then swore as she scalded her tongue with a sip of steaming coffee.

"For the most part," Mae told her. Her own coffee sat cooling in front of her. "And for the most part, women seem to be attracted to mules. You're attracted to him."

Lindsay glanced up, then stared back down at the coffee. "Well…yes. He's a bit different from the men I've known. His life doesn't center around dancing. He's traveled almost everywhere. He's very sure of himself and arrogant in a very controlled sort of way. The only other man I've known who has that sort of confidence is Nick." She smiled, remembering, and her hands floated with the words. "But Nicky has that passionate Russian temper. He throws things, he moans, he shrieks. Even his moods are elaborately orchestrated. Seth is different. Seth would just quietly snap you in two."

"And you respect him for that."

Lindsay looked up again, then laughed. It was the first time she remembered she and her mother having an in-depth discussion on anything that didn't directly involve dancing. "Yes," she agreed. "As ridiculous as it sounds, I do. He's the sort of man who commands respect without demanding it, if you know what I mean." Lindsay sipped her coffee with more caution. "Ruth adores him. It shows in her face whenever she looks at him. The lonely look is fading from her eyes and I'm sure it's his doing." Her voice softened. "He's very sensitive, I think, and very much in control of his emotions. I think if he loved someone, he'd be very demanding because he wouldn't invest his emotions easily. Still, if he weren't so stubborn, I'd send Ruth to Nick. A year's training in New York, and I'm sure she'd be chosen for the *corps*. I mentioned her to him, but..."

"To Nick?" Mae interrupted Lindsay's verbal thoughts. "When?"

She brought herself back with a mental curse. It hadn't been an oversight that she had neglected to mention Nick's call. She had wanted to avoid a topic that brought pain to both of them. Now she shrugged and spoke casually between sips. "Oh, a couple of days ago. He called the studio."

"Why?"

Mae's question was quiet and unavoidable. "To see how I was, to ask after you." The flowers Carol had brought the week before were wilting in the bowl on the table. She rose, taking them with her. "He was always very fond of you."

Mae watched her daughter as she tossed the faded flowers into the trash. "He asked you to come back."

Lindsay placed the bowl in the sink and began to rinse it. "He's excited about a new ballet he's written."

"And he wants you for it." Lindsay continued to rinse the bowl. "What did you tell him?"

She shook her head, wanting only to avoid another strained argument. "Mother, please."

There was silence for a moment with only the sound of water splashing in the sink. It warmed Lindsay's hands.

"I've been thinking I might go to California with Carol."

Surprised by both the statement and the calm tone of her mother's voice, Lindsay turned without switching off the faucet. "That would be wonderful for you. You'd miss the worst of the winter."

"Not for the winter," Mae countered. "Permanently."

"Permanently?" Lindsay's face clouded with confusion. Behind her the water danced against the glass bowl. Reaching back, she twisted the handle of the faucet. "I don't understand."

"She has people there, you know." Mae rose to get more coffee, motioning a protest as Lindsay moved to do it for her. "One of them, a cousin, found a florist who was selling out. Good location. Carol bought it."

"She bought it?" Astonished, Lindsay sat down again. "But when? She hasn't said a word. Andy hasn't said anything either; I just saw him...."

"She wanted everything settled first." Mae interrupted Lindsay's disbelief. "She wants me to be her partner."

"Her partner?" Lindsay shook her head, then pressed fingers to both temples. "In California?"

"We can't go on this way, Lindsay." Mae limped back to the table with her coffee. "Physically, I'm as good as I'm going to be. There's no need for me to be pampered or for you to worry about me anymore. Yes, you do," she continued, even as Lindsay opened her mouth to object. "I'm a long way from where I was when I came out of the hospital."

"I know. I know that, but California...." She sent Mae a helpless look. "It's so far away."

"It's what we both need. Carol told me I was pressuring you, and she's right."

"Mother..."

"No, I do, and I'll keep right on doing it as long as

we're living in each other's pockets this way." After a long breath, Mae pursed her lips. "It's time…for both of us. I've only wanted one thing for you. I haven't stopped wanting it." She took Lindsay's hands, studying the long, graceful fingers. "Dreams are stubborn things. I've had the same one all my life…first for me, then for you. Maybe that's wrong. Maybe you're using me as an excuse not to go back." Even as Lindsay shook her head, she continued. "You took care of me when I needed you, and I'm grateful. I haven't shown it always because the dream got in the way. I'm going to ask you something one last time." Lindsay remained silent, waiting. "Think about what you have, who you are. Think about going back."

There was nothing Lindsay could do but nod. She had thought about it, long and painfully two years before, but she wouldn't shut the door between herself and her mother; it had just worked its way open. "When would you go?"

"In three weeks."

Letting out a quick breath at the reply, Lindsay rose. "You and Carol will make great partners." She suddenly felt lost, alone and deserted. "I'm going for a walk," she said swiftly before the emotions could show on her face. "I need to think."

Lindsay loved the beach when the air hinted at winter. She wore an ancient peacoat against the bite of the cold, and with her hands in her pockets, she walked the low, slow arch of rock and sand. Above the sky was calm and unrelentingly blue. The surf was wild. There was more than the scent of the sea, there was the taste of it. Here the wind blew free, and she felt it would clear her mind.

She had never considered that her mother would make a permanent move away from Cliffside. *She wasn't sure how she felt about it.* A gull swooped low over her head, and Lindsay stopped to watch it wing its way over the rocks. Three years, she thought. Three years of being wrapped up in a routine. She wasn't certain that she could function without it. Bending over, she picked up a smooth, flat stone. It was sand-colored, speckled with black, the size of a silver dollar. Lindsay brushed it clean, then dropped it into her pocket. She kept her hand over it, absently warming it as she walked.

She thought over each stage of her life since her return to Cliffside. Casting her mind back, she recalled her years in New York. Two different lives, Lindsay mused, hunching her shoulders. Perhaps I'm two different people. As she tossed back her head, she saw the Cliff House. It was high above her and still perhaps a quarter of a mile off, but it warmed her as she warmed the stone.

Because it's always there, she decided, because you can depend on it. When everything else goes haywire, it stays constant. Its windows shimmered in the sun as she watched. Puffs of smoke curled, just as they should, from several chimneys. Lindsay sighed, hugging herself.

From far down the beach a movement caught her eye. Seth was walking toward her. He must have come down the beach steps from the house. Shielding her eyes with her hands, she watched him. She was smiling before she was aware of it. Why does he do this to me? she wondered with a shake of her head. Why am I always so terribly glad to see him? He walks with such confidence. No wasted motion, no superfluous movement. I'd like to dance with him, something slow, something dreamy. She felt the tug and sighed. I should run before he gets any closer.

She did. Toward him.

Seth watched her coming. Her hair lifted and streamed behind her. The wind pinched pink into her cheeks. Her body seemed weightless, skimming over the sand, and he was reminded of the evening he had come upon her dancing alone. He wasn't aware that he had stopped walking.

When she reached him, her smile was brilliant. She held out her hands in greeting. "Hi." Rising on her toes, she brushed his mouth with a quick kiss. "I'm so glad to see you. I was lonely." Her fingers laced with his.

"I saw you from the house."

"Did you?" She thought he looked younger with his hair ruffled by the wind. "How did you know it was me?"

There was the faintest of frowns in his eyes, but his voice was untroubled. "The way you move."

"No greater compliment for a dancer. Is that why you came down?" It felt good to feel his hands again, to see the solemn, studying look in his eyes. "To be with me?"

Only his eyebrow moved—in a slight upward tilt—before he answered. "Yes."

"I'm glad." She smiled warmly, without reservation. "I need someone to talk to. Will you listen?"

"All right."

In silent agreement, they began to walk.

"Dancing has always been in my life," Lindsay began. "I can't remember a day without classes, a morning without the barre. It was vital to my mother, who had certain limitations as a dancer, that I go further. It was very fortunate for everyone that I wanted to dance and that I could. It was important to us in different ways, but it was still a bond."

Her voice was quiet but clear against the roar of the sea. "I was only a bit older than Ruth when I joined the company. It's a hard life; the competition, the hours, the pressure. Oh God, the pressure. It begins in the morning, the moment your eyes open. The barre, classes, rehearsals, more classes. Seven days a week. It's your life; there's nothing else. There can't be anything else. Even after you begin to ease your way out of the *corps,* you can't relax. There's always someone behind you, wanting your place. If you miss a class, one class, your body knows it and tortures you. There's pain—in the muscles, the tendons, the feet. It's the price necessary to maintain that unnatural flexibility."

She sighed and let the wind buffet her face. "I loved it. Every moment of it. It's difficult to understand how it feels to be standing there in the wings before your first solo. Another dancer knows. And when you dance, there isn't any pain. You forget it because you have to. Then, the next day, it starts again.

"When I was with the company, I was completely wrapped up in myself, in my work. I rarely thought of Cliffside or anyone here. We were just going into rehearsals for *Firebird* when my parents had the accident." She paused here, and though her voice thickened, it remained steady. "I loved my father. He was a simple, giving man. I doubt if I thought of him more than a dozen times that last year in New York. Have you ever done something, or not done something, that you periodically hate yourself for? Something you can't change, ever?"

"Something that wakes you up at three o'clock in the morning?" Seth slipped an arm around Lindsay's shoulders and drew her closer to him. "A couple of times."

"My mother was in the hospital a long time." For a moment she turned her face into his shoulder. It was more difficult to speak of it than she had anticipated. "She was in a coma, and then there were operations, therapy. It was long and painful for her. There were a lot of arrangements I had to make, a lot of papers I had to go through. I found out they'd taken a second mortgage on the house to finance my first two years in New York." A deep breath helped to hold back tears. "I'd been there, totally fixated on myself, totally involved with my own ambitions, and they were putting up their home."

"It must have been what they wanted to do, Lindsay. And you succeeded. They were obviously proud of you."

"But you see, I just took it from them without any thought, without any gratitude."

"How can you be grateful for something you know nothing about?" he pointed out.

"Logic," Lindsay murmured as a gull screamed over their heads. "I wish I could be more logical. In any case," she continued, "when I came back, I opened the school to keep myself sane and to help with the finances until my mother was well enough for me to leave. At that time I had no plans for staying."

"But your plans changed." Her steps had slowed, and Seth shortened his stride to suit hers.

"The months piled up." Absently, Lindsay pushed at the hair that fluttered into her line of vision. "When my mother finally got out of the hospital, she still needed a great deal of care. Andy's mother was a lifesaver. She split her time between her shop and the house so that I could keep the school going. Then there came a point when I had to face things as they were. Too much time had gone by, and there wasn't an end yet in sight."

She walked for a moment in silence. "I stopped thinking about going back to New York. Cliffside was my home, and I had friends here. I had the school. The lives of professional dancers are very regimented. They take classes every day which is far different from teaching them. They eat a certain way, they think a certain way. I simply stopped being a professional dancer."

"But your mother wouldn't accept that."

Surprised, Lindsay stopped walking and looked up at him. "How did you know?"

He brushed the hair from her cheek. "It isn't difficult."

"Three years, Seth." She shrugged her shoulders. "She isn't being realistic. I'll be twenty-six soon; how can I go back and attempt to compete with girls Ruth's age? And if I could, why should I torture my muscles, destroy my feet and starve myself a second time? I don't even know if I'm capable. I loved it there...and I love it here." She turned to watch the surf spray high over the rocks. "Now my mother plans to move away permanently, to start fresh, and I know, to force me to make a decision. A decision I thought I'd already made."

His hands came to her shoulders, the fingers light and strong. "Do you resent her moving away where you can't take care of her anymore?"

"Oh, you're very perceptive." Lindsay leaned back against him a moment. There was comfort there. "But I want her to be happy—really happy—again. I love her, not in the same uncomplicated way I loved my father, but I do love her. I'm just not sure I can be what she wants."

"If you think being what she wants will pay her back, you're wrong. Life doesn't work that neatly."

"It should." Lindsay frowned at the foaming spray. "It should."

"Don't you think it might be boring if it did?" His voice was quiet and controlled above the screams of the gulls and the roar of the waves. Lindsay was glad, very glad, she had run toward him and not away. "When is your mother leaving?"

"In three weeks."

"Then give yourself some time after she's gone to decide where your life's heading. There's too much pressure on you now."

"I should have known you'd be logical." She turned to him and was smiling again. "Usually, I resent that kind of advice, but this time it's a relief." She slipped her arms around his waist and buried her face in his chest. "Will you hold me? It feels so good to depend on someone else for just a minute."

She seemed very small when his arms came around her. Her slightness appealed to his protective instincts.

Seth rested his cheek on the top of her head and watched the water war against the rocks.

"You smell of soap and leather," Lindsay finally murmured. "I like it. A thousand years from now I'll remember you smelled of soap and leather." She lifted her face and searched deep in his eyes. *I could fall in love with him,* she thought. *He's the first man I could really fall in love with.*

"I know I'm crazy," she said aloud, "but I want you to kiss me. I want so badly to taste you again."

Their mouths met slowly to linger, to savor. They drew away once, far enough to see the need mirrored in each other's eyes, then they joined again, flame for flame. The taste and texture of his mouth was familiar now, but no less exciting. Lindsay clung to him. Their tongues teased only, hinting of what could be. The well of desire was deeper than she had known, and its waters more treacherous. For a moment she gave herself to him utterly. Promises trembled on her lips.

Quickly, Lindsay pushed away, shaking her head. She placed a hand to her head, smoothing her hair back from her face as she took a long breath.

"Oh, I should stay away from you," she whispered. "Very far away."

Seth reached up to cup her face in his hand. "It's too late for that now." Passion was still dark in her eyes. With only the slightest pressure, he brought her back a step.

"Maybe." She placed her hands on his chest but neither pushed away nor drew closer. "In any case, I asked for this."

"If it were summer," he said and trailed his fingers

down her throat, "we'd have a picnic here, late at night with cold wine. Then we'd make love and sleep on the beach until dawn came up over the water."

Lindsay felt the tremors start at her knees. "Oh yes," she said on a sigh. "I should stay away from you." Turning, she sprinted for a clump of rocks. "Do you know why I like the beach best in early winter?" she called out as she scrambled to the top.

"No." Seth walked over to join her. "Why?"

"Because the wind is cold and alive, and the water can be mean. I like to watch it just before a storm."

"You enjoy challenges," Seth remarked, and Lindsay looked down at him. The height gave her a unique perspective. "Yes, I do. So do you, as I recall. I read that you're quite a parachutist."

He held a hand up to her, smiling as their fingers touched. Lindsay wrinkled her nose and jumped lightly to the sand. "I only go as far off the ground as I can without apparatus," she said and cocked a brow. "I'm not about to go leaping out of a plane unless it's parked at the airport."

"I thought you enjoyed a challenge."

"I also enjoy breathing."

"I could teach you," Seth offered, drawing her into his arms.

"You learn to do a *tour en l'air,* and I'll learn to jump. Besides…" Lindsay struggled from his arms as a recollection struck her. "I remember reading that you were teaching some Italian countess to free fall."

"I'm beginning to think you read entirely too much." Seth grabbed her hand and pulled her back.

"I'm surprised you've had time to build anything with such an active social life."

His grin was a quick, youthful flash. "I'm a firm believer in recreation."

"Hmm." Before Lindsay could mull over an answer, a flash of red caught her eye from a short distance down on the beach. "It's Ruth," she said, twisting her head.

Ruth raised her hand once hesitantly as she crossed the sand toward them. Her hair hung loose over a scarlet jacket. "She's a lovely girl." Lindsay turned to face Seth again. She saw as he, too, watched Ruth, but there was a frown in his eyes. "Seth?" He looked down at her. "What is it?" she asked with concern.

"I might have to go away for a few weeks. I worry about her; she's still so fragile."

"You don't give her enough credit." Lindsay tried to ignore the sudden sense of loss his words gave her. *Go away?* Where? When? She focused on Ruth and forced the questions away. "Or yourself," she added. "You've built a relationship. A few weeks won't damage it or Ruth."

Before he could answer, Ruth had joined them.

"Hello, Ms. Dunne." Her smile had become more relaxed since the first time Lindsay had seen it. There was a welcome sparkle of excitement in her eyes. "Uncle Seth, I've just come from Monica's. Her cat had kittens last month."

Lindsay laughed. "Honoria is single-handedly responsible for the feline population explosion in Cliffside."

"Not single-handedly," Seth commented dryly, and Lindsay laughed again.

"She had four," Ruth continued. "And one of them... well..." She glanced from Seth to Lindsay, catching her bottom lip between her teeth. Silently, she pulled open the snaps of her jacket and revealed a tiny bundle of orange fur.

Lindsay let out an inevitable squeal as she reached out and took the velvety kitten from Ruth. She buried her nose in its fur. "He's beautiful. What's his name?"

"Nijinsky," Ruth told her and turned her dark eyes to her uncle. "I'd keep him upstairs in my room where he wouldn't be in Worth's way. He's little and won't be any trouble," she rushed on hopefully.

Lindsay looked up as Ruth spoke. Animation had lit her eyes. In Lindsay's experience with her, only dancing had brought that much life to her face. "Trouble?" she said, automatically allying herself with the girl. "Of course he won't be any trouble. Just look at that face." She pushed the kitten into Seth's hands. Seth took a finger and tilted the kitten's face upward. Nijinsky mewed and settled down to sleep again.

"Three against one," Seth said as he scratched the furry ears. "Some might consider that foul play." He gave the kitten back to Ruth, then ran a hand down her hair. "Better let me handle Worth."

"Oh, Uncle Seth." Cradling the kitten, Ruth tossed her free arm around Seth's neck. "Thank you! Ms. Dunne, isn't he wonderful?"

"Who?" Her eyes danced above Ruth's head. "Nijinsky or Seth?"

Ruth giggled. It was the first time Lindsay had heard the uniquely girlish sound from her. "Both of them. I'm going to take him in." She snapped the small bundle back inside her jacket and began to jog across the sand. "I'll sneak some milk from the kitchen," she called back behind her.

"Such a small thing," Lindsay murmured, watching the bright red jacket disappear down the stretch of sand. She turned to Seth with a nod of approval. "You did that very well. She thinks she persuaded you."

Seth smiled and caught at Lindsay's wind-tossed hair. "Didn't she?"

Lindsay returned his smile and gave in to the urge to touch his cheek. "I like knowing you're a soft touch." She dropped her hand. "I have to go."

"Lindsay." He held her still when she tried to turn away. "Have dinner with me." The look in his eyes was intimate. "Just dinner. I want you with me."

"Seth, I think we both know we wouldn't just have dinner. We'd both want more."

"Then we'll both have more," he murmured, but when he drew Lindsay into his arms, she resisted.

"No, I need to think." For a moment she rested her forehead against his chest. "I don't think clearly when you're touching me. I need some time."

"How much?" He put his hand under her chin to lift her face.

"I don't know." The tears that sprang to her eyes stunned them both. Astonished, Lindsay brushed at them. Seth lifted a finger and trapped one on the tip.

"Lindsay." His voice was gentle.

"No, no, don't be kind. Yell at me. I'll get control of myself if you yell at me." She put both hands to her face and took deep breaths. Quite suddenly, she knew what had brought on the tears. "I have to go. Please let me go, Seth. I need to be alone."

From the pressure of his hands, she was afraid he would refuse. "All right," he said after a long moment. "But I'm not known for my patience, Lindsay."

She didn't respond but turned and fled. Fleeing with her was the realization not only that she could fall in love with Seth Bannion, but that she already had.

Chapter 9

They drove to the airport in the early afternoon. Andy drove with Lindsay beside him and both their mothers in the back seat. The trunk was cramped with luggage. Even after the three weeks of helping her mother prepare for the move, a cloud of disbelief hung over Lindsay. Already, boxes had been shipped ahead to California, and the house she had grown up in was on the market.

When it was sold, she knew her last ties to her childhood would go with it. It's for the best, she thought as she listened to her mother and Carol chatter in the rear seat. Everything I need will fit into the spare room at the school. It'll be more convenient for me, and there isn't any doubt that it's best for Mother.

She watched a plane gliding toward the ground and knew they were almost there. Her thoughts seemed to drift with the aircraft. Since the day Mae had announced her plans, Lindsay hadn't functioned at top level. Too many emotions had surfaced that day. She had tried to lock them away until she could deal with them rationally, but they had been too powerful. Again and again, they had escaped to haunt her dreams, or worse, to catch her unprepared in the middle of a class or conversation. She hadn't wanted to think about Seth, but she had: once when Monica had innocently brought up his name, again when Ruth had smuggled the kitten into class and dozens of other times when something reminded her of him.

It was odd how she could no longer walk into a room where he had been without associating it with him. Even her own studio reminded her of Seth.

After the initial shock had settled, Lindsay had explored the adventure of being in love. It didn't make her light-headed, as some songs promised, but it did make her less attentive to ordinary things. She hadn't lost her taste for food, but sleep had become a problem. She wasn't walking on clouds, but found herself, instead, waiting for the storm to hit. It was not falling in love that dictated her reactions, she decided, but the person with whom she had chosen to fall in love.

Chosen, Lindsay repeated silently, paying no attention as Andy worked his way through airport traffic. If I could have chosen who I'd fall in love with, it would've been someone who adored me, someone who thought I was perfection and whose life would be totally devoted to making mine Utopia.

Oh, no you wouldn't have, she corrected. Her window reflected the ghost of her smile. That would've bored me to death in a week. Seth suits me entirely too well. He's totally in command of himself, very cool, yet sensitive. Trouble is, he's a man who's made a career out of avoiding commitments…except for Ruth. She sighed and touched her own reflection with a fingertip. And there's another problem. It's difficult to be so totally opposed to something that's so important to both of us. How can we get closer when we're on opposite sides of a sixty-foot fence?

It was Andy's voice that brought Lindsay's mind back to present company. Disoriented, she glanced about to see that they had parked and that the others were already climbing out of the car. Quickly, Lindsay got out and tried to catch up with the conversation.

"…since we've already got our tickets and a car waiting at LAX," Carol finished as she pulled a suitcase and tote bag from the trunk.

"You will have to check all this baggage," Andy reminded her, easily hefting three more cases with a garment bag slung over his shoulder. "Catch the trunk, will you, Lindsay?" he asked absently as she was left with only her own purse and a cosmetic case.

"Sure."

Carol winked at Mae as Lindsay slammed the trunk shut and pulled out the keys. The wind billowed the hem of her coat. Glancing up, she scanned the sky. "It'll be snowing by nightfall."

"And you'll be trying on new bathing suits," Lindsay grumbled obligingly as she tried to move the two women along. The air was sharp and stung her cheeks.

Inside the terminal, there was the usual last-minute confusion about locating tickets and securing boarding passes. After checking the luggage, Andy began a detailed verbal listing of the do's and don'ts his mother was to follow.

"Keep the baggage checks in your wallet."

"Yes, Andy."

Lindsay caught the gleam in Carol's eye, but Andy continued to frown.

"And don't forget to call when you get to L.A."

"No, Andy."

"You have to set your watch back three hours."

"I will, Andy."

"And don't talk to strange men."

Carol hesitated. "Define strange," she demanded.

"Mom." His frown turned up into a grin before he enveloped her in a crushing hug.

Lindsay turned to her mother. She wanted it over quickly, without strain. But when they faced each other, her glib parting speech became lost. She was a child again, with words running riot in her mind. Instead of trying to sort through them, she threw her arms around her mother's neck.

"I love you," she whispered, shutting her eyes tight on tears. "Be happy. Please, please, be happy."

"Lindsay." Her name was a softly spoken sigh. After a moment, Mae drew away. They were of the same height, and their eyes were level. It was strange, but Lindsay couldn't remember the last time her mother had looked at her with such total concentration. Not at the dancer, but at her daughter.

"I love you, Lindsay. I might've made mistakes," Mae sighed with the admission. "But I always wanted

the best for you—what I thought was the best. I want
you to know I'm proud of you."

Lindsay's eyes widened, but her throat closed on any
response. Mae kissed both her cheeks, then, taking the
case from her hands, turned to say goodbye to Andy.

"I'm going to miss you," Carol said on a quick, en-
ergetic hug. "Go after that man," she whispered in
Lindsay's ear. "Life's too short." Before Lindsay could
answer, she, too, had kissed her. She walked with Mae
through the gate.

When they were gone, Lindsay turned to Andy. Tears
dampened her lashes, but she managed to prevent them
from rolling down her cheeks. "Should I feel like an
orphan?"

He smiled and slipped an arm around her. "I don't
know, but I do. Want some coffee?"

Lindsay sniffled, then shook her head. "Ice cream,"
she said positively. "A great big ice cream sundae because we should be celebrating for them." She linked
her arm with his as they began to walk away from the
gate. "I'm treating."

Carol's weather forecast was right on the mark. An
hour before sunset, the snow began. It was announced
by Lindsay's evening students as they arrived for class.
For several moments she and her students stood in the
cold of the opened doorway and watched it fall.

There was always something magical about the first
snow, Lindsay thought. It was like a promise, a gift.
By midwinter, snow would bring grumbling and complaints, but now, fresh and soft and white, it brought
dreams.

Lindsay continued the class, but her mind refused to settle. She thought of her mother landing in Los Angeles. It would still be afternoon there, and sunny. She thought of the children here in Cliffside who would be dragging their sleds out of attics and storerooms and sheds in preparation for tomorrow's rides. She thought of taking a long, solitary walk on the snowy beach. She thought of Seth.

It was during the break between classes, when her students were changing shoes for *pointe* class, that Lindsay went to the door again. The wind had picked up, and it tossed snow into her face. There were six inches or more on the ground already, and it was falling thickly. At that rate, Lindsay calculated, there would be well over a foot before the class was finished. Too risky, she decided, and shut the door.

"No *pointe* class tonight, ladies." Rubbing her arms to restore circulation, she moved back into the room. "Who has to call home?"

It was fortunate that the majority of Lindsay's advanced students drove or car pooled to class. Arrangements were soon made for the younger ones to be dispatched, and after the obligatory confusion, the studio was cleared. Lindsay took a deep breath before turning to Monica and Ruth.

"Thanks. That exodus would've taken twice the time if you hadn't helped." She looked directly at Ruth. "Have you called Seth?"

"Yes. I'd already made plans to stay at Monica's tonight, but I checked in."

"Good." Lindsay sat down and began to pull a pair of corduroy slacks over her tights and leg warmers.

"I'm afraid this is going to turn into a solid blizzard in another hour or so. I want to be home with a cup of hot chocolate by then."

"I like the sound of that." Monica zipped up a down-filled parka, then pulled on the hood.

"You look ready for anything," Lindsay commented. She was carefully packing toe and ballet shoes into a tote bag. "What about you?" she asked Ruth as she pulled a ski cap down over her ears. "Ready?"

Ruth nodded and joined the women as they walked to the door. "Do you think classes will be on schedule tomorrow, Ms. Dunne?"

Lindsay opened the door, and the three of them were buffeted by the wind. Wet snow flew into their faces. "Such dedication," Monica mumbled, lowering her head to force her way across the parking lot.

By tacit agreement, all three began by clearing off Monica's car, sharing the broom Lindsay had brought with her from the studio. In short order, the car was un-earthed, but before they could turn to give Lindsay's the same attention, Monica let out a long groan. She pointed to the left front tire.

"Flat," she said dully. "Andy told me it had a slow leak. He told me to keep air in it. Shoot." She kicked the offending tire.

"Well, we'll punish you later," Lindsay decided. She stuck her hands in her pockets, hoping to keep her fingers warm. "Right now, I'll take you home."

"Oh, but Lindsay!" Distress poured from Monica's eyes. "It's so far out of your way."

Lindsay thought a moment, then nodded. "You're right," she said briskly. "Guess you'll have to change that tire. See you tomorrow." Hefting the broom over her shoulder, she started toward her car.

"Lindsay!" Monica grabbed Ruth's hand, and the two ran after the departing figure. Along the way, Monica scooped up a fistful of snow and laughingly tossed it at Lindsay's ski cap. Her aim was flawless.

Lindsay turned, unconcerned. "Want a lift?" The expression on Ruth's face had her bubbling with laughter. "Poor thing, she thought I meant it. Come on." Generously, she handed Monica the broom. "Let's get moving before we're buried in this stuff."

In less than five minutes Ruth was sandwiched between Lindsay and Monica in the front seat. Snow swirled outside the windshield and danced in the stream of the headlights. "Here goes," Lindsay said and took a deep breath as she put the car in first.

"We were in a snowstorm once in Germany." Ruth tried to make herself smaller to avoid cramping Lindsay as she drove. "We had to travel on horseback, and when we reached the village, we were snowbound for three days. We slept on the floor around a fire."

"Got any other bedtime stories?" Monica asked. She closed her eyes against the rapidly falling snow.

"There was an avalanche," Ruth supplied.

"Terrific."

"We haven't had one of those here in years," Lindsay stated as she crept cautiously along.

"I wonder when the snow plows will be out." Monica frowned at the street, then at Lindsay.

"They've already been out; it's just hard to tell. They'll be busy tonight." Lindsay shifted, keeping her eyes on the road. "See if that heater's warmed up yet. My feet are freezing."

Obediently, Ruth switched it on. There was a blast of cold air. "I don't think it's ready," she hazarded, switching it off again. Out of the corner of her eye, Lindsay caught the smile.

"You're just smug because you've battled avalanches."

"I did have on pile-lined boots," Ruth admitted.

Monica wriggled her toes inside her thin loafers. "She's a smart aleck," she said conversationally. "The reason she gets away with it is because she does it with such innocence. Look." She pointed upward and to the right. "You can just see the lights of the Cliff House through the snow."

The urge was irresistible; Lindsay glanced up. The faint brightness of artificial light shone through the curtain of snow. She felt almost as though she were being pulled toward it. The car skidded in response to her inattention. Monica shut her eyes again, but Ruth chattered away, unconcerned.

"Uncle Seth's working on drawings for a project in New Zealand. It's beautiful, even though it's only pictures. You can tell it's going to be fabulous."

Cautiously, Lindsay turned the corner toward Monica's house. "I suppose he's pretty busy these days."

"He closes himself up in his office for hours," Ruth agreed. She leaned forward to try the heater again. This time the air was tepid. "Don't you love winter?" she asked brightly. Monica moaned, and Lindsay burst out laughing. "She is a smart aleck," she agreed. "I might not have noticed if you hadn't pointed it out."

"I didn't detect it myself all at once," Monica told her. She was beginning to breathe a bit easier as they made their way slowly down the block toward her house. When they pulled up in her driveway, Monica heaved a sigh of relief. "Thank goodness!" She shifted in her seat, crushing Ruth as she leaned toward Lindsay. Ruth found she liked the companionable discomfort. "Stay here tonight, Lindsay. The roads are awful."

Lindsay shrugged off the concern. "They're not that bad yet." The heater was humming along nicely now, and she felt warm and confident. "I'll be home in fifteen minutes."

"Lindsay, I'll worry and bite my nails."

"Good grief, I can't be responsible for that. I'll call you the minute I get home."

"Lindsay..."

"Even before I fix the hot chocolate."

Monica sighed, recognizing defeat. "The very minute," she ordered sternly.

"I won't even wipe my feet on the way to the phone."

"Okay." She climbed out of the car and stood amidst the thickly falling snow as Ruth followed. "Be careful."

"I will. Good night, Ruth."

"Good night, Lindsay." Ruth bit her lip at the slip in propriety, but Monica was already closing the door. No one else had noticed. Ruth smiled as she watched Lindsay's headlights recede.

Lindsay backed slowly out of the driveway and headed up the road. She switched on the radio to fill the void left by Monica and Ruth. The roads, as Monica had said, were awful. Though her wipers were working at top speed, they afforded her only scant seconds of vision before the windshield was covered again. It took every bit of her concentration and skill to keep the car from sliding. She was a good driver and knew the roads intimately, yet there was a small knot of tension at the base of her neck. Lindsay didn't mind it. Some people work best under pressure, and she considered herself one of them.

She pondered a moment on why she had refused Monica's invitation. Her own house would be dark and quiet and empty. The refusal had been automatic, and now she found herself regretting it. She didn't want to brood or to be alone. She was tired of thinking.

For a moment she vacillated between going ahead and going back. Before she could reach a firm decision, a large, black shape darted into the road ahead of her. Lindsay's brain barely had enough time to register that the shape was a dog before she was whipping the wheel to avoid a collision.

Once the skid had begun, she had no control. As the car spun, spitting up snow from the wheels, she lost all sense of direction. There was only the blur of white. Firmly, she controlled panic and resisted the urge to slam on the brakes. The fear that bubbled in her throat had no time to surface. It happened fast. The car struck something hard, and there was no slow-motion interlude before it slammed to a halt. She felt a flash of pain and heard the music on the radio turn to static before there was only the silence and the dark....

Lindsay moaned and shifted. There was a fife and drum corps marching inside her head. Slowly, because she knew she'd have to eventually, she opened her eyes.

Shapes floated and dimmed, then swam into focus. Seth frowned down at her. She felt his fingers on the side of her head where the pain was concentrated. Lindsay swallowed because her throat felt dry, but her voice was still husky when she spoke.

"What are you doing here?"

He raised a brow. She watched the change in the slant of its tip. Without speaking, he lifted her lids one at a time and studied her pupils carefully.

"I had no idea you were a complete idiot." The words were calmly spoken. In her dazed state, Lindsay didn't detect the edge of temper. She started to sit up, only to have him place his hand on her shoulders to hold her down. For the moment, she lay back without protest. She was, she discovered, on the sofa in his parlor. There was a fire in the hearth; she could hear its crackle and smell the hint of wood smoke. Its flames cast shadows into a room lit only by two muted china lamps. There was a needleworked pillow under her head, and her coat was still buttoned. Lindsay concentrated on each trivial fact and sensation until her mind began to come to order.

"That dog," she said, abruptly remembering. "Did I hit that dog?"

"What dog?" Impatience was evident in Seth's voice, but she plunged on.

"The dog that jumped out in front of the car. I think I missed him, but I can't be sure...."

"Do you mean to tell me that you ran into a tree to avoid hitting a dog?" If Lindsay had possessed all her faculties, she would have recognized the danger of the icy calm. Instead, she reached up gingerly to finger the ache at her temple.

"Is that what I hit? It feels more like I ran into an entire forest."

"Lie still," he ordered, leaving Lindsay staring as he strode from the room.

Cautiously, she persuaded her body into a sitting position. Her vision remained clear, but her temple throbbed abominably. Leaning her head back against the cushions, she closed her eyes. As a dancer, she was used to pain and to coping with it. Questions began to form in her mind. Lindsay let them shape and dissolve and regroup until Seth came back into the room.

"I thought I told you to lie still."

Lindsay opened her eyes and gave him a wan smile. "I'll do better sitting up, really." She accepted the glass and pills he thrust at her. "What are these?"

"Aspirin," he muttered. "Take them." Her brow lifted at the command, but the ache in her head persuaded her to give in gracefully. Seth watched her swallow before he walked across the room to pour brandy. "Why the hell didn't you stay at Monica's?"

Lindsay shrugged, then leaned back against the cushion again. "I was asking myself that same question when the dog jumped into the road."

"And you hit the brakes in a snowstorm to avoid running into him." The disgust was ripe in his tone. Lindsay opened one eye to stare at his back, then closed it again.

"No, I turned the wheel, but I suppose it amounts to the same thing. I didn't think, though I imagine I'd have done the same thing if I had. In any case, I don't think I hit him, and I'm not damaged much, so there's little harm done."

"Little harm done?" Seth paused in the act of handing her a brandy. The tone of his words caused both of her eyes to open. "Do you have any idea what might have happened to you if Ruth hadn't called and told me you'd driven her to Monica's?"

"Seth, I'm not really very clear on what happened other than that I lost control of my car and hit a tree. I think you'd better clear up the basic facts before we argue."

"Drink some of this." He gave her the brandy snifter. "You're still pale." He waited until she obeyed, then went back to pour his own. "Ruth phoned to let me know she was safe at Monica's. She told me you'd driven them, then insisted on driving yourself home."

"I didn't insist, exactly," Lindsay began, then, noting Seth's expression, she shrugged and sampled the brandy again. It wasn't the hot chocolate she had envisioned, but it was warming.

"Monica was quite naturally worried. She said you'd be driving past shortly and asked, since I've such a good view of the road, if I'd keep a lookout for you. We assumed there wouldn't be much traffic in this miserable weather." He paused to drink, then swirled the remaining brandy while he looked at her. Faint color was returning to her cheeks. "After I hung up, I went to the window, just in time, it seems, to see your headlights. I watched them veer, then circle, then stop dead." After setting the brandy down, he thrust his hands into his pockets. "If it hadn't been for that phone call, you could very well still be in that car unconscious. Thank God you at least had enough sense to wear your seat belt, otherwise you'd have a great deal more than a bump on your head."

She bristled defensively. "Listen, I hardly intended to knock myself unconscious, and I…"

"But you did," Seth inserted. His tone was quiet and clipped.

"Seth, I'm trying very hard to be grateful, as I assume it was you who got me out of the car and up to the house." She drank the rest of her brandy, then set down the snifter. "You're making it difficult."

"I'm not interested in your gratitude."

"Fine, I won't waste it, then." Lindsay rose. The movement was too swift. She had to dig her nails into her palms to drive away the dizziness. "I'd like to call Monica so she won't be worried."

"I've already called." Seth watched the color the brandy had restored drain. "I told her you were here, that you had car trouble. It didn't seem necessary to tell her what kind. Sit down, Lindsay."

"That was very sensible of you," she returned. "Perhaps I could impose further on you to drive me back to Monica's."

Seth walked to her, placed his hands on her shoulders, and meeting her angry eyes, shoved her back down on the sofa. "Not a chance. Neither one of us is going back out in that storm."

Lindsay lifted her chin and aimed a glare. "I don't want to stay here."

"At this point, I don't think you have much choice," he retorted.

Lindsay shifted, crossing her arms over her chest.

"I suppose you'll have Worth make up a room in the dungeon."

"I might," he agreed. "But he's in New York seeing to some business for me." He smiled. "We're quite alone."

Lindsay tried to make an unconcerned gesture with her shoulders, but the movement came off as a nervous jerk. "It doesn't matter; I can walk to Monica's in the morning. I suppose I could use Ruth's room."

"I suppose."

She rose, but more slowly than the first time. The throbbing was down to a dull ache, easily ignored. "I'll go up, then."

"It's barely nine." The hand on her shoulder was light but enough to stop her. "Are you tired?"

"No, I..." The truth was out before she thought to prevaricate.

"Take off your coat." Without waiting for her response, he began undoing the buttons himself. "I was too preoccupied with trying to bring you around to worry about it before." As he slipped the coat from her shoulders, his eyes came back to hers. Gently, he touched a finger to the bruise on her temple. "Hurt?"

"Not much now." Lindsay's pulse rate had quickened. There was no use trying to blame it on the shock of the accident. Instead, she admitted to the feelings that were beginning to swim inside her and met his eyes directly. "Thank you."

He smiled as he ran his hands up her arms, then back down to her fingers.

A moan escaped when he lifted both of her hands to kiss the insides of her wrists. "Your pulse is skittish."

"I wonder why," she murmured. Pleased, Seth gave a low laugh as he released her hands.

"Have you eaten?"

"Eaten?" Lindsay's mind tried to focus on the word, but her senses were still dominating her system.

"Food," Seth supplied. "As in dinner."

"Oh, no, I've been at the studio since this afternoon."

"Sit down, then," he ordered. "I'll go see if Worth left anything palatable."

"I'll come with you." She placed her hand on his to halt his objection. "Seth, we dancers are a sturdy breed. I'm fine."

He studied her face critically, then nodded. "All right, but my way." In an unexpected move, he swept her up in his arms. "Humor me," he said, anticipating her objection.

Lindsay found the sensation of being pampered delicious and settled back to enjoy it. "Have you eaten?"

Seth shook his head. "I've been working…. Then I was distracted."

"I've already thanked you," Lindsay pointed out. "I won't apologize on top of it. It was the dog's fault anyway."

Seth nudged open the kitchen door with his shoulder. "It wouldn't be an issue if you'd done the sensible thing and stayed at Monica's."

"There you go, being logical again." Lindsay heaved a sigh as he set her down at the kitchen table. "It's a nasty habit, but I'm certain you could break it." She smiled up at him. "And if I'd stayed at Monica's, I wouldn't be here right now being waited on. What are you going to fix me?"

Seth captured her chin in his hand and examined her closely. "I've never known anyone like you."

His voice was brooding, so she touched his hand with hers. "Is that good or bad?"

He shook his head slowly, then released her. "I haven't made up my mind."

Lindsay watched him walk to the refrigerator. It was hard for her to believe how much she loved him—how complete and solid the love had already become.

And what do I do about it? she asked herself. Do I tell him? How embarrassing that would be for him, and how completely I would ruin what seems to be the beginning of a great friendship. Isn't love supposed to be unselfish and understanding? Spreading her fingers on the table's surface, she stared at them. But is it supposed to hurt one minute and make you feel like flying the next?

"Lindsay?"

She looked up sharply, suddenly aware that Seth had spoken to her. "I'm sorry." She smiled. "I was daydreaming."

"There's a platter of roast beef, a spinach salad and a variety of cheeses."

"Sounds terrific." Lindsay stood, holding up a hand to quiet his protest. "I'm off the critical list, I promise. I'll trust you to put all that together while I set the table." She walked to a cupboard and began searching.

"How do you feel about washing dishes?" Lindsay asked while Seth made after-dinner coffee.

"I've given the subject very little thought." He glanced back over his shoulder. "How do you feel about it?"

Lindsay leaned back in her chair. "I've just been in an accident. Very traumatic. I doubt whether I'm capable of manual labor just yet."

"Can you walk into the other room?" he asked dryly. He lifted a tray. "Or shall I take the coffee in and come back for you?"

"I'll try." Lindsay pushed herself away from the table. She held open the door and allowed Seth to pass through.

"Actually, most people wouldn't bounce back as quickly as you have." They moved down the hall together. "You took a pretty good whack, from the size of the bump on your head. And from the look of your car, you're lucky it wasn't more."

"But it wasn't," Lindsay pointed out as they came to the parlor. "And please, I don't want to know about my car until I have to. That could send me into severe depression." Sitting on the sofa, she gestured for Seth to set the tray on the table in front of her. "I'll pour. You take cream, don't you?"

"Mmm." Seth moved over to toss another log on the fire. Sparks shot out before the log hissed and caught. When he came back to her, Lindsay was pouring her own cup. "Are you warm enough?"

"Oh yes, the fire's wonderful." She sat back without touching her coffee. "This room's warm even without it." Snug and relaxed, she allowed her eyes to wander and appreciate. "When I was a teenager, I used to dream about sitting here just like this…a storm outside, a fire in the grate and my lover beside me."

The words tumbled out without thought. The moment

they had, Lindsay's cheeks went wild with color. Seth touched the back of his hand to her face.

"A blush is something I didn't expect to see on you." Lindsay caught the hint of pleasure in his voice. She shifted away.

"Maybe I'm feverish."

"Let me see." Seth turned her back to face him. Firmly, he held her still, but the mouth that lowered to her brow was gentle as a whisper. "You don't seem to be." One hand trailed up to the pulse at her throat. His fingers pressed lightly. "Your pulse isn't steady."

"Seth…" She let his name trail off into silence as he slid a hand under her sweater to caress her back. He ran a fingertip along the path where the leotard gave way to flesh.

"But perhaps you're too warm with this heavy sweater."

"No, I…" Before she could prevent him, he had expertly slipped it over her head. Her skin was rosy warm beneath.

"That's better." He kneaded her bare shoulders briefly, then turned back to his coffee. Every nerve in Lindsay's body had been awakened. "What else did you dream about?" As he drank, his eyes sought hers. Lindsay wondered if her thoughts were as transparent as she feared.

"About dancing with Nicky Davidov."

"A realized dream," Seth commented. "Do you know what fascinates me about you?"

Intrigued, Lindsay shook her head. At her stern orders, her nerves began to settle. "My stunning beauty?" she suggested.

"Your feet."

"My feet!" She laughed on the words, automatically glancing down at the canvas slip-ons she wore.

"They're very small." Before Lindsay had any notion of his intent, he had shifted her feet into his lap. "They should belong to a child rather than a dancer."

"But I'm lucky enough to be able to support them on three toes. A lot of dancers can only use one or two. Seth!" She laughed again as he slipped her shoes off.

The laughter stilled as he trailed a finger down her instep. Incredibly, she felt a fierce rush of desire. It poured into her, then spread like wildfire through her system. Her quiet moan was involuntary and irrepressible.

"They appear very fragile," Seth commented, cupping her arch in his palm. "But they must be strong." Again he lifted his eyes to hers. His thumb trailed over the ball of her foot, and she shuddered. "And sensitive." When he lifted her feet and kissed both of her ankles, Lindsay knew she was lost.

"You know what you do to me, don't you?" she whispered. It was time to accept what had to be between them.

There was a gleam of triumph in his eyes as he lifted his head again. "I know that I want you. And that you want me."

If it were only that simple, Lindsay thought. If I didn't love him, we could share each other with total freedom, without regrets. But I do love him, and one day I'll have to pay for tonight. There was a light flutter of fear in her chest at the thought of what the price might be.

"Hold me." She went into his arms and clung. "Hold me." While the snow lasts, she told herself, we're alone. There's no one else in the world, and this is our time. There's no tomorrow. There's no yesterday.

She tilted back her head until she could see his face. With a fingertip, she slowly traced the curves and angles until she knew every inch was carved in her memory.

"Love me, Seth," she said with her eyes wide. "Make love with me."

There was no time for a gentleness neither of them wanted. Passion sets its own rules. His mouth was avid, burning on hers before her words had dissolved in the air. His hunger was unbearably arousing. But she sensed he was in control, still the captain of their destiny. There was no fumbling as he undressed her. His hands caressed her as each layer of clothing was removed, inciting desire wherever they touched. When she struggled to release the buttons of his shirt, he helped her. There was fire and need and spiraling pleasure.

Touching him, exploring the taut flesh of his chest and shoulders, Lindsay felt yet a new sensation. It was one of possession. For now, for the moment, he belonged to her, and he owned her absolutely. And they were flesh to flesh without barriers, naked and hungry and tangled together. His mouth roamed down feverishly to taste her breast, then lingered there, savoring, while his hands brought her trembling delight. His tongue was excitingly rough. As he nuzzled, she moved under him, powered by needs that grew in velocity and strength.

Her breath came in whimpers as she urged his lips back to hers. They came on a slow journey, pausing at her throat, detouring to her ear until she was near madness for the taste of him. Ravenously, she took his mouth with hers, shuddering now with a passion more all-consuming than anything she had ever experienced. In the dance, she remained one unit. The pleasure and dreams were hers and within her control. Now, she was joined to another, and pleasure and dreams were a shared thing. The loss of control was a part of the ecstasy.

She felt strong, more powerful than it seemed possible for her to be. Her energy was boundless, drawn from the need to have, the need to give. Their passion flowed sweet as honey; she was molten in his arms.

Chapter 10

Lindsay dreamed she was lying in a big, old bed, wrapped in quilts and in her lover's arms. It was a bed that knew their bodies well, one she had awakened in morning after morning over the years. The sheets were Irish linen and soft as a kiss. The quilt was an heirloom she would pass on to her daughter. The lover was a husband whose arms became only more exciting over the years. When the baby cried, she stirred, but lazily, knowing that nothing could disturb the tranquil beauty in which she lived. She snuggled deep into the arms that held her and opened her eyes. Still dreaming, she smiled into Seth's.

"It's morning," she murmured and found his mouth warm and soft and delightful. She ran her fingertips down his spine, smiling when his lips became more insistent. "I've got to get up," she whispered, nestling as his hand cupped her breast. She could still hear the faint, plaintive cry of the baby.

"Uh-uh." His lips moved to her ear. Slowly, his tongue began to awaken her fully. Passion rekindled the night's embers.

"Seth, I have to, she's crying."

With a half-hearted oath, Seth rolled over and reached down to the floor. Rolling back, he plopped Nijinsky the cat on Lindsay's stomach. She blinked, disoriented and confused as the kitten mewed at her, making sounds like a baby. The dream shattered abruptly.

Lindsay reached up to drag a hand through her hair and took a long breath.

"What's the matter?" Seth tangled his hand in her hair until she opened her eyes.

"Nothing." She shook her head, stroking the kitten so that he purred. "I was dreaming. It was silly."

"Dreaming." He brushed his lips over her naked shoulder. "About me?"

Lindsay turned her head until their eyes met again. "Yes." Her lips curved. "About you."

Seth shifted, bringing her to rest in the curve of his shoulder. Nijinsky moved to curl at their feet. He circled twice, pawed the quilt, then settled. "What was it about?"

She burrowed into the column of his throat. "My secret." His fingers were trailing soothingly over her shoulder and upper arm.

I belong to him, she thought, *and can't tell him.* Lindsay stared at the window, seeing that though the snow was thinning, it fell still. There's only the two of us, she reminded herself. Until the snow stops, there's just we two. *I love him so desperately.* Closing her eyes, she ran her hand up his chest to his shoulder. There were muscles there she wanted to feel again. With a smile, she pressed her lips against his throat. There was today. *Only today.* She moved her mouth to his, and their lips joined.

Their kisses were short, quiet tastes. The rush—the desperation—of the night before had mellowed. Now desire built slowly, degree by degree. It smoldered, it teased, but it didn't overpower. They took time to enjoy. Seth shifted so that she lay across his chest.

"Your hands," he murmured as he brought one to his lips, "are exquisite. When you dance, they seem to have no bones." He spread his hand over hers, palm to palm.

Her hair cascaded around her shoulders to fall on his. In the soft, morning light it was as pale as an illusion. Her skin was ivory with touches of rose just under the surface. It was a fragile, delicately boned face, but the eyes were vivid and strong. Lindsay lowered her mouth and kissed him, long and lingeringly. Her heartbeat quickened as she felt his hunger build.

"I like your face." She took her mouth from his to softly kiss his cheeks and eyelids and jaw. "It's strong and just a bit wicked." She smiled against his skin, remembering. "You terrified me the first time I saw you."

"Before or after you ran out in the road?" He trailed one hand up her back while the other stroked her hair. It was a lazy, comfortable loving.

"I did not run out in the road," Lindsay nipped at his chin. "You were driving too fast." She began to plant kisses down the length of his chest. "You looked awfully tall when I was sitting in that puddle."

She heard him chuckle as he ran a hand down the arch of her back, then slowly reacquainted himself with the slight flare of her hips, the long length of her thighs.

He shifted, and they moved as one until their positions were reversed. The kiss deepened. The touch of hands to flesh was still gentle but more demanding now. Conversation lapsed into a soft slumber. Passion rose like a tropical wave, warm and steep. It crested, then receded....

Dressed in jeans and a flannel shirt borrowed from Ruth's wardrobe, Lindsay skipped down the main stairway. There was a chill in the house which told her the fires had yet to be lit. Only the one in the master bedroom crackled. The first stage of her plan was to start one in the kitchen hearth. She hummed an impromptu tune as she pushed open the door.

It surprised her that Seth was there ahead of her. She could smell the coffee.

"Hi!" Walking over, she wrapped her arms around his waist, resting her cheek on his back. "I thought you were still upstairs."

"I came down while you were using Ruth's barre." Turning, he gathered her close. "Want some breakfast?"

"Maybe," she murmured, nearly exploding with joy at the simple intimacy. "Who's going to fix it?"

He tilted her chin. "We both are."

"Oh." Her brows lifted. "I hope you like cold cereal and bananas. That's my specialty."

Seth grimaced. "Can't you do anything with an egg?"

"I make really pretty ones at Easter time."

"I'll scramble," he decided, then kissed her forehead. "Can you handle toast?"

"Possibly." With her head resting against his chest, she watched the snow fall.

The trees and lawn resembled a stage set. The white blanket on the ground lay completely unmarred. The evergreen shrubs Seth had planted were wrapped in their own snowy coats; towering above them nearby, the trees stood as snow-covered giants. And still it fell.

"Let's go outside," Lindsay said impulsively. "It looks wonderful."

"After breakfast. We'll need more wood, in any case."

"Logical, logical." Lindsay wrinkled her nose at him. "Practical, practical." She let out a quick cry when he tugged her earlobe playfully.

"Architects have to be logical and practical, otherwise buildings fall down and people get upset."

"But your buildings don't look practical," Lindsay told him. She watched him as he walked to the refrigerator. Who, exactly, was this man she was in love with? Who was the man who had laid claim to her emotions and her body? "They always look beautiful, never like those steel and glass boxes that rob cities of their character."

"Beauty can be practical, too." He turned back with a carton of eggs in one hand. "Or perhaps it's better to say practicality can be beautiful."

"Yes, but I should think it more difficult to make a really good building appealing to the eye as well as functional."

"If it isn't difficult, it's hardly worth the trouble, is it?"

Lindsay gave a slow nod. That she understood. "Will you let me see your drawings of the New Zealand project?" She wandered to the bread box. "I've never seen the conception of a building before."

"All right." He began to break eggs into a bowl.

They prepared and ate the meal in easy companionship. Lindsay thought the kitchen smelled of family; coffee and toast and singed eggs. She logged the scent in her memory file, knowing it would be precious on some future morning. When they had eaten and set the kitchen to rights, they piled on layers of outdoor clothing and left the house.

Lindsay's first step took her thigh-deep in snow. Laughing, Seth gave her a nudge that sent her sprawling backward. She was quickly up to her shoulders. The sound of his laughter hit the wall of snow and bounced back, accentuating their solitude.

"Maybe I'd better put a bell around your neck so I can find you," he called out, laughing.

Lindsay struggled to stand up. Snow clung to her hair and crusted her coat. Seth's grin widened as she scowled at him. "Bully," she said with a sniff before she began to trudge through the snow.

"The wood pile's over here." Seth caught her hand. After giving token resistance, Lindsay went with him.

Their world was insular. Snow tumbled from the sky to disappear into the thick blanket around them. She could barely hear the sea. Ruth's boots came to her knees, but with every step, snow trickled inside the tops. Her face was rosy with cold, but the view outbalanced every discomfort.

The whiteness was perfect. There was no glare to

sting the eyes, nor any shadows to bring variations in shade. There was simply white without relief, without obstruction.

"It's beautiful," Lindsay murmured, pausing as they reached the woodpile. She took a long, sweeping view. "But I don't think it could be painted or photographed. It would lose something in the duplication."

"It'd be flat," Seth told her. He stacked wood into her arms. Lindsay's breath puffed out in front of her as she gazed beyond his shoulder.

"Yes, that's it exactly." The agreement pleased her. "I'd rather remember it than see it in one dimension." With Seth alongside, she made slow progress to the back door. "But you must be an expert at visualizing reality from a flat drawing."

"You've got it backwards." They stacked the wood behind the utility room door. "I make drawings from a reality I visualize."

Lindsay stopped a moment, a bit breathless from the exertion of wading through thigh-deep snow. "Yes." She nodded. "I can understand that." Studying him, she smiled. "You've snow on your eyelashes."

His eyes searched hers questioningly. She tilted her head, inviting the kiss. His lips lowered to touch hers, and she heard him suck in his breath as he lifted her into his arms.

He carried her over the threshold and through the door. When he continued through the utility room into the kitchen, Lindsay roused herself to object. "Seth, we're covered with snow. It's going to drip everywhere."

"Yep."

They were in the hall, and she pushed the hair from her eyes. "Where are you going?"

"Upstairs."

"Seth, you're crazy." She bounced gently on his shoulder as he climbed the main staircase. "We're making a mess. Worth's going to be very upset."

"He's resilient," Seth stated, turning into the master bedroom. He placed Lindsay onto the bed. From her reclining position she pushed herself up onto her elbows.

"Seth." He had removed his coat and was working on his boots. Lindsay's eyes widened, half in amusement, half in disbelief. "Seth, for goodness sake, I'm covered with snow."

"Better get out of those wet things, then." He tossed his boots aside, then moved to her to unbutton her coat.

"You're mad," she decided, laughing as he drew off her coat and tossed it on the floor to join his boots.

"Very possibly," he agreed. In two quick tugs, he had removed her boots. The thick wool socks she wore were stripped off before he began to massage warmth back into her feet. He felt her instant response to his touch.

"Seth, don't be silly." But her voice was already husky. "Snow's melted all over the bed."

With a smile, he kissed the balls of her feet and watched her eyes cloud. Moving to her side, he gathered her into his arms. "The rug is dry," he said as he lowered her. Slowly, his fingers following his mouth, he undid the buttons of her shirt. Beside them, the fire he had built before breakfast sizzled.

He parted her shirt, not yet removing it. With a tender laziness he began kissing her breasts while Lindsay floated on the first stage of pleasure. She sighed once, then, touching his cheek with her hand, persuaded his mouth to hers. The kiss began slowly, but the quality changed without warning. His mouth became desperate on a groan that seemed to come from somewhere deep inside him. Then he was tugging at the rest of her clothes, impatient, tearing the seam in Ruth's shirt as he pulled it from Lindsay's shoulder.

"I want you more than before," he mumbled as his teeth and lips grew rough at her neck. "More than yesterday. More than a moment ago." His hands bruised as they took possession of her body.

"Then have me," she told him, drawing him closer, wanting him. "Have me now."

Then his mouth was on hers and there were no more words.

The phone woke Lindsay. Drowsily, she watched Seth rise to answer it. He wore the forest green robe he had slipped on when he had rebuilt the fire. She had no sense of time. Clocks were for a practical world, not for dreams.

She stretched slowly, vertebra by vertebra. If forever could be a moment, she would have chosen that one. She felt soft and warm and well-loved. Her body was heavy with pleasure.

Lindsay watched Seth without hearing the words he spoke into the phone. He stands so straight, she thought and smiled a little. And he so rarely uses gestures with his words. Gestures can betray feelings, and his are very private. He holds his own leash. Her smile sweetened. And I like knowing I can take him to the end of it.

His voice intruded into her musings as snatches of

his conversation leaked through. It's Ruth, she realized, distracted from her concentrated study of his face. After sitting up, Lindsay drew the quilt around her shoulders. Before she looked to the window, she knew what she would see. The snow had stopped while they slept. She waited for Seth to hang up the phone.

She managed to smile at him while her mind worked feverishly to gather impressions; the way his hair fell over his forehead, the glint of the sun on it as light spilled through the window, the straight, attentive way he stood. Her heart seemed to expand to hold new degrees of love. She fought to keep her face composed.

Don't spoil it, she ordered herself frantically. *Don't spoil it now.* It seemed to Lindsay that Seth was studying her with even more than his usual intensity. After a long moment, he crossed to where she sat on the floor, cocooned by quilts and pillows.

"Is she coming home?" Lindsay asked when Seth replaced the receiver.

"She and Monica are driving over shortly. The county's been on the ball, it seems, and the roads are nearly clear."

"Well." Lindsay pushed at her hair before she rose, still tented by the quilt. "I suppose I'd better get ready, then. It seems I'll have evening classes."

There was a sudden outrageous desire to weep. Lindsay battled against it, bundling herself up in the quilt as she gathered her clothes. Be practical, she instructed. Seth is a practical man. He'd hate emotional scenes. She swallowed hard and felt control returning. While slipping into her tights and leotard, she continued to talk.

"It's amazing how quickly these road crews work.

I can only hope they didn't bury my car. I suppose I'll have to have it towed. If it's only a minor disaster, I shouldn't be without it for long." Dropping the quilt, she slipped her sweater over her head. "I'll have to borrow Ruth's brush," she continued, pulling her hair out from the collar. Suddenly, she stopped to face Seth directly. "Why do you just look at me?" she demanded. "Why don't you say something?"

He stood where he was, still watching her. "I was waiting for you to stop babbling."

Lindsay shut her eyes. She felt completely defenseless. She had, she realized, made an utter fool of herself. This was a sophisticated man, one used to casual affairs and transitory relationships. "I'm simply no good at this sort of thing," she said. "I'm not good at it at all." He reached for her. "No, don't." Quickly, she jerked away. "I don't need that now."

"Lindsay." The annoyance in his tone made it easier for her to control the tears.

"Just give me a few minutes," she snapped at him. "I hate acting like an idiot." With this, she turned and fled the room, slamming the door behind her.

In fifteen minutes Lindsay stood in the kitchen pouring Nijinsky a saucer of milk. Her fine hair was brushed to fall neatly down her back. Her nerves, if not quiet, were tethered. Her hands were steady.

The outburst had been foolish, she decided, but maybe it had helped ease her into the first stage of her return to the outside world.

For a moment she lost herself in a dream as she gazed out on the world of white. She knew, though he made no sound, the moment Seth stepped into the room. Lindsay took an extra second, then turned to him. He was dressed in dark brown corduroy slacks and a vee-neck sweater over a pale blue shirt. She thought he looked casually efficient.

"I made some coffee," she said in a carefully friendly voice. "Would you like some?"

"No." He came toward her purposefully; then, while she was still wondering what he would do, he brought her close. His hands circled her upper arms. The kiss was searing and long and enervating. When he drew her away, Lindsay's vision dimmed and then refocused.

"I wanted to see if that had changed," he told her while his eyes seemed to spear into hers. "It hasn't."

"Seth..." But his mouth silenced hers again. Protest became hungry response. Without thought, she poured every ounce of her feelings into the kiss, giving him all. She heard him murmur her name before he crushed her against him. Again, all was lost. The flashes of paradise came so swiftly, Lindsay could only grasp at them without fully taking hold. Drawn away again, she stared up at him, not seeing, only feeling.

Another woman, she thought dazedly, would be content with this. Another woman could continue to be his lover and not hurt for anything else. Another woman wouldn't need so much from him when she already has so much. Slowly, Lindsay brought herself back. The only way to survive was to pretend she was another woman.

"I'm glad we were snowbound," she told him, pulling gently from his arms. "It's been wonderful being here with you." Keeping her voice light, she walked back to the coffeepot. When she poured, she noticed her hand was no longer steady.

Seth waited for her to turn back, but she continued to face the stove. "And?" he said, slipping his hands into his pockets.

Lindsay lifted the coffee cup and sipped. It was scalding. She smiled when she turned. "And?" she repeated. The hurt was thudding inside her throat, making the word painful.

His expression seemed very much as it had the first time she had seen him. Stormy and forbidding. "Is that all?" he demanded.

Lindsay moistened her lips and shrugged. She clung to the cup with both hands. "I don't think I know what you mean."

"There's something in your eyes," he muttered, crossing to her. "But it keeps slipping away. You won't let me know what you're feeling. Why?"

Lindsay stared into the cup, then drank again. "Seth," she began calmly and met his eyes again. "My feelings are my business until I give them to you."

"Perhaps I thought you had."

The hurt was unbelievable. Her knees trembled from it. His eyes were so steady, so penetrating. Lindsay took her defense in briskness. "We're both adults. We were attracted to each other, we have been for some time...."

"And if I want more?"

His question scattered her thoughts. She tried to draw them back, tried to see past the guard that was now in his eyes. Hope and fear waged war inside her. "More?" she repeated cautiously. Her heart was racing now. "What do you mean?"

He studied her. "I'm not certain it's an issue if I have to explain it."

Frustrated, Lindsay slammed her cup back on the counter. "Why do you start something and not finish it?"

"Exactly what I'm asking myself." He seemed to hesitate, then lifted a hand to her hair. She leaned toward him, waiting for a word. "Lindsay..."

The kitchen door swung open in front of Ruth and Monica.

"Hi!" Ruth's greeting trailed off the moment she took in the situation. She searched quickly for a way to back out, but Monica was already passing her to go to Lindsay.

"Are you okay? We saw your car." Concern dominated her tone as she reached out to touch her friend. "I knew I should've made you stay."

"I'm fine." She gave Monica a kiss for reassurance. "How're the roads now?"

"Pretty good." She jerked her head at Ruth. "She's worried about missing class."

"Naturally." Lindsay gave her attention to the girls until her pulse leveled. "That shouldn't be a problem."

Attracted by Ruth's voice, Nijinsky wandered over to circle her legs until she obliged him by picking him up. "Are you sure you feel up to it?"

Lindsay read the knowledge in Ruth's eyes and reached for her cup again. "Yes. Yes, I'm fine." Automatically she went to the sink for a cloth to wipe up the coffee she had spilled. "I guess I should call a tow truck."

"I'll see to it." Seth spoke for the first time since the interruption. His tone was formal and distant.

"That isn't necessary," Lindsay began.

"I said I'll see to it. I'll take you all to the studio when you're ready." He walked from the room, leaving the three of them staring at the swinging door.

Chapter 11

Monica and Ruth rode in the back of Seth's car on the drive to the studio. Ruth was conscious of a definite, pronounced tension between her uncle and Lindsay. Whatever was between them, she concluded, had hit a snag. Because she was fond of both of them, Ruth did her best to ease the strained atmosphere. "Is Worth due back tonight?"

Seth met her eyes briefly in the rearview mirror. "In the morning."

"I'll fix you coq au vin tonight," she volunteered, leaning forward onto the front seat. "It's one of my best dishes. But we'll have to eat late."

"You have school tomorrow."

"Uncle Seth." Her smile was tolerant. "I'm graduating from high school, not elementary school.

"Monica showed me her brother's yearbook last

night," she continued, turning her attention to Lindsay. "The one from the year you and Andy graduated."

"Andy looked great in his football jersey, didn't he?" Lindsay shifted in her seat so that she faced Ruth.

"I liked your picture best." She pushed her hair back over her shoulder. Lindsay saw that all her shyness had fled. Her eyes were as open and friendly as her smile. "You should see it, Uncle Seth. She's on the steps leading into the auditorium. She's doing an *arabesque*."

"Smart aleck Tom Finley told me to do a little ballet."

"Is that why you were sticking out your tongue?"

Lindsay laughed. "It added to the aesthetic value of the photograph."

"It sounds like a good likeness," Seth commented, turning both Lindsay's and Ruth's attention to himself. "The *arabesque* was in perfect form, I imagine. You could dance in the middle of an earthquake."

Lindsay kept her eyes on his profile, not certain if he was praising her or criticizing her. "It's called concentration, I suppose."

"No." Seth took his eyes from the road long enough to meet her gaze. "It's called love. You love to dance. It shows."

"I don't think there's a better compliment," Ruth said. "I hope someone says that to me one day."

All the things she wanted to say raced through Lindsay's mind, but none would remain constant. Instead, she laid her hand on the back of his. Seth glanced at their hands, then at Lindsay. "Thank you," she said.

Her heart caught when he turned his hand over to grip hers. He brought it to his lips. "You're welcome."

Ruth smiled at the gesture, then settled back as they

turned into the school parking lot. Someone had made a halfhearted attempt to clear the snow, and Lindsay knew immediately that it must have been the neighborhood kids.

"Someone's here," Ruth commented when she spotted the sleek foreign car parked in the lot.

Lindsay absently glanced away from Seth as he stopped the car. "I wonder who…" The words stumbled to a halt, and her eyes widened. She shook her head, certain she was wrong, but climbed slowly out of the car. The man in the black overcoat and fur hat stepped away from the studio door and walked to her. The moment he moved, Lindsay knew she wasn't mistaken.

"Nikolai!" Even as she shouted his name, she was racing through the snow. She saw only a blur of his face as she flung herself into his arms. Memories poured over her.

He had held her before; the prince to her Giselle, the Don to her Dulcinea, Romeo to her Juliet. She had loved him to the fullest extent of friendship, hated him with the pure passion of one artist for another, worshipped his talent and despaired of his temper. As he held her again, everything they had shared, everything she had felt in her years with the company, flooded back to her. The wave was too quick and too high. Weeping, she clung to him.

Nick laughed, pulling her away to give her a boisterous kiss. He was too absorbed with Lindsay to hear Ruth's reverently whispered *"Davidov"* or to see Seth's concentrated study.

"Hello, *ptichka,* my little bird." His voice was high

and rich with Russian inflection. Lindsay could only shake her head and bury her face in his shoulder.

The meeting was unexpected, whipping up her already heightened emotions. But when he drew her away again, she saw through her blurred vision that he was precisely the same. Though he had a deceptively innocent boy's face, he could tell ribald jokes and swear in five languages. His thickly lashed blue eyes crinkled effectively at the corners. His mouth was generous, romantically shaped, and there was the charm of two slight dimples when he smiled. His hair was dark blond, curling and thick. He left it tousled to his advantage. He skimmed under six feet, making him a good partner for a dancer of Lindsay's size.

"Oh, Nick, you haven't changed." Lindsay touched his face with both hands. "I'm so, so glad you haven't."

"But you, *ptichka,* you have changed." The potent choirboy grin lit his face. "You are still my little bird, my *ptichka,* but how is it you are still more beautiful?"

"Nick." Tears mixed with laughter. "How I've missed you." She kissed his cheeks, then his mouth. Her eyes, washed with tears, were shades deeper. "What are you doing here?"

"You weren't home, so I came here." He shrugged at the simplicity. "I told you I'd come in January. I came early."

"You drove from New York in all this snow?"

Nikolai took a deep breath and looked around. "It felt like Russia, your Connecticut. I like to smell the snow." His eyes alit on Seth and Ruth. "Your manners are revolting, *ptichka,*" he said mildly.

"Oh, I'm sorry! I was so surprised…." She felt flustered and brushed at her tears with the back of her hand. "Seth, Ruth, this is Nikolai Davidov. Nicky, Seth and Ruth Bannion. She's the dancer I told you about."

Ruth stared at Lindsay. In that moment, she became Lindsay's willing slave.

"A pleasure to meet friends of Lindsay's." He shook hands with Seth. A small line appeared between his brows as he studied him. "You are not perhaps the architect Bannion?"

Seth nodded while Lindsay watched the men measure each other. "Yes."

Nick beamed with pleasure. "Ah, but I have just bought a house of your design in California. It's on the beach with many windows so that the sea is in the living room."

He's so effusive, Lindsay thought of Nick. So different from Seth, and yet they remind me of each other.

"I remember the house," Seth acknowledged. "In Malibu?"

"Yes, yes, Malibu!" Obviously delighted, Nick beamed again. "I'm told it's early Bannion, reverently, as though you were long dead."

Seth smiled as people invariably did with Nick. "The more reverently, the higher the market value."

Nikolai laughed offhandedly, but he had caught the expression in Lindsay's eyes when she looked at Seth. So, he thought, that's the way the wind blows. "And this is the dancer you want to send me." He turned his attention to Ruth, taking both hands in his. He saw a small, dark beauty—with good bones and narrow hands—who trembled like a leaf. The face would be exotic with the right makeup and lighting, he decided. And her size was good.

"Mr. Davidov." Ruth struggled not to stutter. To her, Nikolai Davidov was a legend, a figure larger than life. To be standing toe to toe with him, her hands held by his, seemed impossible. The pleasure was excruciating.

He chafed her hands, and his smile was personal. "You must tell me if Lindsay's manners are always so appalling. How long does she usually keep her friends standing out in the cold?"

"Oh, blast!" Lindsay fumbled for her keys. "You completely stun me by popping up from nowhere, then expect me to behave rationally." She pushed open the front door. "I was right," she told him over her shoulder, "you haven't changed."

Nikolai wandered past her into the room's center without speaking. Pulling off his gloves, he tapped them idly against his palm as he surveyed the studio. Ruth hung on his every movement.

"Very good," he decided. "You've done well here, *ptichka.* You have good students?"

"Yes." Lindsay smiled at Ruth. "I have good students."

"Have you found a teacher to run your school when you come back to New York?"

"Nick." Lindsay paused in the act of unbuttoning her coat. "I haven't agreed to come back."

"That is nonsense." He dismissed her objection with a flick of the wrist. It was a gesture Lindsay remembered well. An argument now would be heated and furious. "I must be back in two days. I direct *The Nut-cracker.* In January I begin staging for my ballet." As he spoke, he shrugged out of his coat. He wore a simple gray jogging suit and looked, to Ruth's mind, magnificent. "With you as my Ariel, I have no doubt as to its success."

"Nick…"

"But I want to see you dance first," he said over her protest, "to make certain you haven't gone to pot."

"Gone to pot?" Incensed, Lindsay tossed her coat over a chair. "You'll be writing Russian phrase books long before I go to pot, Davidov."

"That's yet to be seen." He turned to Seth as he slipped off his hat. "Tell me, Mr. Bannion, do you know my *ptichka* well?"

Seth turned his eyes to Lindsay, holding them there until she flushed. "Fairly well." His gaze slid back to Nikolai. "Why?"

"I wonder if you could tell me if she has kept her muscles as well-exercised as her temper. It's important that I know how much time I must spend whipping her back into shape."

"Whipping me back into shape!" Knowing she was being maneuvered didn't prevent Lindsay from falling into the trap. "I don't need you or anyone to whip me into shape."

"Okay." He nodded as he looked down at her feet. "You need toe shoes and tights, then."

Lindsay turned on her heel and headed for her office. Still fuming, she slammed the door behind her. Nick grinned at Seth and Ruth.

"You know her very well," Seth commented.

Nikolai gave a quick chuckle. "As I know myself. We are very much the same." Reaching into a deep pocket of his coat, he produced a pair of ballet shoes. He sat on a chair to change into them. "You've known Lindsay long?" Nikolai knew he was prying and realized from the lift of Seth's brow that the bluntness had been acknowledged.

He is a private, self-contained man, Nikolai decided. But his thoughts are on Lindsay. If it was a man who was keeping her from resuming her profession, he wanted to know it and to understand the man. He concluded that Seth wouldn't be an easy man to understand. Complications, he knew, appealed to Lindsay.

"A few months," Seth answered at length. The artist in him recognized an extraordinarily beautiful man. The sensitive face held just enough puckishness to keep it from being too smooth. It was a face easily cast as a fairy-tale prince. A difficult face to dislike. Seth slipped his hands into his pockets. He, too, felt a desire to understand the man.

"You worked together for some time in New York."

"I've had no better partner in my career," he said simply. "But I could never say so to my *ptichka*. She works best when her passions are aroused. She has great passions." He smiled as he rose. "Like a Russian."

Lindsay came back into the room wearing black tights and a leotard with white leg warmers and *pointe shoes*. Her chin was still lifted.

"You've put on some weight," Nikolai commented as he gave her willow slim figure a critical survey.

"I'm a hundred and two," she said defensively.

"You'll need to drop five pounds," he told her as he walked to the barre. "I'm a dancer, not a weight-lifter." He *pliéd* while Lindsay caught her breath in fury.

"I don't have to starve myself for you anymore, Nick."

"You forget, I'm director now." He smiled at her blandly and continued to warm up.

"You forget," she countered, "I'm not with the company now."

"Paperwork only." He gestured for her to join him.

"We'll leave you two alone." Lindsay turned to Seth as he spoke. Nikolai watched the contact of their eyes. *This man gives nothing away,* he decided. "And give you some privacy."

"Please," Nikolai interrupted Lindsay's response. "You must stay."

"Yes, Nick never could perform without an audience." She smiled, reaching out to touch Seth's hand. "Don't go."

"Please, Uncle Seth." Enraptured by the possibility of watching her two favorite artists perform impromptu, Ruth clung to Seth's arm. Her eyes were dark with excitement.

Seth hesitated. He looked once at Lindsay, long and deep. "All right."

The formality was back in his tone and troubled her. Why, she thought as she walked to join Nikolai, was the closeness between them so elusive? She spoke to Nick casually as they loosened and warmed their muscles, but he noted how often her eyes drifted to Seth's reflection in the glass.

"How long have you loved him?" he murmured in a voice only Lindsay could hear. She glanced up sharply. "You could never hold a secret from me, *ptichka.* A friend often sees more clearly than a lover."

"I don't know." Lindsay sighed, feeling the weight of it settle on her. "Sometimes it feels like forever."

"And your eyes are tragic." He stopped her from turning away by placing a hand to her cheek. "Is love so tragic, my little bird?"

Lindsay shook her head, trying to dispel the mood. "What sort of question is that from a Russian? Love is meant to be tragic, isn't it?"

"This isn't Chekhov, *ptichka.*" After patting her cheek, he walked to the CD player. "Perhaps Shakespeare would suit you." He glanced up from the CDs he sifted through. "Do you remember the second *pas de deux* from *Romeo and Juliet?*"

Lindsay's eyes softened. "Of course I do. We rehearsed endlessly. You pulled my toes when they cramped, then threw a sweaty towel at me when I missed a *sauté.*"

"Your memory is good." He inserted the CD and programmed the selection. "Come then, dance with me now, *ptichka,* for old times and for new." Nikolai held out his hand. There was magic when they came together.

Their fingers touched, then parted. Lindsay felt it instantly: the youth, the hope, the poignancy of first love. Her steps were instinctive. They flowed with the music and paired fluidly with Nick's. When he lifted her the first time, she felt as though she was lost forever in the music, in the emotion.

Ruth watched them, hardly daring to breathe. Although the dance looked deceptively simple, her training gave her a complete appreciation of its intricacies and difficulties. It was romance in its purest form: a man and a woman irresistibly drawn together, testing the waters of new love. The music vibrated with the emotion of a love deep and doomed. It shone naked in Lindsay's eyes when she looked at Davidov. Here was not the teasing sauciness of her Dulcinea, but the vulnerabilities of a girl loving for the first time. And when they knelt on the floor, fingertips reaching for fingertips, Ruth's heart nearly burst from the glory of it.

For several seconds after the music ended, the dancers remained still, eyes locked, fingers just touching. Then Davidov smiled, and moving close, pulled her to him. She trembled lightly under his palm.

"It seems you haven't gone to pot after all, *ptichka*. Come back with me. I need you."

"Oh, Nick." Drained, she laid her head on his shoulder. She had forgotten the depth of the pleasure that was hers when she danced with him. And yet, the very essence of the dance had intensified her feelings for Seth.

If she could have gone back to the snowbound house, cut off from all in the world but him, she would have done so blindly. Her mind seemed almost drugged with wants and doubts. She clung to Nick as if he were an anchor.

"She was not too bad." Over Lindsay's head, he grinned at Seth and Ruth.

"She was wonderful," Ruth responded in a voice husky with feeling. "You were both wonderful. Weren't they, Uncle Seth?"

Slowly, Lindsay lifted her head. When she looked up at him, her eyes were still brimming with love. "Yes."

Seth watched her, but there was no expression on his face. "I've never seen two people move together more perfectly." He stood, lifting his coat as he did so.

"I have to go." He laid his hand on Ruth's shoulder as he heard her murmur of disappointment. "Perhaps Ruth could stay. There's only an hour or so before her class."

"Yes, of course." Lindsay stood, uncertain how to deal with the distance that was suddenly between them. Her body still quivered with emotions that belonged to him. "Seth…" She said his name, knowing nothing else.

"I'll pick her up tonight." He shifted his attention to Nikolai, who had risen to stand beside Lindsay. "A pleasure meeting you, Mr. Davidov."

"And for me," Nikolai responded. He could feel the vibrations of distress from Lindsay as Seth turned away.

She took a step, then stopped herself. The night had been her dream, the dance her fantasy. She closed her eyes tight as the door shut behind him.

"Lindsay." Nick touched her shoulder, but she shook her head furiously.

"No, please. I—I have to make some phone calls." Turning, she fled into her office.

Nick sighed as the door clicked shut. "We are an emotional lot, dancers," he commented as he turned to Ruth. Her eyes were dark and wide and young. "Come, then, you will show me why Lindsay would send you to me."

Stunned, Ruth stared at him. "You want—you want me to dance for you?" Her limbs turned to lead. Never would she be able to lift them.

Nick nodded briskly, suddenly all business. "Yes." His eyes drifted to the closed door as he moved back to the CD player. "We will give Lindsay the time she needs for her phone calls, but we need not waste it. Change your shoes."

Chapter 12

Ruth couldn't believe what was happening. As she hurried to exchange boots for ballet shoes, her fingers seemed numbed and unable to function. *Davidov* wanted to see her dance. It was a dream, she was certain. The fantasy was so long-standing and far-fetched that she was positive she would wake up at any moment in her high, soft bed at the Cliff House.

But she was sitting in Lindsay's studio. To reassure herself, Ruth put her mind to work fiercely, checking and rechecking all points of reference while her hands tugged at the boots. There was the long, inescapable wall of mirrors; the shining, always spotless wood floor. She looked at the familiar sheet music piled on the piano, the CDs scattered on the stand. The struggling plant Lindsay had nursed so carefully sat in front of the east window. Ruth could see that another leaf had wilted. She could hear the click and hum of the heater, which had been switched on. The fan whirred softly.

Not a dream, she told herself. This was real. Her trembling hand slipped the favored ballet shoes onto her feet. She rose, daring at last to look at Davidov.

He should have been undistinguished in the plain gray jogging suit, but he wasn't. Ruth, despite her youth, recognized that certain men could never be ordinary. Some drew notice without effort. It was more than his face and physique, it was his aura.

When he had danced with Lindsay, Ruth had been transported. He was no teenage Romeo but twenty-eight, perhaps at the zenith of his career as a dancer. But she had believed him because he had exuded tender youth and the wonder of first love. No one would question any role Nick Davidov chose to portray. Now she tried to see the man but was almost afraid to look. The legend was very important to her. She was still young enough to want indestructible heroes.

She found him remarkably beautiful, but the demand of his eyes and the slight crookedness of his nose prevented it from being too smooth a face. Ruth was glad without knowing why. Now she could see only his profile as he poured over Lindsay's collection of CDs. There was a faint gleam of perspiration on his forehead testifying to the exertion of the dance he had just completed. His eyebrows were lowered, and though he studied the CD insert in his hand, Ruth wondered if his mind was on it. He seemed distant, in a world of his own. She thought perhaps that was how legends should be: remote and unapproachable.

Yet Lindsay had never been, she reflected. And

Davidov had not seemed so at first. He had been friendly, she remembered. He had smiled at her.

Perhaps he's forgotten about me, she thought, feeling small and foolish. Why should he want to see me dance? Her spine straightened with a surge of pride. He asked, she reminded herself. He *ordered,* was more accurate. And he's going to remember me when I'm finished, she determined as she walked to the barre to warm up. And one day, she thought, taking first position, I'll dance with him. Just as Lindsay did.

Without speaking, Davidov set down the CD he was holding and began to pace the studio. His movements were those of a caged animal. Ruth lost her timing in simple awe. She'd been wrong; he hadn't forgotten about her, but his thoughts were focused on the woman behind the office door. He hated the look of hurt and desolation he had seen in Lindsay's eyes as she had rushed from the room.

What a range of emotions her face had held in one short afternoon, Nick mused. He'd watched Lindsay and enjoyed her surprised joy when she had seen him outside for the first time. Her eyes had brimmed with feeling. Being an emotional man, Davidov understood emotional people. He admired Lindsay's abilities to speak without words and to speak passionately.

There had been no mistaking Lindsay's feelings for Seth Bannion. He had seen it instantly. And though Seth was a controlled man, Nikolai had felt something there, too—a slight current, like a soft breath in the air. But Seth had left Lindsay without an embrace or a touch and barely a word. Nikolai felt he would never understand restrained Americans and their hesitancy to touch each other.

Still, he knew the cool departure would have hurt Lindsay. But it wouldn't have devastated her. She was too strong for that. There was something more, he was certain, something deeper. His impulses urged him to walk through the office door and demand to know the problem, but he knew Lindsay needed time. So he would give it to her.

And there was the girl.

He turned to watch Ruth warming up at the barre. The sun, slanting through the windows, flashed in the mirrors. It glowed around Ruth as she brought her leg up to an almost impossible ninety-degree angle. She held it there poised, effortlessly.

Nikolai frowned, narrowing his eyes. When he had looked at her outside, he had seen a lovely girl with exotic features and good bones. But he had seen a child, not yet out of the schoolroom; now he saw a beautiful woman. A trick of the light, he thought, taking a step closer. Something stirred inside him which he quickly suppressed.

Ruth moved, and the angle of the sun altered. She was a young girl again. The tension in Nick's shoulders evaporated. He shook his head, smiling at his own imagination. Sternly professional again, he walked over and selected a CD.

"Come," he said commandingly. "Take the room's center. I'll call the combination."

Ruth swallowed, trying to pretend it was every day that she danced in front of Nikolai Davidov. But she found that even taking a step from the barre was impossible. Nikolai smiled, suddenly recognizing the girl's nervousness.

"Come," he said again with more gentleness. "I rarely break the legs of my dancers."

He was rewarded by a quick, fleeting smile before Ruth walked to the center of the studio. Programming the CD selection, he began.

Lindsay had been right. Nikolai saw that within moments, but the pace of his instructions remained smooth and steady. Had Ruth been able to study him, she might have thought him displeased. His mouth was sternly set, and his eyes held an unfathomable, closed look. Those who knew him or had worked with him would have recognized unswerving concentration.

Ruth's initial terror had passed. She was dancing, and she let the music take her. An *arabesque,* a *soubresaut,* a quick, light series of *pirouettes.* She gave what he demanded her to give without question. When the instructions stopped, so did she, but only to wait. She knew there would be more. She sensed it.

Nick moved back to the CD player without a glance or a word for Ruth. He sifted quickly through the CDs until he found what he wanted. *"The Nutcracker.* Lindsay does it for Christmas?" It was more of a statement than a question, but Ruth answered it.

"Yes." Her voice came strong and smooth with no more trembling nerves. She was the dancer now, the woman in control.

"You're Carla," he said with such casual confidence that Ruth thought Lindsay must have told him she had been cast in the role. He gave the combination quickly. "Show me," he demanded and folded his arms.

* * *

Inside her office, Lindsay sat silently at her desk. Nikolai's instructions to Ruth came clearly enough through the closed door, but they didn't register. She was astonished by the depth of the pain. And it kept coming—wave after wave of it. She had been so certain that she could cope with the end of her idyll with Seth, just as she had coped with the snow. She hadn't realized how much hurt there would be.

The hideous battle with tears had almost passed. She could feel the outrageous need to shed them lessen. She had sworn when she had given herself to Seth that she would never regret it and never weep. She was comforted by the knowledge that there would be memories when the pain subsided—sweet, precious memories. She had been right, she was convinced, not to have thrown herself into his arms confessing her love as she had longed to do. It would have been unbearable for both of them. She had made it easy on him by giving a casual tone to their time together. But she hadn't expected the coldness or the ease with which he had walked out of her studio—and her life. She had thought for a moment, standing in his kitchen and again in the car driving to the studio, that perhaps she had been wrong after all. Imagination, Lindsay told herself with a quick shake of her head. Wishful thinking.

What had been between them had been wonderful: now it was over. That's what she had said to Seth, that's what she would have to remember.

She straightened, trying desperately to act with the same dispassion she had seen in Seth's eyes as he had turned to leave the studio. But her hands tightened into fists as emotions rose again to clog her throat. Will I stop loving him? she wondered despairingly. Can I?

Her eyes drifted to the phone, and she uncurled her hand and touched the receiver. She longed to phone him, just to hear his voice. If she could just hear him say her name. There must be a dozen excuses she could manufacture.

Idiot! She scolded herself and squeezed her eyes tightly shut. He's hardly had time to drive across town, and already you're prepared to make a fool of yourself.

It will get easier, she told herself firmly. It has to.

Rising, Lindsay moved to the window. Ice had formed along the edges of the pane. Behind the school was a high, sloping hill that curved into a narrow field. Already more than a dozen children were sledding madly. They were much too far away for her to hear the screams and laughter that must have echoed in the clear air. But she could sense the excitement, the freedom. There were trees here and there, mantled as they should be, heavy with snow and glistening in the strong sunlight.

Lindsay watched for a long time. A blur of red flew down the hill, then slowly made the trudge back to the summit. A flash of green followed to overturn halfway down and tumble to the bottom. For a moment Lindsay wanted almost desperately to run out and join them. She wanted to feel the cold, the sharp bite of snow as it hurled into her face, the breath-stealing surge of speed. She wanted the long, aching trudge back to the top. She felt too warm—too isolated—behind the window glass.

Life goes on, she mused, leaning her brow against the cool glass. And since it won't stop for me, I'd better keep up with the flow. There isn't any backing away from it, no hiding from it. I have to meet it head on. Then she heard the evocative music of *The Nutcracker*.

And this is where I begin.

Lindsay went to her office door, opened it and walked into the studio.

Neither Nikolai nor Ruth noticed her, and not wanting to disturb them, Lindsay came no farther into the room but stood watching Ruth who, smiling a dreamy half-smile, moved effortlessly and gracefully to Nikolai's command. Nick watched without comment.

No one, Lindsay decided, could tell by looking at him just what was going on in his head.

It was part of his character to be as open as the wind one moment, as mysterious as the sphinx the next. Perhaps that was why he attracted women, she thought. Suddenly it occurred to her that he was not so very different from Seth. But it was not what she wanted to ponder at the moment, and she turned back to watch Ruth.

How young she was! Hardly more than a child despite her wise and tragic eyes. For her there should be high school proms, football games and soft summer nights. Why should the life of a seventeen-year-old be so complicated?

Lindsay pressed her fingers to her temple, trying to remember herself at the same age. She'd already been in New York, and life had been simple but very, very demanding, both for the same reason. Ballet. It was going to be the same for Ruth.

Lindsay continued to watch her dance. For some, she decided, life is not meant to be easy. She thought of herself as much as Ruth. For some it's meant to be hard, but the rewards can be so, so sweet. Lindsay remembered the incredible exhilaration of dancing on stage, the culmination of hours of work and rehearsals, the payment for all the pain and all the sacrifice. Ruth would have it as well. She was destined to. Lindsay shunned the knowledge that in order to secure what she felt was Ruth's right, she herself would have to face Seth. And in facing him, she would have to be very strong. There would be time enough to think of that in the nights ahead when she was alone. She was certain that in a few days she could cope, that she would be able to deal with her own emotions. Then she would speak to Seth about Ruth.

When the music ended, Ruth held the final position for several seconds. As she lowered her arms, the next movement began, but Nick didn't speak to her. He gave no instruction, no comment, but went instead to switch off the CD player.

Ruth, her breath coming quickly, moistened her lips. Now that the dance was finished and she could relax her concentration, every other part of her tensed. Her fingers, which had been superbly graceful during the dance, now began to tremble.

He thinks I was dreadful, and he'll tell me so, she agonized. He'll feel sorry for me and say something pacifying and kind. Both alternatives were equally horrifying to her. A dozen questions came to her mind. She wished for the courage to voice them but could only grip one hand with the other. It seemed to her that her very life was hanging in the balance, waiting for one man's opinion, one man's words.

Davidov looked over suddenly and locked eyes with

her. The intensity of his gaze frightened her, and she gripped her hands together more tightly. Then the mask was gone, and he smiled at her. Ruth's heart stopped.

Here they come, she thought dizzily. Those kind, terrible words.

"Mr. Davidov," she began, wanting to stop him before he could begin. She would prefer a quick, clean cut.

"Lindsay was right," he interrupted her. "When you come to New York, come to me."

"To you?" Ruth repeated stupidly, not certain she had heard him correctly, not daring to believe.

"Yes, yes, to me." Nikolai appeared amused by Ruth's response. "I know a few things about ballet."

"Oh, Mr. Davidov, I didn't mean…" She came to him then, propelled by horrified distress. "I was just… I only meant…"

Nikolai took her hands to quiet her disjointed explanation. "How large your eyes are when you're confused," he said, giving her hands a quick squeeze. "There's still much I haven't seen, of course." He dropped her hands to take her chin and begin a thorough impassive study of her face. "How you dance on *pointe,*" he continued. "How you dance with a partner. But what I've seen is good."

She was speechless. Good from Davidov was the highest of accolades.

Lindsay moved forward then, and Nikolai looked up from his study of Ruth's face. *"Ptichka?"* Releasing the girl's chin, he went to Lindsay.

Her eyes were composed and dry without any trace of red, but her face was pale. Her hand was not lifeless in his; the fingers interlocked, but they were cold. He placed his other hand over them as if to warm them.

"So, you're pleased with my prize student." There was the slightest of signals, a glimpse in her eyes there, then gone, that said what had happened was not now to be discussed.

"Did you doubt I would be?" he countered.

"No." She smiled, turning her face to Ruth. "But I'm sure she did." Lindsay looked back at Nick, and the smile was wry. "You're every bit as intimidating as your reputation, Nikolai Davidov."

"Nonsense." He shrugged off Lindsay's opinion and shot Ruth a grin. "I'm as even-tempered as a saint."

"How sweetly you lie," Lindsay said mildly. "As always."

To this he merely grinned at her and kissed her hand. "It's part of my charm."

His comfort and his friendship were easing the pain. Lindsay pressed his hand to her cheek in gratitude. "I'm glad you're here." Then, releasing his hand, she walked to Ruth. "You could use some tea," she suggested but restrained herself from touching the girl's shoulder. She wasn't yet certain the gesture would be welcomed. "Because if memory serves me, your insides are shaking right now. Mine were the first time I danced in front of him, and he wasn't nearly the legend he is now."

"I've always been a legend, *ptichka,*" Nikolai corrected. "Ruth is merely better schooled in the art of respect than you were. This one," he told Ruth with a jerk of the thumb at Lindsay, "likes to argue."

"Especially with the mighty," Lindsay agreed.

Ruth laughed a breathy, relieved, wondering sound.

Could all this really be happening? she wondered. Am I actually standing here with Dunne and Davidov being treated as a professional? Looking into Lindsay's eyes, Ruth saw understanding and the faintest hint of sadness.

Uncle Seth, she remembered abruptly, ashamed of her own self-absorption. She recalled how crushed Lindsay had looked when Seth had closed the studio door behind him. Tentatively, she reached out and touched her mentor's hand.

"Yes, please, I would like some tea now."

"Russian tea?" Nikolai demanded from across the room.

Lindsay gave him a guileless smile. "Rose hips."

He made a face. "Perhaps vodka, then?" His brow rose in mild question.

"I wasn't expecting any Russian celebrities," Lindsay apologized with a smile. "There's a possibility I could dig up a diet soda."

"Tea is fine." He was studying her again, and Lindsay knew his thoughts had drifted. "Later I'll take you out for dinner, and we'll talk." He paused when Lindsay eyed him suspiciously. "Like old times, *ptichka,*" he told her innocently. "We have much to catch up on, don't we?"

"Yes," Lindsay agreed cautiously, "we do." She started to go back into her office to make the tea, but Ruth stopped her.

"I'll do it," she volunteered, recognizing that they could speak more openly without her standing between them. "I know where everything is." She darted quickly away before Lindsay could assent or decline.

Casually Nikolai slipped a CD at random from its

case and inserted it into the player. The quiet romance of Chopin was enough to help insure a more private conversation. "A lovely girl," he said. "I congratulate you on your judgment."

Lindsay smiled, glancing at the door that Ruth had left partly ajar. "She'll work harder than ever now after what you said to her. You'll take her into the company, Nick," she began, suddenly eager, wanting to seal Ruth's happiness. "She…"

"That isn't a decision to be made in the snap of a finger," he interrupted. "Nor is it only mine to make."

"Oh, I know, I know," she said impatiently, then grabbed both of his hands. "Don't be logical, Nick, tell me what you feel, what your heart tells you."

"My heart tells me you should come back to New York." He held her fingers tighter as she started to withdraw them from his. "My heart tells me you're hurt and confused and still one of the most exquisite dancers I've ever partnered."

"We were talking about Ruth."

"You were talking about Ruth," he countered. *"Ptichka."* The quiet sound of his voice brought her eyes back to his. "I need you," he said simply.

"Oh, don't." Lindsay shook her head and closed her eyes. "That's not fighting fair."

"Fair, Lindsay?" He gave her a quick shake. "Right or wrong isn't always fair. Come, look at me." She obeyed, letting his direct, blue eyes look deep into hers. "This architect," he began.

"No," Lindsay said quickly. "Not now, not yet."

She looked pale and vulnerable again, and he lifted a hand to her cheek. "All right. Then I'll ask you this:

Do you think I would want you back in the company, dancing the most important role of my first ballet, if I had any doubts about your talent?" She started to speak, but a lift of his brow halted her. "Before you talk of sentiment and friendship, think."

Taking a deep breath, Lindsay turned away from him and walked to the barre. She knew Nikolai Davidov and understood his utter selfishness when dancing was involved. He could be generous, giving, charmingly selfless personally. When it suited him. But when the dance was involved, he was a strict professional. Ballet held the lion's share of his heart. She rubbed the back of her neck, now tense again. It all seemed too much to think about, too much to cope with.

"I don't know," she murmured. Nothing seemed as clear or as certain as it had only hours before. Turning back to Nick, Lindsay lifted both hands, palms up. "I just don't know."

When he came to her, she lifted her face. He could see that hurt was still mixed with confusion. The shrill whistle of the teakettle in her office momentarily drowned out Chopin. "Later we'll talk more," he decided and slipped an arm around her. "Now we'll relax before your classes begin."

They walked across the room to join Ruth in Lindsay's office. Stopping, she gave him a quick kiss. "I am glad you're here."

"Good." He gave her a hug in return. "Then after class you can buy me dinner."

Chapter 13

On the day after Christmas, snow lay in drifts on the side of the road. Thick icicles glinted from eaves of houses while multitudes of tiny ones clung to tree branches. The air was crisp and cold, the sunlight thin.

Restless and more than a little bored, Monica walked to the town park. The playground looked abandoned and pitiful. Brushing the snow off a wooden swing, she sat down. She kicked at the snow with her boots and set herself in motion. She was worried about Lindsay.

There had been a change, a change of some magnitude. It had started right after the first snow of the season. She was not sure whether it had been brought about by the time Lindsay had spent with Seth or the visit from Nick Davidov. Moodiness was simply not a characteristic trait of Lindsay's. But time had passed, and the moodiness remained. Monica wondered if she was more sensitive to Lindsay's mood because her own was so uncertain.

Monica had been shocked to realize that the long-standing crush she had on Andy had developed into full-blown love. She had hero-worshipped him from the first day he had come home with her brother wearing his high school football jersey. She had been ten to his fifteen. Ironically, the major obstacle in her path was the person she felt closest to: Lindsay.

Why couldn't Lindsay see how crazy Andy was about her? Monica leaned far back in the swing, enjoying the flutter in her stomach as the sky tilted with her movements. It was pale blue. Why hadn't he told her? Monica pushed harder.

During the years of Lindsay's absence from Cliffside, Monica had been a love-struck teenager whom Andy had treated kindly with absent pats on the head. Since Lindsay's return, he hadn't appeared to notice that his friend's little sister had grown up. No more, Monica thought grouchily, than Lindsay had noticed Andy's heart on his sleeve.

"Hi!"

Turning her head, Monica got a quick glimpse of Andy's grin before she flew forward. On the backswing, it was still there. She dragged her feet on the ground and slowed. "Hi," she managed as he settled in her line of vision.

"You're up early for a Saturday," he commented, idly running his hand down the chain of the swing. "How was your Christmas?"

"Fine—good." She cursed herself and tried to speak coherently. "You're up early, too."

Andy shrugged, then sat on the swing beside her. Monica's heart trembled. "Wanted a walk," he murmured. "Still giving piano lessons?"

Monica nodded. "I heard you were expanding the flower shop."

"Yeah, I'm adding a whole section of house plants."

Monica studied the hands on the chains of the swing beside her. It was amazing that such large and masculine hands could arrange flowers with incredible delicacy. They were gentle hands. "Aren't you opening today?"

"This afternoon, for a while, I thought." He shrugged his broad shoulders. "Doesn't look like anybody's up but you and me." He turned his head to smile at her. Monica's heart cartwheeled.

"I—I like getting up early," she mumbled.

"Me, too." Her eyes were soft and vulnerable as a puppy's.

Monica's palms were hot in the December air. She rose to wander restlessly around the playground.

"Do you ever think about moving away from Cliffside?" she asked after a short silence.

"Sure." Andy pushed off the swing to walk with her. "Especially when I'm down. But I don't really want to leave."

She looked up at him. "I don't, either." Her foot kicked an abandoned ball half-buried in the snow. Stooping, Monica picked it up. Andy watched the thin winter sunlight comb through her hair. "I remember when you and my brother used to practice in the backyard." She tossed the small ball lightly. "Sometimes you'd throw me one."

"You were pretty good, for a girl," Andy acknowledged and earned a scowl. He laughed, feeling lighter than he had when he started on his walk. Monica always made him feel good. As she tossed the ball up again, he grabbed it. "Want to go out for one?"

"Okay." She jogged across the snow, then ran laterally, remembering the moves from years before. Andy drew back, and the ball sailed toward her in a sweeping arch. Perfectly positioned, she caught the ball handily.

"Not bad," Andy yelled. "But you'll never score."

Monica tucked the ball under her arm. "Watch me," she yelled back and raced through the trampled snow.

She ran straight for him, then veered off to the left before he could make the touch. Her agility surprised him, but his reflexes were good. He turned, following her zigzagging pattern. Caught up in the chase, he threw himself out, nipping her by the waist and bringing her down. They hit the snow with a muffled thud. Instantly horrified, Andy rolled her over. Her face was pink under a coating of snow.

"Oh, wow, Monica, I'm sorry! Are you okay?" He began to brush the snow from her cheeks. "I wasn't thinking. Did I hurt you?"

She shook her head but hadn't yet recovered the breath to speak. He lay half across her, busily brushing the snow from her face and hair. Their breath puffed out and merged. She smiled at his expression of horrified concern, and their eyes met. Suddenly Andy gave way to impulse and placed a light, hesitant kiss on her lips.

"Sure you're okay?" His taste was much sweeter than Monica had imagined. She tasted it again when he lowered his mouth a second time.

"Oh, Andy!" Monica threw her arms around his neck and rolled until he was positioned beneath her. Her lips descended to his, but there was nothing light or hesitant about her kiss. Snow slipped down Andy's collar, but he ignored it as his hand went to the back of her head to prolong the unexpected. "I love you," she said as her mouth roamed his face. "I love you so much."

He stroked her hair. Monica felt weightless. He seemed determined to lie there forever as Monica, soft and scented, clung to his neck. Then he sat up, still cuddling her, and looked down at her eyes, dark and wet and beautiful. He kissed her again. "Let's go to my house." His arm went around her shoulders to draw her close to his side.

Driving by, Lindsay passed Andy and Monica and absently lifted her hand in a wave. Neither of them saw her. Her mind crowded with thoughts, she drove on toward the Cliff House. She had to speak with Seth. Time, she felt, was running out for her, for them, for Ruth. Nothing seemed to be going the way it should… not since the afternoon the first snow had stopped.

Seth had gone away almost immediately to his New Zealand site and hadn't returned until a few days before Christmas. He hadn't written or called, and while Lindsay hadn't expected him to, she had hoped for it nonetheless. Missing him was painful. She wanted to be with him again, to recapture some of the happiness, some of the closeness they had shared. Yet she knew that once they had spoken, they could be farther apart than ever. She had to convince him, by whatever means possible, to let Ruth go. Her last conversation with Nick had persuaded her that it was time to press for what was needed, just as it had convinced her it was time to make a final decision about her own life. She wanted Ruth in New York with her.

She took the long curve of Seth's driveway slowly, watching the house as the road rose. Because her heart was thumping inside her chest, she took an extra moment to breathe after she stopped the car. She didn't want to make a fool of herself when she saw Seth again. Ruth's chances depended on her being strong enough to convince him that she knew what the girl needed.

Lindsay got out of the car, nervously clutching her purse in both hands as she walked to the front door. Relax, she told herself. She couldn't allow her feelings for him to ruin what she had come to do.

The wind pinched color into her face, and she was grateful. She had braided her hair and coiled it neatly at her neck so the wind wouldn't disturb it. Composure, at the moment, was vital to her. She knew that the memories of what she had shared with Seth were dormant and would overwhelm her the moment she stepped into the house. She lifted a gloved finger and pushed the doorbell. The wait was mercifully short before Worth answered.

He was dressed much as before. The dark suit and tie were impeccable. The white shirt crisp. The beard was neatly trimmed, his expression inscrutable.

"Good morning, Miss Dunne." There was nothing in his voice to indicate his curiosity at her early call.

"Good morning, Mr. Worth." Lindsay could prevent her hands from nervously twisting her bag, but some of her anxiety escaped into her eyes. "Is Seth in?"

"He's working, I believe, miss." Politely he moved back to allow her entrance into the warmth of the house. "If you'd care to wait in the parlor, I'll see if he can be disturbed."

"Yes, I…please." She bit her lip as she followed his straight back. Don't start babbling, she admonished herself.

"I'll take your coat, miss," he offered as she stepped over the parlor threshold. Wordlessly, Lindsay slipped out of it. The fire was crackling. She could remember making love with Seth here for the first time while the fire hissed and the mantel clock ticked away the time they had together.

"Miss?"

"Yes? Yes, I'm sorry." She turned back to Worth, suddenly aware that he had been speaking to her.

"Would you care for some coffee while you wait?"

"No, nothing. Thank you." She pulled off her gloves and walked to the window. She wanted to regain her composure before Seth joined her. Setting the purse and gloves on a table, she laced her fingers.

It was difficult waiting there, she discovered, in the room where she had first given her love to him. The memories were painfully intimate. Priorities, she reminded herself. I have to remember my priorities. In the window glass she could see just the ghost of her reflection: the trimly cut gray trousers, the burgundy mohair sweater with its full, cuffed sleeves. She looked composed, but the composure, like the woman in the glass, was all illusion.

"Lindsay."

She turned, thinking herself prepared. Seeing him

again sent a myriad of feelings washing over her. But the most dominant was an all-encompassing joy. She smiled, filled with it, and crossed the room to him. Her hands sought him without hesitation.

"Seth. It's so good to see you."

She felt his hands tighten on hers before he released them to say, "You're looking well," in a casually distant tone that had her battling back the words that trembled on her tongue.

"Thank you." Turning, she walked to the fire, needing to warm herself. "I hope I'm not disturbing you."

"No." Seth stayed where he was. "You're not disturbing me, Lindsay."

"Did things go well in New Zealand?" she asked, facing him again with a more reserved smile. "I imagine the weather was different there."

"A bit," he acknowledged. He moved closer then but kept a safe distance between them. "I have to go back after the first of the year for a few weeks. Things should settle down when that's over. Ruth tells me your house is sold."

"Yes." Lindsay tugged at the collar of her sweater, wishing she had something to fill her hands. "I've moved into the school. Everything changes, doesn't it?" He inclined his head in agreement. "There's plenty of room there, of course, and the house seemed terribly empty when I was alone. It'll be simpler to organize things when I go to New York…."

"You're going to New York?" he interrupted her sharply. Lindsay saw his brows draw together. "When?"

"Next month." She roamed to the window, unable

to keep still any longer. "Nick starts staging his ballet then. We reached an agreement on it, finally."

"I see." Seth's words came slowly. He studied the long slope of her neck until she turned back to him. "Then you've decided to go back."

"For one performance." She smiled, trying to pretend it was a casual conversation. Her heart was knocking at her ribs. "The premiere performance is going to be televised. I've agreed, since I was Nick's most publicized partner, to dance the lead for it. The reunion aspect will bring it more attention."

"One performance," Seth mused. He slipped his hands into his pockets as he watched her. "Do you really believe you'll be able to stop at that?"

"Of course," Lindsay tried to say evenly. "I've a number of reasons for doing it. It's important to Nick." She sighed. Thin rays of sunlight passed through the window and fell on her hair. "And it's important to me."

"To see if you can still be a star?"

She lifted her brow with a half-laugh. "No. If I'd had that sort of ego, things would've been different all along. That part of it wasn't ever important enough to me. I suppose that's why my mother and I couldn't agree."

"Don't you think that'll change once you're back living in that kind of world again?" There was an edge to his voice which brought a frown to Lindsay. "When you danced with Davidov in the studio, everything you were was bound up in it."

"Yes, that's as it should be." She closed some of the distance between them, wanting him to understand. "But dancing and performing aren't the same thing always. I've had the performing," she reminded him. "I've had the spotlight. I don't need it anymore."

"Simple enough to say here now. More difficult after you've stood in the spotlight again."

"No." Lindsay shook her head. "It depends on the reasons for going back." She stepped to him, touching the back of his hand with her fingers. "Do you want to know mine?"

He studied her for a long, silent moment, then turned away. "No. No, I don't believe I do." He stood facing the fire. "What if I asked you not to go?"

"Not to go?" Her voice reflected her confusion. She walked to him, laying her hand on his arm. "Why would you?"

Seth turned, and their eyes met. He didn't touch her. "Because I'm in love with you, and I don't want to lose you."

Lindsay's eyes widened. Then she was in his arms, clinging with all her strength. "Kiss me," she demanded. "Before I wake up."

Their lips met with mutual need, tasting and parting to taste again until the sharp edge of hunger had subsided. She pressed her face into his shoulder a moment, hardly daring to believe what she had heard. She felt his hands roam down the softness of her sweater, then under it and upon the softness of her skin.

"I've missed touching you," he murmured. "There were nights I could think of nothing else but your skin."

"Oh, Seth, I can't believe it." She tangled both hands in his hair as she drew her face away from his shoulder. "Tell me again."

He kissed her temple before he drew her close again.

"I love you." She felt his body relax as she heard his sigh. "I've never said that to a woman before."

"Not even an Italian countess or a French movie star?" Lindsay's voice was muffled against his throat.

He pulled her away far enough so that their eyes could meet, then he held her there with a look deep and intent. "No one's ever touched me the way you have. I could say I've spent my life looking for someone like you, but I haven't." He smiled, running his hands up her arms until they framed her face. "I didn't know there was anyone like you. You were a surprise."

"That's the nicest thing anyone's ever said to me." She turned her face and kissed the palm of his hand. "When I knew I loved you, I was afraid because it meant needing you so much." She looked at him, and everything in his face pulled at her. He had laid claim not only to her heart and body, but to her mind as well. The depth of it seemed awesome. Suddenly she pressed against him, her pulse speeding wildly. "Hold me," she whispered, shutting her eyes. "I'm still afraid."

Her mouth sought his, and the kiss that ensued was electric. They took each other deep until neither could rise to the surface alone. It was a kiss of total dependence. They held each other and gave.

"I've been half-alive since you walked out of the studio that day," she confessed. The planes of his face demanded the exploration of her fingertips. "Everything's been flat, like the photograph of the snow would have been."

"I couldn't stay. You had told me that what had happened between us had been nice. Two adults, alone, attracted to each other. Very simple." He shook his head, pulling her closer possessively. "That caught me by the throat. I loved you, I needed you. For the first time in my life, it wasn't simple."

"Can't you tell when someone's lying?" she asked softly.

"Not when I'm trying to deal with being in love."

"If I had known…" Her voice trailed as she nestled, listening to the sound of his heartbeat.

"I wanted to tell you, but then I watched you dance. You were so exquisite, so perfect." He breathed in her scent again, holding her close. "I hated it. Every second I watched you go further away."

"No, Seth." She silenced him with her fingertips on his lips. "It's not like that. It's not like that at all."

"Isn't it?" He took her by the shoulders, holding her away. "He was offering you a life you could never share with me. He was offering you your place in the lights again. I told myself I had to do the right thing and let you walk away. I've stayed away from you all these weeks. But I knew the moment I saw you standing here today that I couldn't let you go."

"You don't understand." Her eyes were sad and pleading. "I don't want that life again, or the place in the lights, even if I could have it. That's not why I'm going back to do this ballet."

"I don't want you to go." His fingers tightened on her shoulders. "I'm asking you not to go."

She studied him for a moment with all the emotion still brimming in her eyes. "What if I asked you not to go to New Zealand?"

Abruptly he released her and turned away. "That's not the same thing. It's my job. In a few weeks it would

be over and I'd be back. It's not a life-ruling force."
When he turned back to her, his hands were balled in
his pockets. "Would there be room for me and for children in your life if you were prima ballerina with the
company?"

"Perhaps not." She came closer but knew from the
look in his eyes that she dared not touch him. "But I'll
never be prima ballerina with the company. If I wanted
it with all my heart, it still couldn't be. And I don't want
it. Why can't you understand? I simply haven't the need
for it. I won't even officially be with the company for
this performance. I'll have guest status."

This time it was she who turned away, too filled
with emotions to be still. "I want to do it, for Nick, because he's my friend. Our bond is very special. And for
myself. I'll be able to close out this chapter of my life
with something beautiful instead of my father's death.
That's important to me; I didn't know myself how important until recently. I have to do it, or else I'd live
forever with regrets."

In the silence a log shifted and spewed sparks against
the screen.

"So you'll go, no matter how I feel."

Lindsay turned slowly. Her eyes were dry and direct. "I'll go, and I'll ask you to trust me. And I want
to take Ruth."

"No." His answer came immediately and with an
edge. "You ask for too much. You ask for too damn
much."

"It isn't too much," she countered. "Listen to me.
Nick asked for her. He watched her dance; he tested
her here, and he wants her. She could have a place in

the *corps* by summer, Seth, she's that good. Don't hold her back."

"Don't talk to me about holding her back." Fury licked at the words. "You've described to me the life she'd lead, the physical pain and emotional anguish, the pressures, the demands. She's a child. She doesn't need that."

"Yes, she does." Lindsay paced back to him. "She's not a child; she's a young woman, and she needs it all if she's going to be a dancer. You haven't the right to deny her this."

"I have every right."

Lindsay breathed deeply, trying to keep control. "Legally, your right will run out in a few months. Then you'll put her into a position of having to go against your wishes. She'll be miserably unhappy about that, and it could be too late for her. Nikolai Davidov doesn't volunteer to train every young dancer he runs across. Ruth is special."

"Don't tell me about Ruth!" His voice rose, surprising her. "It's taken nearly a year for her to begin to be happy again. I won't push her into the kind of world where she has to punish herself every day just to keep up. If it's what you want, then take it. I can't stop you." He took her by the arm and pulled her to him. "But you won't live out your career vicariously through Ruth."

Color fled from Lindsay's face. Her eyes were huge and blue and incredulous. "Is that what you think of me?" she whispered.

"I don't know what I think of you." His face was as alive with fury as hers was cold with shock. "I don't understand you. I can't keep you here; loving you isn't enough. But Ruth's another matter. You won't keep your spotlight through her, Lindsay. You'll have to fight for that yourself."

"Let me go, please." This time it was she who possessed the restraint and control. Though she trembled, her voice was utterly calm. When Seth had released her, she stood for a moment, studying him. "Everything I've told you today is the truth. Everything. Would you please have Worth bring my coat now? I have classes very soon." She turned to the fire; her back was very straight. "I don't think we have anything more to say to each other."

Chapter 14

It was very different being the student rather than the teacher. Most of the women in Lindsay's classes were years younger than her; girls, really. Those who had reached their mid-and late twenties had been on the professional circuit all along. She worked hard. The days were very long and made the nights easier to bear.

The hours were filled with classes, then rehearsals and yet more classes. She roomed with two members of the company who had been friends during her professional days. At night she slept deeply, her mind dazed with fatigue. In the morning her classes took over her body. Her muscles grew familiar with aches and cramps again as January became February. The routine was the same as it had always been: impossible.

The studio window was darkened by an ice storm, but no one seemed to notice as they rehearsed a dance from the first act of Davidov's *Ariel*. The music was fairylike, conjuring up scenes of dusky forests and wild flowers. It was here that the young prince would meet Ariel. Mortal and Sprite would fall in love. The *pas de deux* was difficult, demanding on the female lead because of its combinations of *soubresauts* and *jetés*. High-level energy was required while keeping the moves light and ethereal. Near the end of the scene, Lindsay was to leap away from Nikolai, turning in the air as she did so in order to be facing him, teasingly, when she touched ground again. Her landing was shaky, and she was forced to plant both feet to prevent a spill. Nick cursed vividly.

"I'm sorry." Her breath came quickly after the exertion of the dance.

"Apologies!" He emphasized his anger with a furious flick of his hand. "I can't dance with an apology."

Other dancers in the room glared at Lindsay with varying degrees of sympathy. All of them had felt the rough edge of Davidov's tongue. The pianist automatically flipped back to the beginning of the suite.

Lindsay's body ached from a twelve-hour, punishing day. "My feet hardly touch the ground in the whole third scene," she tossed back at him. Someone handed her a towel, and gratefully she wiped sweat from her neck and brow. "I haven't got wings, Nick."

"Obviously."

It amazed her that his sarcasm wounded. Usually it touched off anger, and the row that would ensue would clear the air. Now she felt it necessary to defend herself. "It's difficult," she murmured, pushing loosened wisps of hair behind her ear.

"Difficult!" He roared at her, crossing the room to stand in front of her. "So it is difficult. Did I bring you here to watch you do a simple pirouette across the stage?" His hair curled damply around his face as his eyes blazed at her.

"You didn't bring me," she corrected, but her voice was shaky, without its usual strength. "I came."

"You came." He turned away with a wide gesture. "To dance like a truck driver."

The sob came too quickly for her to prevent it. Appalled, she pressed her hands to her face. She had just enough time to see the stunned look on Nikolai's face before she fled the room.

Lindsay let the door to the rest room slam behind her. In the far corner was a low bench. Lindsay curled up on it and wept as if her heart would break. Unable to cope any longer, she let the hurt pour out. Her sobs bounced off the walls and came back to her. When an arm slipped around her, Lindsay turned into it, accepting the offered comfort blindly. She needed someone.

Nikolai rocked and stroked her until the passion of her tears lessened. She had curled into him like a child, and he held her close, murmuring in Russian.

"My little dove." Gently he kissed her temple. "I've been cruel."

"Yes." She used the towel she had draped over her shoulders to dry her eyes. She was drained, empty, and if the pain was still there, she was too numb to feel it.

"But always before, you fight back." He tilted her chin. Her eyes were brilliant and wet. "We are very volatile, yes?" Nikolai smiled, kissing the corners of her mouth. "I yell at you, you yell at me, then we dance."

To their mutual distress, Lindsay buried her face in his shoulder and began to cry again. "I don't know why I'm acting this way." She took deep breaths to stop herself. "I hate people who act this way. It just all seems so crazy. Sometimes it feels like it's three years ago and nothing's changed. Then I see girls like Allyson Gray." Lindsay sniffed, thinking of the dancer who would take over the part of Ariel. "She's twelve years old."

"Twenty," Nikolai corrected, patting her hair.

"She makes me feel forty. And the classes seem hours longer than they ever did before."

"You're doing beautifully; you know that." He hugged her and kissed the top of her head.

"I feel like a clod," she said miserably. "An uncoordinated clod."

Nikolai smiled into her hair but kept his voice sympathetic. "You've lost the five pounds."

"Six," she corrected, and sighing, wiped her eyes again. "Who has time to eat? I'll probably keep on shrinking until I disappear." She glanced around, then her eyes widened. "Nick, you can't be in here, this is the ladies' room."

"I'm Davidov," he said imperially. "I go anywhere."

That made her laugh, and she kissed him. "I feel like a total fool. I've never fallen apart at a rehearsal like that before."

"It's not any of the things we talked about." He took her shoulders, and now his look was solemn. "It's the architect."

"No," she said too quickly. Only his left brow moved. "Yes." She let out a long breath and closed her eyes. "Yes."

"Will you talk about it now?"

Opening her eyes, Lindsay nodded. She settled back in the curve of his shoulder and let the silence hang for a moment. "He told me he loved me," she began. "I thought, this is what I've waited for all my life. He loves me, and life's going to be perfect. But love isn't enough. I didn't know that, but it's not. Understanding, trust…love is a closed hand without those."

She paused in silence, remembering clearly every moment of her last meeting with Seth. Nikolai waited for her to continue. "He couldn't deal with my coming back for this ballet. He couldn't—or wouldn't—understand that I had to do it. He wouldn't trust me when I told him it was only for this one time. He wouldn't believe that I didn't want this life again, that I wanted to build one with him. He asked me not to go."

"That was selfish," Nikolai stated. He frowned at the wall and moved Lindsay closer to him. "He's a selfish man."

She smiled, thinking how simple it had been for Nick to demand that she come. It seemed she was caught between two selfish men. "Yes. But perhaps there should be some selfishness in love. I don't know." She was calm now, her breathing steady. "If he had believed me, believed that I wasn't going back to a life that would exclude him, we might have come to an understanding."

"Might?"

"There's Ruth." A new weight seemed to drag on her heart. "There was nothing I could say that would convince him to send her here. Nothing that could make him see that he was depriving her of everything she was, everything she could be. We argued about her often, most violently the last time I saw him."

Lindsay swallowed, feeling some of the pain return. "He loves her very much and takes his responsibility for her very seriously. He didn't want her to deal with the hardships of the life we lead here. He thinks she's too young, and…" Lindsay was interrupted by a Russian curse she recognized. It lightened her mood a little, and she relaxed against him again. "You'd see it that way, of course, but for an outsider, things look differently."

"There is only one way," he began.

"Davidov's," Lindsay supplied, adoring him for his perfect confidence.

"Naturally," he agreed, but she heard the humor in his voice.

"A non-dancer might disagree," she murmured. "I understand how he feels, and that makes it harder, I suppose, because I know, regardless of that, that Ruth belongs here. He feels…" She bit her lip, remembering. "He thinks I want to use her, to continue my career through her. That was the worst of it."

Davidov remained silent for several moments, digesting all Lindsay had told him, then adding it to his own impressions of Seth Bannion. "I think it was a man very hurt who would say that to you."

"I never saw him again after that. We left each other hurting."

"You'll go back in the spring, when your dance is over." He tilted her face. "You'll see him then."

"I don't know. I don't know if I can." Her eyes were tragic. "Perhaps it's best to leave things as they are, so we don't hurt each other again."

"Love hurts, *ptichka*," he said with a broad shrug. "The ballet hurts you, your lover hurts you. Life. Now, wash your face," he told her briskly. "It's time to dance again."

Lindsay faced herself at the barre. She was alone now in a practice room five stories above Manhattan. It was night, and the windows were black. On the CD player, the music came slowly, a piano only. Turning out, she began to lift her right leg. It seemed straight from the hip to the toe, one long line. Keeping her eyes locked on her eyes in the mirror, she took the leg behind her into an *attitude* position, then rose slowly onto her toe. She held it firm, refusing to let her muscles quiver, then brought her leg back painstakingly on the return journey. She repeated the exercise with her left leg.

It had been nearly a week since her outburst at rehearsal. Every night since then she had used the practice room when everyone had gone. An extra hour of reminding her body what was expected of it, an extra hour of keeping her mind from drifting back to Seth. *Glissade, assemblé, changement, changement.* Her mind ordered, and her body obeyed. In six weeks she would be performing for the first time in more than three years. For the last time in her life. She would be ready.

She took herself into an achingly slow *grand plié,* aware of each tendon. Her leotard was damp from her efforts. As she rose again, a movement in the mirror broke her concentration. She would have sworn at the interruption, but then her vision focused.

"Ruth?" She turned just as the girl rushed toward her. Enveloped in a tight hug, Lindsay was thrown back to the first time they had met. She had touched Ruth's shoulder and had been rejected. How far she's come, Lindsay thought, returning the hug with all her strength. "Let me look at you." Drawing away, Lindsay framed her face. It was animated, laughing, the eyes dark and bright. "You look wonderful. Wonderful."

"I missed you. I missed you so much!"

"What are you doing here?" Lindsay took her hands, automatically chafing the cold from them. "Seth. Is Seth with you?" Hoping, fearing, she looked to the doorway.

"No, he's at home." Ruth saw the answer to the question she harbored. She was still in love with him. "He couldn't get away right now."

"I see." Lindsay brought her attention back to Ruth and managed a smile. "But how did you get here? And why?"

"I came by train," Ruth answered. "To study ballet."

"To study?" Lindsay became very still. "I don't understand."

"Uncle Seth and I had a long talk a few weeks ago before he went back to New Zealand." She unzipped her corduroy jacket and slipped out of it. "Right after you'd left for New York, actually."

"A talk?" Lindsay moved to the CD player to switch off the music. She used a towel to dry her neck, then left it draped over her shoulders. "What about?"

"About what I wanted in my life, what was important to me and why." She watched Lindsay carefully remove the CD from the player. She could see the nerves in the movements. "He had a lot of reservations about letting me come here. I guess you know that."

"Yes, I know." Lindsay slipped the disc back into its case.

"He wanted what was best for me. After my parents were killed, I had a hard time adjusting to things. The first couple of months, he dropped everything just to be with me when I needed him. And even after, I know he rearranged his life, his work, for me." Ruth laid her coat over the back of a wooden chair. "He's been so good to me."

Lindsay nodded, unable to speak. The wound was opening again.

"I know it was hard for him to let me come, to let me make the choice. He's been wonderful about it, taking care of all the paperwork with school, and he arranged for me to stay with a family he knows. They have a really great duplex on the East Side. They let me bring Nijinsky." She walked to the barre, and in jeans and sneakers, began to exercise.

"It's so wonderful here." Her expression shone radiant as Lindsay watched it in the glass. "And Mr. Davidov said he'd work with me in the evenings when he has time."

"You've seen Nick?" Lindsay crossed over so that they both stood at the barre.

"About an hour ago. I was trying to find you." She smiled, her head dipping below Lindsay's as she bent her knees. "He said I'd find you here, that you come every evening to practice. I can hardly wait until the ballet. He said I could watch it from backstage if I wanted."

"And, of course, you do." Lindsay touched her hair, then walked to the bench to change her shoes.

An Important Message from the Editors

Dear Nora Roberts Fan,

*Because you've chosen to read one of our fine novels, we'd like to say "thank you!" And, as a **special** way to thank you, we're offering to send you <u>two more</u> of the books you love so well **plus** two exciting Mystery Gifts — absolutely <u>FREE!</u>*

Please enjoy them with our compliments...

Pam Powers

Lift **here**

Peel off seal and place inside...

The Editor's "Thank You" Free Gifts Include:
- **2 Romance books!**
- **2 exciting mystery gifts!**

Yes! I have placed my
Editor's "Thank You" seal in the
space provided at right. Please send
me 2 free books and 2 fabulous
mystery gifts. I understand I am
under no obligation to purchase
any books, as explained on the
back of this card.

PLACE
FREE GIFTS
SEAL
HERE

194/394 MDL F45D

FIRST NAME

LAST NAME

ADDRESS

APT.#   CITY

STATE/PROV.   ZIP/POSTAL CODE

Thank You!

▲ If offer card is missing write to: Harlequin Reader Service, P.O. Box 1867, Buffalo, NY 14240-1867 or visit www.ReaderService.com ▼

BUSINESS REPLY MAIL
FIRST-CLASS MAIL   PERMIT NO. 717   BUFFALO, NY

POSTAGE WILL BE PAID BY ADDRESSEE

HARLEQUIN READER SERVICE
PO BOX 1341
BUFFALO NY 14240-8571

NO POSTAGE
NECESSARY
IF MAILED
IN THE
UNITED STATES

"Aren't you terribly excited?" Ruth did three *pirouettes* to join her. "Dancing the lead in Davidov's first ballet."

"Once," Lindsay reminded her, undoing the satin ribbons on her shoes.

"Opening night," Ruth countered. Clasping her hands together, Ruth looked down at Lindsay. "How will you be able to give it up again?"

"It's not again," she corrected. "It's *still*. This is a favor for a friend, and for myself." She winced, slipping the shoe from her foot.

"Hurt?"

"Oh, God, yes."

Ruth dropped to her knees and began to work Lindsay's toes. She could feel the tension in them. With a sigh Lindsay laid her head against the wall and closed her eyes.

"Uncle Seth's going to try to come spend a few days with me in the spring. He isn't happy."

"He'll miss you." The cramps in Lindsay's feet were subsiding slowly.

"I don't mean about that."

The words caused Lindsay to open her eyes. Ruth was watching her solemnly, though her fingers still worked at the pain. "Did he say anything? Did he send a message?"

Ruth shook her head. Lindsay shut her eyes again.

Chapter 15

Lindsay found that a three-year absence hadn't made her any less frantic during the hours before a performance. For the past two weeks she had endured hours of interviews and photography sessions, questions and answers and flashing cameras. The reunion of Dunne and Davidov for a one-time performance of a ballet he himself had written and choreographed was news. For Nick and for the company, Lindsay made herself available for any publicity required. Unfortunately, it added to the already impossibly long days.

The performance was a benefit, and the audience would be star-studded. The ballet would be televised, and all proceeds would be donated to a scholarship fund for gifted young dancers. Publicity could encourage yet more donations. For this, Lindsay wanted success.

If the ballet was well-received, it would be incorporated into the program for the season. Nick would broaden himself immeasurably in the world of dance. For him, and for herself, Lindsay wanted success.

There had been a phone call from her mother and a visit from Ruth in her dressing room. The phone call had had a warm tone, without pressures.

Mae was as pleased about the upcoming performance as she could have been; but to Lindsay's surprise and delight, her own responsibilities and new life demanded that she remain in California. Her heart and thoughts would be there with Lindsay, she promised, and she would view the ballet on television.

The visit from Ruth had been a breath of fresh air. Ruth had become star-struck at the mechanics of back-stage life. She was a willing slave for anyone who asked. Next year, Lindsay thought, watching her bustle about carrying costumes and props, she would be fussing over her own costumes.

Taking a hammer, she took a new pair of toe shoes, sat on the floor and began to pound them. She would make them supple before sewing on the ribbons. Her costumes hung in order in the closet. Backstage ca-cophony accompanied the sound of hammer against wood. There was makeup and hair styling yet to be seen to, and dressing in the white tutu for the first act. Lindsay went through each process, aware of the video cameras that were recording the preperformance stage of the ballet. Only her warmups were done in private, at her insistence. Here, she would begin to focus the concentration she would need to carry her through the following hours.

The pressure in her chest was building as she walked

down the corridor toward the wings at stage left. Here, she would make her entrance after the opening dance by the forest ensemble. The music and lights were already on her. She knew Nick would be waiting in the wings at stage right, anticipating his own entrance. Ruth stood beside her, gently touching her wrist as if to wish her luck without speaking the words. Superstitions never die in the theater. Lindsay watched the dancers, the women in their long, bell-like white dresses, the men in their vests and tunics.

Twenty bars, then fifteen, and she began taking long, slow breaths. Ten bars and then five. Her throat went dry. The knot in her stomach threatened to become genuine nausea. The cold film on her skin was terror. She closed her eyes briefly, then ran onto the stage.

At her entrance, the rising applause was a welcome wave. Lindsay never heard it. For her, there was only the music. Her movements flowed with the joy of the first scene. The dance was short but strenuous, and when she ran back into the wings, beads of moisture clung to her brow. She allowed herself to be patted dry and fed a stingy sip of water as she watched Nick take over the second scene. Within seconds, he had the audience in the palm of his hand.

"Oh yes," Lindsay breathed, then turned to smile at Ruth. "It's going to be perfect."

The ballet revolved around its principals, and it was rare for one or both of them not to be onstage. In the final scene the music slowed and the lights became a misty blue. Lindsay wore a floating knee-length gown. It was here that Ariel had to decide whether to give up her immortality for love; to marry the prince, she had to become mortal and renounce all her magic.

Lindsay danced alone in the moonlit forest, recalling the joy and simplicity of her life with the trees and flowers. To have love—mortal love—she had to turn her back on everything she had known. The choice brought great sadness. Even as she despaired, falling on the ground to weep, the prince entered the forest. He knelt beside her, touching her shoulder to bring her face to his.

The *grand pas de deux* expressed his love for her, his need to have her beside him. She was drawn to him, yet afraid of losing the life she had always known, afraid of facing death as a mortal. She soared with freedom, through the trees and the moonlight that had always been hers, but again and again, she was pulled back to him by her own heart. She stopped, for dawn was breaking, and the time for decision had come.

He reached out to her, but she turned away, uncertain, frightened. In despair, he started to leave her. At the last moment, she called him back. The first rays of sunlight seeped through the trees as she ran to him. He lifted her into his arms as she gave him her heart and her life.

The curtain had closed, but still Nick held her. Their pulses were soaring, and for the moment, they had eyes only for each other.

"Thank you." And he kissed her softly, as a friend saying goodbye.

"Nick." Her eyes filled with emotion after emotion, but he set her down before she could speak.

"Listen," he ordered, gesturing to the closed curtain.

The sound of applause battered against it. "We can't keep them waiting forever."

Flowers and people. It seemed that no more of either could be crammed into Lindsay's dressing room. There was laughter, and someone poured her a glass of champagne. She set it down untasted. Her mind was already drunk with the moment. She answered questions and smiled, but nothing seemed completely in focus. She was still in costume and makeup, still part Ariel.

There were men in tuxedos and women in sparkling evening dress mingling with elves and wood sprites. She had spoken to an actor of star magnitude and a visiting French dignitary. All she could do was hope her responses had been coherent. When she spotted Ruth, Lindsay hailed her, the look in her eyes entreating.

"Stay with me, will you?" she asked when the girl managed to plow her way through the crowd. "I'm not normal yet; I need someone."

"Oh, Lindsay." Ruth threw her arms around her neck. "You were so wonderful! I've never seen anything more wonderful."

Lindsay laughed and returned the hug. "Just bring me down. I'm still in the air." She was interrupted by the assistant director, who brought more flowers and champagne.

It was more than an hour before the crowd thinned. By then, Lindsay was feeling the weariness that follows an emotional high. It was Nick, who had managed to work his way out of his own dressing room to find her, who cleared the room. Seeing the telltale signs of fatigue on her face, he reminded those remaining of a reception being held at a nearby restaurant.

"You must go so *ptichka* can change," he said jovially, patting a back and nudging it out the door. "Save us some champagne. And caviar," he added, "if it's Russian."

Within five minutes, only he and Ruth joined Lindsay in the flower-filled room.

"So," he addressed Ruth, coming over to pinch her chin. "You think your teacher did well tonight?"

"Oh, yes." Ruth smiled at Lindsay. "She did beautifully."

"I mean me." He tossed back his hair and looked insulted.

"You weren't too bad," Lindsay informed him.

"Not too bad?" He sniffed, rising to his full height. "Ruth, I would ask you to leave us a moment. This lady and I have something to discuss."

"Of course."

Before Ruth could step away, Lindsay took her hand. "Wait." From her dressing table she took a rose, one that had been thrown at her feet after the performance. She handed it to Ruth. "To a new Ariel, another day."

Wordlessly, Ruth looked down at the rose, then at Lindsay. Her eyes were eloquent, though she could only nod her thanks before she left the room.

"Ah, my little bird," Nick took her hand and kissed it. "Such a good heart."

She squeezed his fingers in return. "But you will cast her in it. Three years, perhaps two."

He nodded. "There are some who are made for such things." His eyes met hers. "I will never dance with a more perfect Ariel than I have tonight."

Lindsay leaned forward so that their faces were close.

"Charm, Nick, for me? I had thought I was through with bouquets tonight."

"I love you, *ptichka*."

"I love you, Nicky."

"Will you do me one last favor?"

She smiled, leaning back in her chair again. "How could I refuse?"

"There is someone else I would like you to see tonight."

She gave him a look of good-humored weariness. "I can only pray it's not another reporter. I'll see whomever you like," she agreed recklessly. "As long as you don't expect me to go to that reception."

"You are excused," he said with a regal inclination of his head. He went to the door, and opening it, turned briefly to look at her.

She sat, obviously exhausted in the chair. Her hair flowed freely over the shoulders of the thin white gown, her eyes exotic with their exaggerated lines and coloring. She smiled at him, but he left without speaking again.

Briefly, Lindsay closed her eyes, but almost instantly a tingle ran up her spine. Her throat went dry as it had before her first dance of the ballet. She knew who would be there when she opened her eyes.

She rose when Seth closed the door behind him, but slowly, as if measuring the distance between them. She was alert again, sharply, completely, as if she had awakened from a long, restful sleep. She was suddenly aware of the powerful scent of flowers and the masses of color they brought to the room. She was aware that his face was thinner but that he stood straight and his eyes were still direct and serious. She was aware that her love for him hadn't lessened by a single degree.

"Hello." She tried to smile. Formal clothing suited him, she decided as she laced her fingers together. She remembered, too, how right he had looked in jeans and a flannel shirt. There are so many Seth Bannions, she mused. And I love them all.

"You were magnificent," he said. He came no closer to her but stood, seeming to draw every inch of her through his eyes. "But I suppose you've heard that too often tonight."

"Never too often," she returned. "And not from you." She wanted to cross the room to him, but the hurt was still there, and the distance was so far. "I didn't know you were coming."

"I asked Ruth not to say anything." He came farther into the room, but the gap still seemed immense. "I didn't come to see you before the performance because I thought it might upset you. It didn't seem fair."

"You sent her…I'm glad."

"I was wrong about that." He lifted a single rose from a table and studied it a moment. "You were right, she belongs here. I was wrong about a great many things."

"I was wrong, too, to try to push you too soon." Lindsay unlaced her fingers, then helplessly, she laced them again. "Ruth needed what you were giving her. I don't think she'd be the person she is right now if you hadn't had those months with her. She's happy now."

"And you?" He looked up again and pinned her with his gaze. "Are you?"

She opened her mouth to speak, and finding no words, turned away. There on the dressing table was a half-filled bottle of champagne and her untouched glass. Lindsay lifted the glass and drank. The bubbles soothed the tightness in her throat. "Would you like some champagne? I seem to have plenty."

"Yes." He took the last steps toward her. "I would."

Nervous now that he stood so close, Lindsay looked around for another glass. "Silly," she said, keeping her back to him. "I don't seem to have a clean glass anywhere."

"I'll share yours." He laid a hand on her shoulder, gently turning her to face him. He placed his fingers over hers on the stem. He drank, keeping his eyes on hers.

"Nothing's any good without you." Her voice broke as he lowered the glass. "Nothing."

His fingers tightened on hers, and she saw something flash in his eyes. "Don't forgive me too quickly, Lindsay," he advised. The contact was broken when he placed the glass back on the table. "The things I said..."

"No. No, they don't matter now." Her eyes filled and brimmed over.

"They do," he corrected quietly. "To me. I was afraid of losing you and pushed you right out of my life."

"I've never been out of your life."

She would have gone to him then, but he turned away. "You're a terrifying person to be in love with, Lindsay, so warm, so giving. I've never known anyone like you." When he turned back, she could see the emotions in his eyes, not so controlled now, not so contained. "I've never needed anyone before, and then I needed you and felt you slipping away."

"But I wasn't." She was in his arms before he could

say another word. When he stiffened, she lifted her face and found his mouth. Instantly, the kiss became avid and deep. The low sound of his breath sent pleasure through her. "Seth. Oh, Seth, I've been half-alive for three months. Don't leave me again."

Holding her close, he breathed in the scent of her hair. "You left me," he murmured.

"I won't again." She lifted her face so that her eyes, huge and brilliant, promised him. "Not ever again."

"Lindsay." He reached up to frame her face. "I can't…I won't ask you to give up what you have here. Watching you tonight…"

"You don't have to ask me anything." She placed her hands on his wrists, willing him to believe her. "Why can't you understand? This isn't what I want. Not now, not anymore. I want you. I want a home and a family."

He looked at her deeply, then shook his head. "It's difficult to believe you can walk away from this. You must have heard that applause."

She smiled. It should be so simple, she thought. "Seth, I pushed myself for three months. I worked harder than I've ever worked in my life to give one performance. I'm tired; I want to go home. Marry me. Share my life."

With a sigh, he rested his forehead on hers. "No one's ever proposed to me before."

"Good, then I'm the first." It was so easy to melt in his arms.

"And the last," he murmured between kisses.

* * * * *

DANCE OF DREAMS

For Cora Spasibo.

Chapter 1

The cat lay absolutely still on his back, eyes closed, front paws resting on his white chest. The last rays of the sun slanted through the long vertical blinds and shone on his orange fur. He was undisturbed by the sound of a key in the lock which broke the silence of the apartment. He half-opened his eyes when he heard his mistress's voice but closed them again, just as lazily, when he noted she was not alone. She'd brought that man home with her again, and the cat had no liking for him. He went back to sleep.

"But Ruth, it's barely eight o'clock. The sun's still up."

Ruth dropped her keys on the dainty Queen Anne table beside the door, then turned with a smile. "Donald, I told you I had to make it an early evening. Dinner was lovely. I'm glad you talked me into going out."

"In that case," he said, taking her into his arms in a practiced move, "let me talk you into extending the evening."

Ruth accepted the kiss, enjoyed the gentle surge of warmth just under her skin. But when he pulled her closer, she drew away. "Donald." Her smile was the same easy one she had worn before the kiss. "You really have to go."

"A nightcap," he murmured, kissing her again, lightly, persuasively.

"Not tonight." She moved firmly out of his arms. "I have an early class tomorrow, Donald, plus a full day of rehearsals and fittings."

He gave her a quick kiss on the forehead. "It'd be easier for me if it were another man, but this passion for dancing…" He shrugged before reluctantly turning to leave. Was he losing his touch? he wondered.

Ruth Bannion was the first woman in over ten years who had held him off so consistently and successfully. Why, he asked himself, did he keep coming back? She opened the door for him, giving him one last, lingering smile as she urged him through. A glimpse of her silhouette in the dim light before she shut the door on him answered his question. She was more than beautiful—she was unique.

Ruth was still smiling as she hooked the chain and security lock. She enjoyed Donald Keyser. He was tall and dark and stylishly handsome, with an acerbic humor and exquisite taste. She respected his talents as a designer, wore a number of his creations herself and was able to relax in his company—when she found the time.

Of course, she was aware that Donald would have pre-ferred a more intimate relationship.

It had been a simple matter for Ruth to decide against it. She was attracted to Donald and was fond of him. But he simply did not stir her emotions. While she knew he could make her laugh, she doubted very much that he could make her cry. Turning into the darkened apart-ment, Ruth felt a twinge of regret. She felt abruptly, unexpectedly alone.

Ruth turned to study herself in the gilt-framed, rect-angular mirror that hung in the hallway. It was one of the first pieces she had bought when she had moved into the apartment. The glass was old, and she had paid a ridiculous price for it, despite the dark spots near the top right-hand corner. It had meant a great deal to Ruth to be able to hang it on the wall of her own apartment, her own home. Now, as the light grew dim, she stared at her reflection.

She had left her hair down for the evening, and it flowed over her shoulders to swing past her elbows. With an impatient move, she tossed it back. It lifted, then settled behind her, black and thick. Her face, like her frame, was small and delicate, but her features weren't even. Her mouth was generous, her nose small and straight, her chin a subtle point. Though the bones in her face were elegant, the deep brown eyes were huge and slanted catlike. The brows over them were dark and straight. An exotic face, she had been told, yet she saw no beauty in it. She knew that with the right makeup and lighting she could look stunning, but that was dif-ferent. That was an illusion, a role, not Ruth Bannion.

With a sigh, Ruth turned away from the mirror and

crossed to the plush-covered Victorian sofa. Knowing she was now alone, Nijinsky rolled over, stretched and yawned luxuriously, then padded over to curl in her lap. Ruth scratched his ears absently. Who was Ruth Bannion? she wondered.

Five years before, she had been a very green, very eager student beginning a new phase of her training in New York. *Thanks to Lindsay,* Ruth remembered with a smile. Lindsay Dunne, teacher, friend, idol—the finest classical ballerina Ruth had ever seen. She had convinced Uncle Seth to let her come here. It warmed Ruth to think of them now, married, living in the Cliff House in Connecticut with their children. Every time she visited them, the love and happiness lingered with her for weeks afterward. She had never seen two people more right for each other or more in love. Except perhaps her own parents.

Even after six years, thinking of her parents brought on a wave of sadness—for herself and for the tragic loss of two bright, warm people. But in a strange way Ruth knew it had been their death that had brought her to where she was today.

Seth Bannion had become her guardian, and their move to the small seacoast town in Connecticut had brought them both to Lindsay. It had been through Lindsay that Seth had been made to see Ruth's need for more training. Ruth knew it hadn't been easy for her uncle to allow her to make the move to New York when she had been only seventeen. She had, of course, been well cared for by the Evanstons, but it had been difficult for Seth to give her up to a life he knew to be so difficult and demanding. It was love that had made him hesitate and love that had ultimately ruled his decision. Her life had changed forever.

Or perhaps, Ruth reflected, it had changed that first time she had walked into Lindsay's school to dance. It had been there that she had first danced for Davidov.

How terrified she had been! She had stood there in front of a man who had been heralded as the finest dancer of the decade. A master, a legend. Nikolai Davidov, who had partnered only the most gifted ballerinas, including Lindsay Dunne. Indeed, he had come to Connecticut to convince Lindsay to return to New York as the star in a ballet he had written. Ruth had been overwhelmed by his presence and almost too stunned to move when he had ordered her to dance for him. But he had been charming. A smile touched Ruth's mouth as she leaned her head back on the cushions. And who, she thought lazily, could be more charming than Nick when he chose to be? She had obeyed, losing herself in the movement and the music. Then he had spoken those simple, stunning words.

"When you come to New York, come to me."

She had been very young and had thought of Nikolai Davidov as a name to be whispered reverently. She would have danced barefoot down Broadway if he had told her to.

She had worked hard to please him, terrified of the sting of his temper, unable to bear the coldness of his disapproval. And he had pushed her. Ruth remembered how he had been constantly, mercilessly demanding. There had been nights she had curled up in bed, too exhausted to even weep. But then he would smile or toss off a compliment, and every moment of pain would vanish.

She had danced with him, fought with him, laughed with him, watching the gradual changes in him over the years, and still, there was an elusive quality about him.

Perhaps that was the secret of his attraction for women, she thought: the subtle air of mystery, his foreign accent, his reticence about his past. She had gotten over her infatuation with him years ago. She smiled, remembering the intensity of her crush on him. He hadn't appeared to even notice it. She had been scarcely eighteen. He'd been nearly thirty and surrounded by beautiful women. And *still is,* she reminded herself, smiling in rueful amusement as she stood to stretch. The cat, now dislodged from her lap, stalked huffily away.

My heart's whole and safe, Ruth decided. Perhaps too safe. She thought of Donald. Well, it couldn't be helped. She yawned and stretched again. And there was that early class in the morning.

Sweat dampened Ruth's T-shirt. Nick's choreography for *The Red Rose* was complicated and strenuous. She took a much-needed breather at the barre. The remainder of the cast was scattered around the rehearsal hall, either dancing under Nick's unflagging instructions or waiting, as she did, for the next summons.

It was only eleven, but Ruth had already worked through a two-hour morning class. The long, loose T-shirt she wore over her tights was darkened by patches of perspiration; a few tendrils of her hair had escaped from her tightly secured bun. Still, watching Nick demonstrate a move, any thought of fatigue drained from her. He was, she thought as she always did, absolutely fabulous.

As artistic director of the company and as established creator of ballets, he no longer had to dance to remain in the limelight. He danced, Ruth knew, because he was born to do so. He skimmed just under six feet, but his lean, wiry build gave an illusion of more height. His hair was like gold dust and curled carelessly around a face that had never completely lost its boyish charm. His mouth was beautiful, full and finely sculpted. And when he smiled...

When he smiled, there was no resisting him. Fine lines would spread out from his eyes, and the large irises would become incredibly blue.

Watching him demonstrate a turn, Ruth was grateful that at thirty-three, with all his other professional obligations, he still continued to dance.

He stopped the pianist with a flick of his hand. "All right, children," he said in his musically Russian-accented voice. "It could be worse."

This from Davidov, Ruth mused wryly, was close to an accolade.

"Ruth, the *pas de deux* from the first act."

She crossed to him instantly, giving an absent brush at the locks of hair that danced around her face. Nick was a creature of moods—varied, mercurial, unexplained moods. Today he appeared to be all business. Ruth knew how to match his temperament with her own. Facing, they touched right hands, palm to palm. Without a word, they began.

It was an early love scene, more a duel of wits than an expression of romance. But Nick hadn't written a fairy tale ballet this time. He had written a passionate one. The characters were a prince and a gypsy, each fiercely flesh and blood. To accommodate them the dances were exuberant and athletic. They challenged each other; he demanded, she defied. Now and then a toss of the head or a gesture of the wrist was employed to accent the mood.

The late summer sun poured through the windows, patterning the floor. Drops of sweat trickled unheeded, unfelt, down Ruth's back as she turned in, then out of Nick's arms. The character of Carlotta would enrage and enrapture the prince throughout the ballet. The mood for their duel of hearts was set during their first encounter.

It was at times like this, when Ruth danced with Nick, that she realized she would always worship him, the dancer, the legend. To be his partner was the greatest thrill of her life. He took her beyond herself, beyond what she had ever hoped to be. On her journey from student to the *corps de ballet* to principal dancer, Ruth had danced with many partners, but none of them could touch Nick Davidov for sheer brilliance and precision. And endurance, she thought ruefully as he ordered the *pas de deux* to begin again.

Ruth took a moment to catch her breath as the pianist turned back the pages of the score. Nick turned to her, lifting his hand for hers. "Where is your passion today, little one?" he demanded.

It was a salutation Ruth detested, and he knew it. The grin shot across his face as she glared at him. Saying nothing, she placed her palm to his.

"Now, my gypsy, tell me to go to the devil with your body as well as your eyes. Again."

They began, but this time Ruth stopped thinking of her pleasure in dancing with him. She competed now, step for step, leap for leap. Her annoyance gave Nick precisely what he wanted. She dared him to best her. She spun into his arms, her eyes hot. Poised only a moment, she spun away again and with a *grand jeté,* challenged him to follow her.

They ended as they had begun, palm to palm, with her head thrown back. Laughing, Nick caught her close and kissed her enthusiastically on both cheeks.

"There, now, you're wonderful! You spit at me even while you offer your hand."

Ruth's breath was coming quickly after the effort of the dance. Her eyes, still lit with temper, remained on Nick's. A swift flutter raced up her spine, distracting her. She saw that Nick had felt it, too. She saw it in his eyes, felt it in the fingers he pressed into the small of her back. Then it was gone, and Nick drew her away.

"Lunch," he stated and earned a chorus of approval. The rehearsal hall began to clear immediately. "Ruth." Nick took her hand as she turned to join the others. "I want to talk to you."

"All right, after lunch."

"Now. Here."

Her brows drew together. "Nick, I missed breakfast—"

"There's yogurt in the refrigerator downstairs, and Perrier." Releasing her hand, Nick walked to the piano. He sat and began to improvise. "Bring some for me, too."

Hands on her hips, Ruth watched him play. Of

course, she thought wrathfully, he'd never consider I'd say no. He'd never think to ask me if I had other plans. He expects I'll run off like a good little girl and do his bidding without a word of complaint.

"Insufferable," she said aloud.

Nick glanced up but continued to play. "Did you speak?" he asked mildly.

"Yes," she answered distinctly. "I said, you're insufferable."

"Yes." Nick smiled at her good-humoredly. "I am."

Despite herself, Ruth laughed. "What flavor?" she demanded and was pleased when he gave her a blank look. "Yogurt," she reminded him. "What flavor yogurt, Davidov."

In short order Ruth's arms were ladened with cartons of yogurt, spoons, glasses and a large bottle of Perrier. There was the sound of chatter from the canteen below her mingling with Nick's playing the piano from the hall above. She climbed the stairs, exchanging remarks with two members of the *corps* and a male soloist. The music Nick played was a low, bluesy number. Because she recognized the style, Ruth knew it to be one of his own compositions. No, not a composition, she corrected as she paused in the doorway to watch him. A composition you write down, preserve. This is music that comes from the heart.

The sun's rays fell over his hair and his hands— long, narrow hands with fluid fingers that could express more with a gesture than the average person could with a speech.

He looks so alone!

The thought sped into her mind unexpectedly, catching her off balance. It's the music, she decided. It's only because he plays such sad music. She walked toward him, her ballet shoes making no sound on the wood floor.

"You look lonely, Nick."

From the way his head jerked up, Ruth knew she had broken into some deep, private thought. He looked at her oddly a moment, his fingers poised above the piano keys. "I was," he said. "But that's not what I want to talk to you about."

Ruth arched a brow. "Is this going to be a business lunch?" she asked him as she set cartons of yogurt on the piano.

"No." He took the bottle of Perrier, turning the cap. "Then we'd argue, and that's bad for the digestion, yes? Come, sit beside me."

Ruth sat on the bench, automatically steeling herself for the jolt of electricity. To be where he was was to be in the vortex of power. Even now, relaxed, contemplating a simple dancer's lunch, he was like a circuit left on hold.

"Is there a problem?" she asked, reaching for a carton of yogurt and a spoon.

"That's what I want to know."

Puzzled, she turned her head to find him studying her face. He had bottomless blue eyes, clear as glass, and the dancer's ability for complete stillness.

"What do you mean?"

"I had a call from Lindsay." The blue eyes were fixed unwaveringly on hers. His lashes were the color of the darkest shade of his hair.

More confused, Ruth wrinkled her brow. "Oh?"

"She thinks you're not happy." He was still watching her steadily: the pressure began to build at the base of her neck. Ruth turned away, and it lessened immediately. There had never been anyone else who could unnerve her with a look.

"Lindsay worries too much," she said lightly, dipping the spoon into the yogurt.

"Are you, Ruth?" Nick laid his hand on her arm, and she was compelled to look back at him. "Are you unhappy?"

"No," she said immediately, truthfully. She gave him the slow half smile that was so much a part of her. "No."

He continued to scan her face as his hand slid down to her wrist. "Are you happy?"

She opened her mouth, prepared to answer, then closed it again on a quick sound of frustration. Why must those eyes be on hers, so direct, demanding perfect honesty? They wouldn't accept platitudes or pat answers. "Shouldn't I be?" she countered. His fingers tightened on her wrist as she started to rise.

"Ruth." She had no choice but to face him again. "Are we friends?"

She fumbled for an answer. A simple yes hardly covered the complexities of her feelings for him or the uneven range of their relationship. "Sometimes," she answered cautiously. "Sometimes we are."

Nick accepted that, though amusement lit his eyes. "Well said," he murmured. Unexpectedly, he gathered both of her hands in his and brought them to his lips. His mouth was soft as a whisper on her skin. Ruth didn't pull away but stiffened, surprised and wary. His eyes met hers placidly over their joined hands, as if he were unaware of her would-be withdrawal. "Will you tell me why you're not happy?"

Carefully, coolly, Ruth drew her hands from his. It was too difficult to behave in a contained manner when touching him. He was a physical man, demanding physical responses. Rising, Ruth walked across the room to a window. Manhattan hustled by below.

"To be perfectly honest," she began thoughtfully, "I haven't given my happiness much thought. Oh, no," she laughed and shook her head. "That sounds pompous." She spun back to face him, but he wasn't smiling. "Nick, I only meant that until you asked me, I just hadn't thought about being unhappy." She shrugged and leaned back against the window sill. Nick poured some fizzing water and rising, took it to her.

"Lindsay's worried about you."

"Lindsay has enough to worry about with Uncle Seth and the children and her school."

"She loves you," he said simply.

He saw it—the slow smile, the darkening warmth in her eyes, the faintly mystified pleasure. "Yes, I know she does."

"That surprises you?" Absently, he wound a loose tendril of her hair around his finger. It was soft and slightly damp.

"Her generosity astonishes me. I suppose it always will." She paused a moment, then continued quickly before she lost her nerve. "Were you ever in love with her?"

"Yes," he answered instantly, without embarrassment or regret. "Years ago, briefly." He smiled and pushed one of Ruth's loosened pins back into her hair. "She was always just out of my reach. Then before I knew it, we were friends."

"Strange," she said after a moment. "I can't imagine you considering anything out of your reach."

Nick smiled again. "I was very young, the age you are now. And it's you we're speaking of, Ruth, not Lindsay. She thinks perhaps I push you too hard."

"Push too hard?" Ruth cast her eyes at the ceiling. "*You,* Nikolai?"

He gave her his haughtily amused look. "I, too, was astonished."

Ruth shook her head, then moved back to the piano. She exchanged Perrier for yogurt. "I'm fine, Nick. I hope you told her so." When he didn't answer, Ruth turned, the spoon still between her lips. "Nick?"

"I thought perhaps you've had an unhappy…relationship."

Her brows lifted. "Do you mean, Am I unhappy over a lover?"

It was instantly apparent that he hadn't cared for her choice of words. "You're very blunt, little one."

"I'm not a child," she countered testily, then slapped the carton onto the piano again. "And I don't—"

"Do you still see the designer?" Nick interrupted her coolly.

"The designer has a name," she said sharply. "Donald Keyser. You make him sound like a label on a dress."

"Do I?" Nick gave her a guileless smile. "But you don't answer my question."

"No, I don't." Ruth lifted the glass of Perrier and sipped calmly, though a flash of temper leaped into her eyes.

"Ruth, are you still seeing him?"

"That's none of your business." She made her voice light, but the steel was beneath it.

"You are a member of the company." Though his eyes blazed into hers, he enunciated each word carefully. "I am the director."

"Have you also taken over the role of Father Confessor?" Ruth tossed back. "Must your dancers check out their lovers with you?"

"Be careful how you provoke me," he warned.

"I don't have to justify my social life to you, Nick," she shot back without a pause. "I go to class, I'm on time for rehearsals. I work hard."

"Did I ask you to justify anything?"

"Not really. But I'm tired of you playing the role of stern uncle with me." A frown line ran down between her brows as she stepped closer to him. "I have an uncle already, and I don't need you to look over my shoulder."

"Don't you?" He plucked a loose pin from her hair and twirled it idly between his thumb and forefinger while his eyes pierced into hers.

His casual tone fanned her fury. "No!" She tossed her head. "Stop treating me like a child."

Nick gripped her shoulders, surprising her with the quick violence. She was drawn hard against him, molded to the body she knew so well. But this was different. There were no music or steps or storyline. She could feel his anger—and something more, something just as volatile. She knew he was capable of sudden bursts of rage, and she knew how to deal with them, but now...

Her body was responding, astonishing her. Their

hearts beat against each other. She could feel his fingertips digging into her flesh, but there was no pain. The
hands she had brought up to shove him away with were
now balled loosely into fists and held motionlessly aloft.

He dropped his eyes to her lips. A sharp pang of
longing struck her—sharper, sweeter than anything
she had ever experienced. It left her dazed and aching.

Slowly, knowing only that what she wanted was a
breath away, Ruth leaned forward, letting her lids sink
down in preparation for his kiss. His breath whispered
on her lips, and hers parted. She said his name once,
wonderingly.

Then, with a jerk and a muttered Russian oath, Nikolai pushed her away. "You should know better," he said,
biting off the words, "than to deliberately make me
angry."

"Was that what you were feeling?" she asked, stung
by his rejection.

"Don't push it." Nick tossed off the American slang
with a movement of his shoulders. Temper lingered in
his eyes. "Stick with your designer," he murmured at
length in a quieter tone as he turned back to the piano.
"Since he seems to suit you so well."

He sat again and began to play, dismissing her with
silence.

Chapter 2

She must have imagined it. Ruth relived the surge of concentrated desire she had experienced in Nick's arms. No, I'm wrong, she told herself again. I've been in his arms countless times and never, never felt anything like that. And, Ruth reminded herself as she showered off the grime of the day, I was in his arms a half-dozen times after, when we went back to rehearsal.

There had been something, she admitted grudgingly as she recalled the crackling tension in the air when they had gone over a passage time and time again. But it had been annoyance, aggravation.

Ruth let the water flow and stream over her, plastering her hair to her naked back. She tried, now that she was alone, to figure out her reaction to Nick's sudden embrace.

Her response had been nakedly physical and shockingly urgent. On the other hand, she could recall the warm pleasure of Donald's kisses—the soft, easily resisted temptation. Donald used quiet words and gentle persuasion. He used all the traditional trappings of seduction: flowers, candlelight, intimate dinners. He made her feel—Ruth grasped for a word. *Pleasant.* She rolled her eyes, knowing no man would be flattered with that description. Yet she had never experienced more than *pleasant* with Donald or any other man she had known. And then, in one brief moment, a man she had worked with for years, a man who could infuriate her with a word or move her to tears with a dance, had caused an eruption inside her. There had been nothing *pleasant* about it.

He never kissed me, she mused, losing herself for a moment in the remembering. Or even held me, really—not as a lover would, but...

It was an accident, she told herself and switched off the shower with a jerk of her wrist. A fluke. Just a chain reaction from the passion of the dance and the anger of the argument.

Standing naked and wet, Ruth reached for a towel to dry herself. She began with her hair. Her body was small and delicately built, thin by all but a dancer's standards. She knew it intimately, as only a dancer could. Her limbs were long and slender and supple. It had been her classical dancer's build—and the fateful events of her life—that had brought her to Lindsay years before.

Lindsay, Ruth smiled, remembering vividly her fiery dancing in *Don Quixote*, a ballet Lindsay had starred in before she and Ruth had met. Ruth's smile became wry as she recalled her first face-to-face meeting with the older dancer. It had been years later, in Lindsay's small ballet school. Ruth had been both awed and terrified. She had stated boldly that one day she, too, would dance in *Don Quixote!*

And she had, Ruth remembered, wrapping a towel around her slim body. And Uncle Seth and Lindsay had come, even though Lindsay had been nearly eight months pregnant at the time. Lindsay had cried, and Nick had joked and teased her.

With a sigh, Ruth dropped the towel in a careless heap and reached for her robe. Only Lindsay would have guessed that all was not quite right. Ruth belted the thin fuchsia robe and picked up a comb. She had spoken of Donald, she remembered, playing back their last phone conversation. She had told them about the fabulous little chest she had found in the Village. They had chatted about the children, and Uncle Seth had begged her to come visit them her first free weekend.

And through all the tidbits and family gossip, Lindsay sensed something she hadn't even realized herself. Ruth frowned. That she wasn't happy. Not unhappy, she thought and took the comb smoothly through her long, wet hair. Just dissatisfied. Silly, she decided, annoyed with herself. She had everything she'd ever wanted. She was a principal dancer with the company, a recognized name in the world of ballet. She would be starring in Davidov's latest ballet. The work was hard and demanding, but Ruth craved it. It was the life she had been born for.

But still, sometimes, she longed to break the rules, to race back to the vagabond time she had known as a child. There had been such freedom, such adventure.

Her eyes lit with the memories: skiing in Switzerland where the air was so cold and clean it had hurt her throat to breathe it; the smells and colors of Istanbul. The thin, large-eyed children in the streets of Crete; a funny little room with glass doorknobs in Bonn. All those years she had traveled with her journalist parents. Had they ever been more than three months in one place? It had been impossible to form any strong attachments, except to each other. And to the dance. That had been her constant childhood companion, traveling with her in an ever-changing environment. The teachers had spoken with different voices, different accents, in different languages, but the dance had remained there for her.

The years of travel had given Ruth an early maturity; there was no shyness, only self-sufficiency and caution. Then came her life with Seth, then Lindsay, and her years with the Evanston family that had opened her up, encouraging her to offer trust and affection. Still her world remained insular, as only the world of ballet can be. Perhaps because of this she was an inveterate observer. Watching and analyzing people was more than a habit with Ruth; it had become her nature.

And it was this that had led to her further annoyance with Nick. She had watched him that afternoon and sensed disturbances, but she hadn't been able to put a name to them. What he had been thinking and feeling remained a mystery. Ruth didn't care for mysteries.

That's why Donald appeals to me, she mused with a half-smile. She toyed with the bottles of powder and scent on her dressing table. He's so unpretentious, so predictable. His thoughts and feelings are right on the surface. No eddies, no undercurrents. But with a man like Nick...

She poured lotion into her palm and worked it over her arms. A man like Nick, she thought, was totally unpredictable, a constant source of annoyance and confusion. Volatile, unreasonable, exhausting. Just trying to keep up with him wore her out. And it was so difficult to please him! She had seen many dancers push themselves beyond endurance to give him what he wanted. She did it herself. What was it about him that was endlessly fascinating?

A knock on her door broke into Ruth's thoughts. She shrugged, turning away from the dressing table. It was no use trying to dissect Nikolai Davidov. She flipped on a light in the living room as she rushed through it to the front door. Her glance through the peephole surprised her. She drew the chain from the door.

"Donald, I was just thinking about you."

She was swept up in his arms before she had the chance to offer him a friendly kiss. "*Mmm,* you smell wonderful."

Her laugh was smothered by his lips. The kiss grew long, deeper than the casual greeting Ruth had intended. Yet she allowed the intimacy, encouraging it with her own seeking tongue. She wanted to feel, to experience more than the warm pleasure she was accustomed to. She wanted the excitement, the tingling touch of fear she had felt only that afternoon in another man's arms. But when it was over, her heartbeat was steady, her blood cool.

"Now that," Donald murmured and nuzzled her neck, "is the way to say hello."

Ruth stayed in his arms a moment, enjoying his solidarity, the unspoken offer of protection. Then, pulling away, she smiled into his eyes. "It's also a way of saying it's nice to see you, but what are you doing here?"

"Taking you out," he said and swung her further into the room. "Go put on your prettiest dress," he ordered, giving her cheek a brief caress. "One of mine, of course. We're going to a party."

Ruth pushed her still-damp hair away from her face. "A party?"

"*Hmm*—yes." Donald glanced at Nijinsky, who lay sprawled in sleep on Ruth's small, glass-topped dinette table. "A party at Germaine Jones's," he continued as he and the cat ignored each other. "You remember, the designer who's pushing her short, patterned skirts and knee socks."

"Yes, I remember." Ruth had the quick impression of a short, pixielike redhead with sharp green eyes and thick, mink lashes. "I wish you'd called first."

"I did—or tried to," he put in. "It's a spur-of-the-moment thing, but I did phone the rehearsal hall. I missed you there and you hadn't gotten home yet." He shrugged away the oversight as he drew out his slim, gold cigarette case. "Germaine's throwing the party together at the last minute, but a lot of important people will show. She's hot this season." Donald slipped the case back into the inside pocket of his smartly tailored slate-colored suit jacket, then flicked on his lighter.

"I can't make it tonight."

Lifting a brow, Donald blew out a stream of smoke. "Why not?" He took in her wet hair and thin robe. "You don't have plans, do you?"

Ruth was tempted to contradict him. He was beginning to take too much for granted. "Is that such a remote possibility, Donald?" she asked, masking her annoyance with a smile.

"Of course not." He grinned disarmingly. "But somehow I don't think you do. Now be a good girl and slip into that red slinky number. Germaine's bound to have on one of her famous ensembles. You'll make her look like a misplaced cheerleader."

She studied him a moment, with her dark eyes thoughtful. "You're not always kind, are you, Donald?"

"It's not a kind business, darling." He shrugged an elegant shoulder.

Ruth bit back a sigh. She knew he was fond of her and undeniably attracted, but she wondered if he would be quite so fond or so attracted if he didn't consider her to be an asset when she wore one of his designs. "I'm sorry, Donald, I'm just not up to a party tonight."

"Oh, come on, Ruth." He tapped his cigarette in the ashtray, his first sign of impatience. "All you have to do is look beautiful and speak to a few of the right people."

Ruth banked down on a rising surge of irritation. She knew Donald had never understood the demands and rigors of her profession.

"Donald," she began patiently. "I've been working since eight this morning. I'm bone tired. If I don't get the proper rest, I won't be able to function at top level tomorrow. I have a responsibility to the rest of the company, to Nick and to myself."

Carefully, Donald stubbed out the cigarette. Smoke hung in the air a moment, then wafted out through an open window. "You can't tell me you won't do any so-cializing, Ruth. That's absurd."

"Not as absurd as you think," she returned, crossing to him. "There're less than three weeks until the ballet opens, Donald. Parties simply have to wait until after."

"And me, Ruth?" He pulled her into his arms. Underneath his calm, civilized exterior, she sensed the anger. "How long do I have to wait?"

"I've never promised you anything, Donald. You've known from the beginning that my work is my first priority. Just as your work is for you."

"Does that mean you have to keep denying that you're a woman?"

Ruth's eyes remained calm, but her tone chilled. "I don't believe I've done that."

"Don't you?" Donald's hold on her tightened, just as Nick's had hours before. She found it interesting that the two men should draw two such differing responses from her. With Nick she had felt equal anger and a sharp attraction. Now she felt only impatience touched with fatigue.

"Donald, I'm hardly denying my womanhood by not going to bed with you."

"You know how much I want you." He pulled her closer. "Every time I touch you, I feel you give up to a certain point. Then it stops, just as if you've thrown up a wall." His voice roughened with frustration. "How long are you going to lock me out?"

Ruth felt a pang of guilt. She knew he spoke the truth, just as she knew there was nothing she could do to alter it. "I'm sorry, Donald."

He read the regret in her eyes and changed tactics. Drawing her close again, he spoke softly, his eyes warming. "You know how I feel about you, darling." His lips took hers quietly, persuasively. "We could leave the party early, bring a bottle of champagne back here."

"Donald. You don't—" she began. Another knock at the door interrupted her. Distracted, she didn't bother with the peephole before sliding the chain. "Nick!" She stared at him foolishly, her mind wiped clean.

"Do you open the door to everyone?" he asked in mild censure as he entered without invitation. "Your hair's wet," he added, taking a generous handful. "And you smell like the first rain in spring."

It was as if the angry words had never been spoken, as if the simmering, restrained passion had never been. He was smiling down at her, an amused, cocky look in his eyes. Bending, he kissed her nose.

Ruth made a face as she pulled her thoughts into order. "I wasn't expecting you."

"I was passing," he said, "and saw your lights."

At the sound of Nick's voice, Nijinsky leaped from the table to rub affectionate circles around the dancer's ankles. Stooping, Nick stroked him once from neck to tail and laughed when the cat rose on his hind legs to jump at him affectionately. Nick rose, with Nijinsky purring audibly in his arms, then spotted Donald across the room.

"Hello." There was no apparent change in his amiability.

"You remember Donald," Ruth began hurriedly, guilty that for a moment she had completely forgotten him.

"Naturally." Nick continued to lazily scratch Nijinsky's ears. Purring ferociously, the cat stared with glinted amber eyes at the other man. "I saw a dress of your design on a mutual friend, Suzanne Boyer." Nick smiled with a flash of white teeth. "They were both exquisite."

Donald lifted a brow. "Thank you."

"But you don't offer me a drink, Ruth?" Nick commented, still smiling affably at Donald.

"Sorry," she murmured, automatically turning toward the small bar she had arranged on a drop leaf table in a corner. She reached for the vodka and poured. "Donald?"

"Scotch," he said briefly, trying to maintain some distance from Nick's cheerful friendliness.

Ruth handed Donald his Scotch and walked to Nick.

"Thanks." Accepting the glass, Nick sat in an overstuffed armchair and allowed the cat to walk tight circles on his lap. Nijinsky settled back to sleep while Nick drank. "Your business goes well?" he asked Donald.

"Yes, well enough," Donald responded to Nick's inquiry. He remained standing and sipped his Scotch.

"You use many plaids in your fall designs." Nick drank the undiluted vodka with a true Russian disregard for its potency.

"That's right." A hint of curiosity intruded into Donald's carefully neutral voice. "I didn't imagine you'd follow women's fashions."

"I follow women," Nick countered and drank again deeply. "I enjoy them."

It was a flat statement meant to be taken at face value. There were no sexual overtones. Nick enjoyed many women, Ruth knew, on many levels—from warm, pure friendships, as his relationship with Lindsay, to hot, smoldering affairs like that with their mutual friend Suzanne Boyer. His romances were the constant speculation of the tabloids.

"I think," Nick continued, disrupting Ruth's thoughts, "that you, too, enjoy women—and what makes them beautiful, interesting. It shows in your designs."

"I'm flattered." Donald relaxed enough to take a seat on the sofa.

"I never flatter," Nick returned with a quick, crooked smile. "A waste of words. Ruth will tell you I'm a very frugal man."

"Frugal?" Ruth lifted a brow, pursing her lips as if tasting the word. "No, I think the word is egocentric."

"The child had great respect once upon a time," Nick said into his empty glass.

"When I was a child, yes," she retorted. "I know you better now."

Something flashed in his eyes as he looked at her; anger, challenge, amusement—perhaps all three. She wasn't certain. She kept her eyes level.

"Do you?" he murmured, then set the glass aside. "You would think she'd have more awe for men of our age," he said mildly to Donald.

"Donald doesn't demand awe," she returned, hardly realizing how quickly she was becoming heated. "And he doesn't care for me to think of him as aged and wise."

"Fortunate," Nick decided as neither of them so much as glanced at the man they were discussing. "Then he won't have to adjust his expectations." He gently stroked Nijinsky's back. "She has a nasty tongue as well."

"Only for a select few," Ruth responded.

Nick tilted his head, shooting his disarmingly charming smile. "It's my turn to be flattered, it seems."

Blast him! she thought furiously. Never at a loss for an answer.

Regally, Ruth rose. Her body moved fluidly under the silk of her robe. Donald's gaze flicked down a moment, but Nick's remained on her face. "Like you," she said to him with a cool smile, "I find flattery a waste of time and words. You'll have to excuse me," she continued. "Donald and I are going to a party. I have to change."

There was some satisfaction to be gained from turning her back on him and walking away. She closed her bedroom door firmly. Impatiently, she grabbed the red dress out of her closet, pulled lingerie from her drawers and flung the heap onto the bed. Stripping out of the robe, she started to toss it aside when she heard the doorknob turn. Instinctively she held the robe in front of her, clutching it with both hands at her breasts. Her eyes were wide and astonished as Nick stalked into the room. He shut the door behind him.

"You can't come in here," she began on a rush, too surprised to be outraged or embarrassed.

Ignoring her, Nick crossed the room. "I am in here."

"Well, you can just turn around and get out." Ruth shifted the robe higher, realizing impotently that she was at a dead disadvantage. "I'm not dressed," she pointed out needlessly.

Nick's eyes flicked briefly and without apparent interest over her naked shoulders. "You appear adequately covered." The eyes shot back to her face and locked on hers. "Isn't a twelve-hour day enough for you, Ruth? You have an eight o'clock class in the morning."

"I know what time my class is," she retorted. Cautiously, she took one hand from the robe to push back her hair. "I don't need you to remind me of my schedule, Nick, any more than I need your approval of what I do with my free time."

"You do when it interferes with your performance for me."

She frowned as he stepped onto artistic ground. "You've had no reason to complain about my performance."

"Not yet," he agreed. "But I want your best—and you can hardly give me that if you exhaust yourself with these silly parties—"

"I have always given you my best, Nick," she tossed back. "But since when has every ounce of effort and sweat been enough for you?" She started to swirl away from him, remembered the robe no longer covered her flank and simmered in frustrated rage. "Would you please go?"

"I take what I need," he shot back, again overlooking her heated request. "Not so many years ago, *milaya,* you were eager to give it to me."

"That's not fair!" The jibe stung. "I still am. When I am working, there's nothing I won't give to you. But my private life is just that—private. Stop playing daddy, Nick. I've grown up."

"Is that all you want?" His burst of fury stunned her, so that she took an automatic step back. "Is being treated as a woman what is important to you?"

"I'm sick of you treating me as if I were still seven-

teen and ready to bend at the knee when you walk into
a room." Her anger grew to match his. "I'm a responsible adult, able to look after myself."

"A responsible adult." His eyes narrowed, and Ruth
recognized the danger signals. "Shall I show you how I
treat responsible adults who also happen to be women?"

"No!"

But she was already in his arms, already molded
close. It wasn't the hard, overpowering kiss she might
have expected and fought against. He kissed as if he
knew she would respond to him with equal fervor. It
was a man's mouth seeking a woman's. There was no
need for persuasion or force.

Ruth's lips parted when his did. Their tongues met.
Her thoughts, her body, her world concentrated fully
and completely on him. The scent of her bath rose between them. Reaching up to draw him closer, Ruth took
her hands from the robe. It dropped unheeded to the
floor. Nick ran his hands down her naked back, much
as he had done to the cat, in one long, smooth stroke.
With a low sound of pleasure, Ruth pressed closer.

And as he ran his hands up her sides to linger there,
the kiss grew deeper, beyond what she knew and into
the uncharted.

Her head fell back in submission as she tangled her
fingers in his hair. She pulled him closer, demanding
that he take all she offered. It was a dark, pungent world
she had never tasted, and she yearned. Her body quivered with hot need as his hands ran over her. She had
felt them on her countless times in the past, steadying
her, lifting her, coaching her. But there was no music

to bring them together here, no planned choreography, only instinct and desire.

When she felt herself being drawn away from him, Ruth protested, straining closer. But his hands came firmly to her shoulders, and they were separated.

Ruth stood naked before him, making no attempt to cover herself. She knew he had already seen her soul; there was no need to conceal her body. Nick took his eyes down her, slowly, carefully, as if he would memorize every inch. Then his eyes were back on hers, darkened, penetrating. There was fury in them. Without a word, he turned and left the room.

Ruth heard the front door slam, and she knew he had gone.

Chapter 3

And one, and two, and three, and four. Ruth made the moves to the time Nick called. After hours of dancing, her body was beyond pain. She was numb. The scant four hours sleep had not given her time to recharge. It had been her own anger and a need to defy which had kept her at the noisy, smoke-choked party until the early hours of the morning. She knew that, just as she knew her dancing was well below par that day.

There was no scathing comment from Nick, no bout of temper. He simply called out the combinations again and again. He didn't shout when she missed her timing or swear when her *pirouettes* were shaky. When he partnered her, there were no teases, no taunts in her ear.

It would be easier, Ruth thought as she stretched to a slow *arabesque,* if he'd shouted or scolded her for doing what he had warned her against. But Nick had simply lowered her into a fish dive without saying a word.

If he had shouted, she could have shouted back and released some of her self-disgust. But he gave her no excuse through the classes and hours of rehearsals to lose her temper. Each time their eyes met, he seemed to look through her. She was only a body, an object moving to his music.

When Nick called a break, Ruth went to the back of the room and, sitting on the floor, brought her knees to her chest and rested her forehead on them. Her feet were cramping, but she lacked the energy to massage them. When someone draped a towel around her neck, she glanced up.

"Francie." Ruth managed a grateful smile.

"You look bushed."

"I am," Ruth returned. She used the towel to wipe perspiration from her face.

Francie Myers was a soloist, a talented, dedicated dancer and one of the first friends Ruth had made in the company. She was small and lean with soft, fawn-colored hair and sharp, black eyes. She was constantly acquiring and losing lovers with perpetual cheerfulness. Ruth admired her unabashed honesty and optimism.

"Are you sick?" Francie asked, slipping a piece of gum into her mouth.

Ruth rested her head against the wall. Someone was idling at the piano. The room was abuzz with conversation and music. "I was at a miserably crowded party until three o'clock this morning."

"Sounds like fun." Francie stretched her leg up to touch the wall behind her, then back. She glanced at

Ruth's shadowed eyes. "But I don't think your timing was too terrific."

Ruth shook her head on a sigh. "And I didn't even want to be there."

"Then what were you doing there?"

"Being perverse," Ruth muttered, shooting a quick glance at Nick.

"That takes the fun out of it." Francie's eyes darted across the room and landed on an elegant blonde in a pale blue leotard. "Leah's had a few comments about your style today."

Ruth followed Francie's gaze. Leah's golden hair was pulled back from a beautifully sculptured ivory-skinned face. She was talking to Nick now, gesturing with her long, graceful hands.

"I'm sure she did."

"You know how badly she wanted the lead in this ballet," Francie went on. "Even dancing Aurora hasn't pacified her. Nick isn't dancing in *Sleeping Beauty*."

"Competition keeps the company alive," Ruth said absently, watching Nick smile and shake his head at Leah.

"And jealousy," Francie added.

Ruth turned her head again, meeting the dark, sharp eyes. "Yes," she agreed after a moment. "And jealousy."

The piano switched to a romantic ballad, and someone began to sing.

"Nothing's wrong with a little jealousy." Francie rhythmically circled her ankles one at a time. "It's healthy. But Leah…" Her small, piquant face was abruptly serious. "She's poison. If she wasn't such a beautiful dancer, I'd wish her in another company.

Watch her," she added as she rose. "She'll do anything to get what she wants. She wants to be the prima ballerina of this company, and you're in her way."

Thoughtfully, Ruth stood as Francie moved away. The attractive dancer rarely spoke ill of anyone. Perhaps she was overreacting to something Leah had said. Ruth had felt Leah's jealousy. There was always jealousy in the company, as there was in any family. It was a fact of life. Ruth also knew how badly Leah had wanted the part of Carlotta in Nick's new ballet.

They had competed for a great number of roles since their days in the *corps*. Each had won, and each had lost. Their styles were diverse, so that the roles each created were uniquely individual. Ruth was an athletic, passionate dancer. Leah was an elegant dancer—classic, refined, cool. She had a polished grace that Ruth admired but never tried to emulate. Her dancing was from the heart; Leah's was from the head. In technical skills they were as equal as two dancers could be. Ruth danced in *Don Quixote*, while Leah performed in *Giselle*. Ruth was the Firebird, while Leah was Princess Aurora. Nick used them both to the best advantage. And Ruth would be his Carlotta.

Now, watching her across the room, Ruth wondered if the jealousy was more deeply centered than she had sensed. Though they had never been friends, they had maintained a certain professional respect. But Ruth had detected an increase of hostility over the past weeks. She shrugged, then pulled the towel from her shoulders. It couldn't be helped. They were all there to dance.

"Ruth."

She jolted and spun around at the sound of Nick's

voice. His eyes were cool on her face, without expression. A wave of anxiety washed over her. He was cruelest when he controlled his temper. She had been in the wrong and was now prepared to admit it. "Nick," Ruth began, ready to humble herself with an apology.

"Go home."

She blinked at him, confused. "What?"

"Go home," he repeated in the same frigid tone.

Her eyes were suddenly round and eloquent. "Oh, no, Nick, I—"

"I said go." His words fell like an axe. "I don't want you here."

Even as she stared at him, she paled from the hurt. There was nothing, nothing he could have done to wound her more deeply than to send her away. She felt both a rush of angry words and a rush of tears back up in her throat. Refusing to give way to either, she turned and crossed the room. Picking up her bag, Ruth walked to the door.

"Second dancers, please," she heard Nick call out before she shut it behind her.

Ruth slept for three hours with Nijinsky curled into the small of her back. She had closed the blinds in her bedroom, and fresh from a shower, lay across the spread. The room was dim, and the only sound was the cat's gentle snoring. When she woke, she woke instantly and rolled from her stomach to her back. Nijinsky was disturbed enough to pad down to the foot of the bed. Huffily, he began to clean himself.

Nick's words had been the last thing she had thought of before slumber and the first to play in her mind when she awoke. She had been wrong. She had been punished. No one she knew could be more casually cruel than Nikolai Davidov. She rose briskly to open the blinds, determined to put the afternoon's events behind her.

"We can't lie around in the dark all day," she informed Nijinsky, then flopped back on the bed to ruffle his fur. He pretended to be indignant but allowed her to fondle and stroke. At last, deciding to forgive her, he nudged his forehead against hers. The gesture brought Nick hurtling back into Ruth's mind.

"Why do you like him so much?" she demanded of Nijinsky, tilting his head until the unblinking amber eyes were on hers. "What is it about him that attracts you?" Her brows lowered, and she began to scratch under the cat's chin absently as she stared into the distance. "Is it his voice, that musical, appealingly accented voice? Or is it the way he moves, with such fluidly controlled grace? Or how he smiles, throwing his whole self into it? Is it how he touches you, with his hands so sure, so knowing?"

Ruth's mind drifted back to the evening before, when Nick had stood holding her naked in his arms. For the first time since the impulsive, arousing kiss, Ruth allowed herself to think of it. The night before, she had dressed in a frenzy and had rushed off to the party with Donald, not giving herself a chance to think. She had come home exhausted and had fought with fatigue all day. Now rested, her mind clear, she dwelled on the matter of Nick Davidov. There was no question: She had seen desire in his eyes. Ruth curled on the spread again, resting her cheek on her hand. He had wanted her. *Desire.* Ruth rolled the word around in her mind. Is that what I saw in his eyes? The thought had warmth creeping under her skin. Then, like a splash of ice water, she remembered his eyes that afternoon. No desire, no anger, not even disapproval. Simply nothing.

For a moment Ruth buried her face in the spread. It still hurt to remember his dismissal of her. She felt as though she had been cast adrift. But her common sense told her that one botched rehearsal wasn't the end of the world, and one kiss, she reminded herself, wasn't the beginning of anything.

The poster on the far wall caught her eye. Her uncle had given it to her a decade before. Lindsay and Nick were reproduced in their roles as Romeo and Juliet. Without a second thought, Ruth reached over, picked up the phone and dialed.

"Hello." The voice was warm and clear.

"Lindsay."

"Ruth!" There was surprise in the voice, followed by a quick rush of affection. "I didn't expect to hear from you before the weekend. Did you get Justin's picture?"

"Yes." Ruth smiled, thinking of the boldly colored abstract her four-year-old cousin had sent to her. "It's beautiful."

"Naturally. It's a self-portrait." Lindsay laughed her warm, infectious laugh. "You've missed Seth, I'm afraid. He's just run into town."

"That's all right." Ruth's eyes were drawn back to the poster. "I really called just to talk to you."

There was only the briefest of pauses, but Ruth sensed Lindsay's quick understanding. "Trouble at rehearsal today?"

Ruth laughed. She tucked her legs under her. "Right. How did you know?"

"Nothing makes a dancer more miserable."

"Now I feel silly." Ruth gathered her hair in her hand and tossed it behind her back.

"Don't. Everyone has a bad day. Did Nick shout at you?" There was a trace of humor rather than sympathy; that in itself was a balm.

"No." Ruth glanced down at the small pattern of flowers in the bedspread. Thoughtfully, she traced one with her thumbnail. "It'd be so much easier if he had. He told me to go home."

"And you felt as though someone had knocked you down with a battering ram."

"And then ran over me with a truck." Ruth smiled into the phone. "I knew you'd understand. What made it worse, he was right."

"He usually is," Lindsay said dryly. "It's one of his less endearing traits."

"Lindsay…" Ruth hesitated, then plunged before she could change her mind. "When you were with the company, were you ever—attracted to Nick?"

Lindsay paused again, a bit longer than she had the first time. "Yes, of course. It's impossible not to be, really. He's the sort of man who draws people."

"Yes, but…" Ruth hesitated again, searching for the right words. "What I meant was—"

"I know what you meant," Lindsay said, sparing her. "And yes, I was once very attracted."

Ruth glanced back up at the poster again, studying the star-crossed lovers. She dropped her eyes. "You're closer to him, I think, than anyone else."

"Perhaps," Lindsay considered a moment, weighing Ruth's tone and her own choice of words. "Nick's a very private person."

Ruth nodded. The statement was accurate. Nick could give of himself to the company, at parties, to the press and to his audience. He could flatter the individual with personal attention, but he was amazingly reticent about his personal life. Yes, he was careful about who he let inside. Suddenly Ruth felt alone.

"Lindsay, please, will you and Uncle Seth come to the opening? I know it's difficult, with the children and the school and Uncle Seth's work, but...I need you."

"Of course," Lindsay agreed without hesitation, without questions. "We'll be there."

Hanging up a few moments later, Ruth sat in silence. I feel better, she decided, just talking to her, making contact. She's more than family, she's a dancer, too. And she knows Nick.

Lindsay had been a romantically lovely Juliet to Nick's Romeo. It was a ballet Ruth had never danced with him. Keil Lowell had been her Romeo; a dark whip of a dancer who loved practical jokes. Ruth had danced with Nick in *Don Quixote*, in *The Firebird* and in his ballet *Ariel*, but in her mind, Juliet had remained Lindsay's role. Ruth had searched for one of her own. She believed she had found it in Carlotta of *The Red Rose*.

It was hers, she thought suddenly. And she had better not forget it. Jumping from the bed, she pulled tights from her dresser drawer and began to tug them on.

When Ruth entered the old, six-story building that housed the company, it was past seven, but there were still some members of the troupe milling about. Some hailed her, and she waved in return but didn't stop. Newer members of the *corps* watched her pass. *Someday,* they thought. Ruth might have felt their dreams rushing past her if she hadn't been so impatient to begin.

She took the elevator up, her mind already forming the moves she would demand of her body. She wanted to work.

She heard the music before she pushed open the door of the studio. It always seemed larger without the dancers. She stood silently by the door and watched.

Nikolai Davidov's leaps were like no one else's. He would spring as if propelled, then pause and hang impossibly suspended before descending. His body was as fluid as a waterfall, as taut as a bow string. He had only to command it. And there was more, Ruth knew, just as mesmerized by him as she had been the first time she'd seen him perform; there was his precision timing, his strength and endurance. And he could act—an essential part of ballet. His face was as expressive as his body.

Davidov was fiercely concentrating. His eyes were fixed on the mirrored wall as he searched for faults. He was perfecting, refining. Sweat trickled down his face despite the sweatband he wore. There was virility as well as poetry in his moves. Ruth could see the rippling, the tightening of muscles in his legs and arms as he threw himself into the air, twisting and turning his body, then landing with perfect control and precision.

Oh God, she thought, forgetting everything but sheer admiration. *He is magnificent.*

Nick stopped and swore. For a moment he scowled at himself in the glass, his mind on his own world. When he walked back to the CD player to replay the selection, he spotted Ruth. His eyes drifted over her, touching on the bag she had slung over her shoulder.

"So, you've rested." It was a simple statement, without rancor.

"Yes." She took a deep breath as they continued to watch each other. "I'm sorry I wasn't any good this morning." When he didn't speak, she walked to a bench to change her shoes.

"So, now you come back to make up?" There was a hint of amusement in his voice.

"Don't make fun of me."

"Is that what I do?" The smile lingered at the corners of his mouth.

Her eyes were wide and vulnerable. She dropped them to the satin ribbons she crossed at her ankles. "Sometimes," she murmured.

He moved softly. Ruth wasn't aware he had come to her until he crouched down, resting his hands on her knees. "Ruth." His eyes were just below hers now, his tone gentle. "I don't make fun of you."

She sighed. "It's so difficult when you're so often right." She made a face at him. "I wasn't going to that silly party until you made me so mad."

"Ah." Nick grinned, squeezing her knee companionably. "So, it's my fault, then."

"I like it better when it's your fault." She pulled the towel from her bag and used it to dry his damp face. "You work too hard, Davidov," she said. Nick lifted his hands lightly to her wrists.

"Do you worry about me, *milaya?*"

His eyes were thoughtful on hers. They're so blue,

Ruth thought, like the sea from a distance or the sky in summer. "I never have before," she mused aloud. "Wouldn't it be strange if I started now? I don't suppose you need anyone to worry about you."

He continued to look at her, then the smile slid into his eyes. "Still, it's a comfortable feeling, yes?"

"Nick." He had started to rise, but Ruth put a hand to his shoulder. She found herself speaking quickly while the courage was with her. "Last night—why did you kiss me?"

He lifted a brow at the question, and though his eyes never left hers, she felt the rest of her body grow warm from them. "Because I wanted to," he told her at length. "It's a good reason." He rose then, and she got up with him.

"But you never wanted to before."

The smile was quick, speeding across his face. "Didn't I?"

"Well, you never kissed me before, not like that." She turned away, pulling off the T-shirt she wore over her bone-colored leotard.

He studied the graceful arch of her back. "And do you think I should do everything I want?"

Ruth shrugged. She had come to dance, not to fence. "I imagined you did," she tossed back as she approached the barre. As she went into a deep *plié,* she cast a look back over her shoulder. "Don't you?"

He didn't smile. "Do you mean to be provocative, Ruth, or is it an accident?"

She sensed the irritation in his voice but shrugged again. Perhaps she did. "I haven't tried it very often before," she said carelessly. "It might be fun."

"Be careful where you step," he said quietly. "It's a long fall."

Ruth laughed, enjoying the smooth response of her muscles to her commands. "Being safe isn't my goal in life, Nikolai. You'd understand if you'd known my parents. I'm a born adventurer."

"There are different kinds of danger," he pointed out, moving back to the CD player. "You might not find them all pleasurable?"

"Do you want me to be afraid of you?" she asked, turning.

The player squawked when he pressed the fast forward button. "You would be," he told her simply, "if it were what I wanted."

Their eyes met in the mirror. It took all of Ruth's concentration to complete the leg lift. *Yes,* she admitted silently, keeping her eyes on his. *I would be.* There's no emotion he can't rip from a person. That, along with his technical brilliance, makes him a great dancer. But I won't be intimidated. She dipped to the ground again, her back straight.

"I don't frighten easily, Nick." In the glass, her eyes challenged.

He pushed the button, stopping the machine. The room was thrown into silence while the last of the sun struggled into the window.

"Come." Nick again pressed a button on the player. Music swelled into the room. Walking to the center, Nick held out a hand. Ruth crossed to him, and without speaking they took their positions for the *grand pas de deux.*

Nick was not only a brilliant dancer, he was a demanding teacher. He would have each detail perfect, each minute gesture exact. Again and again they began the movement, and again and again he stopped to correct, to adjust.

"No, the head angle is wrong. Here." He moved her head with his hands until he was satisfied. "Your hands here, like so." And he would position her as he chose.

His hands were professional, adjusting her shoulders, skimming lightly at her waist as she spun, gripping her thigh for a lift. She was content to be molded by him. Yet it seemed she could not please him. He grew impatient, she frustrated.

"You must *look* at me!" he demanded, stopping her again.

"I was," she tossed back, frowning.

With a quick Russian oath he walked over and punched the button to stop the music. "With no feeling! You feel nothing. It's no good."

"You keep stopping," she began.

"Because it's wrong."

She glared at him briefly. "All right," she muttered and wiped the sweat from her brow with her forearm. "What do you want me to feel?"

"You're in love with me." Ruth's eyes flew up, but he was already involved with the CD player. "You want me, but you have pride, spirit. You won't be taken, do you see? Equal terms or nothing." He turned back, his eyes locking on hers. "But the desire is there. Passion, Ruth. It smolders. *Feel* it. You tell me you're a woman, not a child. Show me, then."

He crossed back to her. "Now," he said, putting a hand to her waist. "Again."

This time Ruth allowed her imagination to move her. She was a gypsy in love with a prince, fiercely proud, deeply passionate. The music was fast, building the mood. It was an erotic dance, with a basic sexuality in the steps and gestures. There was a great deal of close work, bodies brushing, eyes locking. She felt the very real pull of desire. Her blood began to hum with it.

Eagerly, as if to burn out what she was feeling, she executed the *soubresauts* trapped somewhere between truth and fantasy. She did want him and was no longer sure that she was feeling only as Carlotta. He touched her, drew her, and always she retreated—not running away but simply standing on her own.

The music built. They spun further and further away from each other, each rejecting the attraction. They leaped apart, but then, as if unable to resist, they came back full circle. Back toward each other and past, then, with a final turn, they were in each other's arms. The music ended with the two wrapped close together, face to face, heart to heart.

The silence came as a shock, leaving Ruth dazed between herself and the role. Both she and Nick were breathing quickly from the demands of the dance. She could feel the rapid beat of his heart against hers. Her eyes, as she stood on pointe were almost level with his. He looked into hers as she did into his—searching, wondering. Their lips met; the time for questions was passed.

This time she felt the hunger and impatience she had only sensed before. He seemed unable to hold her close enough, unable to taste all he craved. His mouth was everywhere, running wildly over her face and throat.

White heat raced along her skin in its wake. She could smell the muskiness of his sweat, taste the salty dampness on his face and throat as her own lips wandered. Then his mouth came back to hers, and they joined in mutual need.

He murmured something, but she couldn't understand. Even the language he spoke was a mystery. Their bodies fused together. Only the thin fabric of her leotard and tights came between his hands and her skin. They pressed here, touched there, lingered and aroused. His lips were at her ear, his teeth catching and tugging at the lobe. He murmured to her in Russian, but she had no need to understand the words.

His mouth found hers again, hotter this time, more insistent. Ruth gave and took with equal urgency, shuddering with pleasure as he slid a hand to her breast for a rough caress while her mouth, ever searching, ever questing, clung to his.

When he would have drawn her away, Ruth buried her face in his shoulder and strained against him. Nothing had ever prepared her for the rapid swing of strength to weakness. Even knowing she was losing part of herself, she was unable to stop it.

"Ruth." Nick drew her away, his hands gentle now. He looked at her, deep into the cloudy depths of her eyes. She was too moved by what was coursing through her to read his expression. "I didn't mean that to happen."

She stared at him. "But it did." It seemed so simple. She smiled. But when she lifted a hand to touch his cheek, he stopped her by taking her wrist.

"It shouldn't have."

She watched him, and her smile faded. Her eyes became guarded. "Why not?"

"We've a ballet to do in less than three weeks." Nick's voice was brisk now, all business. "This isn't the time for complications."

"Oh, I see." Ruth turned away so that he wouldn't see the hurt. Walking back to the bench, she began to untie her shoes. "I'm a complication."

"You are," he agreed and moved to the player again. "I haven't the time or the inclination to indulge you romantically."

"Indulge me romantically," she repeated in a low, incredulous voice.

"There are women who need a candlelight courtship," he continued, his back still to her. "You're one of them. At this point I haven't the time."

"Oh, I see. You only have time for more basic relationships," she said sharply, tying her tennis shoes with trembling fingers. How easily he could make her feel like a fool!

Nick turned to her now, watchful. "Yes."

"And there are other women who can provide that."

He gave a slight shrug. "Yes. I apologize for what happened. It's easy to get caught up in the dance."

"Oh, please." She tossed her toe shoes into the bag. "There's no need to apologize. I don't need you to indulge me romantically, Nick. Like you, I know others."

"Like your designer?"

"That's right. But don't worry, I won't blow any more rehearsals. I'll give you your ballet, Nick." Her voice was thickening with tears, but she was helpless to prevent it. "They'll rave above it, I swear it. It's going to make me the most important prima ballerina in the country." The tears came, and though she despised them, she didn't brush them aside. They rolled silently down her cheeks. "And when the season's over, I'll never dance with you again. *Never!*"

She turned and ran from the studio without giving him a chance to respond.

Chapter 4

The backstage cacophony penetrated Ruth's closed dressing room door. It was closed, uncharacteristically, for only one reason: She wanted to avoid Nick.

He was always everywhere before a performance—popping into dressing rooms, checking costumes and makeup, calming preperformance jitters. No detail was too insignificant to merit his attention, no problem too small for him to seek the solution. He always had and always would involve himself.

In the past Ruth had cherished his brief, explosive visits. His energy was an inspiration and settled her own anxieties. Now, however, she wanted as much distance between herself and the company star and artistic director as possible. During the past weeks of rehearsal that hadn't been possible physically, but she would attempt an emotional distance nevertheless.

She felt reasonably certain that although Nick wouldn't normally respect a closed door, he would, in this case, take her point. The small gesture satisfied her.

Perhaps because of her turmoil and needs, Ruth had worked harder on the role of Carlotta than on any other role in her career. She was determined not just to make it a success, but to make it an unprecedented triumph. It was a gesture of defiance, a bid for independence. These days the character of the sultry gypsy suited her mood exactly.

In the three weeks since her last informal rehearsal with Nick, both dancers had kept their relationship stringently professional. It hadn't always been easy, given the roles they were portraying, but they had exchanged no personal comments, indulged in none of their usual banter. When she had felt his eyes follow her, as she had more than once, Ruth forced herself not to flinch. When she felt his desire draw her, she remembered his last private words to her. That had been enough to stiffen her pride. She had clamped down on her habit of speculating what was in his mind. She'd told herself she didn't need to know, didn't want to know. All she had to do was dance.

Now, dressed in a plain white terry robe, she sat at her dressing table and sewed the satin ribbons onto her toe shoes. The simple dancer's chore helped to relax her.

The heat of the bright, round bulbs that framed her mirror warmed her skin. Already in stage makeup, she had left her hair loose and thick. It was to fly around her in the first scene, as bold and alluring as her character. Her eyes had been darkened, accentuating their shape and size, her lips painted red. The brilliantly colored, full-skirted dress for the first scene hung on the back of her door. Flowers had already begun to arrive, and the room was heavy with scent. On the table at her elbow were a dozen long-stemmed red roses from Donald. She smiled a little, thinking he would be in the audience, then at the reception afterward. She'd keep his roses in her dressing room for as long as they lived. They would help her to remember that not all men were too busy to indulge her romantically.

Ruth pricked her finger on the needle and swore. Even as she brought the wound to her mouth to ease the sting, she caught the glare of her own eyes in the glass.

Serves you right, she told herself silently, for even thinking of him. Indulging her romantically indeed! She picked up her second toe shoe. He made me sound as though I were sixteen and needed a corsage for the prom!

Her thoughts were interrupted by a knock on the door. Ruth put down her shoe. She rose and went to the door. If it were Nick, she wanted to meet him on her feet. She lifted her chin as she turned the knob.

"Uncle Seth! Lindsay!" She launched herself into her uncle's arms, then flung herself at the woman beside him. "Oh, I'm so very glad you're here!"

Lindsay found the greeting a bit desperate but said nothing. She only returned the hug and met her husband's eyes over Ruth's head. Their communication was silent and perfectly understood. Ruth turned to give Seth a second hug.

"You both look wonderful!" she exclaimed as she drew them into the room.

Ruth had been close to Seth Bannion during much of

her adolescence, but it hadn't been until she'd gone out on her own that she had truly appreciated the changes he had made in his own lifestyle to care for her. He was a highly successful architect and had been a sought-after bachelor and world traveler. He had taken a teenager into his home, adjusted his mode of living and made her his priority. Ruth adored him.

She clasped her hands and admired them both with her eyes. "You look so beautiful, Lindsay," Ruth enthused, turning to take her in. "I never get used to it." Lindsay was small and delicately built. Her pale hair and ivory skin set off her deep blue eyes. She was the warmest person Ruth knew; a woman capable of rich emotions and unlimited love. She wore a filmy smoke-gray dress that seemed to swirl from her shoulders to her feet.

Lindsay laughed and caught Ruth's hands in hers. "What a marvelous compliment. Seth doesn't tell me so nearly enough."

"Only daily," he said, smiling into Lindsay's eyes.

"This is the same dressing room you used for *Ariel*," Seth commented, glancing around. "It hasn't changed."

"You should know," Lindsay said. "I proposed to you here."

He grinned. "So you did."

"I didn't know that."

They both turned, shifting their attention to Ruth. Lindsay laughed again. "I've never been very good about tradition," she said and wandered over to pick up one of Ruth's toe shoes. "And he didn't ask me soon enough."

The shoes that lined the dressing table stirred memories. What a life, Lindsay thought. *What a world.* She had once been as much a part of it as Ruth was now. Her eyes lifted and fixed on the dark ones reflected in the glass.

"Nervous?"

Ruth's whole body seemed to sigh. "Oh, yes." She grimaced.

"It's a good ballet," Lindsay said with certainty. She took the quality of Nick's work on faith. She had known him for too long to do otherwise.

"It's wonderful. But…" Ruth shook her head and moved back to her chair. "In the second act there's a passage where I never seem to stop. There are only a few seconds for me to catch my breath before I'm off again."

"Nick doesn't write easy ballets."

"No." Ruth picked up her needle and thread again. "How are the children?"

The quick change of subject was noted. Again Lindsay met Seth's eyes over Ruth's head.

"Justin's a terror," Seth stated wryly with fatherly pride. "He drives Worth mad."

Ruth gave a low, gurgling laugh. "Is Worth maintaining his professional dignity?"

"Magnificently," Lindsay put in. "'Master Justin,'" she quoted, giving a fair imitation of the butler's cultured British tones. "'One must not bring one's pet frog into the kitchen, even when it requires feeding.'" Lindsay laughed, watching Ruth finish the last stitches. "Of course, he dotes on Amanda, though he pretends not to."

"And she's as big a terror as Justin!" Seth commented.

"What a way to describe our children," Lindsay said, turning to him.

"Who dumped the entire contents of a box of fish food into the goldfish bowl?" he asked her, and she lifted a brow.

"She was only trying to be helpful." A smile tugged at Lindsay's mouth. "Who took them to the zoo and stuffed them with hot dogs and caramel corn?"

"I was only trying to be helpful," he countered, his eyes warm on hers.

Watching them, Ruth felt both a surge of warmth and a shaft of envy. What would it be like to be loved that way? she wondered. *Enduringly.* The word suited them, she decided.

"Shall we clear out?" Lindsay asked her. "And let you get ready?"

"No, please stay awhile. There's time." Ruth fingered the satin ribbons nervously.

Nerves, Lindsay thought, watching her.

"You're coming to the reception, aren't you?" Ruth glanced up again.

"Wouldn't miss it." Lindsay moved over to knead Ruth's shoulders. "Will we meet Donald?"

"Donald?" Ruth brought her thoughts back. "Oh, yes, Donald will be there. Shall we get a table together? You'll like him," she went on without waiting for an answer. Her eyes sought Lindsay's, then her uncle's. "He's very—nice."

"Lindsay!"

Nick stood in the open doorway. His face was alive with pleasure. His eyes were all for Lindsay. She ran into his arms.

"Oh, Nick, it's wonderful to see you! It's always too long."

He kissed her on both cheeks, then on the mouth. "More beautiful every time," he murmured, letting his eyes roam her face. "*Ptichka,* little bird." He used his pet name for her, then kissed her again. "This architect you married—" he shot a quick grin at Seth "—he makes you happy still?"

"He'll do." Lindsay hugged Nick again, fiercely. "Oh, but I miss you. Why don't you come see us more often?"

"When would I find the time?" He kept his arm around Lindsay's waist as he held out a hand to Seth. "Marriage agrees with you. It's good to see you."

Their handshake was warm. Seth knew he shared the two women he loved with the Russian. A part of Lindsay had belonged to Nick before he had known her. Now Ruth was part of his world.

"Are you giving us another triumph tonight?" Seth asked.

"But of course." Nick grinned and shrugged. "It is what I do."

Lindsay gave Nick a squeeze. "He never changes." She rested her head on his shoulder a moment. "Thank God."

Throughout the exchange Ruth said nothing. She observed something rare and special between Lindsay and Nick. It emanated from them so vividly, she felt she could almost touch it. It only took seeing them side by side to remember how perfectly they had moved together on the stage. Unity, precision, understanding. She stopped listening to what they were saying, entranced by their unspoken rapport.

When Nick's eyes met hers, Ruth could only stare. Whatever she had been trying to dissect, to absorb, was forgotten. All she knew was that she had unwittingly allowed the ache to return. His eyes were so blue, so powerful, she seemed unable to prevent him from peeling away the layers and reaching her soul. Marshalling her strength, she pulled herself out of the trance.

It would have been impossible not to have witnessed the brief exchange. Lindsay and Seth silently communicated their concern.

"Nadine will be at the reception, won't she?" Lindsay attempted to ease the sudden tension.

"Hmm?" Nick turned his attention back to her. "Ah, yes, Nadine." He realigned his thoughts and spoke smoothly. "Of course, she will want to bask in the glory before she launches her next fund drive."

"You always were hard on her." Lindsay smiled, remembering how often Nick and Nadine Rothchild, the founder of the company, had disagreed.

"She can take it," he tossed off with a jerk of his shoulder. "I'll see you at the reception?"

"Yes." Lindsay watched his eyes drift back to Ruth's. He hadn't spoken a word to her, nor had Ruth said anything to him. They communicated with their eyes only. He held the contact for several long seconds before turning back to Lindsay.

"I'll see you after the performance," he said, and Ruth quietly let out her breath. "I must go change. *Do svidanya.*"

He was gone before they could answer his goodbye. From down the corridor, they could hear someone calling his name.

Seth walked to Ruth and, putting his hands on her shoulders, bent to kiss the crown of her head. "You'd better be changing."

Ruth tried to pull herself together. "Yes, I'm in the first scene."

"You're going to be terrific." He squeezed her shoulders briefly.

"I want to be." Her eyes lifted to his and held before sweeping to Lindsay. "I have to be."

"You will be," Lindsay assured her, holding out a hand for Seth's even as her eyes stayed on Ruth's. "It's what you were born for. Besides, you were my most gifted pupil."

Ruth turned in the chair and gave Lindsay her first smile since Nick's appearance. She lifted her face to Lindsay's quick kiss. *"Do svidanya!"* Lindsay said, smiling as she and Seth left arm in arm.

Slowly Ruth moved to the door and shut it. For a moment she simply stood, contemplating the colorful costume that would make her Carlotta. She was Ruth Bannion, a little unsure of her emotions, a little afraid of the night ahead. To put on the costume was to put on the role. Carlotta has her vulnerabilities, Ruth mused, fingering the fabric of the skirt, but she cloaks them in boldness and audaciousness. The thought made Ruth smile again. *Oh yes,* she decided, *she's for me.* Ruth began to dress.

When she left the room fifteen minutes later, she could hear the orchestra tuning up. She was in full costume. Her skirt swayed saucily at her hips, a slash of a red scarf defined her waist. Her hair streamed freely down her back. She hurried past the dancers warming up for the first scene and those idling in the doorways. She spotted Francie sitting cross-legged on the floor in a corner, breaking in her toe shoes with a hammer.

Ruth went to a convenient prop crate and used it for a barre as she began to warm up. She could already smell the sweat and the lights.

Her muscles responded, tightening, stretching, loosening at her command. She concentrated on them purposefully, keeping her back to the stage, the better to concentrate on her own body. Each performance was important to her, but this one was in a class by itself. Ruth had something to prove—to Nick and to herself. She would flaunt her professionalism. Whatever her feelings were for Nick, she would forget them and concentrate only on interpreting Nick's ballet. Nothing would interfere with that.

It had been a bad moment for her in the dressing room when his eyes had pinned hers. Something inside her had wanted to melt and nearly had. Pride had held her aloof, as it had for weeks. He hadn't wanted her— not wholly, not exclusively—the way she had wanted him. The fact that he had so easily agreed that any number of women could give him what he needed had stung.

Scowling, Ruth curled her leg up behind her, pulling and stretching.

It was time someone taught that arrogant Russian a lesson, she thought as she switched legs. Too many women had fallen at his feet. He expected it, just as he expected his dancers to do things his way.

Ruth lifted her chin and found her eyes once again locked tight on Nick's.

He had come out of his dressing room clad in the glittering white and gold tunic he would wear in the first act. Spotting Ruth, he had stopped to stand and watch her. He wondered if the passion he saw in her face was her own or, like the costume, assumed for her role as Carlotta. He thought that there, in the dim backstage corridor, with the gypsy costume and smoldering eyes, she had never looked more alluring. It was at that moment that Ruth had lifted her eyes to his.

Each felt the instant attraction; each felt the instant hostility. Ruth tossed her head, glared briefly, then whirled away in a flurry of color and skirts. Her unconscious mimicry of the character she was about to play amused him.

All right, little one, Nick thought with the ghost of a smile. We'll see who comes out on top tonight. Nick decided he would rather enjoy the challenge.

He followed Ruth to the wings, dismissing with a wave of his hand one or two who tried to detain him. Reaching Ruth, he spun her around and caught her close, heedless of the backstage audience. She was caught completely off guard. Her reflexes had no time to respond or to reject before his mouth, arrogant and sure, demanded, plundered, then released.

Nick kept his hands on her forearms for a moment, arrogantly smiling. "That should put you in the mood," he said jauntily before turning to stride away.

Furious, Ruth could only stare hotly after his retreating back. There was scattered laughter that her glare did nothing to suppress before she whirled away again and stalked out onto the empty, black stage.

She waited while the stage hands drew the heavy curtain. She waited for the orchestra—strings only, as they played her entrance cue. She waited until she was fully lighted by the single spot before she began to dance.

Her opening solo was short, fast and flamboyant. When she had finished, the stage was lit to show the set of a gypsy camp. The audience exploded into applause.

While the *corps* and second dancers took over, Ruth was able to catch her breath. She waited, half-listening to the praise of Nick's assistant choreographer. Across the long stage she could see Nick waiting in the opposite wing for his entrance.

Top that, Davidov, she challenged silently. Ruth knew she had never danced better in her life. As if he had heard the unspoken dare, Nick grinned at her before he made his entrance.

He was all arrogance, all pride; the prince entering the gypsy camp to buy baubles. He cast aside the trinkets they offered with a flick of the wrist. He dominated the stage with his presence, his talent. Ruth couldn't deny it. It made her only more determined to outdo him. She waited while he dismissed offer after offer, waited for him to make it plain that the gypsies had nothing he desired. Then she glided on stage, her head held high. A red rose was now pinned at her ear.

Their mutual attraction was instant as their eyes met for the first time. The moment was accentuated by the change of lighting and the orchestra's crescendo. Carlotta, seeing the discarded treasures, turned her back on him to join a group of her sisters. The prince, intrigued, approached her for a closer study.

Ruth's mutinous eyes met Nick's again, and she had no trouble jerking her head haughtily away when he took her chin in his hand. Something in Nick's smile made her eyes flare more dramatically as he turned to the dancer who played her father. The prince had found something he desired. He offered his gold for Carlotta.

She defied him with pride and fury. No one could buy her; no one could own her. Taunting him, arousing him, she agreed to sell him a dance for his bag of gold. Enraged yet unable to resist, the prince tossed his gold onto the pile of rejected trinkets. They began their first *pas de deux,* palm to palm, with heated blood and angry eyes.

The high-level pace was maintained throughout the ballet. The competition between them remained sharp, each spurring the other to excel. They didn't speak between acts, but once, as they danced close, he whispered annoyingly in her ear that her *ballottés* needed polishing.

He lifted her, and she dipped, her head arched down, her feet up, so that he was holding her nearly upside down. Six, seven, eight slow, sustained beats, then she was up like lightning again in an *arabesque.* Her eyes were like flame as she executed a double turn. When she leaped offstage leaving him to his solo, Ruth pressed her hand to her stomach, drawing exhausted breaths.

Again and again, the stage burned from their heated dancing. When the ballet finally ended, the two in each other's arms, she managed to pant: "I dislike you intensely, Davidov."

"Dislike all you please," he said lightly as applause and cheers erupted. "As long as you dance."

"Oh, I'll dance, all right," she assured him breathlessly and dipped into a deep, smiling curtsy for the audience.

Only she could have heard his quiet chuckle as he scooped up a rose that had been tossed onstage and presented it to her with a bow.

"My *ballottés* were perfect," she hissed between gritted teeth as he kissed her hand.

"We'll discuss it in class tomorrow." He bowed and presented her to the audience again.

"Go to hell, Davidov," she said, smiling sweetly to the "bravos" that showered over them.

"After the season," he agreed, turning for another bow.

Chapter 5

Nick and Ruth took eleven curtain calls. An hour after the final curtain came down, her dressing room was finally cleared so that she could change from her costume. Now she wore a long white dress with narrow sleeves and a high collar. The only jewelry she added were the sleek gold drop earrings that Lindsay and Seth had given her on her twenty-first birthday. Triumph had made her eyes dark and brilliant and had shot a flush of rose into her cheeks. She left her hair loose and free, as Carlotta's had been.

"Very nice," Donald commented when she met him in the corridor.

Ruth smiled, knowing he spoke of the dress, his design, as much as the woman in it. She slipped her arm through his. "Like it?" Her eyes beamed up into his. "I found it in this little discount dress shop in the clothing district."

He pinched her chin as punishment, then kissed her. "I know I said it before, darling, but you were wonderful."

"Oh, I could never hear that too often." With a laugh she began to lead the way to the stage door. "I want champagne," she told him. "Gallons of it. I think I could swim in it tonight."

"Let's see if it can be arranged."

They moved outside, where his car was waiting. "Oh, Donald," Ruth continued, the moment they had settled into it. "It never felt more *right*. Everything just seemed to come together. The music—the music was so perfect."

"You were perfect," he stated, steering the car into Manhattan traffic. "They were ready to tear the walls down for you."

Much too excited to lean back, Ruth sat on the edge of her seat and turned toward him. "If I could freeze a moment in time, with all its feelings and emotions, it would be this ballet. Tonight. Opening night."

"You'll do it again tomorrow," he told her.

"Yes, and it'll be wonderful, I know. But not like this." Ruth wished he could understand. "I'm not sure it can ever be exactly like this again, or even if it should be."

"I'd think you might get a bit weary of doing the same dance night after night after a couple of weeks."

He pulled over to the curb, and Ruth shook her head. Why did she want him to understand? she wondered as the doorman helped her alight. For all his creative talents as a designer, Donald was firmly rooted to the earth. But tonight she was ready to fly.

"It's hard to explain." She allowed him to lead her through the wide glass doors and into the hotel lobby. "Something just happens when the lights come on and the music starts. It's always special. Always."

The banquet room was ablaze with light and already crowded with people. Cameras began to click and flash the moment Ruth stepped into the doorway. The applause met her.

"Ruth!" Nadine walked through the crowd with the assurance of a woman who knew people would step aside for her. She was small, with a trim build and grace that revealed her training as a dancer. Her hair was sculptured and palely blond, her skin smooth and pink. The angelic face belied a keen mind. More than she ever had as a dancer, Nadine Rothchild, as company founder, devoted her life to the ballet.

Ruth turned to find herself embraced. "You were beautiful," Nadine said. Ruth knew this to be her highest compliment. Pulling her away, Nadine stared for several long seconds directly into her eyes. It was a characteristic habit. "You've never danced better than you danced tonight."

"Thank you, Nadine."

"I know you want Lindsay and Seth." She began to lead Ruth across the room, leaving Donald to follow in her wake. "We're all sitting together."

Ruth's eyes met Lindsay's first. What she read there was the final gratification. Lindsay held out both her hands, and Ruth extended hers to join them. "I'm so proud of you." Her voice was thick with emotion.

Seth laid his hands on his wife's shoulders and looked at his niece. "Every time I watch you perform, I think you'll never dance any better than you do at that moment. But you always do."

Ruth laughed, still gliding, and lifted her face for a kiss. "It's the most wonderful part I've ever had." She turned then, and taking Donald's arm, made quick introductions.

"I'm a great admirer of your designs." Lindsay smiled up at him. "Ruth wears them beautifully."

"My favorite client. I believe you could easily become my second favorite," Donald returned the compliment. "You have fantastic coloring."

"Thank you." Lindsay recognized the professional tone of the compliment and was more amused than flattered. "You need some champagne," she said, turning to Ruth.

Before they could locate a waiter, the sound of applause had them turning back toward the entrance. Ruth knew before she saw him that it would be Nick. Only he could generate such excitement. He was alone, which surprised her. Where there was Davidov, there were usually women. Ruth knew his eyes would find hers.

Nick quickly dislodged himself from the crowd and slowly, with the perfectly controlled grace of his profession, walked to her, holding a single red rose, which he handed to Ruth. When she accepted it, he took her other hand and lifted it to his lips. He didn't speak, nor did his eyes leave hers, until he turned and walked away.

Just theatrics, she told herself, but she couldn't resist breathing in the scent of the rose. No one knew how to set the stage more expertly than Davidov. Her eyes shifted to Lindsay's. In them Ruth could read both understanding and concern. She barely prevented herself from shaking her head in denial. She forced a bright smile.

"What about that champagne?" she demanded.

Ruth toyed with her dinner, barely eating, too excited for food. It was just as well; she sat at the table with Nadine, and it was a company joke that Nadine judged her dancers by the pound.

Nadine gave Lindsay's dish of chocolate mousse a frowning glance. "You have to watch those rich desserts, dear."

With a laugh Lindsay leaned over and kissed Nadine's cheek. "You're so wonderfully consistent, Nadine. There's too much in the world that's unpredictable."

"You can't dance with whipped cream in your thighs," Nadine pointed out and sipped at her champagne.

"You know," Lindsay said to Ruth, "she caught me once with a bag of potato chips. It was one of the most dreadful experiences of my life." She shot Nadine a grin and licked chocolate from her spoon. "It completely killed my taste for them."

"My dancers look like dancers," Nadine said firmly. "Lots of bone and no bulges. Proper diet is as essential as daily class—"

"And daily class is as essential as breathing," Lindsay finished and laughed again. "Can it really be eight years since I was with the company?"

"You left a hole. It wasn't easy to fill it."

The unexpected compliment surprised Lindsay. Nadine was a pragmatic, brisk woman who took her dancers' talent for granted. She expected the best and rarely considered praise necessary.

"Why, thank you, Nadine."

"It wasn't a compliment but a complaint," Nadine countered. "You left us too soon. You could still be dancing."

Lindsay smiled again. "You seem to have plenty of young talent, Nadine. Your *corps* is still the best."

Nadine acknowledged this with a nod. "Of course." She paused a moment, looking at Lindsay again as she sipped her wine. "Can you imagine how many Juliets I've watched in my lifetime, Lindsay?"

"Is that a loaded question?" she countered and grinned at Seth. "If I say too many, she'll complain that I'm aging her. Too few, and I'm insulting her."

"Try 'a considerable number,'" he suggested, adding champagne to his wife's glass.

"Good idea." Lindsay shifted her attention back to Nadine. "A considerable number."

"Quite correct." Nadine set down her glass and laid her hands on Lindsay's. Her eyes were suddenly intense. "You were the best. The very best. I wept when you left us."

Lindsay opened her mouth, then shut it again on words that wouldn't come. She swallowed and shook her head.

"Excuse me, please," she murmured. Rising, she hurried across the room.

There were wide glass doors leading to a circling balcony. Lindsay opened them and stepped outside. Leaning on the rail, she took a deep breath. It was a clear night, with stars and moonlight shedding silver over Manhattan's skyline. She looked out blindly.

After all the years, she thought, and all the distance. I'd have cut off an arm to have heard her say that ten years ago. She felt a tear run down her cheek and closed her eyes. Oh, God, how badly I once needed to know what she just told me. And now...

At the touch of a hand on her shoulder, she started. Lindsay turned into Nick's arms. For a moment she said nothing, letting herself lean on him and remember. She had been his Juliet in that other life, that world she had once been a part of.

"Oh, Nick," she murmured. "How fragile we are, and how foolish."

"Foolish?" he repeated and kissed the top of her head. "Speak for yourself, *ptichka*. Davidov is never foolish."

She laughed and looked up at him. "I forgot."

"Foolish of you." He pulled her back into his arms, and she rose on her toes so that her cheek brushed his. "Nick. You know, no matter how long you're away, no matter how far you go, all of this is still with you. It's more than in your blood, it's in the flesh and muscle." With a sigh, she drew out of his arms and again leaned on the rail. "Whenever I come back, part of me expects to walk into class again or rush to make company calls. It's ingrained."

Nick rested a hip on the rail and studied her profile. There was a breeze blowing her hair back, and he thought again that she was one of the most beautiful women he had ever known. Yet she had always seemed unaware of her physical appeal.

"Do you miss it?" he asked her, and she turned to look at him directly.

"It's not a matter of missing it." Lindsay's brows drew together as she tried to translate emotions into words. "It's more like putting part of yourself in storage. To be honest, I don't think about the company much at home. I'm so busy with the children and my students. And Seth is…" She stopped, and he watched the smile illuminate her face. "Seth is everything." Lindsay turned back to the skyline. "Sometimes, when I come back here to watch Ruth dance, the memories are so vivid, it's almost unreal."

"It makes you sad?"

"A little," she admitted. "But it's a nice feeling all the same. When I look back, I don't think there's anything in my life I'd change. I'm very lucky. And Ruth…" She smiled again, gazing out at New York. "I'm proud of her, thrilled for her. She's so good. She's so incredibly good. Somehow I feel like a part of it all over again."

"You're always a part of it, Lindsay." He caught at the ends of her hair. "Talent like yours is never forgotten."

"Oh, no, no more compliments tonight." She gave a shaky laugh and shook her head. "That's what got me started." Taking a deep breath, she faced him again. "I know I was a good dancer, Nick. I worked hard to be. I treasure the years I was with the company—the ballets I danced with you. My mother still has her scrapbook, and one day my children will look through it." She gave him a puzzled smile. "Imagine that."

"Do you know, I'm always amazed to think of you with two growing children."

"Why?"

He smiled and took her hand. "Because it's so easy to remember you the first time I saw you. You were still a soloist when I came to the company. I watched you rehearsing for *Sleeping Beauty*. You were the flower fairy, and you were dissatisfied with your *fouettés*."

"How do you remember that?"

Nick lifted a brow. "Because my first thought was how I would get you into my bed. I couldn't ask you— my English was not so good in those days."

Lindsay gave a choked laugh. "You learned quickly enough, as I remember. Though as I recall, you never, in any language, suggested I come into your bed."

"Would you have?" He tilted his head as he studied her. "I've wondered for more than ten years."

Lindsay searched her heart even as she searched his face. She could hear laughter through the windows and the muffled drone of traffic far below. She tried to think of the Lindsay Dunne who had existed ten years before. Ultimately, she smiled and shook her head. "I don't know. Perhaps it's better that way."

Nick slipped an arm around her, and she leaned against his shoulder. "You're right. I'm not sure it would be good to know one way or the other."

They fell silent as their thoughts drifted.

"Donald Keyser seems like a nice man," Lindsay murmured. She felt the fractional stiffening of Nick's arm.

"Yes."

"Ruth's not in love with him, of course, but he isn't

in love with her, either. I imagine they're good company for each other." When he said nothing, Lindsay tilted her head and looked at him. "Nick?"

He glanced down and read her unspoken thoughts clearly. "You see too much," he muttered.

"I know you—I know Ruth."

He frowned back out at the skyline. "You're afraid I'll hurt her."

"The thought crossed my mind," Lindsay admitted. "As it crossed my mind that she might hurt you." Nick looked back at her, and she continued. "It's difficult when I love you both."

After a shrug, he thrust his hands into his pockets and turned to take a few steps away. "We dance together, that's all."

"That's hardly all," Lindsay countered, but as he turned back, annoyed, she continued. "Oh, I don't mean you're lovers, nor is it any of my business if you are. But Nick." She sighed, recognizing the anger in his eyes. "It's impossible to look at the two of you and not see."

"What do you want?" he demanded. "A promise I won't take her to bed?"

"No." Calmly, Lindsay walked to him. "I'm not asking for promises or giving advice. I only hope to give you support if you want it."

She watched the anger die as he turned away again. "She's a child," he murmured.

"She's a woman," Lindsay corrected. "Ruth was barely ever a child. She was grown up in a number of ways when I first met her."

"Perhaps it is safer if I consider her a child."

"You've argued with her."

Nick laughed and faced Lindsay again. "*Ptichka,* I always argue with my partners, yes?"

"Yes," Lindsay agreed and decided to leave it at that. Instead of pressing him, she held out her hand. "We had some great arguments, Davidov."

"The best." Nick took the offered hand in both of his. "Come, let me take you back in. We should be celebrating."

"Did I tell you how wonderful you were tonight or how brilliant your ballet is?"

"Only once." He gave her his charming smile. "And that was hardly enough. I have a very big ego." The creases in his cheeks deepened. "How wonderful was I?"

"Oh, Nick." Lindsay laughed and threw her arms around him. "As wonderful as Davidov can possibly be."

"A suitable compliment," he decided, "as that is a great deal more brilliant than anyone else."

Lindsay kissed him. "I'm so glad you don't change."

They both turned as the door opened. Seth stepped out on the balcony.

"Ah, we're caught," Nick stated, grinning as he kept Lindsay in his arms. "Now your architect will break both my legs."

"Perhaps if you beg for mercy," Lindsay told him, smiling over at Seth.

"Davidov beg for mercy?" Nick rolled his eyes and released her. "The woman is mad."

"Often," Seth agreed. "But I make allowances for it." Lindsay's hand slipped into his. "People are asking for you," he told Nick.

Nick nodded, casting a quick glance toward the dining room. "How long are you staying?"

"Just overnight," Seth answered.

"Then I will say goodbye now." He held out a hand to Seth. "*Do svidanya, priyatel.*" He used the Russian term for friend. "You're a man to be envied. *Do svidanya, ptichka.*"

"Good-bye, Nick." Lindsay watched him slip back into the dining room. She sighed.

"Feeling better?" Seth asked her.

"How well you know me," she murmured.

"How much I love you," he whispered as he pulled her into his arms.

"Seth. It's been a lovely evening."

"No regrets?"

Lindsay knew he spoke of her career, the choices she had made. "No. No regrets." She lifted her face and met his mouth with hers.

The kiss grew long and deep with a hint of hunger. She heard his quiet sound of pleasure as he drew her closer. Her arms slipped up around his back until her hands gripped his shoulders. It's always like the first time, she thought. Each time he kisses me, it's like the first.

"Seth," she murmured against his mouth as they changed the angle of the kiss. "I'm much, much too tired for a party tonight."

"*Hmm.*" His lips moved to her ear. "It's been a long day. We should just slip up to our room and get some rest."

Lindsay gave a low laugh. "Good idea." She brought

her lips teasingly back to his. "Maybe we could order a bottle of champagne—to toast the ballet."

"A magnum of champagne," Seth decided, drawing her back far enough to smile down into her face. "It was an excellent ballet, after all."

"Oh, yes." Lindsay cast an eye toward the doors that separated them from the crowd of people. She smiled back at her husband. "I don't think we should disturb the party, do you?"

"What party?" Seth asked. Taking her arm, he walked past the doors. "There's another set of doors on the east side."

Lindsay laughed. "Architects always know the most important things," she murmured.

Chapter 6

By the end of the first week, *The Red Rose* was an established success. The company played to a full house at every performance. Ruth read the reviews and knew it was the turning point of her career. She gave interviews and focused on promoting the ballet, the company and herself. It was a simple matter to engage herself in her work and in her success. It was not so simple to deal with her feelings when she danced, night after night, with Nick.

Ruth told herself they were Carlotta's feelings; that it was merely her own empathy with the role she played. To fall in love with Davidov was impossible.

He was absorbed with ballet. So was she. He was only interested in brief physical relationships. Should she decide to involve herself with a man, she wanted emotions—deep, lasting emotions. The example of her own parents and Lindsay and Seth had spoiled her for anything less. Nick was demanding and selfish and unreasonable—not qualities she looked for in a lover. He found her foolish and romantic.

She needed to remember that after each performance when her blood was pumping and the need for him was churning inside her. She needed to remind herself of it when she lay awake at night with her mind far too wide awake.

They met on stage almost exclusively, so that when they came together face to face, the temptation was strong to take on the roles of the characters they portrayed. Whenever Ruth found herself too close to losing Carlotta's identity or her distance from Nick, she reviewed his faults. She had plans for her life, both professionally and personally. She was aware that Nick was the one man who could interfere with them.

She considered herself both self-sufficient and independent. She had had to be, growing up without an established home and normal childhood routines. There had been no lasting playmates in her young years, and she had taught herself not to form sentimental attachments to the homes her parents had rented, for they had never been homes for long. Ruth's apartment in New York was the first place she had allowed herself to grow attached to. It was hers—paid for with money she earned, filled with the things that were important to her. In the year she had lived there, she had learned that she could make it on her own. She had confidence in herself as a woman and as a dancer. It infuriated her that Nick was the only person on earth who could make her feel insecure in either respect.

Professionally, he could either challenge or intimidate her by a choice of words or with a facial expression. And Ruth was well aware of the confusion he aroused in her as a woman.

The girlhood crush was long over. For years, her passions had been centered on dancing. The men she had dated had been companions, friends. Nick had been the *premier danseur,* a mentor, a professional partner. It seemed strange to her that her feelings for him could have changed and intensified so quickly.

Perhaps, she thought, it would be easier to fall in love with a stranger rather than be in the embarrassing position of being suddenly attracted to a man she had known and worked with for years. There was no escape from the constant daily contact.

If it had been just a matter of physical attraction, Ruth felt she could have handled it. But it was the emotional involvement that worried her. Her feelings for Nick were complex and deep. She admired him, was fascinated by him, enraged by him, and trusted him without reservation—professionally. Personally, she knew he could, by the sheer force of his personality, overwhelm and devour. She wasn't willing to be the victim. Love, she feared, meant dependence, and that meant a lack of control.

"How far away are you?"

Ruth spun around to see Francie standing in her dressing room doorway. "Oh, miles," she admitted. "Come on in and sit down."

"You seem to have been thinking deep thoughts," Francie commented.

Ruth began to brush her hair back into a ponytail.

"Mmm," she said noncommittally. "Wednesdays are the longest. Just the thought of doing two shows makes my toes cramp."

"Seven curtain calls for a matinee isn't anything to sneeze at." Francie sank down on a handy chair. "Poor Nick is at this moment giving another interview to a reporter from *New Trends.*"

Ruth gave a half-laugh as she tied her hair back with a leather strap. "He'll be absolutely charming, and his accent will get more and more incomprehensible."

"Spasibo," Thank you, Francie said. "One of my few Russian words."

"Where did you learn that?" Ruth turned to face her.

"Oh, I did a bit of Russian cramming a couple of years ago when I thought I might enchant Nick." Grinning, Francie reached in her pocket for a stick of gum. "It didn't work. He'd laugh and pat me on the head now and again. I had delusions of gypsy violins and wild passion." She lifted her shoulders and sighed. "Nick always seems to be occupied, if you know what I mean."

"Yes." Ruth looked at her searchingly. "I never knew you were—interested in Nick that way."

"Honey." Francie gave her a pitying smile. "What female over twelve wouldn't be? And we all know my track record." She laughed and stretched her arms to the ceiling. "I like men; I don't fight it." She dropped her arms into her lap. "I just ended my meaningful relationship with the dermatologist."

"Oh. I'm sorry."

"Don't be sorry. We had fun. I'm considering a new meaningful relationship with the actor I met last week.

He's Price Reynolds on *A New Breed*." At Ruth's blank look, she elaborated. "The soap opera."

Ruth shook her head while a smile tugged at her mouth. "I haven't caught it."

"He's tall, with broad shoulders and dark, sleepy eyes. He might just be the one."

Ruth bit her bottom lip in thought. "How do you know when he is?" She met Francie's eyes again. "What makes you think he might be?"

"My palms sweat." She laughed at Ruth's incredulous face. "No, really, they do. Every time. It wouldn't work for you." Francie stopped smiling and leaned forward as she did when she became serious. "It wouldn't be enough for you to think a man *might* be the one. You'd have to *know* he was. I've been in love twice already this year. I was in love at least four or five times last year. How many times have you been in love?"

Ruth looked at her blankly. "Well, I…" Never, she realized. There had been no one.

"Don't look devastated." Francie popped back out of the chair with all the exuberance she showed on stage. "You've never been in love because there's only one meaning of the word for you. You'll know it when it happens." She laid a friendly hand on Ruth's shoulders. "That's going to be it. You're not insecure, like me. You know what you want, what you need. You're not willing to settle for anything less."

"Insecure?" Ruth gave her friend a puzzled smile. "I've never imagined you as insecure."

"I need someone to tell me I'm pretty, I'm clever, I'm loved. You don't." She took a breath. "When we were in the *corps,* you knew you weren't going to stay there.

You never had any doubt." She smiled again. "And neither did anyone else. If you found a man who meant as much to you as dancing does, you'd have it all."

Ruth dropped her eyes. "But he'd have to feel the same about me."

"That's part of the risk. It's like pulling a muscle." Francie grinned again. "It hurts like crazy, but you don't stop dancing. You haven't pulled a muscle yet."

"You're a great one with analogies."

"I only philosophize on an empty stomach," Francie told her. "Want lunch?"

"I can't. I'm meeting Donald." Ruth picked up her watch from the dressing table. "And I'm already late."

"Have fun." Francie headed for the door. "George is picking me up after tonight's show. You can get a look at him."

"George?"

"George Middemeyer." Francie tossed a grin over her shoulder. "Doctor Price Reynolds. He's a neurosurgeon with a failing marriage and a conniving mistress who might be pregnant. Tune in tomorrow."

With that, she was gone. Ruth laughed and grabbed her purse.

The delicatessen where Ruth was to meet Donald was two blocks away. She hurried toward it. She was aware that she was ten minutes late and that Donald was habitually prompt. She had little enough time before she had to report back for company calls.

The rich, strong smells of corned beef and Kosher pickles greeted her the moment she opened the door. The deli wasn't crowded, as the lunch rush was over, but a few people lingered. Two old men played a slow-moving game of checkers at a far table littered with the remnants of their lunch.

Ruth's glance swept over them and found Donald sitting back in his chair, smoking. She walked lightly, with rippling, unconscious confidence through the rows of tiny tables. "I'm sorry, Donald, I know I'm late." She leaned over to give him a quick kiss before she sat. "Have you ordered?"

"No." He tapped his cigarette. "I waited for you."

Ruth lifted a brow. There was something underlying the casual words. Knowing Donald, she told herself to wait. Whatever he had to say he would say in his own time.

She glanced over as the rotund, white-aproned man behind the counter shuffled over to their table. "What'll ya have?"

"Fruit salad and tea, please," Ruth told him, giving him a smile.

"Whitefish and coffee." Donald didn't glance at him. The man gave a little snort before shuffling off again. Ruth grinned at his retreating back.

"Have you ever been in here at lunch time?" she asked Donald. "It's a madhouse. He has a boy helping out during the rush, but they both move at the same pace. *Adagio.*"

"I rarely eat in places like this," Donald commented, taking a last drag before crushing out his cigarette.

Again Ruth detected undercurrents but waited. "It's really all I have time for today, Donald. Today must be pretty frantic for you, too, with your fashion show and reception tonight." She settled her purse strap over the back of her chair, then leaned her elbows on the table. "Is everything going well?"

"It appears to be. Some last-minute mayhem, naturally. Temperamental disagreements between my senior cutter and my head seamstress." He shrugged. "The usual."

"But this show is quite important, isn't it?" She tilted her head at his offhand tone.

"Yes, it's important." He shot her a direct look. "That's why I wanted you there with me."

Ruth met the look but kept her silence as the food was set unceremoniously on the table in front of them. Deliberately, she picked up her spoon but left the salad untouched. "You know why I can't, Donald. We've already discussed it."

He spilled a generous spoonful of sugar into his black coffee. "I also know you've got an understudy. One missed performance wouldn't matter that much."

"An understudy is for serious problems. I can't take a night off because I want to go out on a date."

"It's not quite movies and pizza," he said crossly.

"I know that, Donald." Ruth sipped the tea. A light throbbing had begun behind her eyes. "I'd be there if I could."

"I didn't let you down on opening night."

"That's hardly fair." Ruth set down her cup. She could see by the cool, set look on his face that his mind was already made up. "If you'd had a show scheduled to conflict with mine, you wouldn't have missed it, and I wouldn't have expected you to."

"You're not willing to make adjustments for me or for my work."

Ruth thought of the parties and functions she had attended at his insistence. "I give you what I can, Donald. You knew my priorities when we started seeing each other."

Donald stopped stirring his coffee and set the spoon on the table. "It isn't enough," he said coldly. Ruth felt her stomach tighten. "I want you with me tonight."

Her brow lifted. "An ultimatum?"

"Yes."

"I'm sorry, Donald." Her voice was low but without apology. "I can't."

"You won't," he countered.

"It hardly matters which way you put it," she said wearily.

"I'll be taking Germaine to the showing tonight."

Ruth looked at him. His choice showed a certain shrewdness. His biggest competitor would probably be more useful to him than a dancer.

"I've taken her out a few times recently," he explained. "You've been busy."

"I see." Ruth's response was noncommittal, although his words hurt.

"You've been too self-absorbed lately. There's nothing for you in your life but ballet. You refuse to make room in it for me, for any man. You've a selfish streak, Ruth. Class after class after class, with rehearsals and performances thrown in. Dancing's all you have, all you want."

His words shocked her at first, then cut. Ruth fumbled behind her for her purse, but Donald caught her arm.

"I'm not finished." He held her firmly in her chair.

"You stand in front of those mirrors for hours, and what do you see? A body that waits to be told what to do by a choreographer. How often do you move on your own, Ruth? How often do you feel anything that isn't programmed into you? What will you have when the dancing stops?"

"Please." She bit down hard on her lip, trying without success to stop a flow of tears. "That's enough."

He seemed to focus on her face all at once. On a sharp breath, Donald released her arm. "Damn it, Ruth, I'm sorry."

"No." Frantically shaking her head, she pushed back her chair and rose. "Don't say any more." In a flash, she darted out the door.

The steamy summer air struck her like a blast. For a moment she looked up and down the street, confused, before turning toward the studio.

She hurried past the sea of strangers. The barbs that Donald had aimed had struck home—struck deep. Was she just an automaton? An empty body waiting to be filled by the bid of choreographers and composers? Was that how people from the outside saw her—as a ballerina on a music box, pirouetting endlessly until the music stopped?

She wondered how much truth had been in his angry words. Bursting through the front door of the building, she headed straight for her dressing room.

Once inside, she closed her door and leaned back against it. She was shaking from head to foot. A few short remarks from Donald had dehumanized her. Ruth moved slowly to her mirror and switched on all the lights. With hard, searching eyes, she studied her face.

Had her love and devotion for dancing made her selfish and one-dimensional? Was she really unable to feel deeply for a man, to make a positive commitment?

Ruth pressed her hands to her cheeks. The skin was soft, smooth, the scent on her hands was feminine. *But was she?* Ruth could read the panic in her eyes. Where did the dancer end and the woman begin? She shook her head and turned away from her own image.

Too many mirrors, she thought suddenly. There were too many mirrors in her life, and she was no longer certain what they reflected. What would she be in a decade, when the dancer faced the twilight of her career? Would memories and clippings be all she had?

Closing her eyes, Ruth forced herself to take several long breaths. She had three hours until curtain. There was no time to dwell on problems. She would look for the answers after the performance.

Deciding what she needed was the lunch that had been so recently pushed aside, Ruth went down to the canteen for tea and an apple. The simple familiarity of the place helped level her. There were complaints about strained muscles, impossible dance combinations, Nadine's tight purse strings and the uncertain state of the plumbing on the fourth floor. By the time she was back at her dressing room door, she was steadier.

"Ruth!"

She looked over her shoulder as she placed her hand on the knob.

"Hello, Leah." Ruth tried to drum up some enthusiasm upon seeing the elegant blond dancer.

"Your reviews are marvelous." Leah eased her way into the dressing room as Ruth opened the door and entered. Too well, she knew the blonde's penchant for stirring up trouble. Ruth felt she had had her fair share for one day.

"Roses for the whole ballet," Ruth agreed, walking over to take a seat at her dressing table as Leah settled into a chair. "But I don't imagine you found ballet reviews in there." She let her eyes fall on the tabloid Leah had in her hand.

"You never know whose name's going to pop up in here." She smiled at Ruth, then began thumbing through the paper. "I just happened to see a friend of yours mentioned in here. Let's see now, where...?" She trailed off as she scanned the print. "Oh, yes, here it is. 'Donald Keyser,'" she quoted, "'top designer, has been seen recently escorting his fiery-headed competitor, Germaine Jones. Apparently his interest in ballet has waned.'" Leah lifted her eyes, moving her lips into a sympathetic little smile. "Men are such pigs, aren't they?"

Ruth swallowed her temper. "Aren't they."

"And it's so demeaning to be dumped in print, too."

Ruth's spine snapped straight. Color flowed in, then out of her cheeks. "I was dumped in the flesh as well," she said with the calm of determination. "So it hardly matters."

"He was terribly good-looking," Leah commented, meticulously folding the paper. "Of course, someone else is bound to come along."

"Haven't I told you about the Texan?" Ruth surprised herself, but the blank, then curious expression on Leah's face was motivation enough to maintain the pretense.

"Texan? What Texan?"

"Oh, we've been keeping a low profile," Ruth ad-libbed airily. "He can't afford to have his name splashed around in print until the divorce is final. Just piles of money, you know, and his second wife's not being very cooperative." She managed a slow smile. "You wouldn't believe the settlement. He offered her the villa in southern Italy, but she's holding out for his art collection. French impressionists."

"I see." Leah narrowed her eyes to a feline slit. "Well, well, aren't you the quiet one."

"Like a sphinx."

"You'll have to be careful how much Nick finds out," Leah warned, then ran the tip of her tongue over her top lip. "He really detests nasty publicity. He'll want to be particularly careful now that he's finalizing plans for that big special on cable television."

"Special?" Ruth echoed.

"Didn't you know?" Leah looked pleased again. "Featuring the company, of course, and spotlighting the principal dancers. I'll do Aurora, naturally, probably the wedding scene. I believe Nick plans to do a *pas de deux* from *Le Corsaire*, and, of course, one from *The Red Rose*. He hasn't chosen his partners yet." She paused deliberately and smiled. "We have two full hours of air time. Nick's very excited about filling it." She slanted Ruth a glance. "Strange he hasn't mentioned it to you, but perhaps he thought you wouldn't be up to it after the strain of these last few weeks."

Leah rose to leave. "Don't worry, darling, he'll be making the announcement in a few days. I'm sure he'll use you somewhere." She dropped the paper into the chair. "Dance well," she said and left, closing the door quietly behind her.

Chapter 7

Ruth sat staring at the closed door for several long minutes. How could Leah know about such an enormously important project and she be left in the dark? *Unless Nick intended to exclude her.*

She knew she and Nick were having their personal problems, but professionally... Professionally, she remembered, she had told him that after this run she'd never dance with him again. Ruth recalled her own words and knew she had meant them, at least at that moment. But did that mean she was not to be partnered by anyone else? Could Nick be so vindictive?

Ruth knew that she was a good dancer. Would Nick drop her for personal reasons? After all, she had threatened him. Ruth closed her eyes and tried to control the rising sickness in her stomach.

He had barely spoken to her since that night. Was

this his way of punishing her for claiming not to want or need him as a partner? Would he let someone else dance Carlotta? The thought was more than Ruth could bear. Over and over she told herself she was a fool to allow herself to grow so attached to a part. Many other women would become Carlotta; she had simply been the first. Yet Ruth knew she had had a hand in creating the role as much as Nick had. She had put her soul into it.

Opening her eyes, Ruth looked directly at the copy of *Keyhole* that was left on the chair. Leah had done her work well, Ruth realized on a long breath. She had wanted to upset Ruth before the performance, and she had succeeded. Everything Donald had said—every feeling of doubt and inadequacy—had been reinforced. Now she feared that Nick would release her from the company when *The Red Rose*'s engagement was finished.

Ruth buried her face in her hands a moment and tried to push it all away. She had a performance to give; nothing could interfere with that. She was a dancer. That couldn't be taken from her.

Less than an hour later Ruth stepped out of her dressing room to warm up backstage. Still shaken, she tried to focus all her power of concentration on the role she was to portray. On another night she would have left Ruth Bannion behind in the dressing room. But not this time. Tonight Carlotta's free-spirited confidence and verve would be difficult to capture.

Ruth loosened her muscles automatically, trying to block out Donald's and Leah's words, but they continued to play through her thoughts.

The sounds of the orchestra tuning brought her back to the moment. It all felt wrong—the costume, the lights, the whine of strings as they were tested. She was cold, numb. She forgot the first movements of the ballet.

Nick came out of his dressing room. His eyes sought Ruth. It was a habitual practice of his, and it annoyed him. A sign of weakness in himself, however slight, irritated him. Ruth Bannion was becoming a weakness. She was as cool as autumn offstage and as sultry as summer on it. The transition was playing havoc with his nerves. He didn't care for it one bit.

It was difficult to deal with desire that would not abate even when she appeared to be indifferent to him, then challenged him to take her the moment she moved on stage. No woman had made him feel curb and spur at the same time before.

Nick could see the tension in her back, although he couldn't see her face. Her body spoke volumes. "Ruth."

Her already tense shoulders went rigid at the sound of his voice. Slowly, fighting to compose her features, she turned. Something flickered over his face before it became closed and still.

"What's wrong?"

"Nothing." Ruth hoped her voice sounded casual. She didn't flinch when he took her chin in his hand to study her face. Beneath the makeup her skin was pale, her eyes dark and miserable.

"Are you ill?" Had there been concern in his voice, she might have collapsed.

"No."

Nick gave her a long, thorough study before dropping his hand. "Then snap out of it. You have to dance in a moment. If you had a fight with your boyfriend, your tears have to wait."

He heard her sharp intake of breath, saw the simultaneous cloud of hurt in her eyes. "I'll dance, don't worry. No one you've got lined up to replace me will ever dance this part better."

Nick's gaze narrowed as he curled his fingers around her arm. "What are you talking about?"

"Don't." Ruth jerked her arm free. "I've had enough dumped on me tonight. I don't need any more." Her voice broke, and cursing herself, Ruth walked to the wings to wait for her cue. She took long, steadying breaths and forced as much as possible out of her mind.

Her opening dance did not go well. Ruth comforted herself, as she stood again in the wings, that only the sharpest eyes would have detected any flaws. Technically her moves had been perfect, but Ruth knew a dancer had to give more than body to the dance. Her mind and heart had not flowed with her. Her inability to give her best shook her all the more.

She made her second entrance and moments later was dancing with Nick.

"Put some life into it," he demanded in low tones as she spun in a double *pirouette*. He lifted her into an *arabesque*. "You dance like a robot."

"Isn't that what you want?" she hissed back. *Jeté, jeté, arabesque,* and she was back in his arms.

"Be angry," he murmured, lifting her again. "Hate me, but think of me. *Of me.*"

It was difficult to think of anything else. His eyes alone demanded it throughout the performance. Ruth's nerves were stretched to the breaking point by the last act. Emotions were churning inside her until she feared she would be physically sick. Never before had she prayed for a performance to end. Her head pounded desperately, but she fought to the finish. She sagged against Nick when the curtains closed.

"You said you weren't ill." He took her by the shoulders. Ruth shook her head. "Can you take curtain calls?"

"Yes. Yes, of course." She tried to pull out of his arms. He resisted her efforts, then, when her eyes lifted questioningly to his, he released her to take her hand.

The applause was muffled against the heavy curtain, but with a nod from Nick, the drape was lifted. The applause was thunderous. Ruth winced at the volume of noise. Again and again she made her curtsies, hanging on to the knowledge that the long day was almost at an end.

"Enough," Nick said curtly when the applause battered against the curtain yet again. He began to lead her offstage left.

"Nick," Ruth began, confused because her dressing room was in the opposite direction.

"Ms. Bannion is ill," he told the stage manager as they brushed past. "She goes home. She sees no one."

"Nick, I can't," Ruth protested. "I have to change."

"Later." He all but pushed her into the elevator. "We're going up to my office." He punched a button, and the doors slid shut. "We'll talk."

"I can't," Ruth began in rising panic. "I won't."

"You will. For now, be quiet. You're shaking."

Because she knew he wasn't above force to get his own way, Ruth subsided when the doors opened and he propelled her down the hall. The entire floor was dark and deserted. Without the least hesitation, he located the door to his office. Pushing her through, Nick flipped on the lights, then closed and locked the door. "Sit," he ordered shortly, then moved to a low, ornate cabinet.

Ruth had rarely been inside the room. It bespoke a different aspect of Nikolai Davidov, the dancer, the choreographer. This was his executive domain. Here he dealt with the rich, urging money from them to keep the company alive. Ruth could easily imagine him sitting behind the huge, old oak desk, radiating charm and coaxing dollars from patrons. Hadn't she heard Nadine state that Nick was as valuable to the company behind a desk as he was on stage?

Charm. Charisma. That generous, intimate smile that made it impossible to say no. Yes, it was a talent, just as double *tours en l'air* required talent. And style. What was talent without style? Davidov had an abundance of both.

Ruth glanced around the stately office with its old, tasteful furniture and fat, leather chairs. How many thousands of dollars had begun their journey in this office from silk-lined pockets to props, costumes and lights? What elegant balletomane had paid for the costume she was wearing at that moment?

"I said *sit*."

Nick's curt order broke into Ruth's thoughts. She turned, but before she could speak, she found herself being turned toward the sofa. The unarguable pressure on her shoulder convinced her to sit. A brandy snifter, a quarter full, was thrust into her hands.

"Drink." So saying, Nick moved back to the cabinet

for his own brandy. When he was sitting next to her, Nick leaned back into the curve of the sofa arm and watched her. A lift of his brow repeated his order, and Ruth sipped at the brandy.

Silently, he continued to study her while he swirled his own. The quiet was absolute. Ruth drank again, focusing her entire concentration on a scar in the wood of his desk.

"So." The word brought her eyes flying back to his face. He kept his own on hers while he lifted his glass. "Tell me," he ordered.

"There's nothing to tell."

"Ruth." He glanced down at the liquor in his glass as if considering its vintage. "You know at times I am a patient man. This," he said and brought his eyes back to hers, "is not one of those times."

"I'm glad you clarified that." Ruth finished off the brandy recklessly, then set down the snifter. "Well, thanks for the drink." She hadn't even started to rise when his hand clamped over her wrist.

"Don't press your luck," he warned softly. He kept her prisoner while he leisurely sipped his drink. "Answers," he told her. "Now."

"May I have the question first, please?" Ruth kept her voice light, but her pulse betrayed her by beating fitfully against his fingers.

"What was wrong with you tonight?"

"I was a little off." She made an impatient move with her shoulders.

"Why?"

"It was a mood. I have them." She tried, without success, to free her arm. The ease with which he prevented this was infuriating. "Aren't I entitled to any privacy?" she demanded. "Any personal feelings?"

"Not when it interferes with your work."

"I can't dance on automatic." The passion she tried to control slipped into her voice. Her eyes flared with it. "No matter what anyone thinks. I'm not just a body that dances when someone plays the tune. Oh, let me go!" She tugged on her hand again. "I don't want to talk to you."

Ignoring this demand, Nick set down his glass. "Who puts these thoughts into your head?" He took her shoulders, keeping her facing him when she would have turned away. "Your designer?" Her expression gave her away even as she shook her head.

Nick swore quietly in Russian. He increased the pressure of his fingers. "Look at me," he demanded. "Don't you know nonsense when it falls on your ears?"

"He said I had no feelings," she said haltingly, trying to control the tears that thickened her voice and blurred her vision. "That my life, my emotions were all bound up in ballet and without it…" She trailed off and shook her head.

"What does he know?" Nick gave her a quick, exasperated shake. "He's not a dancer. How does he know what we feel? Does he know the difference between jumping and soaring?" There was another quick, concise oath. "He's jealous. He wants to cage you."

"He wants more than I've given him," Ruth countered. "He's entitled to more. I do care about him, but—" She pushed her hair back from her face with both hands.

"You're not in love with him," Nick finished.

"No. No, I'm not. Maybe I'm just not capable of that kind of feeling. Maybe he's right, and I—"

"Stop!" He shook her again, harder than before. Springing up, he prowled the room. Ruth heard him muttering in Russian as he paced. "You're a fool to let anyone make you believe such things. Because you are not in love with a man, you let him convince you you're less than a woman?" He made a sound of disgust and whirled back to her. "What's wrong with you? Where's your spirit? Your temper? If I had said such things to you, you wouldn't have allowed it!"

Ruth pressed her fingers to her temple and tried to rearrange her thoughts. "But you would never have said those things to me."

"No." The answer was quiet. Nick walked back to her. "No, because I know you, understand what's in you. We have this, you see." He took her hand and laced their fingers. Ruth stared at the joined hands. "You have your world and your designer has his. If there was love, you could live in both."

Ruth took a moment, carefully thinking over his words. "Yes, I'd want to," she said slowly. "I'd try to. But—"

"No. No buts. Buts tire me." He sank back down beside her, managing to make the inelegant movement graceful. "So you fought with your designer, and he said stupid things. Is this enough to make you pale and sick?"

"It didn't help to have my replacement shoved down my throat," Ruth shot back. "I didn't care for being taunted with a copy of *Keyhole* chatting about his new relationship an hour before curtain."

"Keyhole?" Nick frowned in confusion. "What is this *Keyhole?* Ah," he said, remembering before Ruth could elaborate. "The silly newspaper with the very bad pictures?"

"The silly newspaper that speculated Donald Keyser had lost interest in the ballet."

"Ah." Nick pressed his fingertips together. "He brought that by your dressing room?"

"No, not Donald…" Ruth broke off, alerted by the sharpening of his eyes. Quickly she moistened her lips and rose. "It doesn't matter; it was stupid to let it upset me."

"Stop." The quiet order froze her. "Who?" Ruth felt the warning feather up her spine. "Who brought the paper to you before the performance?"

"Nick, I—"

"I asked you a question." He rose, too. "It's inexcusable for a member of the company to deliberately set out to disturb another before a performance. I do not permit it."

"I won't tell you. No, I won't," she added firmly as she saw the temper leap into his eyes. "I should've handled it better. I will next time. In any case, there was something more than Donald that upset me tonight." Ruth stood her ground, not so much wanting to protect Leah but more unwilling to subject anyone to the full force of Davidov's temper. She knew he could be brutal.

"I want a name."

"I won't give you one. I can't." She touched his arm and found the muscles rigid. "I just can't," she murmured, using what power she knew her eyes possessed. "There's something more important that we have to settle."

He became very still. Ruth searched his face, but his expression was guarded. Whatever his thoughts, they remained his alone. Feeling the withdrawal, Ruth took her hand from his arm.

"What?"

Ruth caught herself before she moistened her lips again. Her heart was beginning to pound furiously against her ribs. "I think I'd like another brandy first."

She waited for an angry, impatient refusal, but after a brief hesitation he picked up the snifters and went back to the liquor cabinet. The only sound was the splash of liquid as it hit the glass. She accepted the drink when he offered it, then sipped. She took a deep breath.

"Do you plan to release me from the company?"

Nick's own snifter paused on the way to his lips. "What did you say?"

This time Ruth spoke more firmly. "I said, do you plan to release me from the company?"

"Do I look like a stupid man?" he demanded.

In spite of her tension, the incredulity in his tone made her smile. "No, Davidov."

"*Khorosho.* Good. For once, we agree." He flicked his wrist in angry confusion. "And since I am not a stupid man, why would I release from the company my finest ballerina?"

Ruth stared at him. Shock shot through her body and was plain on her face. "You never said that before," she whispered.

"Said what?"

Shaking her head, she pressed her fingers between

her brows, then turned away. "As long as I can remember, I've wanted to dance." Ruth gave a muffled laugh as tears began to flow. "All these years, I've pushed myself—for myself, yes—for the dance and for you. And you never said anything like that to me before." She took a small, shuddering breath. "After a day like this, after tonight's performance, you stand there and very casually tell me I'm the finest ballerina you have." Ruth wiped tears away with a knuckle. "Only you, Nikolai, would choose such a time."

Though she hadn't heard him move, Ruth wasn't surprised when his hands touched her shoulders. "If I hadn't said so before, I should have. But then, I haven't always considered words so very important."

Nick ran his fingers through her hair, watching the light glint on it. "You're very important to me. I will not lose you."

Ruth felt her heart stop beating. Then, like thunder, it began to roar in her ears. We're only speaking of the company, she reminded herself. Of dancing only. She turned.

"Will you replace me as Carlotta for television?"

"For television?" he repeated. He struggled, as he had to do from time to time, to think in precise English. "Do you mean the cable?" Reading the answer in her eyes, he continued. "But that is not yet finalized, how would you…?" He stopped. "So that's what you meant before you went on tonight. And this information, I imagine, came from the same person who brought you the little *Doorknob*?"

"*Keyhole,*" Ruth corrected, but he was swearing

suddenly in what she recognized as full-blown Russian rage.

"This is not permitted. I will not have my dancers sniping at each other before a performance. I will tell you this: What plans I made, and what casting I do, *I* do." He glared at her, caught up in fury. "My decision. *Mine.* If I chose you to dance Carlotta, then you dance Carlotta."

"I said I wouldn't dance with you again," Ruth began. "But—"

"I care *that* for what you said," Nick told her with a snap of his fingers. "If I tell you to dance with me, then you do. You have no say in this."

His temper was in full swing, and Ruth's flared to match it. "I have a say in my own life."

"To go or to stay, yes," he agreed. "But if you stay, you do as you're told."

"You haven't told me anything," she reminded him. "I have to hear of your big plans less than an hour before curtain. You've barely spoken to me in weeks."

"I've had nothing to say to you. I don't waste my time."

"You arrogant, insufferable pig! I've poured everything I have into this ballet. I've bled for it. If you think I'm going to let you hand it over to someone else without a fight, you *are* stupid. I don't care if it's a two-minute *pas de deux* or the whole ballet. It's mine!"

"You think so, little one?" His tone was deceptively gentle.

"I know so," she tossed back. "And don't call me little one. I'm a woman, and Carlotta's mine until I can't dance her anymore." She took a quick breath before continuing. "I'll be dancing her years after you're finished with Prince Stefan."

"Really?" He circled her throat with his hand and squeezed lightly. The meaning pierced through her fury. "And do you forget, *milaya,* who composed the ballet? Who choreographed it and cast you as Carlotta?"

"No. And don't you forget who danced it!"

"You have a lovely, slender neck," he murmured. His fingers caressed it. "Don't tempt me to break it."

"I'm too mad to be frightened of you, Davidov. I want a simple answer. Do I dance Carlotta on this special or not?"

His eyes roamed over her furious face. "I'll let you know. You've just under a week left in this run. We can discuss future plans when it's finished." He cocked a brow when she let out a furious sigh. "Incentive. Now you'll dance your heart out for me."

"You always know what to say, don't you, Nick?" Ruth started to turn away, but he stopped her.

Very slowly, very deliberately, he lowered his mouth until it hovered an inch above hers. After a long, breathless moment, his lips descended. He heard her draw in her breath at the contact. He could feel her pulse beat against his palm, but still he did not increase the pressure.

Caressingly, the tip of his tongue traced her lips until, with a quiet sigh, they parted and invited him to enter. He had never kissed her with such care before, with such aching tenderness. Was there a defense against such tenderness? Always before, there had been heat and fire and hints of fear. Now she felt nothing but mindless pleasure.

He nipped her bottom lip, stopping just before the point of pain, then he replaced his teeth with his tongue. There was a strong scent of stage makeup and sweat to mix with the taste of brandy. Weak and weightless, she let her head fall back, inviting his complete control.

Their lips clung a few seconds longer as he began to draw her away. Nick felt the quiet release of her breath as she opened heavy eyes to look at him. In them he saw that she was his. He had only to lower her to the couch or pull her to the floor. They were alone, she was willing. He could still taste her, a dark, wild honey flavor that taunted him.

"Little one," he murmured and slid his hand from her throat to stroke her cheek. "What have you eaten today?"

Ruth's thoughts were thrown into instant confusion. "Eaten?" she repeated dumbly.

"Yes, food." There was a hint of impatience in his voice as he scooped up his brandy again. "What food have you had today?"

"I…" Ruth's mind was a total blank. "I don't know," she said finally with a helpless gesture. Her body was still throbbing.

"When's the last time you had a steak?"

"A steak?" Ruth ran a hand through her hair. "Years," she decided with an exasperated laugh.

"Come, you need a good meal." He held out a hand. "I'll take you to dinner."

"Nick, I don't understand you." Bewildered, Ruth ignored his outstretched hand, but he took hers firmly in his and was soon pulling her toward the door.

"Five minutes to change."

"Nick." Ruth stopped in the doorway to study him. "Will I ever understand you?"

His brows lifted and fell at the question. "I'm Davidov," he said with a quick grin. "Is that not enough?"

She laughed shakily. "Too much," she answered. "Too much…"

Chapter 8

Dinner with Nick had been enjoyable but hardly illuminating. Looking back, Ruth realized that they hadn't
spoken of ballet at all. After a wild cab ride home, which
Nick had apparently enjoyed, he had deposited her at
her door with a very quick, passionless kiss.

Ruth had slept until the ring of her alarm clock the
following morning. Emotional exhaustion and rich food
had proven an excellent tranquilizer.

The next day, routine had taken over. Though her
mind still fretted for answers, Ruth knew Nick well
enough to realize he intended to make her wait for them.
The more she pressed, the more reticent he became.

As the two-week run of *The Red Rose* came to an
end, Ruth dealt with the familiar let-down feeling that
came with the completion of an engagement. She would

be in limbo for a time, waiting for Nick to assign her another role. It was one more unanswered question.

Ruth hung up Carlotta's costume on closing night and felt as though she was losing part of herself. She was in no mood to go to the cast party, though she knew she should at least put in an appearance.

I'd be lousy company, she told herself with a wry smile. No champagne tonight, she decided quickly as she creamed off her makeup. Just a huge glass of milk and an entire bag of cookies, all to myself. No one to share them with but Nijinsky. Ruth pulled on jeans. No brooding, just gorging.

"Come on in!" she called out when there was a knock on her door. She pulled a T-shirt down over her hips as Francie popped her head in.

"Where are you hiding?" she demanded. "They're already into the champagne."

"I'm skipping out," Ruth told her, picking up her purse.

"Oh, but you can't." Francie was still in full costume and make-up. Her darkened lips pouted. "I want you to meet my neurosurgeon."

"Can't tonight." Ruth shot her a grin and a wink. "Big plans."

"Oh?" Francie drew out the word knowingly. "Why didn't you bring him by?"

"I'm not sharing with anyone," she told her. She let out a big, anticipatory sigh. "All mine."

"Wow." Francie's brows shot up. "What's he like?"

"Delicious." Ruth couldn't resist as she swung through the door. "Absolutely delicious."

"Have I seen him?" Francie called out, but Ruth just laughed and dashed for the stage door.

Two hours later Ruth sat in a living room chair. Nijinsky lay sprawled at her feet, belly up, his front paws posed like a fighter's, ready to lead with the left.

Ruth yawned. The old movie on TV wasn't holding her attention. Still she was glad she had slipped out on the party. Her mood had been wrong. The crowds and the laughter and the company jokes would have depressed her, while the solitary time had lifted her spirits. She thought of taking the free hours she would have the next day to go shopping for something useless. Nick would be working her again soon enough. It might be fun to rummage through antique shops for a candle snuffer or pillbox.

Closing her eyes, she stretched luxuriously. Maybe this was the time to steal a couple of days and drive up to see Lindsay and Seth. She frowned when Nick's image flew into her mind.

His quiet, gentle kiss had cracked the very foundations of her defense against him. For days she hadn't allowed herself to think of him in anything but professional terms. He was the main reason, she was finally forced to admit, that she hadn't been able to face the cast party.

She wanted him. No matter how many times, over the past days and weeks, she had refused to accept that thought, her desire simply hadn't changed. But yes, it had—she wanted him more. The longing was difficult enough, but when hints of something else, something more complicated, intruded, Ruth tightly closed the door on it.

"I'm too tired to think about that now," she told a totally disinterested Nijinsky. "I'm going to bed." When he made no sign of acknowledgment, Ruth rose and stepped over him to switch off the television. Leaving the plate of cookie crumbs for morning, she flicked off all the lights on her way to bed.

Nick stared up at the dark windows of Ruth's apartment. It's one o'clock in the morning, and she's asleep. If I had any brains, I'd be asleep, too, he said fiercely to himself.

He jammed his hands into his pockets and started to walk. You've no business here, Davidov, he told himself. You've known that all along. The night was cooling with the first true hint of fall. He hunched his shoulders against it. He'd been an idiot to come. He had told himself that over and over as he had steadily walked the blocks to her apartment building.

If she had been at the party, if he could just have looked at her... Oh, God, he thought desperately, he was long past the time when looking was enough. The nights were driving him mad, and no other woman would do. He needed Ruth.

How long had it been going on? he demanded of himself, never giving a glance as a police car sped by, sirens screaming. A month, a year? Five years? Since that moment in Lindsay's studio when he had first watched Ruth at the barre? He should have known, with that first impossible stir of desire. Good Lord, she'd only been seventeen!

How was he to have known she would taste that way when he kissed her? Or that she would respond as if she had only been sleeping—waiting for him? How was he to have known that the sight of that small, slim body would torment him day after day, night after night? Even when he danced with her, the thought of taking her, of having her melt against him, throbbed through him until he knew he would go mad. He began to walk away.

Nick stopped and turned around. Good God, he wanted her. Now. Tonight.

The banging at her door had Ruth sitting straight up in bed. What was the dream she had been having? *Nick?* She shook her head to clear it. Even as she reached for the clock, the banging started again. Sliding from the bed, she groped for her robe.

"I'm coming!" she called, urged to hurry by the ferocity of the banging. Pulling the robe on as she went, she rushed through the darkened apartment. "For heaven's sake, you're going to wake the neighborhood!" Ruth peered through the peephole, blinked and peered again. She fumbled for the chain; he pounded again.

They stared at each other when the door was opened. Ruth stood bewildered by the traces of temper she saw in his eyes. Her hair was a riot of confusion over the hastily drawn on robe. Her cheeks were still flushed with sleep, her eyes heavy. Nick took a step forward, knowing he had crossed over the line.

"I need you."

Her heart skidded at the three simple words spoken quietly, roughly, as if they fought to be said. Before she knew what she was doing, Ruth held out her arms to him.

Then they were pressed together, mouth to mouth. The hunger was raw, unbelievably strong. It was a devouring kiss—long, desperate, deep. Ruth clung to the wildness of it. She felt his hand tighten its grip on her hair, pulling her head back as if in fury. His mouth left hers only to change angles and probe deeper. There was a hint of brutality, as if he would assuage all his needs by a single kiss.

"I want you." It was a groan from well within him as he drew her away. His eyes were dark and burning. "God, too much."

Ruth gripped the front of his sweater until her fingers hurt. "Not too much," she whispered. She drew him inside.

Her throat was dry with the pounding of her heart as she closed the door and turned to him. They were only silhouettes as they stood, inches apart, in the dark.

She swallowed, sensing his struggle for control. It wasn't control she wanted from him. Not tonight. She wanted him to be driven—for her, by her. The overwhelming need to have him touch her was terrifying. Slowly, hardly conscious of her actions, Ruth reached up to draw the robe from her shoulders. She let it slide soundlessly to the floor as it left her naked.

"Love me," she murmured.

She heard his low groan of surrender as he drew her into his arms. His mouth was hot, his hands rough and possessive. She could feel the urgency of his need.

Ruth tugged at his sweater as they moved toward the bedroom. Somewhere in the hallway she pulled it over his head and threw it to the floor. His muscles flowed under her hands.

They were at the bedroom door when she fumbled with the snap of his jeans. She felt his stomach suck in as her fingers glided over it and heard the hoarse, muffled Russian as his teeth nipped into her shoulder. His hips were narrow, the skin warm. He dug his fingers into her back when she touched him.

"Milenkaya," he said and managed a rough laugh. "Let me get my shoes off."

"I can't." The need was overpowering. She'd already waited so long. "Lie with me." She pulled him toward the bed. "Take me now, Nick. I'll go mad if you don't."

Then they were naked, and he was on top of her. Ruth could hear his heart's desperate race, his ragged breath against her ear. He was trembling, she realized, as he entered her. Her body took over, knowing its own needs, while her mind shuddered with the onslaught of sensations. One moment she was strong, the next weak and spent. Nick lay atop her, his face buried in her hair.

"Sweet God, Ruth." He heaved out the words on labored breaths. "Untouched. Untouched and I take you like a beast!" Nick rolled from her, running a hand through his hair. When he sat up, Ruth could see just the outline of his chest and shoulders, the glimmer of his eyes. "I should have known better. There's no excuse for it. I must have hurt you."

"No." She felt drugged and dizzy, but there was no pain. "No."

"It should never have been like this."

"Are you saying you're sorry this happened?"

"Yes, by God!"

The answer hurt, but she sat up and spoke calmly. "Why?"

"It's obvious, isn't it?" He rose. "I come to your door in the middle of the night and push you into bed without the smallest show of..." He groped for a word, struggling for the English equivalent of his meaning.

"Pushed me into bed?" Ruth repeated. "And of course, I had nothing to do with it." She kneeled on the bed and tossed back her hair. Nick saw the glimmer of her angry eyes. "You conceited ass! Who pushed whom into bed? Let's just get the facts straight, Davidov. *I* opened the door, *I* told you what I wanted, *I* took your clothes off. So don't act like this was all your idea. If you want to be sorry you made love with me, go right ahead." She continued to storm before he could open his mouth to speak. "But don't hide behind guilt just because I was a virgin. I was a virgin because I wanted to be. I chose the time to change it. *I* seduced *you!*" she finished furiously.

"Well." Nick spoke again after a long moment of silence. "It seems I've been put in my place."

Ruth gave a short laugh. She was angry and hurt and still throbbing. "That'll be the day."

Nick walked back to the bed and touched her hair with his hand. There were times he thought it would be easier to speak in Russian. His feelings were more clearly articulated in his native tongue.

"Ruth, it is sometimes, when I am upset, difficult to make myself understood." He paused a moment, working out the way to make himself clear. "I'm not sorry to have made love with you. This is something I've wanted for a very long time. I am sorry that your first experience in love had to be so lacking in romance. Do you see?" He cupped her face in his hands and lifted it.

"This was not the way to show an innocent the delights of what a man and woman can have."

Ruth looked at him. She could see more clearly now as her eyes grew accustomed to the dark. His face was a pale shadow, but his eyes were vital and alive. She felt the warmth flowing back. She smiled.

"There's another way?" she asked, keeping the smile from her voice.

His fingers traced her cheekbones. "Many other ways."

"Then I think you owe it to me to show me." She slipped her arms around his neck. "Now."

"Ruth—"

"Now," she repeated before she pressed her mouth to his. With a groan, Nick let her taste fill him again. He lingered over the kiss, exciting her with his lips and teeth and tongue. Ruth felt her blood begin to swim.

Gently, so that his thumbs just brushed her nipples, he cupped her breasts. They were small and firm and smooth. The points were taut, and he stroked easily until he heard her breath quicken. Taking his mouth to her ear, he whispered words that meant nothing to her. But the sound of them, the flutter of warm breath, dissolved her. He slid his hands to her back, supporting her as she kneeled on the bed. Already she was trembling, but he used only his lips to entice—waiting, waiting.

Slowly, with infinite care, he began to stroke her until her skin was hot against him. He seemed to find the skin on the inside of her thighs irresistible. Again and again he returned there with teasing touches. Once he caressed the triangle between her legs, and her body shuddered as she pressed against his hand. But he retreated to mold her hips and take her deep with a kiss.

The sound of her own breathing was shouting in her ears. As he pressed her back on the bed, she moaned his name.

"There's more, *milaya*," he murmured, feasting on the flavor of her throat. "Much more."

Her breath caught in a gasp and a moan all at once as he took her nipple between his teeth. His tongue became moist as he suckled. Ruth pressed him closer, unaware of the seductive rhythm her body set under his. He took his mouth to her other breast, and shock coursed through her. She called for him mindlessly, steeped in sensation.

His mouth roamed lower and lower as his hands reached for her breasts, still hot and moist from his mouth. He guided her, as he had once guided her to music, setting the pace for their private *pas de deux*. Again he was the composer, she the dancer, moving to his imagination. Her mind was swept clean. She was utterly his.

She opened for him, and as he entered her, his mouth came greedily down on hers. He moved inside her slowly, ignoring the desperate pressure in his loins for his own release. He took her as though he had a lifetime to savor the ultimate pleasure.

Seconds, minutes, hours, they were joined until both were wild with need. With his mouth still fastened on hers, Nick took them both to the climax.

Drained, aching, Ruth lay tight against him, her head nestled on his chest. He stroked her hair now and then, winding the ends around his fingers. Under her ear Ruth could hear the deep, steady rhythm of his heart. There was no light through the windows. The room was dark and warm and silent.

This, she thought languidly, this is what I've been waiting for. This is the end of my privacy. He knows all my secrets now. Tonight I've given him everything I've ever held inside me. She sighed. "You won't go," she murmured, closing her eyes. "You won't go tonight?"

There was quiet for a moment, their own personal silence. "No," he said softly. "I won't go."

Content, Ruth curled against him and slept.

Chapter 9

Nijinsky leaped onto the bed, wanting his breakfast. He stared, slant-eyed, at Nick for a moment, then calmly padded over his legs and stomach to stand on his chest. Feeling the pressure, Nick stirred and opened his eyes to look straight into the cat's. They regarded each other in silence. Nick brought his hand up and obligingly scratched Nijinsky's ears.

"Well, *priyatel,* you seem to have no objection in finding me here?"

Nijinsky arched his back and stretched, then settled his full length on Nick's chest. Still absently scratching the cat's ears, Nick turned his head to look at Ruth.

She was curled tightly to his side. Indeed, his arm held her firmly there. Her hair looked thick and luxurious spread over the pillowcase. Her breathing was even and deep, her lips slightly parted. She looked impossibly young—too young to feel that wild desire she had shown him. She looked like the sleeping princess, but Nick knew she was more Carlotta than Aurora. She was more fire than flower. He bent down to kiss her.

Ruth awoke to passion, her body tingling into arousal. She sighed and reached for him as his hands began a sure, steady quest. Nijinsky, caught between them, made his disapproval vocal.

Ruth gave a throaty laugh as Nick swore. "He wants his breakfast," she explained. Her eyes were still sleepy as she smiled up at Nick. Experimentally, she lifted her hand to rub his chin with her palm. "I've always wanted to do that," she told him. "Feel a man's beard the first thing in the morning."

Nick slid his hand down to fondle her breast. "I prefer softer things. Your mouth," he specified, lowering his head to nibble at it. "Very soft, very warm."

Nijinsky padded forward to butt his head between theirs. Nick narrowed his eyes at the cat. "My affection for this creature," he stated mildly, "is rapidly fading."

"He likes to keep on schedule," Ruth explained. "He always wakes me right before the alarm goes off." On cue, the clock set off a low, monotonous buzz. "See?" She laughed as Nick reached over her and slammed the button in. "What first?" she asked him. "Shower or coffee?"

He leaned over her still, and his smile was slow. "I had something else in mind."

"Class," she reminded him and slipped quickly from the bed.

Nick watched her walk naked to the closet and pull out a robe. She was slim as a wand, with long legs and no hips—a boyish figure, had it not been for the pure femininity of her gait. As she reached inside the closet, he saw the small thrust of her breast under her outstretched arm. The robe passed over her, and she crossed it in front and belted it. She turned and smiled.

"Well?" she said, flipping her long hair out of the collar of the robe. "Do you want coffee?"

"You are exquisite," he murmured.

Ruth's hands faltered at the knot of the belt. She wondered if she would ever grow used to that tone of voice or that look in his eyes. She knew what would happen if she walked back to the bed. Her body began to tingle, as if his hands were already roaming it. Nijinsky growled.

"Since I'm the first up," she said, casting the cat a rueful glance, "I'll have the shower first." She arched her brows at Nick. "You can make the coffee." As she darted into the bath, she called over her shoulder, "Don't forget to feed the cat."

Ruth turned on the shower and stripped. Should it feel so right? she asked as she bundled her hair on top of her head. When I woke next to him, should I have felt that he simply belonged there? She had experienced no shyness, none of the awkwardness that she had been certain would have come with the morning after her first time. Ruth stepped under the shower and let the water hit her hot and strong.

But I knew it would be him. Somehow I always knew. Shaking her head, she reached for the soap. I must be crazy. How could I know it would be like this? She soaped herself and let her mind drift. They had had meals together between classes and rehearsals. They had been at the same parties. But there had never been any planned, conventional dates between them.

Should there have been? she wondered. Certainly last night had been no ordinary consummation of a typical relationship. Nick had seen her sweat and swear and rage, seen her weep. His hands had worked pain from her calves and feet. But she knew him only as well as he allowed himself to be known.

Ruth shut off the water. It was too soon, she decided, to explore her heart too deeply. She understood pain, had lived with it, but wouldn't deliberately seek it out. Nick could bring her pain. That, too, she had always known.

After toweling briskly, she slipped back into her robe and walked into the bedroom. She could hear Nick talking to Nijinsky in the kitchen. She smiled and began to pull leotards and tights from her drawer. There was something essentially right about Nick's voice carrying to her through the small apartment. She knew the cat would be much too busy attacking his breakfast to enjoy the conversation, but it pleased her. Another small bond. How many mornings had she held conversations with the disinterested cat?

Nick came into the bedroom with two steaming mugs in his hands. He was naked. His body was glorious; lean and muscled from the rigors of his profession. He strode into the room without the slightest hint of self-consciousness. Another man, Ruth mused, would have pulled on his jeans. Not Davidov.

"It's hot," he stated, setting both mugs down on the dresser before pulling Ruth into his arms. "You smell so good," he murmured against her neck. "The scent of you follows me everywhere."

His chin was raspy against her skin. She laughed, enjoying it.

"I must shave, yes?"

"Yes," Ruth agreed before she turned her mouth into the kiss. "It would hardly do for Davidov to come to class unshaven." They kissed again. His hands went to her hips to bring her closer.

"You have a razor?" He took his mouth to her ear.

"*Hmm.* Yes, in the medicine cabinet." Ruth let her fingers trail up his spine. She gave a muffled shriek when he bit her earlobe.

"The shaving will wait," he decided, drawing her away to pick up his coffee. He sipped and then rose.

"Will you have to go to your apartment for clothes?" Ruth watched the easy rhythm of his muscles before he disappeared into the bath.

"I have things at my office." She heard the shower spurt back to life. "And a fresh razor."

He sang in Russian in the shower. Music was an intrinsic part of him. She found herself humming along as she went into the bath to brush her teeth. "What does it mean?" she asked with a mouthful of toothpaste.

"It's old," he told her. "And tragic. The best Russian songs are old and tragic."

"I was in Moscow once with my parents." Ruth rinsed her mouth. "It was beautiful…the buildings, the snow. You must miss it sometimes."

Ruth didn't have time to scream when he grabbed her and pulled her into the shower with him.

"*Nick!*" Blinded by streaming water, she pushed at

her eyes. Her clothes were plastered against her. "Are you crazy?"

"I needed you to wash my back," he explained, drawing her closer. "But now I think there is a better idea."

"Wash your back!" Ruth struggled against him. "You might notice, I'm fully dressed."

"Oh, yes?" He smiled affably. "That's all right, I'll fix that." He pulled the soaked leotard over her shoulders so that her arms were effectively pinned.

"I've already had my shower." Ruth laughed, exasperated, and continued to struggle.

"Now you can have mine. I'm a generous man."

He fastened his mouth on hers as the water poured over them.

"Nick." His hands were wandering, loosening clothes as they went. "We have class." But she had stopped struggling.

"There's time," he murmured, sighing deeply as he found her breast. "We make time."

He drew the tights down over her hips.

Arabesque, pirouette, arabesque, pirouette. Ruth turned and lifted and bent to the commands. The practice was rigorous, as always. Her body, like the bodies of the other students, was drenched with sweat. Every day, seven days a week, they went over and over the basic steps. Professionals. Class was as much a part of a professional dancer's life as shoes and tights.

The small, intimate details were drummed into their minds at the earliest age. Who noticed the two little steps before a *jeté?* Only a dancer.

Muscles must be constantly tuned. The body must

be constantly made to accept the unnatural lines of the dance. *Fifth position. Plié.* Even a day's respite would cause the body to revolt. *Port de bras.* The arms and hands must know what to do. A wrong gesture could destroy the line, shatter a mood. *Attitude.* Hold it—one, two, three, four....

"Thank you."

Company class was over. Ruth went for her towel to mop her face. A shower, she thought, wiping the sweat from her neck.

"Ruth."

She glanced up at Nick. He, too, was wet. His hair curled damply around his sweatband.

"Meet me downstairs. Five minutes."

"Five minutes?" Alerted, she slung the towel over her shoulders. "Is something wrong?"

"Wrong?" He smiled, then bent and kissed her, oblivious to the other members of the company. "What should be wrong?"

"Well, nothing." A bit confused, she frowned up at him. "Why, then?"

"You have nothing scheduled for today." It was a statement, not a question, but she still shook her head. "I've seen that I don't, either." He leaned close. "We're going to play."

A smile began to tug at her mouth. "Play?"

"New York is a very entertaining city, yes?"

"So I've heard."

"Five minutes," he repeated and turned away.

Ruth narrowed her eyes at his back. "Fifteen."

"Ten," Nick countered without stopping.

Ruth dove for her bag and dashed for the showers.

* * *

In somewhere under ten minutes Ruth came downstairs, freshly washed, clad in jeans and a loose mauve sweater. Her hair was as free as her mood. Nick was already waiting, impatient, parrying questions from two male soloists.

"I'll speak to him tomorrow," he said, moving away from them when he spotted Ruth. "You're late," he accused, propelling her toward the door.

"Nope. On the minute."

They pushed through the door together.

The noise level was staggering. Somewhere to the left a road crew was tearing up the sidewalk, and the jackhammer shot its machine-gunning sound through the air. Two cabs screeched to a halt in front of them, nose to nose. Their drivers rolled down the windows and swore enthusiastically. Pedestrians streamed by without notice or interest. From a window across the street poured the hot, harsh sounds of punk rock.

"An entertaining city, yes?" Nick slipped his hand through Ruth's arm to clasp hers. Looking down, he gave her a quick grin. "Today, it's ours."

Ruth was suddenly breathless. None of their years together, none of the wild, searing love-making, had had the impact of that one intimate, breezy look.

"Where—where are we going?" she managed, struggling to come to terms with what was happening to her.

"Anywhere," Nick told her and pulled her to him for a hard kiss. "Choose." He held her tight a moment, and Ruth found she was laughing.

"That way!" she decided, throwing her hand out to the right.

Summer had vanished overnight. The cooler air made the walking easy, and they walked, Ruth was sure, for miles. They investigated art galleries and bookstores, poking here, prodding there and buying nothing. They sat on the edge of a fountain and watched the crowds passing while they drank hot tea laced with honey.

In Central Park they watched sweating joggers and tossed crumbs to pigeons. There was a world to observe.

In Saks, Ruth modeled a glorious succession of furs while Nick sat, fingers steepled together, and watched.

"No," he said, shaking his head as Ruth posed in a hip-length blue fox, "it's no good."

"No good?" She rubbed her chin against the luxurious collar with an unconscious expression of sensual pleasure. "I like it."

"Not the fur," Nick corrected. "You." He laughed as Ruth haughtily raised her brows. "What model walks with her feet turned out like that?"

Ruth looked down at her feet, then grinned. "I suppose I'm more at home in leotards than furs." She did a quick *pirouette* that had the sales clerk eyeing her warily. "And it would be hot in class." She slipped it off, letting the satin lining linger over her skin.

"Shall I buy it for you?"

She started to laugh, then saw that he was perfectly serious. "Don't be silly."

"Silly?" Nick rose as Ruth handed the clerk the fur. "Why is this silly? Don't you like presents, little one?"

She knew he used the term to goad her, but she only gave him a dry look. "I live for them," she said throatily, for the clerk's benefit. "But how can I accept it when we've only just met?" With a smoldering glance, she caressed his cheek. "What would you tell your wife?"

"There are some things wives need not know." His voice was suddenly thickly Russian. "In my country, women know their place."

"Mmm." Ruth slipped her arm through his. "Then perhaps you'll show me mine."

"A pleasure." Nick gave the wide-eyed clerk a wolfish grin. "Good day, madam." He swept Ruth away in perfect Cossack style.

"Such wickedness," he murmured as they walked from the store.

"I just love it when you're Russian, Nikolai."

He cocked an eyebrow. "I'm always Russian."

"Sometimes more than others. You can be more American than a Nebraska farmer when you want to be."

"Is this so?" He looked intensely interested for a moment. "I hadn't thought about it."

"That's why you're so fascinating," Ruth told him. "You don't think about it, you just are." Her hand linked with his as they walked. "I've wondered, do you think in Russian and then have to translate yourself?"

"I think in Russian when I am…" He searched for the word. "Emotional."

"That covers a lot of ground." She grinned up at him. "You're often emotional."

"I'm an artist," he returned with a shrug. "We are entitled. When I'm angry, Russian is easier, and Russian curses have more muscle than American."

"I've often wondered what you were saying when you're in a rage." She gave him a hopeful glance, and he laughed, shaking his head. "You spoke to me in Russian last night."

"Did I?" The look he gave her had Ruth's heart in her throat. "Perhaps you could say I was emotional."

"It didn't sound like cursing," she murmured.

His hand was suddenly at the back of her neck, drawing her near. "Shall I translate for you?"

"Not now." Ruth calculated the distance between Fifth Avenue and her apartment. Too far, she thought. "Let's take a bus." She laughed, her eyes on his.

Nick grinned. "A cab," he countered and hailed one.

Sunlight flooded the bedroom. They hadn't taken the time to draw the blinds. They lay tangled together, naked and quiet after a storm of love-making. Content, Ruth drifted between sleep and wakefulness. Beneath her hand, Nick's chest rose and fell steadily; she knew he slept.

Forever, she thought dreamily. I could stay like this forever. She cuddled closer, unconsciously stroking his calf with the bottom of her foot.

"Dancer's feet," he murmured, and she realized that the small movement had awakened him. "Strong and ugly."

"Thanks a lot." She nipped his shoulder.

"A compliment," he countered, then shifted to look down at her. His eyes were sleepy, half-closed. "Great dancers have ugly feet."

She smiled at his logic. "Is that what attracted you to me?"

"No, it was the back of your knees."

Ruth laughed and turned her face into his neck. "Was it really? What about them?"

"When I dance with you, your arms are soft, and I wonder how the back of your knees would feel." Nick leaned up on his elbow to look at her. "How often have I held your legs—for a lift, to ease a cramp? But always there are tights. And what, I say to myself, would it be like to touch?"

Sitting up, he took her calf in his hand. "Here." His fingers slid up to the back of her knees. "And here." He saw her eyes darken, felt the pulse quicken where his fingers pressed. "So, I am nearly mad from wondering if the softness is everywhere. Soft voice, soft eyes, soft hair."

His voice was low now and quiet. "And I hold your waist to balance you, but there are leotards and costumes. What is the skin like there?" He trailed his hand up over her thigh and stomach to linger at her waist. His fingers followed the contours of her ribcage to reach her breast.

"Small breasts," he murmured, watching her face. "I've felt them pressed against me, seen them lift and fall with your breathing. How would they feel in my hand? What taste would I find there?" He lowered his mouth to let his tongue move lightly over her.

Ruth's limbs felt weighted, as though she had taken some heady drug. She lay still while his hands and mouth explored her, while his voice poured over her. He moved with aching slowness, touching, arousing, murmuring.

"Even on stage, with the lights and the music everywhere, I thought of touching you. Here." His fingers glided over her inner thigh. "And tasting. Here." His mouth moved to follow them. "You would look at me. Such big eyes, like an owl. I could almost see your thoughts and wondered if you could see mine." He pressed his lips against the firm muscles of her stomach and felt her quiver of response. "And what would you do, *milaya,* if you knew how I was aching for you?"

His tongue glided over her navel. She moaned and moved under him. She had never experienced pleasure such as this—a thick, heavy pleasure that made her body hum, that weighed on her mind until even thoughts were sensations.

"So long," he murmured. "Too long, the wanting went on. The wondering."

His hands, though still gentle, became more insistent. They broke through the dark languor that held her. Her body was suddenly fiercely alive. She was acutely aware of her surroundings: the texture of the sheet against her back, the tiny dust motes that spun in the brilliant sunshine, the dull throb of traffic outside the windows. There was an impossible clarity to everything around them. Then it spun into nothing but the hands and mouth which roamed her skin.

She could have been anywhere—in the show, in the desert; Ruth felt only Nick. She heard his breathing, more labored now than it would have been after a strenuous dance. Her own melded with it. With hard, unbridled urgency, he crushed his mouth to hers. His teeth scraped her lips as they parted for him.

The kiss deepened as his hands continued to drive her nearer the edge. Ruth clutched at him, lost in delight. Then he was inside her, and she was catapulted beyond reason into ecstasy.

"Lyubovnitsa." Ruth heard his voice come hoarsely from deep within him. "Look at me."

Her eyes opened heavily as she shuddered again and again with the simultaneous forces of need and delight.

"I have you," he said, barely able to speak. "And still I want you."

She crested on a mountainous peak. Nick buried his face in her hair.

Chapter 10

Francie caught Ruth's arm as they filed in for morning class. "Where'd you disappear to yesterday?" she demanded, pulling Ruth to the barre.

"Yesterday?" Ruth couldn't prevent the smile. "Oh, I went window shopping."

Francie shot her a knowing look. "Sure. Introduce him to me sometime." Her face grew thoughtful at Ruth's quick laugh, but she hurried on. "Have you heard the news?"

Ruth executed her *pliés* as the room began to fill with other company members. Her eyes drifted to Nick, who was in a far corner with several *corps* dancers. "What news?" Look how the sun hits his hair, she thought, as if it were drawn to it.

"The television thing." Francie set herself to Ruth's rhythm so that their heads remained level. "Didn't you hear anything?"

"Leah mentioned something." Ruth sought out the blonde as she remembered the preperformance visit. "I was told nothing was definite yet."

"It is now, kiddo." Francie was gratified to see Ruth's attention come full swing back to her.

"It is?"

"Nadine worked a whale of a deal." Francie bent to adjust her leg warmers. "Of course, she had the main man to dangle in front of their noses."

Ruth was fully aware that Francie spoke of Nick. Again her eyes traveled to him. He had his head together with Leah now. The ballerina was using her fluid hands to emphasize her words.

"What sort of deal?"

"Two hours," Francie said with relish. "Prime time. And Nick has virtually a free hand artistically. He has the name, after all, and not only in the ballet world. People who don't know a *plié* from a *pirouette* know Davidov. It's some kind of package deal where he agrees to do two more projects. It's him they want. Just think what this could mean to the company!"

Francie rose on her toes. "How many people can we reach in two hours on TV compared to those we reach in a whole season on stage? Oh, God, I hope I get to dance!" She lowered into a *plié*. "I'd almost be willing to go back into the *corps* for the chance. You'll do *The Red Rose*." She gave an envious sigh.

Ruth was glad it was time for class to begin.

It was difficult to concentrate. Ruth's body responded to the calls and counts while her mind dashed in a dozen directions. Why hadn't he told her?

Her hand rested on the barre as Madame Maximova

put them through their paces. Ruth was aware that Nick stood directly behind her.

They had been together all day yesterday—and this morning. He had never said a word. Would she dance? Her working leg came up and back in attitude. Will what's happened between us interfere?

As she moved out with the class for center practice, Ruth tried to think logically. It had been hardly a week since he had told her things were still unsettled. She struggled to remember what else he had said, what exactly his mood had been. He had been annoyed because her dancing had been below par—concern that she had been upset. He had been furious when she wouldn't divulge the name of the person who had leaked the information.

What had he done? Snapped his fingers and told her *that* was how much he cared for what she said. He played the tune, and she danced. It was as simple as that. Ruth frowned as she did the combination. But why did everyone seem to know about things before her? she wondered. One minute Nick would tell her she was the finest ballerina in the company, and the next, he didn't even bother to fill her in on what could be the most important company project of the year.

How do you figure out such a man? You don't, she reminded herself. Turning her head, she looked him straight in the eye. He's Davidov.

Nick met the look a bit quizzically, but the tempo suddenly increased from *adagio* to *allegro* and required their attention.

"Thank you," Madame Maximova said to the troupe of dripping bodies thirty minutes later. Her voice, Ruth thought fleetingly, was much more thickly Russian than Nick's, though she had been forty years in America.

"I'd like to see the entire company on stage in fifteen minutes."

Ruth lifted her eyes and caught Nick's in the glass as he made the announcement. The speculative buzzing began immediately. Dancers began to file out in excited groups. Davidov had spoken. Ruth hefted her bag over her shoulder and prepared to join them.

"One moment, Ruth." She stopped obediently at his words. Her training was too ingrained for anything else. He said something to the ballet mistress in quiet Russian which made her chuckle—a formidable achievement. With a brisk nod, she strode from the room as if her bones were a quarter of a century younger than Ruth knew them to be.

Nick crossed to Ruth, absently pulling his towel through his hands. "Your mind was not on class."

"No?"

He recognized her searching look. As usual, it disconcerted him. "Your body moved, but your eyes were very far away. Where?"

Ruth studied him for another moment as she turned over in her mind the best way to broach the subject. She settled on directness. "Why didn't you tell me about the television plans?"

Nick's brow lifted. It was a haughty gesture. "Why should I have?"

"I'm a principal dancer with the company."

"Yes." He waited a beat. "That doesn't answer my question."

"Everyone else seems to know the details." Exasperated, she flared at him. "I'm sure they're avidly discussing it in the *corps*."

"Very likely," he agreed, slinging the towel over his shoulders. "It's hardly a secret, and secrets are always avidly discussed in the *corps*."

"You might have told me yourself," she fumed, pricked by his hauteur. "I asked you about it last week."

"Last week it was not finalized."

"It was certainly finalized yesterday, and you never said a word."

She saw his lids lower—a danger signal. When he spoke, his cool tone was another. "Yesterday we were just a man and a woman." He lifted his hands to the ends of the towel, holding them lightly. "Do you think because we are lovers I should give you special treatment as a ballerina?"

"Of course not!" Ruth's eyes widened in genuine surprise at the question. The thought had simply never occurred to her. "How could you think so?"

"Ah." He gave a small nod. "I see. I'm to trust and respect your integrity, while mine is suspect."

"I never meant—" she began, but he cut her off with that imperious flick of the wrist.

"Get your shower. You've only ten minutes now." He strode away, leaving her staring and open-mouthed.

When Ruth dashed into the theater, members of the company were already sitting on the wide stage or pocketed together in corners. Breathless, she settled down next to Francie.

"So." Nick spared her a brief glance. "We seem to be all here now."

He was standing stage center with his hands tucked

into the pockets of dull gray sweat pants. His hair was still damp from his shower. Every eye was on him. Nadine sat in a wooden chair slightly to his right in a superbly tailored ice blue suit.

"Most of you seem to know at least the bare details of our plans to do a production for WNT-TV." His eyes swept the group, passing briefly over Ruth, then on. "But Nadine and I will now go over the finer points." He glanced at Nadine, who folded her hands and began.

"The company will do a two-hour presentation of ballet, in vignette style. It will be taped here over a two-week period beginning in one month. Naturally, we plan to include many dances from the ballets in our repertoire. Nick and I, along with Mark and Marianne." She glanced briefly at two choreographers, "have outlined a tentative program. We will, of course, work with the television director and staff on time allowances and so forth." She paused a moment for emphasis. "I needn't tell you how important this is to the company and that I expect the best from every one of you."

Nadine fell silent. Nick turned to pick up a clipboard he had left on a tree stump prop from a forest scene in *Sleeping Beauty*.

"Rehearsals begin immediately," he stated and began to read off the list of dances and roles and rehearsal halls.

It was a diversified program, Ruth concluded, trying not to hold her breath. From Tchaikovsky's *Nutcracker*—Francie gave a muffled squeal when her name was called to dance the Sugar Plum Fairy—to de Mille's *Rodeo*. Obviously, Nick wanted to show the variety and universality of ballet.

Choreographers were assigned, scenes listed. Ruth moistened her lips. Leah was Aurora and Giselle, two plum roles but fully expected. Keil Lowell was to partner Leah both as Prince Charming and as Albrecht. A young *corps* member began to weep softly as she was given her first solo.

Nick continued to read without glancing up. "Ruth, the *grand pas de deux* from *The Red Rose* and the second act *pas de deux* from *Le Corsaire*. I will partner."

Ruth let out her breath slowly and felt the tension ease from her shoulders.

"If time permits, we will also do a scene from *Carnival*."

He continued to read in his quiet, melodious voice, but Ruth heard little more. She could have wept like the young *corps* dancer. This was what she had worked for. This was the fruit of almost two decades of training. Yet even through the joy, she could feel Nick's temper lick out at her.

He doesn't understand, she thought, frustrated by his quick, volatile moods. And he's so pig-headed, I'll have to fight my way through to explain. Drawing her knees up to her chest, she studied him carefully.

Strange, she mused, for all his generosity of spirit, he doesn't give his trust easily. She frowned. *Neither do I,* she realized abruptly. We have a problem. She rested her chin on her knees. And I'm not sure yet how to solve it.

The next few weeks weren't going to be easy, personally or professionally. Personally, Ruth knew she and Nick would have to decide what they wanted from each other and what each could give. She tucked the problem away, a little awed by it.

Professionally, it would be a grueling time. Nick as a choreographer or director was difficult enough, but as a partner, he was the devil himself. He accepted no less than perfection and had never been gentle about showing his displeasure with anything short of it. Still, Ruth would have walked over hot coals to dance with him.

Rehearsals would be exhausting for everyone. The time was short, the expectations high, and a good portion of the company were performing *Sleeping Beauty* every night for the next two weeks. Tempers and muscles would be strained. They would be limping home at night to soak their feet in ice or hot baths. They would pull each other's toes and rub each other's calves and live on coffee and nerves. But they would triumph; they were dancers.

Ruth rose with the others when Nick finished. Seeing he was already involved with Nadine, she went to the small rehearsal hall he had assigned to her. She left the door open. Company members streamed down the corridor. There was talk and raised voices. Already the sound of music flowed out from another room down the hall. Stravinsky.

Ruth walked to a bench to change to her toe shoes. She looked at them absently. They would last two or three more days, she decided. They were barely a week old. Idly, she wondered how many pairs she had been through already that year. And how many yards of satin? She crossed the ribbon over her ankle and looked up as Nick walked into the room. He closed the door behind him, and they were cut off from music and voices.

"We do *Le Corsaire* first," he stated, crossing the room to sit on the bench. "We work without an accompanist for now. They are at a premium, and I have still to block it out." He pulled down his sweat pants so that he wore only tights and the unitard.

"Nick, I'd like to talk to you."

"You have a complaint?" He slipped leg warmers over his ankles.

"No. Nick—"

"Then you are satisfied with your assignment? We begin." He rose, and Ruth stood to face him.

"Don't pull your *premier danseur* pose on me," she said dangerously.

He lifted his brow, studying her with cool blue eyes. "I am *premier danseur.*"

"You're also a human being, but that isn't the point." She could feel the temper she had ordered herself to restrain running away with her.

"And what," he said in a tone entirely too mild, "is the point?"

"What I said this morning had nothing to do with the casting." She put her hands on her hips, prepared to plow her way through the wall he had thrown up between them.

"No? Then perhaps you will tell me what it had to do with. I have a great deal to do."

Her eyes kindled. Her temper snapped. "Go do it then. I'll rehearse alone." She turned away, only to be spun back around.

"I say when and with whom you rehearse." His eyes were as hot as hers. "Now say what you will say so we can work."

"All right, then." Ruth jerked her arm from his hold. "I didn't like being kept in the dark about this. I think I should have heard it from you, straight out. Our being lovers has nothing to do with it. We're dance partners, professional partners. If you can tell half the company, why not me?" She barely paused for breath. "I didn't like the way I had to get tidbits, first from Leah, and then—"

"So, it was Leah," Nick interrupted her tirade with quiet words. Ruth let out a frustrated breath. Temper had betrayed her into telling him what she had promised herself she never would.

"It doesn't matter," she began, but the flick of his wrist stopped her again.

"Don't be stupid," he said impatiently. "There is no excuse for a dancer deliberately disturbing another before a performance. You won't tell me it was not intentional?" He waited, watching her face. Ruth opened her mouth and closed it again. She didn't lie well, even in the best of circumstances. "So don't pretend it doesn't matter," Nick concluded.

"All right," she conceded. "But it's done. There's no use stirring up trouble now."

Nick was thoughtful a moment. Ruth saw that his eyes were hard and distant. She knew very well he was capable of handing out punishment without compassion. "No," he said at length, "I have a need for her at the moment. We have no one who does Aurora so well, but…" His words trailed off, and Ruth knew his mind was fast at work. He would find a way of disciplining Leah and keeping his Aurora dancing. A whip in a velvet glove, Ruth thought ruefully. That was Davidov.

"In any case," she continued, bringing his attention back to her, "Leah isn't the point, either."

Nick focused on her again. "No." He nodded, agreeing to this. "You were telling me what was."

Calmer now, Ruth took a moment to curb her tongue. "I was upset when I heard this morning that things had been arranged. I suppose I felt shut out. We hadn't talked reasonably about dancing since the night we rehearsed together for *The Red Rose*. I was angry then."

"I wanted you," he said simply. "It was difficult."

"For both of us." Ruth took a deep breath. "I had never considered you would treat me differently professionally because we've become lovers. I couldn't stand to think you would. But I was nervous about the casting. I always am."

"That was perhaps an unwise thing for me to say."

Ruth smiled. Such an admission from Davidov was closer to an apology than she had hoped for.

"Perhaps," she agreed with her tongue in her cheek.

His brow lifted. "You still have trouble with respect for your elders."

"How's this?" she asked and stuck out her tongue.

"Tempting." Nick pulled her into his arms and kissed her, long and hard. "Now, I will tell you once so that it is understood." He drew her away again but kept his hands on her shoulders. "I chose you for my partner because I chose to dance with the best. If you were less of a dancer, I would dance with someone else. But it would still be you I wanted at night."

A weight was lifted from her shoulders. She was satisfied that Davidov wanted her for herself and danced with her because he respected her talent.

"Only at night?" she murmured, stepping closer.

Nick gave her shoulders a caress. "We will have lit-

tle else but the night for ourselves for some time." He
kissed her again, briefly, roughly, proprietarily. "Now
we dance."

They went to the center of the room, faced the mirrors and began.

Chapter 11

Days passed; long, exhausting days filled with excitement and disappointments. Ruth worked with Nick as he blocked out and tightened their *pas de deux* from *Le Corsaire*. The choreography must suit the camera, he told her. If the dance was to be recorded by a lens, it had to be played to the lens. This was a different prospect altogether from dancing to an audience. Even during their first improvised rehearsal Ruth realized Nick had done his homework. He worked hand in glove with the television director on angles and sequence.

Ruth's days were filled between classes and rehearsals, but her nights were often empty. Nick's duties as choreographer and artistic director kept him constantly busy. There were other rehearsals to oversee, more dances to be blocked out, budget meetings and late-night sessions with the television staff.

There was little time for the two of them at rehearsals. There they worked as dancer to dancer or dancer to choreographer, fitting movement to music. They argued, they agreed. *The Red Rose* posed little problem, though Nick altered a few details to better suit the new medium. *Le Corsaire* took most of their time. The part suited him perfectly. It was the ideal outlet for his creativity. His verve aroused Ruth's competitiveness. She worked hard.

He criticized tiny details like the spread of her fingers, praised the angle of her head and drove her harder. His vitality seemed to constantly renew itself, and it forced her to keep up or be left behind. At times she wondered how he did it: the endless dancing, the back-to-back meetings.

He had told her they would have the nights for each other, but so far that had not been the case. For the first time since she had moved into her apartment, Ruth was lonely. For as long as she could remember, she had been content with her own company. She walked to the window and opened the blinds to gaze out at the darkness. She shivered.

A knock at the door startled her, then she shook her head. No, it's not Nick, Ruth reminded herself as she crossed the room. She knew he had two meetings that night. She glanced through the peephole, then stood for several seconds with her hand on the knob. Taking a breath, she opened the door.

"Hello, Donald."

"Ruth." He smiled at her. "May I come in?"

"Of course." She stepped back to let him enter, then shut the door behind him.

He was dressed casually and impeccably in a leather jacket and twill trousers. Ruth realized suddenly that it had been weeks since they had last seen each other.

"How are you?" she asked, finding nothing else to say.

"Fine. I'm fine."

She detected a layer of awkwardness under his poise. It put her at ease. "Come, sit down. Would you like a drink?"

"Yes, I would. Scotch, if you have it." Donald moved to a chair and sat, watching Ruth pour the liquor. "Aren't you having one?"

"No." She handed him the glass before taking a seat on the sofa. "I've just had some tea." Absently, she passed her hand over Nijinsky's head.

"I heard your company's doing something for television." Donald swirled the Scotch in his glass, then drank.

"News travels fast."

"You're having some new costumes made," he commented. "Word gets around."

"I hadn't thought of that." She curled her legs under her. "Is your business going well?"

Lifting his eyes from the glass, Donald met hers. "Yes. I'm going to Paris at the end of the month."

"Really?" She gave him a friendly smile. "Will you be there long?"

"A couple of weeks. Ruth…" He hesitated, then set down his glass. "I'd like to apologize for the things I said the last time I saw you."

Her eyes met his, calm, searching. Satisfied, Ruth nodded. "All right."

Donald let out a breath. He hadn't expected such easy absolution. "I've missed seeing you. I'd hoped we could have dinner."

"No, Donald," she answered just as mildly. She watched him frown.

"Ruth, I was upset and angry. I know I said some hard things, but—"

"It isn't that, Donald."

He studied her, then let out a long breath. "I see. I should've expected there'd be someone else."

"You and I were never more than friends, Donald." There was no apology in her voice, nor anger. "I don't see why that has to change."

"Davidov?" He gave a quick laugh at her surprised expression.

"Yes, Davidov. How did you know?"

"I've eyes in my head," he said shortly. "I've seen the way he looked at you." Donald took another swallow of Scotch. "I suppose you're well-suited."

Ruth had to smile. "Is that a compliment or an insult?"

Donald shook his head and rose. "I'm not sure." For a moment he looked at her intensely. She met his gaze without faltering. "Good-bye, Ruth."

Ruth remained where she was. "Good-bye, Donald." She watched him cross the room and shut the door behind him.

After a few moments she took his half-filled glass into the kitchen. Pouring the Scotch down the sink, Ruth thought of the time they had spent together. Donald had made her happy, nothing more, nothing less.

Was it true that some women were made for one man? Was she one of them?

Another knock scattered her thoughts. She caught her bottom lip between her teeth. The last thing she wanted was another showdown with Donald. Resolutely, Ruth went to the door and fixed a smile on her face.

"Nick!"

He carried two boxes, one flat, one larger, and a bottle of wine. *"Privet, milenkaya."* He stepped over the threshold and managed to kiss her over the boxes.

"But you're supposed to be in meetings tonight." Ruth closed the door as he dropped the boxes on her dinette table.

"I cancelled them." He gave her a grin and pulled her against him. "I told you artists are entitled to be temperamental." He made up for his brief first kiss with a lingering one. "You have plans for tonight?" he murmured against her ear.

"Well…" Ruth let the word hang. "I suppose I could alter them—with the right incentive." It felt so good to be held by him, to feel his lips on her skin. "What's in the boxes?"

"Mmm. This and that." Nick drew her away. "That is for later," he said, pointing to the large box. "This is for now." With a flourish, he tossed open the lid of the flat one.

"Pizza!"

Nick leaned over, breathing in its aroma with closed eyes. "It is to die over! Go, get plates before it's cold."

Ruth turned to obey.

"I'll sweat it off you in rehearsal tomorrow." He picked up the wine. "I need a corkscrew."

"What's in the other box?" Ruth called out as she clattered dishes.

"Later. I'm hungry." When she came back, hands filled with plates and glasses, he was still holding the wine while stooping over to greet Nijinsky. "You'll have your share." Watching him, Ruth felt her heart expand.

"I'm so glad you're here."

Nick straightened and smiled. "Why?" He took the corkscrew from her fingers.

"I love pizza," Ruth told him blandly.

"So, I win your heart through your stomach, yes? It's an old Russian custom." The cork came out with a muffled pop.

"Absolutely." Ruth began busily to transfer pizza from box to plates.

"Then you'll bounce on stage like a little round meatball." Nick sat across from her and poured the wine. "It seems time permits for *Carnival* as well. You do Columbine."

"Oh, Nick!" Ruth, her mouth full of pizza, struggled to swallow and say more.

"The extra rehearsals will help to keep you from getting chubby."

"Chubby!"

"I don't want to strain my back in the lifts." He gave her a wicked smile.

"And what about you?" she asked sweetly. "Who wants to watch Harlequin with a paunch?"

"My metabolism," he told her smugly, "would never permit it." He wolfed down the pizza and reached for his wine. "I've been watching movies," he told her suddenly. "Fred Astaire, Gene Kelly. Such movement. With the right camera work we see all a dancer is. Angles are the key."

"Did you see *An American in Paris?*" Ruth finished off her slice and reached for the wine. "I'd love to do a time step."

"A new set of muscles," Nick mused, looking through her. "It would be interesting."

"What are you thinking?"

His eyes came back to hers and focused. "A new ballet with some of your typically American moves. It's for later." He shook his head as if filing the idea away. "So, have some more." He slid another piece onto Ruth's plate. "When one sins, one should sin magnificently."

"Another old Russian custom?" Ruth asked with a grin.

"But of course." He poured more wine into her glass.

They finished the pizza, giving the cat a whole piece for himself. Nick filled her in on the progress of rehearsals, dropping little bits of company gossip here and there to amuse her. When he began to question her about dance sequences in movies he hadn't seen, Ruth did her best to describe them.

"Are you thinking of writing this new ballet with television in mind?" she asked as they cleared the dishes. "For one of the other two projects you've agreed to do?"

"Perhaps." He was vague. "Nadine would like also a documentary on the company. It's being considered. I learned some when they taped *Ariel* and other ballets, but the cameras were always apart. Ah…" He groped for the word closer to his meaning. "Remote?" Satisfied, he continued. "This time they'll be everywhere, and this director has more knowledge of the dance than others I've worked with. It makes a difference," he concluded and smiled as Ruth handed him a dish to dry. "I've missed you."

Ruth looked up at him. They had been together for hours every day, but she knew what he meant. There was something steadying about standing together in the kitchen. "I've missed you, too."

"We can make a little time when this is over, before new rehearsals begin. A few days." Nick set down the dish and touched her hair. "Will you come with me to California?"

His house in Malibu, she thought and smiled. "Yes." Forgetting the dishes, she slipped her arms around his waist and held him. They were silent a moment, then Nick bent and kissed the top of her head.

"Don't you want to know what's in the other box?"

Ruth groaned. "I can't eat another thing."

"More wine?" he murmured, moving his lips down her temple.

"No." She sighed. "Just you."

"Come, then." Nick drew her away, then offered his hand. "It's been too long."

They walked from the kitchen, but Ruth's eyes fell on the unopened box. "What *is* in there?"

"I thought you weren't interested."

Unable to restrain her curiosity, Ruth lifted the lid. She stared and made no sound.

There, where she had expected some elaborate pastries or a huge cake, was the soft, thick pelt of the blue fox she had modeled in Saks. Touching it with her fingertips, she looked up at Nick.

"It's not fattening," he told her.

"Nick." Ruth made a helpless gesture and shook her head.

"It suited you best. The color is good with your hair." He caught a generous handful of Ruth's hair and let it fall through his fingers. "It's soft. Like you."

"Nick." Ruth took his hand in hers. "I can't."

He lifted a brow. "I'm not allowed to give you presents?"

"Yes, I suppose." She let out a little breath. "I hadn't thought of it." He was smiling at her, making it difficult to explain logically. "But not a present like this."

"I bought you a pizza," he pointed out and brought her hand to his lips. "You didn't object."

"That's not the same thing." She made a small, exasperated sound as his lips brushed her wrist. "And you ate half of it."

"It gave me pleasure," he said simply, "as it will give me pleasure to see you in the fur."

"It's too expensive."

"Ah, I can only buy you cheap presents." He pushed up her sleeve and kissed the inside of her elbow.

Her brows lowered. "Stop making me sound foolish."

"You don't need my help for that." Before she could retort, he pulled her close and silenced her. "Do you find the fur ugly?" he asked.

"No, of course not. It's gorgeous." With a sigh, Ruth rested her head on his shoulder. "But you don't have to buy me anything."

"Have to? No." He ran a hand down her back to the curve of her hip. "The things I have to do, I know.

This is what I choose to do." He drew her away, smiling again. "Come, try it on for me."

Ruth studied him carefully. The gesture was generous, impulsive and typically Nick. How could she refuse? "Thank you," she said so seriously that he laughed and hugged her.

"You look at me like an owl again, very sober and wise. Now, please, let me see you wear it."

If Ruth had any doubts, the *please* brushed them aside. She was certain she could count on the fingers of one hand the times he had used the word to her personally. With no more hesitation, she dove into the box. Her fingers sank into fur.

"It is gorgeous, Nick. Really gorgeous."

"Not over your robe, *milaya.*" He shook his head as Ruth started to put the coat on. "They don't wear fox with blue terry cloth."

Ruth shot him a look, then undid the knot in her belt. She slipped out of the robe and quickly into the fur. Nick felt his stomach tighten at the brief flashes of her nakedness. Her dark hair fell over the blue-toned white; her eyes shone with excitement.

"I have to see how it looks!" Ruth turned, thinking to dash to the bedroom mirror.

"I love you."

The words stopped her dead. She felt completely winded, as though she had taken a bad fall on stage. Her breath would simply not force its way through her lungs. She closed her eyes. Her fingers were gripping the fur so tightly they hurt. She couldn't relax them. Very slowly, she turned to face him. Her throat was closing, so that when the words came, they were thick. "What did you say?"

"I love you. In English. I've told you in Russian before. *Ya tebya lyublyu.*"

Ruth remembered the words murmured in her ear— words that had jumbled in her brain when he had made love to her, when he had held her close before sleep. Her knees were beginning to shake. "I didn't know what they meant."

"Now you do."

She stared at him, feeling the trembling spread. "I'm afraid," Ruth whispered. "I've waited to hear you say that for so long, and now I'm terrified. Nick." She swallowed as her eyes filled. "I don't think my legs will move."

"Do you want to walk to me or away?"

The question steadied her. Perhaps he was afraid, too. She moved forward. When she stood in front of him, she waited until she thought her voice would be level. "How do I say it in Russian?" she asked him. "I want to say it in Russian first."

"Ya tebya lyublyu."

"Ya tebya lyublyu, Nikolai." She fumbled over the pronunciation. Ruth saw the flash of emotion in his eyes before she was crushed against him. *"Ya tebya lyublyu."* She said again, "I love you."

His mouth was on her hair, her cheeks and eyelids, then bruisingly, possessively on hers. *"Ona-moya,"* he said once, almost savagely. *"She is mine."*

The fur slipped to the floor.

Chapter 12

Ruth knew she had never worked so hard in her life. Performing a full-length ballet was never easy, but dancing for four cameras was very exasperating. Short sequences of step combinations had to be repeated over and over, so that she found it nearly impossible to keep the mood. She was accustomed to the lights, but the technicians' cables and the cameras intruding on the stage were another matter. She felt surrounded by them.

Her muscles cramped from the starting and stopping. Her face had to be remade-up for the closeups and tight shots. The television audience wouldn't care to see beads of perspiration on an elegant ballerina. It was possible, with the distance of a stage performance, to maintain ballet's illusion of effortless fluidity. But the camera was merciless.

Again and again they repeated the same difficult

set of *soubresauts* and *pirouettes*. Nick seemed inexhaustible. The camera work appeared to fascinate him. He showed no sign of annoyance with minor technical breakdowns but simply stopped, talking with the director as the television crew made ready again. Then he would repeat the steps with renewed energy.

They had been taping what would be no more than a three-minute segment for over two hours. It was an athletic piece, full of passion and spirit—the type of dance that was Nick's trademark. Again Ruth turned in a triple *pirouette,* felt a flash of pain and went down hard. Nick was crouched beside her in an instant.

"Just a cramp," she managed, trying to get her breath.

"Here?" Taking her calf, he felt the knotted muscle and began to work it.

Ruth nodded, though the pain was acute. She put her forehead on her knees and closed her eyes.

"Ten minutes, please," she heard Nick call out. "Did you hurt anything when you fell?" he murmured, kneading the muscle. Ruth could only shake her head. "It's a bad one," he said, frowning. "It's difficult without warmers."

"I can't do it!" She suddenly banged a fist on the stage and raised her face. "I just can't do it right!"

Nick narrowed his eyes. "What nonsense is this?"

"It's not nonsense. I can't," Ruth continued wildly. "It's impossible. Over and over, back and forth. How can I feel anything when there's no flow to it? People everywhere, practically under my nose, when I'm supposed to be preparing for a leap."

"Ignore them and dance," he said flatly. "It's necessary."

"Necessary?" she tossed back. "I'll tell you what's necessary. It's necessary to sweat. I'm not even allowed to do that. If that man dusts powder on my face once more, I'll scream." She caught her breath as a cramp shot into her other leg. Her feet were past pain. She lowered her head again. "Oh, Nick, I'm so tired."

"So what do you do? Quit?" His voice was rough as he began to work her other leg. "I need a partner, not a complaining baby."

"I'm not a baby." Her head shot back up. "Nor a machine!"

"You're a dancer." He felt the muscle relaxing under his hand. "So dance."

Her eyes flashed at the curt tone. "Thanks for the understanding." She pushed his hand away and swung to her feet. Her legs nearly buckled under her, but she snapped them straight.

"There's a place for understanding." He rose. "This isn't it. You've work to do. Now, go have the man with the powder fix your face."

Ruth stared at him a moment, then turned and walked offstage without a word.

When she had gone, Nick swore under his breath, then sat down again to work out the pain in his own legs.

"You're a tough man, Davidov."

Nick looked up to see Nadine rise from a chair in the audience. "Yes." He turned his attention back to his leg. "You've told me before."

"It's the way I like you." She walked to the side of the stage and climbed the steps. "But she is still young." Her heels set out an echo as she walked across the stage.

Nadine knelt beside him. She took his leg and

began to competently massage the cramp. "Good feet, wonderful legs, very musical." She gave him a quick smile. "She's not yet as tough as we are."

"Better for her."

"More difficult for you because you love her." Nick gave her an inquiring lift of a brow. "There's nothing about my dancers I don't know," Nadine went on. "Often before they do. You've been in love with her for a long time."

"So?" Nick said.

"Dancers often pair up with dancers. They speak the same language, have the same problems." Nadine sat back on her haunches. "But when it's my *premier danseur* and artistic director involved with my best ballerina, I'm concerned."

"There's no need for it, Nadine." His tone was mild, but there was no mistaking his annoyance.

"Romances can go several ways," she commented. "Believe me, I know very well." Nadine smiled again, a bit ruefully. "Dancers are an emotional species, Nick. I don't want to lose either of you if you have a falling out. This one is destined to be *prima ballerina assoluta.*"

Nick's voice was very cool. "Are you suggesting I stop seeing Ruth?" He rose carefully to his feet. His eyes were very direct and very blue.

Nadine studied him thoughtfully. "How long have I known you, Davidov?"

He smiled briefly. "It would only age both of us, Nadine."

She nodded in agreement, then held up her hand. Nick lifted her lightly to her feet. "A long time. Long enough to know better than to suggest to you." Her look became wry. "I've watched your parade of women over the years."

"Spasibo."

"That wasn't praise," she countered. "It was an observation." She paused again, briefly. "Bannion's different."

"Yes," he said simply. "Ruth's different."

"Be careful, Davidov. Falls are dangerous to dancers." She turned as technicians began to wander back toward the stage. "She'll hate you for a while."

"I'll have to deal with that."

"Of course," Nadine agreed, expecting nothing else.

Very erect, face composed, Ruth walked out of the wings. While her makeup was being repaired, she had forced everything out of her mind but the dance she was to perform. Until it was completed and on tape, she would allow herself no emotion but that which her character would feel. She crossed to Nick.

"I'm ready."

He looked down at her. He wanted to ask if there was still pain, wanted to tell her that he loved her. Instead, he said, "Good, then we start again."

Nearly two hours later Ruth stood under the shower. Her body was too numbed for pain. Her thoughts were fuzzy with fatigue. Only two things were clear: She detested dancing for the camera; and when she had needed Nick, he had stepped away. He had spoken to her as though she had been lazy and weak. That she had lost control in public had humiliated her enough. His cold words had added to it.

Her strength and stamina had always been a source of pride for her. It had been an enormous blow to have fallen to the stage, beaten and hurting. She had wanted comfort, and he had given her disdain.

Ruth stepped from the shower and wrapped herself in a towel just as Leah walked in. Still in street clothes, the blonde leaned against a sink and smiled.

"Hi." She studied Ruth's pale, exhausted face. "Rough day?"

"Rough enough." Ruth walked to her bag to pull out a sweater.

"I heard you had some trouble with your number this afternoon."

Ruth had a moment, as she pulled the sweater over her head, to compose her features. "Nothing major," she said calmly, though the easy words cost her. "*Le Corsaire's* taping is finished."

"I can't wait to see it." Leah smiled, taking out a brush and pulling it lazily through her baby fine hair. "You're looking pale," she observed as Ruth tugged on her jeans. "Lucky you have a couple of days to rest before they start taping *The Red Rose*."

Ruth pulled up her zipper with a jerk. "You keep up with the schedules."

"I make it my business to know what's going on with everybody in the company."

Ruth sat down and took her sneakers from her bag. She put one on, then threw Leah a long, thoughtful look. "What is it you want?"

"Nick," she answered instantly. Her smile deepened as Ruth's eyes glistened. "Not that way, darling, though it's tempting." She smiled. "It appears that being his lover has its advantages."

Ruth struggled with the desire to hurl her other shoe at the smile. Seething, she slipped it on her foot. "What's between Nick and me is personal and has nothing to do with anyone." Blood pounding, Ruth got to her feet.

"Oh, but there's a connection." Leah reached out to touch Ruth's arm as she would have swung from the room.

The violent urge surprised Ruth. Her temper had never been so close to being completely, blindly lost. She let her bag drop noisily to the floor.

"What?"

Leah sat on the edge of the sink and crossed her ankles. "I intend to be *prima ballerina assoluta*."

"Is that supposed to be news?" Ruth countered with an arched brow.

"I'm fully aware," Leah continued smoothly, "that to do that and remain with this company, I need Nick for my partner."

"Then you have a problem." Ruth faced her squarely. "Nick is my partner."

"For now," Leah agreed easily. "He'll certainly drop you when he gets tired of sleeping with you."

"That's my concern," Ruth said softly.

"Nick's lovers never last long. We've all witnessed the ebb and flow over the years. Remember that lawyer six or eight months ago? Very elegant. And there was a model before that. He usually avoids picking from the company. Very fastidious, our Nikolai."

"*My* Nikolai." Ruth picked up her bag again. "You'd better satisfy yourself with the partners you're given."

"He won't be dancing much longer than a couple more years. He's already choreographing most of the time. Two years is all I need," Leah returned flatly.

"Two years." Ruth laughed and swung the bag over her shoulder. "I'll be *prima ballerina assoluta* in six months." She let her own fury guide her words. "After the show is aired, everyone in the country will know who I am. If the competition worries you, try another company."

"Competition!" Leah's eyes narrowed. "You barely made it through your first piece." She gave Ruth one of her glittery smiles. "Nick might be persuaded to cut your other two or give them to someone with a bit more stamina."

"Such as you."

"Naturally."

"In a pig's eye," Ruth said mildly, then, shoving Leah aside, she walked out.

Though the small gesture had helped, her nerves were still stretched to the breaking point. The emotional onslaught had taken her mind off her body, and she moved down the steps oblivious to the ache in her calves. She headed for the street, seething with indignation.

"Ruth." Nick took her arm when she failed to respond the first time he called. "Where are you going?"

"Home," she said shortly.

"Fine." He studied her heated face. "I'll take you."

"I know where it is." She turned toward the door again, but his hand remained firm.

"I said I would take you."

"Very well." She shrugged. "Suit yourself."

"I usually do," he answered coolly and drew her outside and into a cab. Ruth sat in her corner with her bag held primly in her lap. Nick sat back against the seat, making no attempt at conversation. His mind was apparently occupied with his own thoughts. Stubbornness prevented Ruth from speaking.

Her scene with Nick on stage replayed in her head, followed by the scene with Leah. Ruth's anger took the form of stony silence.

When the cab pulled up in front of her apartment, she slid out her side, prepared to bid Nick a cool goodbye. He alighted from the street side, however, and rounding the rear of the cab, took her arm again. His grip was light but unarguable. Making no comment, Ruth walked with him into the building.

She knew she was primed for a fight. It would take only the smallest provocation. Anger was bubbling hot just beneath the surface. She unlocked the door to her apartment. Breezing through, she left Nick to go or come in as he chose.

From his seat on the sofa, Nijinsky rose, arched his back, then leaped soundlessly down. Dutifully, he circled around Ruth's ankles before he moved to Nick. She heard him give the cat a murmured greeting. Staying behind her wall of silence, she went into the bedroom to unpack her bag.

She lingered over the task purposefully. There was no sound from the other room as she carefully placed her toe shoes on her dresser. Meticulously, she took the pins from her hair and let it fall free. A small part of her headache fled with the lack of confinement. She brushed her hair out, letting one long stroke follow the next. The apartment remained absolutely silent.

For a full ten minutes Ruth busied herself around the bedroom, finding a dozen small, meaningless tasks that required her attention. Her nerves began to pound again. Deciding that what she needed was food, Ruth tied her hair back with a ribbon and left the room.

Nick was sound asleep on the couch. He lay on his back with a purring Nijinsky curled in a comfortable ball on his chest. His breathing was slow and even. All her resentment fled.

He's exhausted, she realized. The signs were clear on his face. Why hadn't she noticed them before? Because she had been too involved with her own feelings, she thought guiltily.

The creases were deep in his cheeks. She could see the faint mauve shadows under his eyes. Ruth sighed. She could have wept. No tears, she ordered herself firmly.

Taking a mohair afghan from the back of a chair, she spread it up to Nick's waist. He never moved. Nijinsky opened one eye, sent her an accusing glance and settled back to sleep. Ruth sat in a chair and curled her legs under her. She watched her lover sleep.

It was dark when Nick woke. Disoriented, he pressed his fingers to his eyes. There was a weight on his chest. Moving his hand to it, he discovered a warm ball of fur. He let out a long sigh as Nijinsky experimentally dug his claws in. With a halfhearted oath, Nick pushed the cat aside and sat up. A stream of light fell from the kitchen doorway. He sat for some moments longer before rising and walking to it.

Ruth stood at the stove. With her hair pulled back, Nick could study her profile: delicate bones, lifted jaw, the slight slant of her eyes. Her lips were parted in concentration—soft, generous lips he could taste just by looking. She had the slender, arching neck of a classical ballerina. He knew the precise spot where the skin was most sensitive.

She looked very young in the harsh kitchen light, much as she had looked the first time he had seen her— in the glare of sun on snow in the parking lot of Lindsay's school. Ruth turned suddenly, sensing him. Their eyes locked.

She moistened her lips. "You were stirring. I thought you'd be hungry. Are omelets all right?"

"Yes. Good."

He leaned on the door jamb as she went back to her preparation. A glance at his watch told him it was barely nine o'clock. He had slept for just under two hours. He was as refreshed as if it had been a full night.

"Can I help?"

Ruth kept her eyes on the eggs growing firm in the pan. "You could get out the plates. I'm almost done." Beside her on the counter the percolator began to pop. Nick got out plates and cups. "Do you want anything else?" she asked, hating the strained politeness of her voice.

"No. This is fine."

Expertly, Ruth flipped the first omelet from pan to plate. "Go ahead and get started. I'll just be another minute." Beaten eggs sizzled as she poured them into the pan. "I'll bring the coffee."

Nick took his plate into the dining room. Ruth continued to work, focusing all her concentration on her cooking. The percolator became more lively. She slid the eggs from the pan. Unplugging the coffee, she took it into the dining room.

Nick glanced up as she came in.

"Is it all right?" She set down her plate, then poured coffee into the waiting cups.

"It's good." He forked another mouthful. Ruth avoided his eyes and set the percolator on a trivet. Taking the seat across from him, she began to eat.

"I have to thank you for letting me sleep." Nick watched her push the eggs around on her plate. "I needed it. And this."

"You looked so tired," she murmured. "It never occurred to me that it's difficult for you."

"Ah," he said with light amusement. "Davidov the indestructible."

Ruth lifted her eyes at that. "I suppose that's how I've always seen you. How all of us see you."

His glance was steady. "But then, you are not all of us." He saw the tears spring to her eyes. Something tightened inside his stomach. "You should eat," he said briskly. "It's been a long day."

Ruth picked up her coffee cup, struggling for composure. She'd had enough scenes for one day. "I'm not really hungry."

Nick shrugged and went back to his meal. "Something's burning," he commented. With a cry, Ruth leaped up and dashed into the kitchen.

The omelet pan smoked in a steady column, its surface crackling from the heat. Swearing, she flicked off the flame she had left burning under it and gave the stove an angry kick.

"Careful," Nick said from the doorway. "I can't use a partner with broken toes."

She rounded on him, wanting to vent her anger somewhere. But he smiled. It was as though he had pulled his finger from the dam.

"Oh, Nick!" Ruth threw herself into his arms and clung. "I was so horrible today. I danced so badly."

"No," he corrected, kissing her hair. "You danced beautifully, better when you were angry with me."

Ruth drew her head back and looked at him. She knew with certainty that he would never lie about her dancing to comfort her. "I shouldn't have been angry with you. I was so wrapped up in myself, in how I was feeling, that I never thought about how difficult it was for you, too. You always make it look so easy."

"You don't like the camera."

"I hate it. It's horrible."

"But valuable."

"I know that. I know it." She drew back to stand away from him. "I hate the way I acted this afternoon, crying in front of all those people, raging at you."

"You're an artist. I've told you, it's expected."

"I don't like public displays." She took a long breath. "I particularly don't like seeing myself as selfish and uncaring."

"You're too hard on yourself, Ruth. The woman I love is not selfish or uncaring."

"I was today." She shook her head. "I didn't stop thinking of myself until I saw you sleeping, looking so utterly exhausted. I know how hard you've been working, not only on our dances but at all the other rehearsals you have to supervise and the meetings and the schedule for the rest of the season. But all I thought about was how I hated those cameras looming everywhere and about how my legs ached." She gave a quiet, shuddering sigh. "I don't like knowing I can be that one-dimensional, too much like what Donald once accused me of."

"Oh, enough." Nick took her shoulders in a firm grip. "We have to think of ourselves, of our own bodies. There's no other way to survive. You're a fool if you believe it makes you less of a person. We're different from others, yes. It's our way."

"Selfish?"

"Must it have a name?" He gave her a little shake, then pulled her against him. "Selfish, if you like. Dedicated. Obsessed. What does it matter? Does it change you? Does it change me?" Suddenly his mouth was on hers.

Ruth moaned with the kiss. His lips were both tender and possessive, sparking small flames deep inside her. He drew her closer, and still closer, until they were molded together.

"This is how I wanted to kiss you when you sat on the stage angry and hurting." His mouth moved over hers with the words. "Do you hate me because I didn't?"

"No. No, but I wanted you to." She held him tighter. "I wanted so badly for you to."

"You would never have finished the dance if I had comforted you then." Nick tilted her head back until their eyes met. "I knew that, because I know you. Does this make me cold and selfish?"

"It makes you Davidov." Ruth sighed and smiled at him. "That's all I want."

"And you are Bannion." He lowered his mouth to hers. "That's all I want."

"You make it sound so simple. Is it simple?"

"Tonight it is simple." He lifted her into his arms.

Chapter 13

Ruth sat six rows back and watched the taping. Her three segments were finished. What would be perhaps nine or ten minutes of air time had taken three grueling days to tape. She had learned to play for the camera, even to tolerate it. But she knew she would never feel the excitement with it that Nick did. He had challenged her to outdo him in their *pas de deux* from *Carnival*. He had been exuberant, incredibly agile in his Harlequin mask and costume, a teasing, free-spirited soul who infused more vitality into her Columbine than she had believed possible.

He simply glows with energy, she mused, watching him on stage. Even when he's not dancing.

The *corps* was doing a scene from *Rodeo*. Amid the cowboy hats and gingham, Nick stood in a characteristically drab sweat suit and instructed the dancers. If he had worn gold or silver, he could not have been more of a focal point.

Ruth knew how little relaxation he had allowed himself over the past weeks. Yet as he coached his dancers a last time, he was as vital and alive as a young boy. How does he do it? she asked herself.

She thought of what Leah had said and wondered: Would he stop dancing in another two years? Ruth hated to think of it. He looked so young. In most other professions he would be considered young, she reflected. As art director, as choreographer, as composer, he could go on indefinitely. But as *danseur noble,* time was precious.

He knew it, of course. Ruth watched as Davidov stepped out of camera range. How did he feel about it? He'd never told her. There were so many things he'd never told her.

Ruth was aware of how smoothly he changed the subject whenever she probed too deeply about his life in Russia. It wasn't a simple matter of curiosity that prompted her to ask. Yet she didn't know how to explain her questions to him.

It frustrated her that he chose to block off a part of himself from her. Privacy was something Ruth valued deeply and respected in others, but loving Nick wholeheartedly, she had the need to know him completely. Yet he continued to draw back from questions or discussions of his early life or his professional career in his own country. Nor had he spoken with her of his feelings about perhaps coming to the end of his active dancing career.

Too often, she decided, he thought of her as a little

girl. How would she convince him to share his problems with her as well as his joys?

Music filled the theater; the quick, raucously Western-American music that set the mood for the dance. Nick watched the *corps* from behind a cameraman, his hands lightly balled at his hips. Ruth drew in her breath.

Will I always feel like this? she wondered. Moved by him, dazed by him? It was frightening to be in love with a legend. Even in the short time they had been together, career demands had pressured them both. Ballet was both a bond and a strain. The time they spent alone in her apartment was another world. They could be any man and woman then. But the music and the lights called them back. And here, in the world that consumed most of their lives, he was Davidov the master.

"He seems to be handling things well, as usual." Nadine slipped into the seat beside her, and Ruth snapped herself back.

The music had stopped. Nick was talking to the dancers again as the director spoke to some invisible technician on his headset. Ruth let her eyes follow Nick. "Yes, he seems to be."

"Like a boy with a new train set."

Ruth gave Nadine a quizzical look. "Train set?"

"The fresh excitement, the enthusiasm," she explained with a sweeping gesture of her hand. "He's loving this."

"Yes." Ruth looked back at Nick. "I can see that."

"Your dances went well." At Ruth's deprecating laugh, Nadine went on. "Oh, I know you had some adjustments to make. That's life."

"Were you watching?"

"I'm always watching."

"You're not usually kind, Nadine," Ruth commented wryly.

"My dear, I'm never kind. I can't afford to be." The music began again, and though Nadine's eyes were on the stage, she spoke to Ruth. "They did go well, all in all. The tape is magnificent."

"You've seen it?" Ruth was all attention now.

Nadine merely lifted her brow in response. "The program should be all we hoped for. I can say frankly that you and Nick together are the best I've seen in some time. I never thought he'd find a partner to equal Lindsay. Of course, your style and hers are very different. Lindsay took to the air as if she were part of it—effortlessly, almost mystically. You challenge it, as if defying gravity."

Ruth pondered over the description. It seemed to make perfect sense. "Lindsay was the most beautiful ballerina I've ever seen."

"We lost her because she allowed her personal life to interfere," Nadine said flatly.

"She didn't have any choice." Ruth rushed to Lindsay's defense. "When her father was killed and her mother so badly hurt, she had to go."

"We make our own choices." Nadine turned to face Ruth directly. "I don't believe in fate. We make things happen."

"Lindsay did what she had to do."

"What she chose to do," Nadine corrected. "We all do." She studied Ruth's frown. "I've had one priority all my life. I'd like to think all my dancers were the same, but I know better. You have the talent, the youth, the drive to make a very important mark in the world of ballet. Lindsay had just begun to make hers when she left. I wouldn't like to lose you."

"Why should you?" Ruth phrased the question carefully, keeping her eyes on Nadine. She was no longer aware of what was happening on stage.

"Temperaments run high in dancers."

"So I've been told," Ruth said dryly. "But that doesn't answer my question."

"I need both you and Nick, Ruth, but I need Nick more." She paused a moment, watching her words sink in. "If the two of you come to a time when things are… no longer as they are, and you can't—or won't—work together, I'd have to make a choice. The company can't afford to lose Nick."

"I see." Ruth turned back to the stage and stared at the dancers.

"I've thought a long time about speaking to you. I felt it best I make my position clear."

"Have you spoken to Nick?"

"No." Nadine looked at Nick as he stood with the technicians. "Not so bluntly. I will, of course, if it becomes necessary. I hope it doesn't."

"Quite a number of dancers in the company become involved with each other," Ruth commented. "Some even marry. Do you make a habit of prying into their private lives?"

"I always thought there was fire behind those scrupulous manners." Nadine smiled thinly. "I'm glad to see it." She paused a moment. "As long as nothing outside interferes with the company, there's no reason to create unhappiness." She gave Ruth another direct look.

"But Nick isn't merely one of my dancers. We both know that."

"I don't think you could say that what's between Nick and me has interfered with the company or with our dancing." Ruth sat stiffly.

"Not yet, no. I'm fond of you, Ruth, which is why I spoke. Now I have to go wring a few more dollars out of a patron." Nadine rose and, without another word, moved up the dark aisle and out of the theater.

On stage, Nick watched his dancers. He saw them both individually and as a group. This one's arm wasn't arched quite right, that one's foot placement was perfect. He kept a close eye on the *corps*. There were two he planned to make soloists soon. There was a young girl, barely eighteen, whom he observed with special interest. She had an ethereal, otherworldly beauty and great speed. She reminded him a bit of Lindsay. Already he saw her as Carla in *The Nutcracker* the following year. He would have to induce Madame Maximova to work with her individually.

The director stopped the tape, and Nick moved forward to correct a few minor details. They had been working nearly two hours and the hot lights shone without mercy.

Nadine, he thought as they began again, is like a hawk hunting chickens when she holds auditions for the *corps*. Poor children; were they ever really aware of the drudgery of dance? So few of them would ever go beyond the *corps*. Again he watched the young girl as she spun into her partner's arms. That one will, he concluded. She'll be chasing after Ruth's heels in two years.

He smiled, remembering Ruth's *corps* days. She'd

been so young and very withdrawn. Only when she had danced had she been truly confident. Even then—yes, even then—he had wanted her, and it had astonished him. He had watched her grow more poised, more open. He'd watched her talent blossom.

Five years, he thought. Five years, and now, at last, I have her. Still it wasn't enough. There were nights his duties kept him late, and he was forced to go home to his own empty apartment knowing Ruth slept far away in another bed.

He wondered whether he was more impatient now because he had waited so long for her. It was a daily struggle to keep from hurrying her into a fuller commitment. He hadn't even meant to tell her he loved her, certainly not in that flat, unadorned manner. The moments before she had turned and given the love back to him had left him paralyzed with fear. Fear was a new sensation and one he discovered he didn't care for.

Part of him resented the hold she had on him. No one woman had ever occupied his thoughts so completely. And still she held part of herself aloof from him. It was tantalizing, infuriating.

He wanted her without reserve, without secrets. The longer they went on, the more impossible it became to prevent himself from pressing her for more. Even now, with his mind crammed with his work, he knew she sat out in the darkened theater. He sensed her.

She shouldn't be allowed to pull at him this way, he thought with sudden anger. Yet he wanted her there. Close. The words he had spoken when he had come to her apartment in the night grew more true as time passed. He needed her.

At last the taping session was completed. Nick spoke with the director as dancers filed off stage. They would cool their bodies under showers and nurse their aches. Ruth rose from her seat in the audience and approached the stage. The musicians were talking among themselves, stretching their backs.

"One hour, please," Nick called to them and received a grumbled response.

Technicians shut off the high wattage lights, and the temperature dropped markedly. The crew was talking about the Italian deli down the street and meatball sandwiches. With a laugh, Nick declined joining them. His offer of yogurt in the company canteen was met with unilateral disgust.

"So." He drew Ruth into his arms when she stepped on stage. "What did you think of it?"

"It was wonderful," she answered truthfully. She tried not to think about her conversation with Nadine as Nick gave her a brief kiss. "Apparently, you have a flair for Americana."

"I always thought I'd make a good cowboy." He grinned and picked up one of the abandoned prop hats. With a flourish, he set it on his head. "Now I only need six-guns."

Ruth laughed. "It suits you," she decided, adjusting the hat lower over his forehead. "Did they have cowboys in Russia?"

"Cossacks," he answered. "Not quite the same." He smiled, running his hands down her arms. "Are you hungry? There's an hour before we begin again."

"Yes."

Slipping an arm around her, he tossed off the hat as

they crossed the stage. "We'll get something and take it up to my office. I want you alone."

Ten minutes later Nick closed his office door behind them. "We should have music for such an elaborate meal, yes?" He moved to the stereo.

Ruth set down their bowls of fruit salad as he switched on Rimsky-Korsakov. After turning the volume low, he came back to her.

"This first." Nick gathered her into his arms. Ruth lifted her mouth to his, hungry for his kiss.

Her demand fanned the banked fires within him. With a low sound of pleasure, he tangled his fingers in her hair and plundered. Her mouth was avid, seeking, as she let the kiss take her. Desire was a fast-driving force that rocketed inside her. She slipped her hands under his sweat shirt to feel the play of muscles on his back. His mouth began to move wildly over her face; her lips ached for his.

"Kiss me," she demanded and stopped his roaming mouth with hers.

The kiss was shattering and stormy. It was as though he poured all his needs into the single meeting of lips. It left her breathless, shaken, wanting more. He probed her lip with his teeth until she moaned in drugged excitement. Then he drove deeper, using his tongue to destroy any hold on sanity. Ruth murmured mindlessly, craving for him to touch her.

As if reading her thoughts, he brought his hand to her breast. She shuddered as the rough fabric of her cotton blouse scraped her skin. With his other hand he tugged it from the waistband of her jeans. His fingers snaked up over her ribcage and found her. Together they caught their breath at the contact.

When the phone on his desk began to ring, Nick let out a steady stream of curses. He spun to answer and yanked the receiver from the cradle.

"What is it?"

Ruth let out a long breath and sat. Her knees were trembling.

"I can't see him now." She had heard that sharp, impatient tone before and felt a small tingle of sympathy for the caller. "No, he'll wait. I'm busy, Nadine."

Ruth's brows shot up. No one spoke to Nadine that way. She sighed then and looked up at Nick. No one else was Davidov.

"Yes, I'm aware of that. In twenty minutes, then. No, twenty." He set the phone down with a final click. When he looked back down at Ruth, the annoyance was still in his eyes. "It seems an open wallet requires my attention." He swore and thrust his hands into his pockets. "There are times when this business of money drives me mad. It must be forever coaxed and tugged. It was simple once just to dance. Now it's not enough. They give us little time, Ruth."

"Come and eat," she said, wanting to soothe him. "Twenty minutes is time enough."

"I don't speak of only now!" The anger rose in his voice, and she braced herself for the torrent. "I wanted to be with you last night and all the other nights I slept alone. I need more than this—more than a few moments in the day, a few nights in the week."

"Nick—" she began, but he cut her off.

"I want you to move in with me. To live with me."

Whatever she had been about to say escaped her. He stood over her, furious and demanding. "Move in with you?" she repeated dumbly.

"Yes. Today. Tonight."

Her thoughts were whirling as she stared up at him. "Into your apartment?"

"Yes." Impatient, he pulled her to her feet. "I cannot—will not—keep going home to empty rooms." His grip was firm on her arms. "I want you there."

"Live with you," Ruth said again, struggling to take it in. "My things…"

"Bring your things." Nick shook her in frustration. "What does it matter?"

Ruth shook her head, lifting a hand to push herself away. "You have to give me time to think."

"Damn it, what need is there to think?" He betrayed the depth of his agitation by swearing in English. She was too confused to notice. She might have been prepared for him to ask her to take such a step, but she hadn't been prepared for him to shout it at her.

"I have a need to think," she shot back. "You're asking me to change my life, give up the only home of my own I've ever had."

"I'm asking you to have a home with me." His fingers dug deeper. "I will not go on stealing little moments of time with you."

"*You* can't, *you* won't! I have the final say in my own life. I won't be pressured this way!"

"Pressured? Hell!" Nick stormed to the window, then back to her. "You speak to me of pressures? Five years, *five years* I've waited for you. I wanted a child and must wait until the child grows to a woman." His English began to elude him.

Ruth's eyes grew enormous. "Are you telling me you felt…had feelings for me since…since the beginning and never told me?"

"What was I to say?" he countered furiously. "You were seventeen."

"I had a right to make my own choice!" She tossed her hair back and glared at him. "You had no right to make it for me."

"I gave you your choice when the time was right."

"You gave!" she retorted. Indignation nearly choked her. "You're the director of the company, Davidov, not of my life. How dare you presume to make any decisions for me!"

"My life was also involved," he reminded her. His eyes glittered as he spoke. "Or do you forget?"

"You always treated me like a child," she fumed, ignoring his question. "You never considered that between my childhood and dancing, I was grown up before I ever met you. And now you stand there and tell me you kept something from me for years for my own good. *And* you tell me to pack my things and move in with you without giving it a thought."

"I had no idea such a suggestion would offend you," he said coldly.

"Suggestion?" she repeated. "It came out as an order. I won't be *ordered* to live with you."

"Very well, do as you wish." He gave her a long, steady look. "I have an appointment."

Her eyes opened wider in fresh rage as he moved

to the door. "I'm taking some time off," she said impulsively.

Nick paused with his hand on the knob and turned to her. "Rehearsals begin again in seven days," he said, deadly calm. "You will be back or you will be fired. I leave the choice to you."

He walked out without bothering to close the door behind him.

Chapter 14

Lindsay hefted Amanda and settled her into the curve of her hip while Justin skidded a car across the wood-planked floor.

"Dinner in ten minutes, young man," she warned, stepping expertly between the wrecked and parked cars. "Go wash your hands."

"They're not dirty." Justin bowed his blond head over a tiny, flashy racer as if to repair the engine.

Lindsay narrowed her eyes while Amanda squirmed for freedom. "Worth might think otherwise," she said. It was her ultimate weapon.

Justin slipped the toy Ferrari into his pocket and got up. With a weighty, world-weary sigh, he walked from the room.

Lindsay smiled after him. Justin had a healthy respect for the fastidious British butler. She listened to the squeak of her son's tennis shoes as he climbed the stairs. He could have used the downstairs bath, but when Justin Bannion was being a martyr, he liked to do it properly.

It amazed Lindsay, when she had time to think of it, that her son was four years old. He had already outgrown the chunky toddler stage and was lean as a whippet. And, she thought, not without pride, he has his mother's hair and eyes. Glancing around the room, she grimaced at the wreckage of cars and small buildings. And his mother's lack of organization, she mused.

"Not like you at all, is he?" She buried her face in her daughter's neck and earned a giggle.

Amanda was dark, the female image of her father. And like Seth, she was meticulous. Armies of dolls were arranged just so in her room. She showed almost a comical knack for neatly stacking her blocks into buildings. Temper perhaps came from both of her parents, as she wasn't too ladylike to chuck a block at her brother if he infringed on her territory.

With a last kiss, Lindsay set Amanda down and began to gather Justin's abandoned traffic jam. She stopped, car in hand, and shot her daughter a look. "Daddy won't like it if I pick these up."

"Justin's sloppy," Amanda stated with sisterly disdain. At two, she had a penchant for picking up telling phrases.

"No argument there," Lindsay agreed and passed a car from hand to hand. "And he certainly has to learn better, but if Worth walks in here…" She let the thought hang, weighing whose disapproval she would rather face. Worth won. Moving quickly, she began scooping up the evidence. "I'll speak to Justin. We won't have to tell Daddy."

"Tell Daddy what?" Seth demanded from the doorway.

"Uh-oh." Lindsay rolled her eyes to the ceiling, then peered over her shoulder. "I thought you were working."

"I was." He took in the tableau quickly. "Covering up for the little devil again, are you?"

"I sent him up to wash his hands." Lindsay pushed the hair out of her eyes and continued to stay on her hands and knees. Amanda walked over to wrap an arm around Seth's leg. Both of them studied her in quiet disapproval. "Oh, please!" She laughed, sitting back on her haunches. "We throw ourselves on the mercy of the court."

"Well." He laid a hand on his daughter's head. "What should the punishment be, Amanda?"

"Can't spank Mama."

"No?" Seth gave Lindsay a wicked grin. Walking over, he pulled her to her feet. "In the interest of justice, I might find it necessary." He gave her a light, teasing kiss.

"Are you open to a bribe?" she murmured.

"Always," he told her as she pressed her mouth more firmly to his.

Justin bounced to the doorway with his freshly scrubbed hands in front of him. He made a face at his parents, then looked down at his sister. "I thought we were going to eat."

An hour later Lindsay rushed down the steps, heading out for her evening ballet class. Spotting another of Justin's cars at the foot of the steps, she picked it up and stuffed it into her bag.

"A life of crime," she muttered and pulled open the front door. "Ruth!" Astonished, she simply stared.

"Hi. Got a room for an escaped dancer and a slightly overweight cat for the weekend?"

"Oh, of course!" She pulled Ruth across the threshold for a huge hug. Nijinsky scrambled from between them, leaped to the floor and stalked away. He wasn't fond of traveling. "It's wonderful to see you. Seth and the children will be so surprised."

Through her first rush of pleasure, Lindsay could feel the hard desperation of Ruth's grip. She drew her away and studied her face. She had no trouble spotting the unhappiness. "Are you all right?"

"Yes." Lindsay's eyes were direct on hers. "No," she admitted. "I need some time."

"All right." She picked up Ruth's bag and closed the door behind them. "Your room's in the same place. Go up and surprise Seth and the children. I'll be back in a couple of hours."

"Thanks."

Lindsay dashed out the door, and Ruth drew a deep breath.

Two days later Ruth sat on the couch, a child on each side of her. She read aloud from one of Justin's books. Nijinsky dozed in a patch of sunlight on the floor. She was feeling more settled.

She should have known that she would find exactly what she had needed at the Cliff House. No questions, no coddling. Lindsay had opened the door, and Ruth had found acceptance and love.

After Ruth had left Nick's office, she'd gone back

to her apartment, packed and come directly to Cliff-side. She hadn't even thought about it, but had simply followed instinct. Now, after two days, Ruth knew her instincts had been right. There were times when only family could heal.

"I thought you must have bound and gagged them," Seth commented as he strode into the room. "They're not this quiet when they're asleep."

Ruth laughed. Both children went to climb into Seth's lap the moment he sat down.

"They're angels, Uncle Seth." She watched him wrap his arms around both his children. "You should be ashamed of yourself, blackening their names."

"They don't need my help for that." He tugged Amanda's hair. "Worth announced that there was a half-eaten lollipop in someone's bed this morning."

"I was going to finish it tonight," Justin stated, looking earnestly up at his father. "He didn't throw it away, did he?"

"Afraid so."

"Nuts."

"He had a few choice things to say about the state of the sheets," Seth added mildly.

Justin set his mouth—his mother's mouth—into a pout. "Do I have to 'pologize again?"

"I should think so."

"I wanna watch." Amanda was already scrambling down in anticipation.

"I'm always 'pologizing," Justin said wearily. Ruth watched him troop from the room with Amanda trotting to keep up.

"You know, of course," Ruth began, "that Worth adores them."

"Yes, but he'd hate to know his secret was out." Seth could hear both sets of feet clattering down the hall toward the kitchen.

"He always awed me." Ruth set the book aside. "All the months I lived with you I never grew completely used to him."

"No one handles him as well as Lindsay does." Seth sat back and let his mind relax. "He's never yet realized he's being handled."

"There's no one like Lindsay," Ruth said.

"No," Seth said in simple agreement. "No one."

"Was it frightening falling in love with someone so—special?"

He could read the question in her eyes and knew what she was thinking. "Loving's always frightening if it's important. Loving someone special only adds to it. Lindsay scared me to death."

"How strange. I always thought of you as invulnerable and fearless."

"Love makes cowards of all of us, Ruth." The memories of his first months with Lindsay, before their marriage, came back to him. "I nearly lost her once. Nothing's ever frightened me more."

"I've watched you for five years." Ruth was frowning in concentration. "Your love's the same as it was in the very beginning."

"No." Seth shook his head. "I love her more, incredibly more. So I have more to lose."

They both heard her burst through the front door.

"God save me from mothers who want Pavlova after five lessons!"

"She's home," Seth said mildly.

"Mrs. Fitzwalter," Lindsay began without preamble as she stormed into the room, "wants her Mitzie to take class with Janet Conner. Never mind that Janet has been taking lessons for two years and Mitzie just started two weeks ago." Lindsay plopped into a chair and glared. "Never mind that Janet has talent and Mitzie has lead feet. Mitzie wants to take class with her best friend, and Mrs. Fitzwalter wants to car pool."

"You, of course, explained diplomatically." Seth lifted a brow.

"I was the epitome of diplomacy. I've been taking Worth lessons." She turned to Ruth. "Mitzie is ten pounds overweight and can't manage first position. Janet's been on toe for two months."

"You might find her another car pool," Ruth suggested.

"I did." Lindsay smiled, pleased with herself. The smile faded as she noted the abnormal quiet. "Where are the children?"

"Apologizing," Seth told her.

"Oh, dear, again?" Lindsay sighed and smiled. Rising, she crossed to Seth. "Hi." She bent and kissed him. "Did you solve your cantilever problem?"

"Just about," he told her and brought her back for a more satisfying kiss.

"You're so clever." She sat on the arm of his chair.

"Naturally."

"And you work too hard. Holed up in that office

every day, and on Saturday." She slipped her hand into his. "Let's all go for a walk on the beach."

Seth started to agree, then paused. "You and Ruth go. The kids need a nap. I think I'll join them."

Lindsay looked at him in surprise. The last thing Seth would do on a beautiful Saturday afternoon was take a nap. But his message passed to her quickly, and she turned to Ruth with no change in rhythm. "Yes, let's go. I need some air after Mrs. Fitzwalter."

"All right. Do I need a jacket?"

"A light one."

Lindsay looked back down at Seth as Ruth went to fetch one. "Have I told you today how marvelous you are and how I adore you?"

"Not that I recall." He lifted his hand to her hair. "Tell me now."

"You're marvelous and I adore you." She kissed him again before she rose. "I should warn you that Justin informed me yesterday that he was entirely too old for naps."

"We'll discuss it."

"Diplomatically?" she asked, smiling over her shoulder as she walked from the room.

The air smelled of the sea. Ruth had nearly forgotten how clean and sharp the scent was. The beach was long and rocky, with a noisy surf. An occasional leaf found its way down from the grove on the ridge. One scuttled along the sand in front of them. "I've always loved it here." Lindsay stuck her hands into the deep pockets of her jacket.

"I hated it when we first came," Ruth mused, gazing

down the stretch of beach as they walked. "The house, the sound, everything."

"Yes, I know."

Ruth cast her a quick look. Yes, she thought, she would have known. "I don't know when I stopped. It seemed I just woke up one day and found I was home. Uncle Seth was so patient."

"He's a patient man." Lindsay laughed. "At times, infuriatingly so. I rant and rave, and he calmly wins the battle. His control can be frustrating." She studied Ruth's profile. "You're a great deal like him."

"Am I?" Ruth pondered the idea a moment. "I wouldn't have thought myself very controlled lately."

"He has his moments, too." Lindsay reached over to pick up a stone and slipped it into her pocket, a habit she had never broken.

"Lindsay, you've never asked why I came so suddenly or how long I intend to stay."

"It's your home, Ruth. You don't have to explain coming here."

"I told Uncle Seth there was no one else like you."

"Did you?" Lindsay smiled at that and brushed some flying hair from her eyes. "That's the best sort of compliment, I think."

"It's Nick," Ruth said suddenly.

"Yes, I know."

Ruth let out a long breath. "I love him, Lindsay. I'm scared."

"I know the feeling. You've fought, I imagine."

"Yes. Oh, there are so many things." Ruth's voice was suddenly filled with the passion of frustration. "I've tried to work it out in my head these past couple of days, but nothing seems to make sense."

"Being in love never makes sense. That's the first rule." They had come to a clump of rocks, and Lindsay sat.

It was right here, she remembered, that Seth and she had stood that day. She had been in love and frightened because nothing made sense. Ruth had come down from the house with a kitten zipped up in her jacket. She'd been seventeen and cautious about letting anyone get too close. Maybe she's still being cautious, Lindsay thought, looking back at her. "Do you want to talk about it?"

Ruth hesitated only a moment. "Yes, I think I would."

"Then sit, and start at the beginning."

It was so simple once begun. Ruth told her of the suddenness of their coming together after so many years of working side by side. She told her of the shock of learning he loved her and of the frustrations at having no time together. She left nothing out: the scenes with Leah, Nick's quick mood changes, her own uncertainties.

"Then, the day I left, Nadine spoke to me. She wanted me to know that if Nick and I had a break-up and wouldn't work together, she'd have to let me go. I was furious that we couldn't seem to keep what we had between us between us." She stared out toward the sound, feeling impotent with frustration.

"Before I had a chance to simmer down, Nick was demanding that I give up my apartment and move in with him. Just like that," she added, looking back at Lindsay. "Demanding. He was so infuriating, standing there, shouting at me about what *he* wanted. He tossed in that he'd wanted me for five years and had never said a word. I could hardly believe it. The nerve!"

She paused, dealing with a fresh spurt of anger. "I couldn't stand thinking he'd been directing my life. He was unreasonable and becoming more Russian by the minute. I was to pack up my things and move in with him without a moment's thought. He didn't even ask; he was ordering, as though he were staging his latest ballet. No," she corrected herself and rose, no longer able to sit, "he's more human when he's staging. He didn't once ask me what my feelings were. He just threw this at me straight after my little session with Nadine and after the dreadful week of taping."

Ruth ran out of steam all at once and sat back down. "Lindsay, I've never been so confused in my life."

Idly, Lindsay jiggled the stone in her pocket. She had listened throughout Ruth's speech without a single interruption. "Well," she said finally, "I have a firm policy against offering advice." Pausing, she gazed out at the sea. "And policies are made to be broken. How well do you know Nick?"

"Not as well as you do," Ruth said without thinking. "He was in love with you." The words were out before she realized she had thought them. "Oh, Lindsay."

"Oh, indeed." She faced Ruth directly. "When I first joined the company, Nadine was struggling to keep it going. Nick's coming gave it much-needed momentum, but there were internal problems, financial pressures outsiders are rarely aware of. I know you think Nadine was hard—she undoubtedly was—but the company is everything to her. It's easier for me to understand that now with the distance. I didn't always.

"In any case," she continued, "Nick's coming was the turning point. He was very young, thrown into the spotlight in a strange country. He barely spoke coherent English. French, Italian, a bit of German, but he had to learn English from the ground up. Of all people, you should understand what it's like to be in a strange country with strange customs, to be the outsider."

"Yes," Ruth murmured. "Yes, I do."

"Well, then." Lindsay wrapped her arms around her knee. "Try to picture a twenty-year-old who had just made the most important decision of his life. He had left his country, his friends, his family. Yes, he has family," Lindsay said, noting Ruth's surprise. "It wasn't easy for him, and the first years made him very careful. There were a lot of people out there who were very eager to exploit him—his story, his background. He learned to edit his life. When I met him, he was already Davidov, a name in capital letters."

She took a moment, watching the surf fly up on the rocks. "Yes, I was attracted to him, very attracted. Maybe half in love for a while. It might have been the same for him. We were dancers and young and ambitious. Maybe if my parents hadn't had the accident, maybe if I had stayed with the company, something would have developed between us. I don't know. I met Seth." Lindsay smiled and glanced back up at the Cliff House. "What I do know is that whatever Nick and I might have had, it wouldn't have been the right choice for either of us. There's no one for me but Seth. Now or ever."

"Lindsay, I didn't mean to pry." Ruth gestured helplessly.

"You're not prying. We're all bound up in this. That's why I'm breaking my policy." She paused another moment. "Nick talked to me in those days because he needed someone. There were very few people he felt he could trust. He thought he could trust me. If there are things he hasn't told you, it's simply because it's become a habit of his not to dwell on what he left behind. Nick is a man who looks ahead. But he feels, Ruth; don't imagine he doesn't."

"I know he does," Ruth said quietly. "I've only wanted to share it with him."

"When he's ready, you will." She said it simply. "Nick made ballet first in his life out of choice or necessity, take your pick. From what you've told me, it appears something else is beginning to take the driver's seat. I imagine it scares him to death."

"Yes." Ruth remembered what her uncle had said to her. "I hadn't thought that he'd feel that way, too."

"When a man, especially a man with a flair for words and staging, asks a woman to live with him so clumsily, I'd guess he was scared right out of his shoes." She smiled a little and touched Ruth's hand. "Now, as for this Leah and the rest of this nonsense about your relationship interfering with your careers or vice versa, you should know better. After five years with the company you should be able to spot basic jealousy when it hits you in the face."

Ruth let out a sigh. "I've always been able to before."

"This time the stakes were higher. Love can cloud

the issue." She studied Ruth in silence for a moment. "And how much have you been willing to give him?"

Ruth opened her mouth to speak, then shut it again. "Not enough," she admitted. "I was afraid, too. He's such a strong man, Lindsay; his personality is overwhelming. I didn't want to lose myself." She looked at Lindsay searchingly. "Is that wrong?"

"No. If you were weak and bent under every demand he handed out, he wouldn't be in love with you." She took Ruth's hand and squeezed it. "Nick needs a partner, Ruth, not a fan."

"He can be so arrogant. So impossible."

"Yes, bless him."

Ruth laughed and hugged her. "Lindsay, I needed to come home."

"You've come." Lindsay returned the hug. "Do you love him?"

"Yes. Yes, I love him."

"Then go pack and go after him. Time's too precious. He's in California." She smiled at Ruth's puzzled face. "I called Nadine this morning. I'd already decided to break my policy."

Chapter 15

Nick's feet pounded into the sand. He was on his third mile. The sun was rising slowly, casting rose-gold glints into the ocean. Dawn had been pale and gray when he had started. He had the beach to himself. It was too early for even the most enthusiastic jogger. He liked the lonely stretch of sand turning gold under the sun, the empty cry of gulls over his head and the whooshing sound of the waves beside him.

The only pressures here were the ones he put on his own body. Like dancing, running could be a solitary challenge. And here, too, he could put his mind above the pain. Today, if he ran hard enough, far enough, he might stop thinking of Ruth.

How could he have been so stupid? Nick cursed himself again and increased his pace. *What timing! What style!* He had meant to give her more space, meant to wait until the scene was right. Nothing had come out the way he had intended. Had he actually ordered her to pack? What had possessed him? Anger, frustration, need. Fear. The choreography he had so carefully devised had become stumbling missteps.

He had wanted to ease her into living with him, letting her grow used to the first commitment before he slid her into marriage. He had destroyed it all with temper and arrogance.

Once he had begun, he had been unable to stop himself. And how she had looked at him! First stunned, then furious. How could he have been so clumsy? There had been countless women in his life, and he had never had such trouble telling them what he felt—what he didn't feel. How many languages could he make love in? Why, when it finally mattered, had he struck out like a blundering fool? Yet it had been so with every step in his courtship of Ruth.

Courtship! He berated himself and kept running as the sun grew higher. He set himself a punishing rhythm. What courtship had he given her? He had taken her like a crazed man the first time, and when he had told her he loved her, had there been any finesse? A schoolboy would have shown more care!

Well out at sea a school of dolphins took turns leaping into the air; a beautifully choreographed water ballet. Nick kept running.

She won't be back, he thought grimly. Then in despair—good God what will I do? Will I bury myself in the company and have nothing else, like poor Nadine? Is this what all the years have been for? Every time I dance, she'll be there, just out of reach. She'll go to another company, dance with Mitchell or Kirminov. The thought made his blood boil.

I'll drag her back. He pounded on, letting the pain fill him. She's so young! What right do I have to force her back to me? Could I? It isn't right; a man doesn't drag a woman back when she leaves him. There's the pride. I won't.

The hell I won't, he thought suddenly and turned back toward the house. He never slackened his pace. *The hell I won't.*

Ruth pulled up in front of the house and sat in the rented car, letting the engine idle. The house was two stories of wind-and salt-weathered cedar and gleaming glass. Very impressive, Uncle Seth, she decided, admiring the clean, sharp lines and lavish use of open space he had used in designing this house.

Swallowing, she wondered for the hundredth time how to approach the situation. All the neat little speeches she had rehearsed on the plane seemed hopelessly silly or strained.

"Nick, I thought we should talk," she tried out loud, then laid her forehead on the steering wheel. Brilliant. Why don't I just use: "Hello, Nick, I was just passing by, thought I'd drop in?" That's original.

Just do it, she told herself. Just go up there and knock on the door and let it happen. Moving quickly, Ruth shut off the engine and slid out of the car. The six steps leading to the front door looked impossibly high. Taking a deep breath, as she had so many other times for a *jeté* from the wings, she climbed them.

Now knock, she ordered herself as she stared at the

door. Just lift your hand, close it into a fist and knock. It took her a full minute to manage it. She waited, the breath backing up in her lungs. No answer. With more determination she knocked again. And waited.

Unable to bear the suspense any longer, Ruth put her hand on the knob and turned. She almost leaped back when it opened to her touch. The locks and bolts of Manhattan were more familiar.

The living room apparently took up the entire first floor. The back wall was almost completely in glass, featuring a stunning panorama of the Pacific. For a moment Ruth forgot her anxiety. She had seen other buildings of her uncle's design, but this was a masterpiece.

The floor was wood, graced by a few very plain buff-colored rugs. He had placed no paintings on the walls. The ocean was art enough. Trinkets were few, but she lifted an exquisite old brass silent butler that pleased her tremendously. There was a bar with shelves behind it lined with glasses of varying colors and shapes. The sofa was thick and deep and piled with pillows. A gleaming mahogany grand piano stood in the back of the room, its top opened wide. Ruth went to it and lifted a sheet of staff paper.

Musical notes dotted it, with Nick's meticulous handwriting in the margins. The Russian writing was unintelligible to her, but she began to pick out the melody on the piano.

His new ballet? She listened carefully to the unfamiliar music. With a smile she set the paper back in place. He was amazing, she decided. Davidov had the greatest capacity for work of anyone she had ever known.

But where was he?

Ruth turned to look around the room again. Could he have gone back to New York? Not with the door unlocked and pages of his new ballet still on the piano! She glanced at her watch and suddenly remembered: She was still on East Coast time. Oh, for heaven's sake, she thought as she quickly calculated the time difference. It was early! He was probably still in bed.

Slowly, Ruth walked to the stairs and peered up. I can't just go up there. She pressed her lips together. I could call. She opened her mouth and shut it again on a sound of annoyance. What could she say? *Yoo-hoo, Nick, time to get up?* She lifted her fingers to her lips to stifle a nervous giggle.

Taking a deep breath, Ruth put her hand on the banister and started to climb.

Nick opened the double glass doors that led from the back deck to the living room. He was breathing hard. His sweat shirt was dampened in a long vee from neck to hem. The exertion had helped. He felt cleaner, clearer. He would go up and have a shower and then work through the day on the new ballet. His plans to go east and drag Ruth back with him were the thoughts of a crazy man.

Halfway into the room, he stopped. The scent of wildflowers overwhelmed him. God! Would he never escape her?

What right had she to do this to him, to haunt him wherever he went? Damn her, he thought furiously. I've had enough of this!

Striding to the phone, he lifted it and punched out Ruth's number in New York. Without any idea of what he would say, Nick waited in blind fury for her to answer. With another curse, he hung up again. Where the devil is she? The company? No, he shook his head immediately. *Lindsay.* Of course, where else would she go?

Nick picked up the phone again and had pushed four numbers when a sound caught his attention. Frowning, he glanced toward the stairs. Ruth walked down, her own face creased in a frown.

Their eyes met immediately.

"So, there you are," she said and hoped the words didn't sound as foolish as they felt. "I was looking for you."

With infinite care Nick replaced the phone receiver on its cradle. "Yes?"

Though his response was far from gracious, Ruth came down the rest of the steps. "Yes. Your door was unlocked. I hope you don't mind that I just came in."

"No."

She fidgeted nervously, concentrating all her effort into a smile. "I noticed you've started work on a new ballet."

"I've begun, yes." The words were carefully spaced. His eyes never left hers.

Unable to bear the contact, Ruth turned to wander the room. "This is a lovely place. I can see why you come whenever you have the chance. I've always loved the ocean. We stayed in a house on the Pacific once in Japan." She began to ramble on, hardly knowing what she said but needing to fill the space with words. Nick remained silent, studying her back as she stared out to sea.

Realizing his muscles were balled tight, Nick forced them to relax. He hadn't heard a word she had said.

"Do you come to enjoy the view?" he demanded, interrupting her.

Ruth winced, then composed her face before she turned. "I came to see you," she told him. "I have things to say."

"Very well." He gestured with his hand. "Say them."

His unconscious gesture stiffened her spine. "Oh, I intend to. Sit down."

His brow lifted at the order. After a moment he moved to the sofa. "I'm sitting."

"Do you practice being insufferable, Davidov, or is it a natural talent?"

Nick waited a moment, then leaned back against the pillows. "You've traveled three thousand miles to tell me this?"

"And more," Ruth shot back. "I've no intention of being buried by you, professionally or personally. We'll speak of the dancing first."

"By all means." Nick lifted his hands and let them fall. "Please continue."

"I'm a good dancer, and whether you partner me or not, I'll continue to be a good dancer. In the company you can tell me to dance until my feet drop off, and I'll do it. You're the director."

"I'm aware of that."

Ruth glared at him. "But that's where it stops. You don't direct my life. Whatever I do or don't do is my choice and my responsibility. If I choose to take a dozen lovers or live like a hermit, you have nothing whatever to say about it."

"You think not?" His words were cool enough, his position still easy against the pillows, but fury had leaped into his eyes.

"I *know* you." Ruth took another step toward him. "As long as I'm free, until I make a personal commitment, no one has any business interfering with how I live, with what I do. No one questions you, Davidov. You wouldn't permit it. Well, neither will I." She put her hands on her hips. "If you think I'll run along like a good little girl and pack my bags because you tell me to, you're sadly mistaken. I'm not a little girl, and I won't be told what to do. I make my own choices." She walked toward him.

"You always expect everyone to cheerfully do your bidding," she continued, still fuming. "But you'd better prepare yourself for a shock. I've no intention of being your underling. Partners, Davidov, in every sense. And I won't live with you; it's not good enough. If you want me, you'll have to marry me. That's it." Ruth crossed her arms over her chest and waited.

Nick straightened slowly, then, taking another moment, rose. "Is that an ultimatum?"

"You bet it is."

"I see." He studied her consideringly. "It seems you give me no choice. You will wish to be married in New York?"

Ruth opened her mouth, and when there were no words, cleared her throat. "Well, yes—I suppose."

"Did you have in mind a small ceremony or something large?"

With the impetus gone, she stared at him in confusion. "I don't know…I hadn't thought…"

"Well, you can decide on the plane, yes?" He gave her an odd smile. "Shall I make reservations for a flight now?"

"Yes. No," she said when he turned for the phone. Nick tilted his head and waited. "All right, yes, go ahead." Ruth went to the windows again and stared out. Why, she asked herself, does it seem so wrong?

"Ruth." He waited until she faced him again. "I've told you I love you, I've said the same words to women I don't even remember. Words mean little."

She swallowed and felt the ache begin. The whole expanse of the room separated them.

"I have not shown you, as I wanted to, the way I felt. You make me clumsy." He spread his fingers. "A difficult thing for a dancer to admit. If I were not clumsy, I could tell you that my life is not my life without you. I could tell you that you are the heart of it, the muscle, the bone. I could tell you there is only emptiness and aching without you. I could tell you that to be your partner, your husband, your lover, is what I want more than breath. But…" He shook his head. "You make me clumsy, and I can only tell you that I love you and hope it is enough."

"Nick!" She ran for him, and he caught her before she was halfway across the room.

He held her tightly, just filling himself with the joy of having her in his arms again. "When I saw you walk down the stairs, I thought it was a dream. I thought I had gone mad."

"I thought you'd still be asleep."

"Sleep? I don't think there has been sleep since you left me." He drew her away. "Never again," he said fiercely. "Hate me, shout at me, but don't leave me again." His mouth came down on hers and smothered her promise.

Her answer was as wild and heated as his demand. She tangled her fingers into his hair, pressing him closer, wanting to drown in the current that raged between them. Need soared through her, a raw, urgent hunger that made her mouth grow more desperate under his. Desire came in an avalanche of sensations; his taste, his scent, the thick soft texture of his hair in her hands.

"I love you." Her mouth formed the words but made no sound. "I want you."

She felt him release the zipper at her back and let the dress slip to the floor. Nick let out a low groaning murmur as he stroked his hands down her sides.

"So small, *lyubovnitsa,* I fear always to hurt you."

"I'm a dancer," she reminded him, thrilling to the touch of his hands over the thin silk of her chemise. "Strong as an ox." They lowered to the sofa and lay tangled together. "I was afraid," she murmured, closing her eyes as his hands gently aroused her. "Afraid to trust you, afraid to love you, afraid to lose you."

"Both of us." He pulled her close and just held her. "No more."

Ruth slipped her hand under his shirt to lay it on his heart. *Davidov,* she thought. How many years had she worshipped the legend? Now the man was hers. And she his. She held his heart and was sure of it. Smiling, she pressed her lips to his neck and lingered there.

"Davidov?"

"Mmm?"

"Are you really going to accept that ultimatum?"

His hand reached for her breast. "I've thought about it. It seems for the best. You were very fierce. I think I'll humor you."

"Oh, do you?" Her smile was in her voice.

"Yes, but I will not permit your dozen lovers unless they are all me." He took his mouth on a teasing journey along her jaw line. "I think I should keep you busy enough."

"Maybe," she said and sighed luxuriously as he began to unlace the front of her chemise.

His mouth came to hers and swept her away even as he continued to undress her. "I will be a very jealous husband. Unreasonable, perhaps violent." He lifted his face to smile down at her. "Very hard to live with. Do I still call for the plane?"

Ruth opened her eyes and looked into his. She smiled. "Yes. Tomorrow."

* * * * *

New York Times bestselling author

SUSAN MALLERY

welcomes readers back to Fool's Gold, where two misfits discover that passion isn't the only thing they have in common!

Felicia Swift never dreamed she'd hear a deep, sexy voice from her past in tiny Fool's Gold, California. The last time Gideon Boylan whispered in her ear was half a world away…on the morning after the hottest night of her life.

And for Gideon, Black Ops taught him that love could be deadly. Now he pretends to fit in while keeping everyone at arm's length. Felicia wants more than he can give—a home, family, love—but she has a lot to learn about men…and Gideon needs to be the man to teach her.

Available wherever books are sold!

Be sure to connect with us at:

Harlequin.com/Newsletters

Facebook.com/HarlequinBooks

Twitter.com/HarlequinBooks

HARLEQUIN® HQN™

www.Harlequin.com

PHSM2

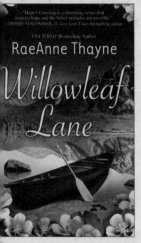

REQUEST YOUR FREE BOOKS!

2 FREE NOVELS
FROM THE ROMANCE COLLECTION
PLUS 2 FREE GIFTS!

YES! Please send me 2 FREE novels from the Romance Collection and my 2 FREE gifts (gifts are worth about $10). After receiving them, if I don't wish to receive any more books, I can return the shipping statement marked "cancel." If I don't cancel, I will receive 4 brand-new novels every month and be billed just $6.24 per book in the U.S. or $6.74 per book in Canada. That's a savings of at least 22% off the cover price. It's quite a bargain! Shipping and handling is just 50¢ per book in the U.S. and 75¢ per book in Canada.* I understand that accepting the 2 free books and gifts places me under no obligation to buy anything. I can always return a shipment and cancel at any time. Even if I never buy another book, the two free books and gifts are mine to keep forever.

194/394 MDN F4X

Name	(PLEASE PRINT)
Address	Apt. #
City	State/Prov.	Zip/Postal Code

Signature (if under 18, a parent or guardian must sign)

Mail to the **Harlequin®** Reader Service:
IN U.S.A.: P.O. Box 1867, Buffalo, NY 14240-1867
IN CANADA: P.O. Box 609, Fort Erie, Ontario L2A 5X3

Want to try two free books from another line?
Call 1-800-873-8635 or visit www.ReaderService.com.

* Terms and prices subject to change without notice. Prices do not include applicable taxes. Sales tax applicable in N.Y. Canadian residents will be charged applicable taxes. Offer not valid in Quebec. This offer is limited to one order per household. Not valid for current subscribers to the Romance Collection or the Romance/Suspense Collection. All orders subject to credit approval. Credit or debit balances in a customer's account(s) may be offset by any other outstanding balance owed by or to the customer. Please allow 4 to 6 weeks for delivery. Offer available while quantities last.

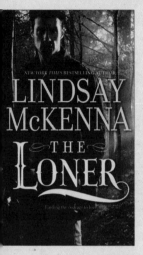

NORA ROBERTS

(limited quantities available)

TOTAL AMOUNT	$	_____
POSTAGE & HANDLING	$	_____
($1.00 FOR 1 BOOK, 50¢ for each additional)		
APPLICABLE TAXES*	$	_____
TOTAL PAYABLE	$	_____

(check or money order—please do not send cash)

To order, complete this form and send it, along with a check or money order for the total above, payable to Harlequin Books, to: **In the U.S.:** 3010 Walden Avenue, P.O. Box 9077, Buffalo, NY 14269-9077. **In Canada:** P.O. Box 636, Fort Erie, Ontario, L2A 5X3.

Name: _____
Address: _____ City: _____
State/Prov.: _____ Zip/Postal Code: _____
Account Number (if applicable): _____

075 CSAS

*New York residents remit applicable sales taxes.
*Canadian residents remit applicable GST and provincial taxes.

Silhouette®
Where love comes alive™